FEA

Break In

Books by Dick Francis

THE SPORT OF QUEENS (autobiography)
DEAD CERT
NERVE
FOR KICKS
ODDS AGAINST
FLYING FINISH
BLOOD SPORT
FORFEIT
ENQUIRY
RAT RACE
BONECRACK
SMOKESCREEN
SLAY-RIDE
KNOCK DOWN
HIGH STAKES
IN THE FRAME
RISK
TRIAL RUN
WHIP HAND
REFLEX
TWICE SHY
BANKER
THE DANGER
PROOF
BREAK IN
LESTER: The Official Biography
BOLT
HOT MONEY
THE EDGE
STRAIGHT
LONGSHOT
COMEBACK
DRIVING FORCE
DECIDER
WILD HORSES
COME TO GRIEF
TO THE HILT
10-lb PENALTY
FIELD OF THIRTEEN
SECOND WIND
SHATTERED

Break In

THE DICK FRANCIS LIBRARY

MICHAEL JOSEPH
an imprint of
PENGUIN BOOKS

MICHAEL JOSEPH
Published by the Penguin Group
Penguin Books Ltd, 80 Strand, London WC2R 0RL, England
Penguin Group (USA) Inc., 375 Hudson Street, New York, New York 10014, USA
Penguin Group (Canada), 90 Eglinton Avenue East, Suite 700, Toronto, Ontario, Canada M4P 2Y3
(a division of Pearson Penguin Canada Inc.)
Penguin Ireland, 25 St Stephen's Green, Dublin 2, Ireland (a division of Penguin Books Ltd)
Penguin Group (Australia), 250 Camberwell Road,
Camberwell, Victoria 3124, Australia (a division of Pearson Australia Group Pty Ltd)
Penguin Books India Pvt Ltd, 11 Community Centre,
Panchsheel Park, New Delhi – 110 017, India
Penguin Group (NZ), cnr Airborne and Rosedale Roads, Albany,
Auckland 1310, New Zealand (a division of Pearson New Zealand Ltd)
Penguin Books (South Africa) (Pty) Ltd, 24 Sturdee Avenue,
Rosebank, Johannesburg 2196, South Africa

Penguin Books Ltd, Registered Offices: 80 Strand, London WC2R 0RL, England

www.penguin.com

First published in Great Britain 1985
Second impression May 1993
Third impression June 1998
Fourth impression December 2005

Printed in England by Antony Rowe Ltd, Chippenham, Wiltshire

A CIP catalogue record for this book is available from the British Library

ISBN-13: 978-0-718-13507-2
ISBN-10: 0-718-13507-5

B000 000 012 7751

With love and thanks
to my son
MERRICK
racehorse trainer

and to

NANCY BROOKS GILBERT
bureau coordinator
for WSVN

ONE

Blood ties can mean trouble, chains and fatal obligation. The tie of twins, inescapably strongest. My twin, my bond.

My sister Holly, sprung into the world ten minutes after myself on Christmas morning with bells ringing over frosty fields and hope still wrapped in beckoning parcels, my sister Holly had through thirty years been cot-mate, puppy-companion, boxing target and best friend. Consecutively, on the whole.

My sister Holly came to Cheltenham races and intercepted me between weighing room and parade ring when I went out to ride in a three-mile steeplechase.

'Kit!' she said intensely, singling me out from among the group of other jockeys with whom I walked, and standing four-square and portentously in my way.

I stopped. The other jockeys walked on, parting like water round a rock. I looked at the lines of severe strain in her normally serene face and jumped in before she could say why she'd come.

'Have you any money with you?' I said.

'What? What for?' She wasn't concentrating on my question but on some inner scenario of obvious doom.

'Have you?' I insisted.

'Well . . . but that's not . . .'

'Go to the Tote,' I said. 'Put all you've got on my horse to win. Number eight. Go and do it.'

'But I don't . . .'

'Go and do it,' I interrupted. 'Then go to the bar and with what's left buy yourself a triple gin. Then come and meet me in the winners' enclosure.'

'No, that's not . . .'

7

I said emphatically, 'Don't put your disaster between me and that winning post.'

She blinked as if awakening, taking in my helmet and the colours I wore beneath my husky, looking towards the departing backs of the other jockeys and understanding what I meant.

'Right?' I said.

'Right.' She swallowed. 'All right.'

'Afterwards,' I said.

She nodded. The doom, the disaster, dragged at her eyes.

'I'll sort it out,' I promised. 'After.'

She nodded dumbly and turned away, beginning almost automatically to open her shoulder bag to look for money. Doing what her brother told her, even after all these years. Coming to her brother, still, for her worst troubles to be fixed. Even though she was four years married, those patterns of behaviour, established in a parentless childhood, still seemed normal to us both.

I'd sometimes wondered what difference it would have made to her if she had been the elder by that crucial ten minutes. Would she have been motherly? Bossy, perhaps. She felt safer, she'd said, being the younger.

I walked on towards the parade ring, putting consciously out of my mind the realisation that whatever the trouble this time, it was bad. She had come, for a start, one hundred and fifty miles from Newmarket to see me, and she disliked driving.

I shook my head physically, throwing her out. The horse ahead, the taxing job in hand, had absolute and necessary priority. I was primarily no one's brother. I was primarily Kit Fielding, steeplechase jockey, some years champion, some years not, sharing the annual honour with another much like myself, coming out top when my bones didn't break, bowing to fate when they did.

I wore the colours of a middle-aged princess of a dispossessed European monarchy, a woman of powerful femininity whose skin was weathering towards sunset like cracked glaze on porcelain. Sable coat, as usual, swinging from narrow shoulders. Glossy dark hair piled high. Plain gold earrings. I walked towards her across the parade-ring grass; smiled, bowed, and briefly shook the offered glove.

'Cold day,' she said; her consonants faintly thick, vowel sounds pure English, intonation as always pleasant.

I agreed.

'And will you win?' she asked.

'With luck.'

Her smile was mostly in the eyes. 'I will expect it.'

We watched her horse stalk round the ring, its liver chestnut head held low, the navy rug with gold embroidered crest covering all else from withers to tail. North Face, she'd named it, from her liking for mountains, and a suitably bleak, hard and difficult customer he'd turned out to be. Herring-gutted, ugly, bad-tempered, moody. I'd ridden him in his three-year-old hurdles, his first races, and on over hurdles at four, five and six. I'd ridden him in his novice steeplechases at seven and through his prime at eight and nine. He tolerated me when he felt like it and I knew his every mean move. At ten he was still an unpredictable rogue, and as clever a jumper as a cat. He had won thirty-eight races over the years and I'd ridden him in all but one. Twice to my fury he had purposefully dropped his shoulder and dislodged me in the parade ring. Three times we had fallen together on landing, he each time getting unhurt to his feet and departing at speed with indestructible legs, indestructible courage, indestructible will to win. I loved him and hated him and he was as usual starting favourite.

The princess and I had stood together in such a way in parade rings more often than one could count, as she rarely kept fewer than twenty horses in training and I'd ridden them constantly for ten years. She and I had come to the point of almost monosyllabic but perfectly understood conversation and, as far as I could tell, mutual trust and regard. She called me 'Kit', and I called her 'Princess' (at her request) and we shared a positive and quite close friendship which nevertheless began and ended at the racecourse gates. If we met outside, as occasionally happened, she was considerably more formal.

We stood alone together in the parade ring, as so often, because Wykeham Harlow, who trained North Face, suffered from migraine. The headaches, I'd noticed, occurred most regularly on the coldest days, which might have been a truly physical phenomenon, but also they seemed to develop in severity in direct ratio to the distance between his armchair and the day's racing. Wykeham Harlow trained south of London and very seldom now made the north-westerly traverse to Cheltenham: he was growing old and wouldn't confess he was nervous about driving home in the winter dark.

The signal was given for jockeys to mount, and Dusty, the travelling head-lad who nowadays deputised for Wykeham more often than not, removed North Face's rug with a flick and gave me a deft leg-up into the saddle.

The princess said, 'Good luck', and I said cheerfully, 'Thank you.'

No one in jump racing said 'Break a leg' instead of 'Good luck', as they did in the theatre. Break a leg was all too depressingly possible.

North Face was feeling murderous: I sensed it the moment I sat on his back and put my feet in the irons. The telepathy between that horse and myself was particularly strong always, and I simply cursed him in my mind and silently told him to shut up and concentrate on winning, and we went out on to the windy track with the mental dialogue continuing unabated.

One had to trust that the urge to race would overcome his grouchiness once the actual contest started. It almost always did, but there had been days in the past when he'd refused to turn on the enthusiasm until too late. Days, like this one, when his unfocussed hatred flowed most strongly.

There was no way of cajoling him with sweet words, encouraging pats, pulling his ears. None of that pleased him. A battle of wills was what he sought, and that, from me, was what he habitually got.

We circled at the starting point, seven runners in all, while the roll was called and girths were tightened. Waited, with jockeys' faces turning pale blue in the chilly November wind, for the seconds to tick away to start-time, lining up in no particular order as there were no draws or stalls in jump races, watching for the starter to raise the tapes and let us go.

North Face's comment on the proceedings took the form of a lowered head and arched back, and a kick like a bronco.

The other riders cursed and kept out of his way, and the starter told me to stay well to the rear.

It was the big race of the day, though heavier in prestige than prize money, an event in which the sponsors, a newspaper, were getting maximum television coverage for minimum outlay. The Sunday Towncrier Trophy occurred annually on a Saturday afternoon (naturally) for full coverage in the *Sunday Towncrier* itself the next morning, with self-congratulatory prose and dramatic pictures jostling scandals on the front page. Dramatic pictures of Fielding being bucked off before the start were definitely not going to be taken. I called the horse a bastard, a sod and a bloody pig, and in that gentlemanly fashion the race began.

He was mulish and reluctant and we got away slowly, trailing by ten lengths after the first few strides. It didn't help that the start was in plain view of the stands instead of decently hidden in some far corner. He gave another two bronco kicks to entertain the multitude, and there weren't actually many horses who could manage that while approaching the first fence at Cheltenham.

He scrambled over that fence, came almost to a halt on landing and bucked again before setting off, shying against coercion from the saddle both bodily and clearly in mind.

Two full circuits ahead. Nineteen more jumps. A gap between me and the other runners of embarrassing and lengthening proportions. I sent him furious messages: Race, you bastard, race, or you'll end up as dogmeat, I'll personally kill you, you bastard, and if you think you'll get me off, think again, you're taking me all the way, you sod, so get on with it, start racing, you sod, you bastard, you know you like it, so get going . . .

We'd been through it before, over and over, but he'd never been worse. He ignored all take-off signals at the second fence and made a mess of it and absolutely refused to gallop properly round the next bend.

Once in the past when he'd been in this mood I'd tried simply not fighting him but letting him sort out his own feelings, and he'd brought himself to a total halt within a few strides. Persevering was the only way: waiting until the demonic fit burned itself out.

11

He stuck his toes in as we approached the next fence as if the downhill slope there alarmed him, which I knew it didn't; and over the next, the water jump, he landed with his head down by his feet and his back arched, a configuration almost guaranteed to send a jockey flying. I knew his tricks so well that I was ready for him and stayed in the saddle, and after that jolly little manoeuvre we were more than three hundred yards behind the other horses and seriously running out of time.

My feelings about him rose to somewhere near absolute fury. His sheer pigheadedness was again going to lose us a race we could easily have won, and as on other similar occasions I swore to myself that I'd never ride the brute again, never. Not ever. Never. I almost believed I meant it.

As if he'd been a naughty child who knew its tantrums had gone too far, he suddenly began to race. The bumpy uneven stride went smooth, the rage faded away, the marvellous surge of fighting spirit returned, as it always did in the end. But we were a furlong and a half to the rear, and to come from more than three hundred yards behind and still win meant theoretically that one could have won by the same margin if one had tried from the start. A whole mile had been wasted; two left for retrieval. Hopeless.

Never give up, they say.

Yard by flying yard over the second circuit we clawed back the gap, but we were still ten lengths behind the last tired and trailing horse in front as we turned towards the final two fences. Passed him over the first of them. No longer last, but that was hardly what mattered. Five horses in front, all still on their feet after the long contest, all intent on the final uphill battle.

All five went over the last fence in front of North Face. He must have gained twenty feet in the air. He landed and strode away with smooth athletic power as if sticky bronco jumps were the peccadillo of another horse altogether.

I could dimly hear the crowd roaring, which one usually couldn't. North Face put his ears back and galloped with a flat, intense, bloody-minded stride, accelerating towards the place he knew was his, that he'd so wilfully rejected, that he wanted in his heart.

I flattened myself forward to the line of his neck to cut the wind resistance; kept the reins tight, my body still, my weight steady over his shoulders, all the urging a matter of mind and hands, a matter of giving that fantastic racing creature his maximum chance.

The others were tiring, the incline slowing them drastically, as it did always to so many. North Face swept past a bunch of them as they wavered and there was suddenly only one in front, one whose jockey thought he was surely winning and had half dropped his hands.

One could feel sorry for him, but he was a gift from heaven. North Face caught him at a rush a bare few strides from the winning post, and I heard his agonised cry as I passed.

Too close for comfort, I thought, pulling up. Reprieved on the scaffold.

There was nothing coming from the horse's mind: just a general sort of haze that in a human one would have interpreted as smugness. Most good horses knew when they'd won: filled their lungs and raised their heads with pride. Some were definitely depressed when they lost. Guilt they never felt, nor shame nor regret nor compassion: North Face would dump me next time if he could.

The princess greeted us in the unsaddling enclosure with starry eyes and a flush on her cheeks. Stars for success, I diagnosed, and the flush from earlier embarrassment. I unbuckled the girths, slid the saddle over my arm and paused briefly before going to weigh in, my head near to hers.

'Well done,' she said.

I smiled slightly. 'I expected curses.'

'He was especially difficult.'

'And brilliant.'

'There's a trophy.'

'I'll come right out,' I said, and left her to the flocking newsmen, who liked her and treated her reverently, on the whole.

I passed the scales. The jockey I'd beaten at the last second was looking ashamed, but it was his own fault, as well he knew. The Stewards might fine him. His owners might sack him. No one else paid much attention either to his loss or to my win. The past was the past: the next race was what mattered.

I gave my helmet and saddle to the valet, changed into different colours, weighed out, put the princess's colours back on, on top of those I would carry in the next race, combed my hair and went out dutifully for the speeches. It always seemed a shame to me when the presentation photographs were taken with the jockey not wearing the winner's colours, and for owners I cared for I did whenever possible appear with the right set on top. It cost me nothing but a couple of minutes, and it was more satisfactory, I thought.

The racecourse (in the shape of the chairman of directors) thanked the *Sunday Towncrier* for its generosity and the *Sunday Towncrier* (in the shape of its proprietor, Lord Vaughnley) said it was a pleasure to support National Hunt racing and all who sailed in her.

Cameras clicked.

There was no sign anywhere of Holly.

The proprietor's lady, thin, painted and good-natured, stepped forward in smooth couturier clothes to give a foot-high gilded statue of a towncrier (medieval version) to the princess, amid congratulation and hand shaking. The princess accepted also a smaller gilt version on behalf of Wykeham Harlow, and in my turn I received the smile, the handshake, the congratulations and the attentions of the cameras, but not, to my surprise, my third set of golden towncrier cufflinks.

'We were afraid you might win them again,' Lady Vaughnley explained sweetly, 'so this year it's a figure like the others,' and she pressed warmly into my hands a little golden man calling out the news to the days before printing.

I genuinely thanked her. I had more cufflinks already than shirts with cuffs to take them.

'What a finish you gave us,' she said, smiling. 'My husband is thrilled. Like an arrow from nowhere, he said.'

'We were lucky.'

I looked automatically to her shoulder, expecting to greet also her son, who at all other Towncriers had accompanied his parents, hovering around and running errands, willing, nice-natured, on the low side of average for brains.

'Your son isn't with you?' I asked.

Most of Lady Vaughnley's animation went into eclipse. She glanced swiftly and uncomfortably across to her husband,

14

who hadn't heard my remark, and said unhappily, 'No, not today.'

'I'm sorry,' I said; not for Hugh Vaughnley's absence, but for the obvious row in the family. She nodded and turned away, blinking, and I thought fleetingly that the trouble must be new and bad, near the surface of tears.

The princess invited Lord and Lady Vaughnley to her box and they happily accepted.

'You as well, Kit,' she said.

'I'm riding in the next race.'

'Come after.'

'Yes. Thank you.'

Everyone left their trophies on the presentation table to be taken away for engraving and I returned to the changing room as the princess moved away with the Vaughnleys.

She always asked me to her box because she liked to discuss her horses and what they'd done, and she had a loving and knowledgeable interest in all of them. She liked most to race where she rented a private box, namely at Cheltenham, Ascot, Sandown and Lingfield, and she went only to other courses where she had standing invitations from box-endowed friends. She was not democratic to the point of standing on the open stands and yelling.

I came out in the right colours for the next race and found Holly fiercely at my elbow immediately.

'Have you collected your winnings?' I asked.

'I couldn't reach you,' she said disgustedly. 'All those officials, keeping everyone back, and the crowds . . .'

'Look, I'm sorry. I've got to ride again now.'

'Straight after, then.'

'Straight after.'

My mount in that race, in contrast to North Face, was unexciting, unintelligent and of only run-of-the-mill ability. Still, we tried hard, finished third, and seemed to give moderate pleasure to owners and trainer. Bread and butter for me: expenses covered for them. The basic fabric of jump racing.

I weighed in and changed rapidly into street clothes, and Holly was waiting when I came out.

'Now, Kit . . .'

'Um,' I said. 'The princess is expecting me.'

15

'No! Kit!' She was exasperated.

'Well . . . it's my job.'

'Don't come to the office, you mean?'

I relented. 'OK. What's the matter?'

'Have you seen this?' She pulled a page torn from a news-paper called the *Daily Flag* out of her shoulder bag. 'Has anyone said anything in the weighing room?'

'No and no,' I said, taking the paper and looking where she was pointing with an agitated stabbing finger. 'I don't read that rag.'

'Nor do we, for God's sake. Just look at it.'

I glanced at the paragraph which was boxed by heavy red lines on a page entitled 'Intimate Details', a page well known to contain information varying from stale to scurrilous and to be intentionally geared to stirring up trouble.

'It's yesterday's,' I said, looking at the date.

'Yes, yes. Read it.'

I read the piece. It said:

Folk say the skids are under Robertson (Bobby) Allardeck (32), racehorse-trainer son of tycoon Maynard Allardeck (50). Never Daddy's favourite (they're not talking), Bobby's bought more than he can pay for, naughty boy, and guess who won't be coming to the rescue. Watch this space for more.

Robertson (Bobby) Allardeck (32) was my sister Holly's husband.

'It's libellous,' I said. 'Bobby can sue.'

'What with?' Holly demanded. 'We can't afford it. And we might not win.'

I looked at the worry in her normally unlined face.

'Is it true, then?' I said.

'No. Yes. In a way. Of course he's bought things he can't pay for. Everyone does. He's bought horses. It's yearling sale time, dammit. Every trainer buys yearlings he can't pay for. It's natural, you know that.'

I nodded. Trainers bought yearlings at auction for their owners, paying compulsorily for them on the spot and relying on the owners to reimburse them fairly soon. Sometimes

16

the owners backed out after a yearling had been bought; sometimes trainers bought an extra animal or two to bring on themselves and have ready for a later sale at a profit. Either way, at sale time, it was more common than not to borrow thousands short term from the bank.

'How many has Bobby bought that he can't sell?' I asked.

'He'll sell them in the end, of course,' she said, staunchly.

Of course. Probably. Perhaps.

'But now?'

'Three. We've got three.'

'Total damage?'

'More than a hundred thousand.'

'The bank paid for them?'

She nodded. 'It's not that it won't be all right in the end, but where did that disgusting rag get the information from? And why put it in the paper at all? I mean, it's pointless.'

'And what's happened?' I asked.

'What's happened is that everyone we owe money to has telephoned demanding to be paid. I mean, horrible threats, really, about taking us to court. All day yesterday ... and this morning the feed-merchant rang and said he wouldn't deliver any more feed unless we paid our bill and we've got thirty horses munching their heads off, and the owners are on the line non-stop asking if Bobby's going to go on training or not and making veiled hints about taking their horses away.'

I was sceptical. 'All this reaction from that one little paragraph?'

'Yes.' She was suddenly close to tears. 'Someone pushed the paper through the letter-box of half the tradesmen in Newmarket, open at that page with that paragraph outlined in red, just like this. The blacksmith showed me. It's his paper. He came to shoe some of the horses and made us pay him first. Made a joke of it. But all the same, he meant it. Not everyone's been so nice.'

'And I suppose you can't simply just pay everyone off and confound them?'

'You know we can't. The bank manager would bounce the cheques. We have to do it gradually, like we always do. Everyone will get paid, if they wait.'

17

Bobby and Holly lived in fairly usual fashion at permanent full stretch of their permitted overdraft, juggling the incoming cheques from the owners with the outgoing expenses of fodder, wages, overheads and taxes. Owners sometimes paid months late, but the horses had to be fed and the lads' wages found to the minute. The cash flow tended to suffer from air locks.

'Well,' I said, 'go for another triple gin while I talk to the princess.'

TWO

The Princess Casilia, Mme de Brescou (to give her her full style), had as usual asked a few friends to lunch with her to watch the races, and her box contained, besides herself and the Vaughnleys, a small assortment of furs and tweeds, all with inhabitants I'd formerly met on similar occasions.

'You know everyone, don't you?' the princess said, and I nodded 'Yes', although I couldn't remember half their names.

'Tea?' she asked.

'Yes, thank you.'

The same waitress as usual smoothly gave me a full cup, smiling. No milk, no sugar, slice of lemon, as always.

The princess had had a designer decorate her boxes at the racecourses and they were all the same: pale peach hessian on the walls, coffee-coloured carpet and a glass-topped dining table surrounded by comfortable chairs. By late afternoon, my habitual visiting time, the table had been pushed to one side and bore not lunch but plates of sandwiches, creamy pastries, assorted alcohol, a box of cigars. The princess's friends tended to linger long after the last races had been run.

One of the women guests picked up a plate of small delicious-looking cakes and offered it to me.

'No, thank you,' I said mildly. 'Not this minute.'

'Not ever,' the princess told her friend. 'He can't eat those. And don't tempt him. He's hungry.'

The friend looked startled and confused. 'My dear! I never thought. And he's so tall.'

'I eat a lot,' I said. 'But just not those.'

The princess, who had some idea at least of the constant struggle I had to stay down at a body weight of ten stone, gave me a glimmering look through her eyelashes, expressing disbelief.

The friend was straightforwardly curious. 'What do you eat most of,' she asked, 'if not cake?'

'Lobster, probably,' I said.

'Good heavens.'

Her male companion gave me a critical glance from above a large moustache and long front teeth.

'Left it a bit late in the big race, didn't you, what?' he said.

'I'm afraid so, yes.'

'Couldn't think what you were doing out there, fiddling about at the back. You nearly bungled it entirely, what? The princess was most uncomfortable, I can tell you, as we all had our money on you, of course.'

The princess said, 'North Face can behave very badly, Jack. I told you. He has such a mind of his own. Sometimes it's hard to get him to race.'

'It's the jockey's job to get him to race,' Jack said to me with a touch of belligerence. 'Don't you agree, what?'

'Yes,' I said. 'I do agree.'

Jack looked fractionally disconcerted and the princess's lips twitched.

'And then you set him alight,' said Lord Vaughnley, over-hearing. 'Gave us a rousing finish. The sort of thing a sponsor prays for, my dear fellow. Memorable. Something to talk about, to refer to. North Face's finish in the Towncrier Trophy. Splendid, do you see?'

Jack saw, chose not to like it, drifted away. Lord Vaughnley's grey eyes looked with bonhomie from his large bland face and he patted me with kindly meant approval on the shoulder.

'Third time in a row,' he said. 'You've done us proud. Would you care, one Saturday night, to see the paper put to bed?'

'Yes,' I said, surprised. 'Very much.'

'We might print a picture of you watching a picture of yourself go through the presses.'

More than bonhomie, I thought, behind the grey eyes: a total newspaperman's mentality.

He was the proprietor of the *Towncrier* by inheritance, the

20

fiftyish son of one of the old-style newspaper barons who had muscled on to the scene in the nineteen thirties and brought new screaming life to millions of breakfasts. Vaughnley Senior had bought a dying provincial weekly and turned it into a lusty voice read nationwide. He'd taken it to Fleet Street, seen the circulation explode, and in due course had launched a daily version which still prospered despite sarcastic onslaughts from newer rivals.

The old man had been a colourful buccaneering entrepreneur. The son was quieter, a manager, an advertising man at heart. The *Towncrier*, once a raucous newsheet, had over the last ten years developed Establishment leanings, a remarkable testimony of the hand-over from the elder personality to the younger.

I thought of Hugh Vaughnley, the son, next in the line: the sweet-tempered young man without strength, at present at odds, it appeared, with his parents. In his hands, if it survived at all, the *Towncrier* would soften to platitude, waffle and syrup.

The *Daily Flag*, still at the brassiest stage, and among the *Towncrier*'s most strident opposition, had been recently bought, after bitter financial intrigues, by a thrusting financier in the ascendant, a man hungry, it was said, for power and a peerage, and taking a well-tried path towards both. The *Flag* was bustling, go-getting, stamping on sacrosanct toes and boasting of new readers daily.

Since I'd met Lord Vaughnley several times at various racing presentation dinners where annual honours were dished out to the fortunate (like champion jockeys, leading trainers, owners-of-the-year, and so on) and with Holly's distress sharp in my mind, I asked him if he knew who was responsible for 'Intimate Details' in the *Flag*.

'Responsible?' he repeated with a hint of holier-than-thou distaste. 'Irresponsible, more like.'

'Irresponsible, then.'

'Why, precisely?' he asked.

'They've made an unprovoked and apparently pointless attack on my brother-in-law.'

'Hm,' Lord Vaughnley said. 'Too bad. But, my dear fellow, pointless attacks are what the public likes to read. Destructive

21

criticism sells papers, back-patting doesn't. My father used to say that, and he was seldom wrong.'

'And to hell with justice,' I said.

'We live in an unkind world. Always have, always will. Christians to the lions, roll up, buy the best seats in the shade, gory spectacle guaranteed. People buy newspapers, my dear fellow, to see victims torn limb from limb. Be thankful it's physically bloodless, we've advanced at least that far.' He smiled as if talking to a child. 'Intimate Details, as you must know, is a composite affair, with a whole bunch of journalists digging out nuggets and also a network of informants in hospitals, mortuaries, night clubs, police stations and all sorts of less savoury places, telephoning in with the dirt and collecting their dues. We at the *Towncrier* do the same sort of thing. Every paper does. Gossip columns would be non-starters, my dear fellow, if one didn't.'

'I'd like to know where the piece about my brother-in-law came from. Who told who, if you see what I mean. And why.'

'Hm.' The grey eyes considered. 'The editor of the *Flag* is Sam Leggatt. You could ask him of course, but even if he finds out from his staff, he won't tell you. Head against brick wall, I'm afraid, my dear fellow.'

'And you approve,' I said, reading his tone. 'Closing ranks, never revealing sources, and all that.'

'If your brother-in-law has suffered real positive harm,' he nodded blandly, 'he should get his solicitor to send Sam Leggatt a letter announcing imminent prosecution for libel unless a retraction and an apology are published immediately. It sometimes works. Failing that, your brother-in-law might get a small cash settlement out of court. But do advise him, my dear fellow, against pressing for a fully-fledged libel action with a jury. The *Flag* retains heavyweight lawyers and they play very rough. They would turn your brother-in-law's most innocent secrets inside out and paint them dirty. He'd wish he'd never started. Friendly advice, my dear fellow, I do assure you.'

I told him about the paragraph being outlined in red and delivered by hand to the houses of tradespeople.

Lord Vaughnley frowned. 'Tell him to look for the informant on his own doorstep,' he said. 'Gossip column items often spring from local spite. So do stories about vicars and their mistresses.' He smiled briefly. 'Good old spite. Whatever would the newspaper industry do without it!'

'Such a confession!' I said with mockery.

'We clamour for peace, honesty, harmony, common sense and equal justice for all,' he said. 'I assure you we do, my dear fellow.'

'Yes,' I said. 'I know.'

The princess touched Lord Vaughnley's arm and invited him to go out on to the balcony to see the last race. He said however that he should return to the *Towncrier*'s guests whom he had temporarily abandoned in a sponsors' hospitality room, and, collecting his wife, he departed.

'Now, Kit,' said the princess, 'while everyone is outside watching the race, tell me about North Face.'

We sat, as so often, in two of the chairs, and I told her without reservation what had happened between her horse and myself.

'I do wish,' she said thoughtfully, at the end, 'that I had your sense of what horses are thinking. I've tried putting my head against their heads,' she smiled almost self-consciously, 'but nothing happens. I get nothing at all. So how do you do it?'

'I don't know,' I said. 'I don't think head to head would work, anyway. It's just when I'm riding them, I seem to know. It's not in words, not at all. It's just there. It just seems to come. It happens to very many riders. Horses are telepathic creatures.'

She looked at me with her head on one side. 'But you, Kit, you're telepathic with people as well as horses. Quite often you've answered a question I was just going to ask. Quite disconcerting. How do you do it?'

I was startled. 'I don't know how.'

'But you know you do?'

'Well ... I used to. My twin sister Holly and I were telepathic between ourselves at one time. Almost like an extra way of talking. But we've grown out of it, these last few years.'

'Pity,' she said. 'Such an interesting gift.'

'It can't logically exist.'

23

'But it does.' She patted my hand. 'Thank you for today, although you and North Face between you almost stopped my heart.'

She stood up without haste, adept from some distant training at ending a conversation gracefully when she wished, and I stood also and thanked her formally for her tea. She smiled through the eyelashes, as she often did with everybody: not out of coquetry but in order, it seemed to me, to hide her private feelings.

She had a husband to whom she went home daily; Monsieur Roland de Brescou, a Frenchman of aristocratic lineage, immense wealth and advanced age. I had met him twice, a frail white-haired figure in a wheel-chair with an autocratic nose and little to say. I asked after his health occasionally: the princess replied always that he was well. Impossible ever to tell from her voice or demeanour what she felt about him: love, anxiety, frustration, impatience, joy ... nothing showed.

'We run at Devon and Exeter, don't we?' she said.

'Yes, Princess. Bernina and Icicle.'

'Good. I'll see you there on Tuesday.'

I shook her hand. I'd sometimes thought, after a win such as that day's, of planting a farewell kiss on her porcelain cheek. I liked her very much. She might consider it the most appalling liberty, though, and give me the sack, so in her own disciplined fashion I made her merely a sketch of a bow, and went away.

'You've been a hell of a long time,' Holly complained. 'That woman treats you like a lap dog. It's sickening.'

'Yeah ... well ... here I am.'

She had been waiting for me on her feet outside the weighing room in the cold wind, not snugly in a chair in the bar. The triple gin anyway had been a joke because she seldom drank alcohol, but that she couldn't even sit down revealed the intensity of her worry.

The last race was over, the crowds streaming towards the car parks. Jockeys and trainers, officials and valets and pressmen bade each other goodnight all around us although it was barely three-forty in the afternoon and not yet dusk. Time to go home from the office. Work was work, even if the end product was entertainment. Leisure was a growth industry, so they said.

'Will you come home with me?' Holly asked.

I had known for an hour that that was what she would want.

'Yes,' I said.

Her relief was enormous but she tried to hide it with a cough, a joke and a jerky laugh. 'Your car or mine?'

I'd thought it over. 'We'll both go to the cottage. I'll drive us in your car from there.'

'OK.' She swallowed. 'And Kit . . .'

'Save it,' I said.

She nodded. We'd had an ancient pact: never say thank you out loud. Thanks came in help returned, unstintingly and at once, when one needed it. The pact had faded into abeyance with her marriage but still, I felt, existed: and so did she, or she wouldn't have come.

Holly and I were more alike in looks than many fraternal twins, but nowhere near identical Viola and Sebastian: Shakespeare, most rarely, got it wrong. We each had dark hair, curly. Each, lightish brown eyes. Each, flat ears, high foreheads, long necks, easily tanned skin. We had different noses and different mouths, though the same slant to the bone above the eye socket. We had never had an impression of looking into a mirror at the sight of the other, although the other's face was more familiar to us than our own.

When we were two years old our young and effervescent parents left us with our grandparents, went for a winter holiday in the Alps, and skied into an avalanche. Our father's parents, devastated, had kept us and brought us up and couldn't in many ways have been better, but Holly and I had turned inward to each other more than might have happened in a normal family. We had invented and spoken our own private language, as many such children do, and from there had progressed to a speechless communication of minds. Our telepathy had been more a matter of knowing what the other was thinking rather than of deliberately planting thoughts in the other's head. More reception than transmission, one might say: and it happened also without us realising it, as over and over again when we'd been briefly apart we had done things

25

like writing in the same hour to our Australian aunt, getting the same book out of the library, and buying identical objects on impulse. We had both, for instance, one day gone separately home with roller skates as a surprise birthday present for the other and hidden them in our grandmother's wardrobe. Grandmother herself by that time hadn't found it strange as we'd done similar things too often, and she'd said that right from when we could talk if she asked, 'Kit, where's Holly?' or, 'Holly, where's Kit?' we would always know, even if logically we couldn't.

The telepathy between us had not only survived the stresses and upheavals of puberty and adolescence but had actually become stronger: also we were more conscious of it, and used it purposely when we wanted, and grew in young adulthood into a new dimension of friendship. Naturally we put up a front to the world of banter, sarcasm and sibling rivalry, but underneath we were solid, never doubting our private certainty.

When I'd left our grandparents' house to buy a place of my own with my earnings, Holly had from time to time lived there with me, working away in London most of the time but returning as of right whenever she wished, both of us taking it for granted that my cottage was now her home also.

That state of affairs had continued until she fell in love with Bobby Allardeck and married him.

Even before the wedding the telepathy had begun to fade and fairly soon afterwards it had more or less stopped. I wondered for a while if she had shut down deliberately, and then realised it had been also my own decision: she was off on a new life and it wouldn't have been a good idea to try to cling to her, or to intrude.

Four years on, the old habit had vanished to such an extent that I hadn't felt a flicker of her present distress, where once I would somehow have had it in my mind and would have telephoned to find out if she was all right.

On our way out to the car park I asked her how much she'd won on North Face.

'My God,' she said, 'you left that a bit late, didn't you?'

'Mm.'

'Anyway, I went to put my money on the Tote but the

26

queues were so long I didn't bother and I went down on to the lawn to watch the race. Then when you were left so far behind I was glad I hadn't backed you. Then those bookies on the rails began shouting five to one North Face. Five to one! I mean, you'd started at odds-on. There was a bit of booing when you came past the stands and it made me cross. You always do your best, they didn't have to boo. So I walked over and got one of the bookies to take all my money at fives. It was a sort of gesture, I suppose. I won a hundred and twenty-five, which will pay the plumber, so thanks.'

'Did the plumber get Intimate Details?'

'Yes, he did.'

'Someone knows your life pretty thoroughly,' I said.

'Yes. But who? We were awake half the night wondering.' Her voice was miserable. 'Who could hate us that much?'

'You haven't just kicked out any grievance-laden employees?'

'No. We've a good lot of lads this year. Better than most.'

We arrived at her car and she drove me to where mine was parked.

'Is that house of yours finished yet?' she asked.

'Getting on.'

'You're bizarre.'

I smiled. Holly liked things secure, settled and planned in advance. She thought it crazy that I'd bought on impulse the roofless shell of a one-storey house from a builder who was going broke. He'd been in the local pub one night when I'd gone in for a steak: leaning on the bar and morosely drowning his sorrows in beer. He'd been building the house for himself, he said, but he'd no money left. All work on it had stopped.

I'd ridden horses for him in his better-off days and had known him for several years, so the next morning I'd gone with him to see the house; and I'd liked its possibilities and bought it on the spot, and engaged him to finish it for me, paying him week by week for work done. It was going to be a great place to live and I was going to move into it, finished or not, well before Christmas, as I'd already exchanged contracts on my old cottage and would have to leave there willy nilly.

'I'll follow you to the cottage,' Holly said. 'And don't drive like you won the Towncrier.'

We proceeded in sedate convoy to the racehorse-training village of Lambourn on the Berkshire Downs, leaving my car in its own garage there and setting off together on the hundred miles plus to the Suffolk town of Newmarket, headquarters of the racing industry.

I liked the informality of little Lambourn. Holly and Bobby swam easily in the grander pond. Or had done, until a pike came along to snap them up.

I told her what Lord Vaughnley had said about demanding a retraction from the *Flag*'s editor but not suing, and she said I'd better tell Bobby. She seemed a great deal more peaceful now that I was actually on the road with her, and I thought she had more faith in my ability to fix things than I had myself. This was a lot different from beating up a boy who pinched her bottom twice at school. A little more shadowy than making a salesman take back the rotten car he'd conned her into buying.

She slept most of the way to Newmarket and I had no idea at all what I was letting myself in for.

We drove into the Allardeck stableyard at about eight o'clock and found it ablaze with lights and movement when it should have been quiet and dark. A large horsebox was parked in the centre, all doors open, loading ramp down. Beside it stood an elderly man watching a stable-lad lead a horse towards the ramp. The door of the place where the horse had been dozing the night away shone as a wide open oblong of yellow behind him.

A few steps away from the horsebox, lit as on a stage, were two men arguing with fists raised, arms gesticulating, voices clearly shouting.

One of them was my brother-in-law, Bobby. The other . . .?

'Oh my God,' Holly said. 'That's one of our owners. Taking his horses. And he owes us a fortune.'

She scrambled out of the car almost before I'd braked to a halt, and ran towards the two men. Her arrival did nothing, as far as I could see, to cool the flourishing row, and to all intents they simply ignored her.

My calm-natured sister was absolutely no good at stalking into any situation and throwing her weight about. She thought privately that it was rather pleasant to cook and keep house and be a gentle old-fashioned woman: but then she was of a generation for whom that way was a choice, not a drudgery oppressively imposed.

I got out of the car and walked across to see what could be done. Holly ran back to meet me.

'Can you stop him?' she said urgently. 'If he takes the horses, we'll never get his money.'

I nodded.

The lad leading the horse had reached the ramp but the horse was reluctant to board. I walked over to the lad without delay, stood in his way, on the bottom of the ramp, and told him to put the horse back where he'd brought it from.

'What?' he said. He was young, small, and apparently astonished to see anyone materialise from the dark.

'Put it back in the box, switch off the light, close the door. Do it now.'

'But Mr Graves told me . . .'

'Just do it,' I said.

He looked doubtfully across to the two shouting men.

'Do you work here?' I said. 'Or did you come with the horsebox?'

'I came with the horsebox.' He looked at the elderly man standing there who had so far said and done nothing. 'What should I do, Jim?'

'Who are you?' I asked him.

'The driver,' he said flatly. 'Keep me out of it.'

'Right,' I said to the lad. 'The horse isn't leaving. Take it back.'

'Are you Kit Fielding?' he said doubtfully.

'That's right. Mrs Allardeck's brother. Get going.'

'But Mr Graves . . .'

'I'll deal with Mr Graves,' I said. 'His horse isn't leaving tonight.'

'Horses,' the boy said, correcting me. 'I loaded the other one already.'

'OK,' I said. 'They're both staying here. When you've put back the one you're loading, unload the first one again.'

The boy gave me a wavering look, then turned the horse round and began to plod it back towards its rightful quarters.

29

The change of direction broke up the slanging match at once. The man who wasn't Bobby broke away and shouted to the lad across the yard, 'Hey, you, what the shit do you think you're doing? Load the horse this minute.'

The lad stopped. I walked fast over to him, took hold of the horse's head-collar and led the bemused animal back into its own home. The lad made no move at all to stop me. I came out. Switched off the light. Shut and bolted the door.

Mr Graves (presumably) was advancing fast with flailing arms and an extremely belligerent expression.

'Who the shit do you think you are?' he shouted. 'That's my horse. Get it out here at once!'

I stood, however, in front of the bolted door, leaning my shoulders on it, crossing one ankle over the other, folding my arms. Mr Graves came to a screeching and disbelieving halt.

'Get away from there,' he said thunderously, stabbing the night air with a forefinger. 'That's my horse. I'm taking it, and you can't stop me.'

His pudgy face rigid with obstinacy, he stood about five feet five from balding crown to polished toecaps. He was perhaps fifty, plump, already out of breath. There was no way whatever that he was going to shift my five feet ten by force.

'Mr Graves,' I said calmly, 'you can take your horses away when you've paid your bill.'

His mouth opened speechlessly. He took a step forward and peered at my face, which I dare say was in shadow.

'That's right,' I said. 'Kit Fielding. Holly's brother.'

The open mouth snapped shut. 'And what the shit has all this to do with you? Get out of my way.'

'A cheque,' I said. 'You do have your chequebook with you?'

His gaze grew calculating. I gave him little time to slide out.

I said, 'The *Daily Flag* is always hungry for tit-bits for its Intimate Details. Owners tying to sneak their horses away at dead of night without paying their bills would be worth a splash, don't you think?'

'That's a threat!' he said furiously.

'Quite right.'

'You wouldn't do that.'

'Oh yes, I certainly would. I might even suggest that if you can't pay this one bill, maybe you can't pay others. Then all your creditors would be down like vultures in a flash.'

'But that's . . . that's . . .'

'That's what's happening to Bobby, yes. And if Bobby has a cash-flow problem, and I'm only saying if, then it's partly due to you yourself and others like you who don't pay when you should.'

'You can't talk to me like that,' he said furiously.

'I don't see why not.'

'I'll report you to the Jockey Club.'

'Yes, you do that.'

He was blustering, his threat a sham. I looked over his shoulder towards Bobby and Holly, who had been near enough to hear the whole exchange.

'Bobby,' I said, 'go and fetch Mr Graves's account. Make sure every single item he owes is on it, as you may not have a second chance.'

Bobby went at a half-run, followed more tentatively by Holly. The lad who had come with the horsebox retreated with the driver into the shadows. Mr Graves and I stood as if in a private tableau, waiting.

While a horse remained in a trainer's yard the trainer had a good chance of collecting his due, because the law firmly allowed him to sell the horse and deduct from the proceeds what he was owed. With the horse whisked away his prospects were a court action and a lengthy wait, and if the owner went bankrupt, nothing at all.

Graves's horses were Bobby's security, plain and simple.

Bobby eventually returned alone bringing a lengthy bill which ran to three sheets.

'Check it,' I said to Graves, as he snatched the pages from Bobby's hand.

Angrily he read the bill through from start to finish and found nothing to annoy him further until he came to the last item. He jabbed at the paper and again raised his voice.

'Interest? What the shit do you mean, interest?'

'Um,' Bobby said, 'on what I've had to borrow because you hadn't paid me.'

31

There was a sudden silence. Respectful, on my part. I wouldn't have thought my brother-in-law had it in him.

Graves suddenly controlled his anger, pursed his lips, narrowed his eyes, and delved into an inner pocket for his chequebook. Without any sign of fury or haste he carefully wrote a cheque, tore it out, and handed it to Bobby.

'Now,' he said to me. 'Move.'

'Is it all right?' I asked Bobby.

'Yes,' he said as if surprised. 'All of it.'

'Good,' I said, 'then go and unload Mr Graves's other horse from the horsebox.'

THREE

'Do what?' Bobby said, astonished.

I remarked mildly, 'A cheque is only a piece of paper until it's been through the bank.'

'That's slander!' Graves said furiously, all his earlier truculence reappearing.

'It's an observation,' I said.

Bobby shoved the cheque quickly into his trouser pocket as if fearing that Graves would try to snatch it back, not an unreasonable suspicion in view of the malevolence facing him.

'Once the cheque's been cleared,' I said to Graves, 'you can come and pick up the horses. Thursday or Friday should do. Bobby will keep them for nothing until then, but if you haven't removed them by Saturday he will begin charging training fees again.'

Bobby's mouth opened slightly and shut purposefully, and he walked without more ado towards the horsebox. Graves scuttled a few steps after him, protesting loudly, and then reversed and returned to me, shouting and practically dancing up and down.

'I'll see the Stewards hear about this!'

'Most unwise,' I said.

'I'll stop that cheque.'

'If you do,' I said calmly, 'Bobby will have you put on the forfeit list.'

This most dire of threats cut off Graves's ranting miraculously. A person placed on the Jockey Club's forfeit list for non-payment of training fees was barred in disgrace from all racecourses, along with his horses. Mr Graves, it seemed, was not quite ready for such a social blight.

'I won't forget this,' he assured me viciously. 'You'll regret you meddled with me, I'll see to that.'

Bobby had succeeded in unloading Graves's first horse and was leading it across to its stable, while the lad and the driver closed the ramp and bolted it shut.

'Off you go, then, Mr Graves,' I said. 'Come back in the daytime and telephone first.'

He gave me a bullish stare and then suddenly went into the same routine as earlier: pursed his mouth, narrowed his eyes and abruptly quietened his rage. I had guessed, the first time, watching him write his cheque without further histrionics, that he had decided he might as well write it because he would tell his bank not to cash it.

It looked very much now as if he were planning something else. The question was, what?

I watched him walk calmly over to the horsebox and wave an impatient hand at the lad and the driver, telling them to get on board. Then he himself climbed clumsily up into the cab after them and slammed the door.

The engine started. The heavy vehicle throbbed, shuddered, and rolled away slowly out of the yard, Graves looking steadfastly ahead as if blinkered.

I detached myself from the stable door and walked across towards Bobby.

'Thanks,' he said.

'Be my guest.'

He looked round. 'All quiet. Let's go in. It's cold.'

'Mm.'

We walked two steps and I stopped.

'What is it?' Bobby asked, turning.

'Graves,' I said. 'He went too meekly.'

'He couldn't have done much else.'

'He could have gone shouting and kicking and uttering last-minute threats.'

'I don't know what you're worrying about. We've got his cheque and we've got his horses ... er, thanks to you.'

His horses.

The breath in my lungs went out in a whoosh, steaming in a vanishing plume against the night sky.

'Bobby,' I said, 'have you any empty boxes?'

'Yes, there are some in the fillies' yard.' He was puzzled. 'Why?'

'We might just put Graves's horses in them, don't you think?'

'You mean ... he might come back?' Bobby shook his head. 'I'd hear him. I heard him before, though I admit that was lucky because we should have been out at a party, but we were too worried about things to go.'

'Could Graves have known you would be out?' I asked.

He looked startled. 'Yes, I suppose he could. The invitation is on the mantelpiece in the sitting room. He came in there last Sunday for a drink. Anyway, I'd hear a horsebox coming back. Couldn't miss it.'

'And if it parked at three in the morning on that strip of grass along from your gate, and the horses were led out in rubber boots to deaden the noise of their hooves?'

Bobby looked nonplussed. 'But he wouldn't. Not all that. Would he?'

'He was planning something. It showed.'

'All right,' Bobby said. 'We'll move them.'

On my way back to fetch the horse I'd been guarding I reflected that Bobby was uncommonly amenable to advice. He usually considered any suggestion from me to be criticism of himself and defensively found sixteen reasons for not doing what I'd mentioned: or at least not until I was well out of sight and wouldn't know. This evening things were different. Bobby had to be very worried indeed.

We walked Graves's horses round to Bobby's second yard behind the main quadrangle and installed them there in two empty boxes, which happened (all to the good, I thought) not to be side by side.

'Does Graves know his horses by sight?' I asked Bobby; which was not by any means a stupid question, as many owners didn't.

'I don't know,' he said dubiously. 'It's never come up.'

'In other words,' I said, 'he always knows them because they're where he expects to see them?'

'Yes. I should think so. But it's not certain. He might know them better than I think.'

'Well ... in that case, how about rigging some sort of alarm?'

Bobby didn't say certainly not, it wasn't necessary, he said, 'Where?'

Incredible.

'On one of the boxes they are normally in,' I said.

'Yes. I see. Yes.' He paused. 'What sort of alarm? I haven't any electric gadgets here. If I need any special tight security before a big race I hire a man with a dog.'

I did a quick mental review of his house and its contents. Saucepan lids? Metal trays? Something to make a noise.

'The bell,' I said. 'Your old school bell.'

'In the study.' He nodded. 'I'll fetch it.'

Bobby's study contained shelves of tidily arranged mementoes of his blameless early life: cricket caps, silver cups won at school sports, team photographs, a rugger ball ... and the hand bell which as a prefect he had rung noisily through his House to send the younger boys to bed. Bobby had been the sort of steadfast team-spirited boy that made the British public school system work: that he had emerged complacent and slightly pompous was probably owing to his many good qualities being manifest to all, including himself.

'Bring a hammer,' I said. 'And some staples if you have any. Nails, if not. And some heavy-duty string.'

'Right.'

He went away and in due course returned carrying the bell quietly by its clapper in one hand and a tool-box in the other. Between us we installed the bell as near to Bobby's house as possible and rigged it in such a way that a good tug to the string tied to its handle would send it toppling and jangling. Then we led the string through a long line of staples to the usual home of one of Graves's horses, and fastened the end of it out of sight to the top of the closed door.

'OK,' I said. 'Go into the house. I'll open this door and you see if you can hear the bell.'

He nodded and went away, and after a fair interval I opened the stable door. The bell fell with a satisfying clamour and Bobby came back saying it would wake the dead. We returned it to its precarious pre-toppling position and with rare accord walked together into the house.

36

There had been Fieldings and there had been Allardecks in racing further back than anyone could remember: two families with some land and some money and a bitter mutual persisting hatred.

There had been a Fielding and an Allardeck knifing each other for favour with King Charles II when he held court not in London but in Newmarket, thereby making foreign ambassadors travel wearily north-east by coach to present their credentials.

There had been an Allardeck who had wagered three hundred sovereigns on a two-horse race on Queen Anne's own racecourse on Ascot Heath and lost his money to a Fielding, who had been killed and robbed before he reached home.

There had been a Mr Allardeck in the Regency years who had challenged a Mr Fielding to a cross-country contest over fearsome jumps, the winner to take the other's horse. Mr Allardeck (who lost) accused Mr Fielding (an easy victor) of taking a cheating short cut, and the dispute went to pistols at dawn, when they each shot carefully at the other and died of their wounds.

There had been a Victorian gentleman rider named Fielding with a wild moustache and a wilder reputation, and an Allardeck who had fallen off, drunk, at the start of the Grand National. Fielding accused Allardeck of being a coward, Allardeck accused Fielding of seducing his (Allardeck's) sister. Both charges were true: and those two settled their differences by fisticuffs on Newmarket Heath, Fielding half killing the (again) drunk and frightened Allardeck.

By Edwardian times the two families were inextricably locked into inherited hostility and would accuse each other of anything handy. A particularly aggressive Fielding had bought an estate next door to the Allardecks on purpose to irritate, and bitter boundary disputes led to confrontations with shotguns and (more tamely) writs.

Bobby's great-grandfather burned down Great-grandfather Fielding's hay-barn (Great-grandfather Fielding having built it where it most spoiled the Allardecks' view) only to find his favourite hunter shot dead in its field a week later.

Bobby's grandfather and Grandfather Fielding had naturally been brought up to hate each other, the feud in their case extending later to bitter professional rivalry, as each (being a second son and not likely to inherit the family estate) had decided to set up as a licensed racehorse trainer. They each bought training stables in Newmarket and paid their lads to spy and report on the other. They cockily crowed when their horses won and seethed when the other's did, and, if coming first and second in the same race, lodged objections against each other almost as a matter of course.

Holly and I, being brought up in Grandfather Fielding's tempestuous household, were duly indoctrinated with the premise that all Allardecks were villainous madmen (or worse) who were to be cut dead at all times in Newmarket High Street.

Bobby and I, I dare say, each having been taught from birth to detest the other, might in our turn have come to fists or fire, were it not for my father dying, and Bobby's father leaving Newmarket with his family and going off into property and commodities. Not that Bobby's father, Maynard, could bear even the mention of the word Fielding: and the reason he was not speaking to Bobby (as truthfully noted in Intimate Details) was because Bobby Allardeck had dared, despite a promise of disinheritance, to defy his father's fury and walk up the aisle with Holly Fielding.

When Holly was thirteen her one absolute heroine had been Juliet in *Romeo and Juliet*. She learned almost the whole play by heart, but Juliet's part particularly, and became hopelessly romantic about the dead young lovers uniting the warring families of Montague and Capulet. Bobby Allardeck, I reckoned, was her Romeo, and she had been powerfully predisposed to fall in love with him, even if he hadn't been, as he was, tall, fair-haired and good-looking.

They had met by chance (or did she seek him out?) in London after several years of not seeing each other, and within a month were inseparable. The marriage had succeeded in its secret purpose to the extent that Bobby and I were now almost always polite to each other and that our children, if we had any, could, if they would, be friends.

Bobby and Holly had returned to Newmarket, Bobby hoping to take over as trainer in his by then ailing grandfather's yard, but the quarrelsome old man, calling his grandson a traitor to

38

the family, had made him pay full market price for the property, and had then died, not leaving him a penny.

Bobby's current financial troubles were not simple. His house and yard (such small part of it as was free from mortgage) would as a matter of course be held by the bank as security for the extra loans they'd made him for the buying of yearlings. If the bank called in the loans, he and Holly would be left with no home, no livelihood, and an extremely bleak future.

As in many racing houses, a great deal of life went on in the kitchen, which in Holly and Bobby's case was typically furnished with a long dining table and a good number of comfortable chairs. A friendly room, with a lot of light pine, warmly lit and welcoming. When Bobby and I went in from the yard Holly was whisking eggs in a bowl and frying chopped onions and green peppers in a large pan.

'Smells good,' I said.

'I was starving.' She poured the eggs over the onions and peppers. 'We must all be.'

We ate the omelette with hot french bread and wine and talked of nothing much until we had finished.

Then Holly, making coffee, said, 'How did you get Jermyn Graves to go?'

'Jermyn? Is that his name? I told him if he stopped the cheque Bobby would put him on the forfeit list.'

'And don't think I haven't thought of it,' Bobby said. 'But of course it's a dead loss from our point of view really.'

I nodded. The Jockey Club would refrain from putting an owner on the forfeit list if he (or she) paid all training fees which had been owing for three months or more. Unfortunately, though, the forfeit list leverage applied to basic training fees only, and not to vets' or blacksmiths' fees or to the cost of transporting horses to racemeetings. Bobby had had to pay out for all those things already for Graves's horses, and putting the owner on the forfeit list wouldn't get them reimbursed.

'Why is he in such a hurry to take his horses away?' I asked.

'He's just using our troubles as an excuse,' Holly said.

Bobby nodded. 'He's done something like this to at least two other trainers. All young and trying to get going, like us.

He runs up big bills and then one day the trainer comes home and finds the horses gone. Then Graves pays the bare training fees to avoid the forfeit list, and the trainer's left with no horses as security and all the difficulties and expense of going to court to try to get what he's owed, and of course it's seldom worth it, and Graves gets away with it.'

'Why did you accept his horses in the first place?' I said.

'We didn't know about him, then,' Holly said gloomily. 'And we're not exactly going to turn away people who ask us to take two horses, are we?'

'No,' I said.

'Anyway,' Holly said, 'Jermyn's just another blow. The worst crisis is the feed-merchant.'

'Give him Graves's cheque,' I said.

Holly looked pleased but Bobby said dubiously, 'Our accountant doesn't like us doing that sort of thing.'

'Yeah, but your accountant hasn't got thirty hungry horses on his doorstep staring at him reproachfully.'

'Twenty-nine, really,' Holly said.

'Twenty-seven,' Bobby sighed, 'when Graves's have gone.'

'Does that include the three unsold yearlings?' I asked.

'Yes.'

I rubbed my nose. Twenty-four paying inmates were basically a perfectly viable proposition, even if in his grandfather's day there had been nearer forty. They were, moreover, just about to enter their annual rest period (as Bobby trained only on the Flat) and would no longer be incurring the higher expenses of the season.

Conversely they could not until the following March win any prize money, but then nor would they be losing any bets.

Winter, in flat-racing stables, was time for equilibrium, for holidays, for repainting, and for breaking in the yearlings, sold or not.

'Apart from the unsold yearlings, how much do you owe?' I asked.

I didn't think Bobby would tell me, but after a pause, reluctantly, he did.

I winced.

'But we can pay everything,' Holly said. 'At our own pace. We always do.'

Bobby nodded.

'And it's so unfair about the yearlings,' my sister said passionately. 'One of our owners told Bobby to go up to fifty thousand to get one particular yearling, and Bobby did, and now the owner's telephoned to say he's very sorry he can't afford it after all; he just hasn't got the money. And if we send it back to the next sale, we'll make a loss. It's always that way. People will think there's something wrong with it.'

'I'll probably be able to syndicate it,' Bobby said. 'Sell twelve equal shares. But it takes time to do that.'

'Well,' I said, 'surely the bank will give you time.'

'The bank manager's panic-stricken by that damned newspaper.'

'Did someone deliver it to him too?' I asked.

Holly said gloomily, 'Someone did.'

I told Bobby what Lord Vaughnley had said about the *Flag*'s informant being someone local with a grudge.

'Yes, but who?' Bobby said. 'We really haven't any enemies.' He gave me a sidelong look in which humour was definitely surfacing. 'Once upon a time it would have been a Fielding.'

'Too true.'

'Grandfather!' Holly said. 'It couldn't be him, could it? He's never forgiven me, but surely . . . he wouldn't?'

We thought of the obstinate old curmudgeon who still trained a yardful of horses half a mile away and bellowed at his luckless lads on the Heath every morning. He was still, at eighty-two, a wiry, vigorous, cunningly intelligent plotter whose chief regret these days was that Bobby's grandfather was no longer alive to be outsmarted.

It was true that Grandfather Fielding had been as outraged as Grandfather Allardeck by the unthinkable nuptials, but the man who brought us up had loved us in his own testy way, and I couldn't believe he would actively try to destroy his granddaughter's future. Not unless old age was warping him into malice, as it sadly could sometimes.

'I'll go and ask him,' I said.

'Tonight?' Holly looked at the clock. 'He'll be in bed. He goes so early.'

'In the morning.'

'I don't want it to be him,' Holly said.

'Nor do I.'

We sat over the coffee for a while, and at length I said, 'Make a list of all the people who you know had the *Flag* delivered to them with that paragraph marked, and I'll go and call on some of them tomorrow. All I can get to on a Sunday.'

'What for?' Bobby said. 'They won't change their minds. I've tried. They just say they want their money at once. People believe what they read in newspapers. Even when it's all lies, they believe it.'

'Mm,' I said. 'But apart from telling them again that they'll be paid OK I'll ask them if any of them saw the paper being delivered. Ask them what time it came. Get a picture of what actually went on.'

'All right,' Holly said. 'We'll make the list.'

'And after that,' I said, 'work out who could possibly know who you deal with. Who could have written the same list. Unless, of course,' I reflected, 'dozens of other people who you don't owe money to got the paper delivered to them as well.'

'I've no idea,' Holly said. 'We never thought of that.'

'We'll find out tomorrow.'

Bobby yawned. 'Scarcely slept last night,' he said.

'Yes. Holly told me.'

There was suddenly a loud clanging from outside, a fierce and urgent alarm, enough to reawaken all the horses, if not the dead.

'God!' Bobby leapt to his feet, crashing his chair over backwards. 'He came back!'

We pelted out into the yard, all three of us, intent on catching Jermyn Graves in the act of trying to steal away his own property; and we did indeed find an extremely bewildered man holding open a stable door.

It was not, however, Jermyn Graves, but Nigel, Bobby's ancient head-lad. He had switched on the light inside the empty box and turned his weatherbeaten face to us as he heard us approach, the light carving deep canyons in his heavy vertical wrinkles.

'Sooty's gone,' he said anxiously. 'Sooty's gone, guv'nor. I

42

fed him myself at half-six, and all the doors were shut and bolted when I went home.' There was a detectable tinge of defensiveness in his voice which Bobby also heard and laid to rest.

'I moved him,' he said easily. 'Sooty's fine.'

Sooty was not the real name of Graves's horse, but the real names of some horses tended to be hopeless mouthfuls for their attendant lads. It was hard to sound affectionate when saying (for instance) Nettleton Manor. Move over Nettleton Manor. Nettleton Manor, you old rogue, have a carrot.

'I was just taking a last look round,' Nigel said. 'Going home from the pub, like.'

Bobby nodded. Nigel, like most head-lads, took the welfare of the horses as a personal pride. Beyond duty, their horses could be as dear to head-lads as their own children, and seeing they were safely tucked up last thing at night was a parental urge that applied to both species.

'Did you hear a bell ring?' Holly said.

'Yes.' He wrinkled his forehead. 'Near the house.' He paused. 'What was it?'

'A new security system we're trying out,' Bobby said. 'The bell rings to tell us someone's moving about the yard.'

'Oh?' Nigel looked interested. 'Works a treat then, doesn't it?'

FOUR

Work a treat the bell might, but no one came in the small hours to tug it again to its sentinel duty. I slept undisturbed in jeans and sweater, ready for battle but not called, and Bobby went out and disconnected the string before the lads arrived for work in the morning.

He and Holly had written out the list of *Flag* recipients, and after coffee, when it was light, I set off in Holly's car to seek them out.

I went first, though, as it was Sunday and early, to every newsagent, both in the town and within a fair radius of the outskirts, asking if they had sold a lot of copies of the *Flag* to any one person two days ago, on Friday, or if anyone had arranged for many extra copies to be delivered on that morning.

The answer was a uniform negative. Sales of the *Flag* on Friday had been the same as Thursday, give or take. None of the shops, big or small, had ordered more copies than usual, they said, and no one had sold right out of the *Flag*. The boys had done their regular delivery rounds, nothing more.

Dead end to the first and easiest trail.

I went next to seek out the feed-merchant, who was not the one who supplied my grandfather. I had been struck at once, in fact, by the unfamiliarity of all the names of Bobby's suppliers, though when one thought about it, it was probably only to be expected. Bobby, taking over from his grandfather, would continue to use his grandfather's suppliers: and never, it seemed, had the lifelong antagonists used the same blacksmith, the same vet, the same anything. Each had always believed the other would spy on him, given the slightest opportunity. Each had been right.

44

No feed-merchant in Newmarket, with several thousand horses round about, would find it strange to have his doorbell rung on his theoretical day of rest. The feed-merchant who waved me into the brick office annexe to his house was young and polished; and in an expensive accent and with crispness he told me it was not good business to allow accounts to run on overdue, he had his own cash-flow to consider, and Allardeck's credit had run out.

I handed him Jermyn Graves's cheque, duly endorsed by Bobby on the back.

'Ah,' said the feed-merchant, brightening. 'Why ever didn't you say so?'

'Bobby hoped you might wait, as usual.'

'Sorry. No can do. Cash on delivery from now on.'

'That cheque is for more than your account,' I pointed out.

'So it is. Right then. Bobby shall be supplied until this runs out.'

'Thank you,' I said, and asked him if he had seen his copy of the *Flag* delivered.

'No. Why?'

I explained why. 'This was a large scale and deliberate act of spite. One tends to want to know who.'

'Ah.'

I waited. He considered.

'It must have been here fairly early Friday morning,' he said finally. 'And it was delivered here to the office, not to the house, as the papers usually are. I picked it up with the letters when I came in. Say about eight-thirty.'

'And it was open at the gossip page with the paragraph outlined in red?'

'That's right.'

'Didn't you wonder who'd sent it?'

'Not really . . .' He frowned. 'I thought someone was doing me a good turn.'

'Mm,' I said. 'Do you take the *Flag* usually?'

'No, I don't. *The Times* and the *Sporting Life*.'

I thanked him and left, and took Holly's winnings to the plumber, who greeted me with satisfaction and gave me some of the same answers as the feed-merchant. The *Flag* had been inside his house on the front door mat by seven o'clock, and he hadn't seen who brought it. Mr Allardeck owed him for some pipework done way back in the summer, and he would admit, he said, that he had telephoned and threatened him pretty strongly with a county court action if he didn't pay up at once.

Did the plumber take the *Flag* usually?

Yes, he did. On Friday, he got two.

'Together?' I asked. 'I mean, were they both there on the mat at seven?'

'Yes. They were.'

'Which was on top of the other?'

He shrugged, thought, and said, 'As far as I remember, the one marked in red was underneath. Funny, I thought it was, that the boy had delivered two. Then I saw the paragraph, and I reckoned one of my neighbours was tipping me off.'

I said it was all very hard on Bobby.

'Yes, well, I suppose so.' He sniffed. 'He's not the only bad payer, by a long shot.' He gave me the beginnings of a sardonic smile. 'They pay up pretty quick when their pipes burst. Come a nice heavy freeze.'

I tried three more creditors on the list. Still unpaid, they were more brusque and less helpful, but an overall pattern held good. The marked papers had been delivered before the newsboys did their rounds and no one had seen who delivered them.

I went back to the largest of the newsagents and asked the earliest time their boys set out.

'The papers reach us here by van at six. We sort them into the rounds, and the boys set off on their bicycles before six-thirty.'

'Thanks,' I said.

They nodded. 'Any time.'

Disturbed by the stealth and thoroughness of the operation I drove finally to see my grandfather in the house where I'd been brought up: a large brick-built place with gables like comic eyebrows peering down at a barbed-wire-topped boundary fence.

The yard was deserted when I drove in, all the horses in their boxes with the top doors closed against the cold. On the day after the last day of the Flat season, no one went out to gallop on the Heath. Hibernation, which my grandfather hated, was already setting in.

I found him in his stable office, typing letters with concentration, the result, I surmised, of the departure of yet another beleaguered secretary.

'Kit!' he said, glancing up momentarily. 'I didn't know you were coming. Sit down. Get a drink.' He waved a thin hand. 'I won't be long. Damned secretary walked out. No consideration, none at all.'

I sat and watched while he hammered the keys with twice the force necessary, and felt the usual slightly exasperated affection for him, and the same admiration.

He loved horses beyond all else. He loved Grandmother next best and had gone very silent for a while the winter she'd died, the house eerily quiet after the years they'd spent shouting at each other. Within a few months he had begun shouting at Holly and me instead, and later, after we'd left, at the secretaries. He didn't intend to be unkind. In an imperfect world he was a perfectionist irritated by minor incompetencies, which meant most of the time.

The typing stopped. He stood up, the same height as myself, white-haired, straight and trim in shirt, tie and excellently cut tweed jacket. Casual my grandfather was not, not in habits or manners or dress, and if he was obsessive by nature it was probably just that factor which had brought him notable success over almost sixty years.

'There's some cheese,' he said, 'for lunch. Are you staying tonight?'

'I'm, er, staying with Holly.'

His mouth compressed sharply. 'Your place is here.'

'I wish you'd make it up with her.'

'I talk to her now,' he said, 'which is more than can be said for that arrogant Maynard with his rat of a son. She comes up here some afternoons. Brings me stews and things sometimes. But I won't have him here and I won't go there, so don't ask.' He patted my arm, the ultimate indication of approval. 'You and I, we get along all right, eh? That's enough.'

He led the way to the dining room where two trays lay on the table, each covered with a cloth. He removed one cloth to reveal a carefully laid single lunch: cheeses, biscuits under clingfilm, pats of butter, dish of chutney, a banana and an apple with a silver fruit knife. The other tray was for dinner.

'New housekeeper,' he said succinctly. 'Very good.'

Long may she last, I thought. I removed the clingfilm and brought another knife and plate, and the two of us sat there politely eating very little, he from age, I from necessity.

I told him about the paragraph in the *Flag* and knew at once with relief that he'd had no hand in it.

'Nasty,' he said. 'Mind you, my old father could have done something like that, if he'd thought of it. Might have done it myself,' he chuckled, 'long ago. To Allardeck.' Allardeck, to Grandfather, was Bobby's grandfather, Maynard's father, the undear departed. Grandfather had never in my hearing called him anything but plain Allardeck.

'Not to Holly,' my grandfather said. 'Couldn't do it to Holly. Wouldn't be fair.'

'No.'

He looked at me searchingly. 'Did she think it might be me?'

'She said it couldn't be, and also that she very much didn't want it to be you.'

He nodded, satisfied and unhurt. 'Quite right. Little Holly. Can't think what possessed her, marrying that little rat.'

'He's not so bad,' I said.

'He's like Allardeck. Just the same. Smirking all over his face when his horse beat mine at Kempton two weeks ago.'

'But you didn't lodge an objection, I noticed.'

'Couldn't. No grounds. No bumping, boring or crossing. His horse won by three lengths.' He was disgusted. 'Were you there? I didn't see you.'

'Read it in the paper.'

'Huh.' He chose the banana. I ate the apple. 'I saw you win the Towncrier yesterday on television. Rotten horse, full of hate. You could see it.'

'Mm.'

'You get people like that, too,' he observed. 'Chockful of ability and too twisted up to do anything worthwhile.'

'He did win,' I pointed out.

'Just. Thanks to you. And don't argue about that, it's

something I enjoy, watching you ride. There never was an Allardeck anywhere near your class.'

'And I suppose that's what you said to Allardeck himself?'

'Yes, of course. He hated it.' Grandfather sighed. 'It's not the same since he's gone. I thought I'd be glad, but it's taken some of the point out of life. I used to enjoy his sour looks when I got the better of him. I got him barred from running his horse in the St Leger once, because my spies told me it had ringworm. Did I tell you that? He would have killed me that day if he could. But he'd stolen one of my gullible lady owners with a load of lies about me never entering her horses where they could win. They didn't win for him either, as I never let him forget.' He cut the peeled banana into neat pieces and sat looking at them. 'Maynard, now,' he said, 'Maynard hates my guts too, but he's not worth the ground Allardeck stood on. Maynard is a power-hungry egomaniac, just the same, but he's also a creeper, which his father never was, for all his faults.'

'How do you mean, a creeper?'

'A bully to the weak but a boot-licker to the strong. Maynard boot-licked his way up every ladder, stamping down on all the people he passed. He was a hateful child. Smarmy. He had the cheek to come up to me once on the Heath and tell me that when he grew up he was going to be a lord, because then I would have to bow to him, and so would everyone else.'

'Did he really?'

'He was quite small. Eight or nine. I told him he was repulsive and clipped his ear. He snitched to his father, of course, and Allardeck sent me a stiff letter of complaint. Long ago, long ago.' He ate a slice of banana without enthusiasm. 'But that longing for people to bow to him, he's still got it, I should think. Why else does he take over all those businesses?'

'To win,' I said. 'Like we win, you and I, if we can.'

'We don't trample on people doing it. We don't want to be bowed to.' He grinned. 'Except by Allardecks, of course.'

We made some coffee and while we drank I telephoned some of Grandfather's traditional suppliers, and his vet and blacksmith and plumber. All were surprised at my question, and no, none of them had received a marked copy of the *Flag*.

'The little rat's got a traitor right inside his camp,' Grandfather said without noticeable regret. 'Who's his secretary?'

'No one. He does everything himself.'

'Huh. Allardeck had a secretary.'

'You told me about fifty times Allardeck had a secretary only because you did. You boasted in his hearing that you needed a secretary as you had so many horses to train, so he got one too.'

'He never could bear me having more than he did.'

'And if I remember right,' I said, 'you were hopping up and down when he got some practice starting stalls, until you got some too.'

'No one's perfect.' He shrugged dismissively. 'If the little rat hasn't got a secretary, who else knows his life inside out?'

'That,' I said, 'is indeed the question.'

'Maynard,' Grandfather said positively. 'That's who. Maynard lived in that house, remember, until long after he was married. He married at eighteen . . . stupid, I thought it, but Bobby was on the way. And then he was in and out for at least another fifteen years, when he was supposed to be Allardeck's assistant, but was always creeping off to London to do all those deals. Cocoa! Did you ever hear of anyone making a fortune out of cocoa? That was Maynard. Allardeck smirked about it for weeks, going on and on about how smart his son was. Well, my son was dead, as I reminded him pretty sharply one day, and he shut up after that.'

'Maynard wouldn't destroy Bobby's career,' I said.

'Why not? He hasn't spoken to him since he took up with Holly. Holly told me if Maynard wants to say anything to Bobby he gets his tame lawyer to write, and all the letters so far have been about Bobby repaying some money Maynard lent him to buy a car when he left school. Holly says Bobby was so grateful he wrote his father a letter thanking him and promising to repay him one day, and now Maynard's holding him to it.'

'I can't believe it.'

'Absolutely true.'

'What a bastard.'

'The one thing Maynard is actually not,' Grandfather said dryly, 'is a bastard. He's got Allardeck's looks stamped all over him. The same sneer. The same supercilious smirk. Lanky hair. No chin. The little rat's just like them, too.'

Bobby, the little rat, was to any but a Fielding eye a man with a perfectly normal chin and a rather pleasant smile, but I let it pass. The sins and shortcomings of the Allardecks, past and present, could never be assessed impartially in a Fielding house.

I stayed with Grandfather all afternoon and walked round the yard with him at evening stables at four-thirty, the short winter day already darkening and the lights in the boxes shining yellow.

The lads were busy, as always, removing droppings, carrying hay and water, setting the boxes straight. The long-time head-lad (at whom Grandfather never shouted) walked round with us, both of them briefly discussing details of each of the fifty or so horses. Their voices were quiet, absorbed and serious, and also in a way regretful, as the year's expectations and triumphs were all over, excitement put away.

I dreaded the prospect of those excitements being put away for ever: of Grandfather ill or dying. He wouldn't retire before he had to, because his job was totally his life, but it was expected that at some point not too very far ahead I would return to live in that house and take over the licence. Grandfather expected it, the owners were prepared for it, the racing world in general thought it a foregone conclusion; and I knew that I was far from ready. I wanted four more years, or five, at the game I had a passion for. I wanted to race for as long as my body was fit and uninjured and anyone would pay me. Jump jockeys never went on riding as long as flat jockeys because crunching to the ground at thirty miles an hour upwards of thirty times a year is a young man's sport, but I'd always thought of thirty-five as approximately hanging-up-the-boots time.

By the time I was thirty-five, Grandfather would be eighty-seven, and even for him . . . I shivered in the cold air and thrust the thought away. The future would have to be faced, but it wasn't upon me yet.

To Grandfather's great disgust I left him after stables and went back to the enemy house, to find the tail end of the same evening ritual still in progress. Graves's horses were still in the fillies' yard, and Bobby was feeling safer because Nigel had told him that Graves had at least twice mistaken other horses for his own when he'd called to see them on Sunday mornings.

I watched Bobby with his horses as he ran his hand down their legs to feel for heat in strained tendons, and peered at the progress of minor skin eruptions, and slapped their rumps as a friendly gesture. He was a natural-born horseman, there was no doubt, and the animals responded to him in the indefinable way that they do to someone they feel comfortable with.

I might find him a bit indecisive sometimes, and not a razor-brain, but he was in truth a good enough fellow, and I could see how Holly could love him. He had, moreover, loved her enough himself to turn his back on his ancestors and estrange himself from his powerful father, and it had taken strength, I reckoned, to do that.

He stood up from feeling a leg and saw me watching him, and with an instinct straight from the subconscious stretched to his full height and gave me a hawk-like look of vivid antagonism.

'Fielding,' he said flatly, as if the word itself was an accusation and a curse: a declaration of continuing war.

'Allardeck,' I replied, in the same way. I grinned slightly. 'I was thinking, as a matter of fact, that I liked you.'

'Oh!' He relaxed as fast as he'd tensed, and looked confused. 'I don't know . . . for a moment . . . I felt . . .'

'I know,' I said, nodding. 'Hatred.'

'Your eyes were in shadow. You looked . . . hooded.'

It was an acceptable explanation and a sort of apology; and I thought how irrational it was that the deep conditioning raised itself so quickly to the surface, and in myself on occasions just the same, however I might try to stop it.

He finished the horses without comment and we walked back towards the house.

'I'm sorry,' he said then, with a touch of awkwardness. 'Back there . . .' He waved a hand. 'I didn't mean it.'

I asked curiously, 'Do you ever think of Holly in that way? As a Fielding? If her eyes are in shadow, does she seem a menace?'

52

'No, of course not. She's different.'

'How is she different?'

He glanced at my face and seemed to find it all right to explain. 'You,' he said, 'are strong. I mean, in your mind, not just muscles. No one who's talked to you much could miss it. It makes you . . . I don't know . . . somehow people notice when you're there, like in the weighing room, or somewhere. People would be able to say if you'd been at a particular race meeting or not, or at a party, even though you don't try. I suppose I'm not making sense. It's what's made you a champion jockey, I should think, and it's totally *Fielding*. Well, Holly's not like that. She's gentle and calm and she hasn't an ounce of aggressiveness or ambition, and she doesn't want to go out and beat the world on horses, so she isn't really a Fielding at heart.'

'Mm.' It was a dry noise from the throat more than a word. Bobby gave me another quick glance. 'It's all right,' I said. 'I'll plead guilty to my inheritance, and also exonerate her from it. But she does have ambition.'

'No.' He shook his head positively.

'For you,' I said. 'For you to be a lasting success. For you both to be. To prove you were right to get married.'

He paused with his hand on the knob of the door which led from the yard to the kitchen. 'You were against it, like all the others.'

'Yes, for various reasons. But not now.'

'Not on the actual day,' he said with fairness. 'You were the only one that turned up.'

'She couldn't walk up that aisle by herself, could she?' I said. 'Someone had to go with her.'

He smiled as instinctively as before he'd hated.

'A Fielding giving a Fielding to an Allardeck,' he said. 'I wondered at the time if there would be an earthquake.'

He opened the door and we went in. Holly, who bound us together, had lit the log fire in the sitting room and was trying determinedly to be cheerful.

We sat in armchairs and I told them about my morning travels, and also assured them of Grandfather's non-involvement.

'The marked copies of the *Flag* were on people's mats at

least by six,' I said, 'and they came from outside, not from Newmarket. I don't know what time the papers get to the shops in Cambridge, but not a great deal before five, I shouldn't think, and there couldn't have been much time for anyone to buy twenty or so papers in Cambridge and deliver them, folded and marked, to addresses all over Newmarket, twenty miles away, before the newsboys here started on their rounds.'

'London?' Holly said. 'Do you think someone brought them up direct?'

'I should think so,' I nodded. 'Of course that doesn't necessarily mean that it wasn't someone from here who arranged it, or even did it personally, so we're not much further ahead.'

'It's all so pointless,' Holly said.

'No one seems to have been looking out of their windows by six,' I went on. 'You'd think someone would be, in this town. But no one that I asked had seen anyone walking up to anyone's door with a newspaper at that time. It was black dark, of course. They said they hardly ever see the newsboys themselves, in winter.'

The telephone on the desk beside Bobby's chair rang, and Bobby stretched out a hand to pick up the receiver with a look of apprehension.

'Oh . . . hello, Seb,' he said. There was some relief in his voice, but not much.

'Friend,' Holly said to me. 'Has a horse with us.'

'You saw it, did you?' Bobby made a face. 'Someone sent you a copy . . .' He listened, then said, 'No, of course I don't know who. It's sheer malice. No, of course it's not true. I'm here in business to stay, and don't worry, your mare is very well and I was just now feeling her tendon. It's cool and firm and doing fine. What? Father? He won't guarantee a penny, he said so. Yes, you may well say he's a ruthless swine . . . No, there's no hope of it. In fact on the contrary he's trying to squeeze out of me some money he lent me to buy a car about fourteen years ago. Yes, well . . . I suppose it's that sort of flint that's made him rich. What? No, not a fortune, it was a second-hand old banger, but my first. I suppose I'll have to pay him in the end just to get his lawyers off my back.

Yes, I told you, everything's fine. Pay no attention to the *Flag*. Sure, Seb, any time. Bye.'

He put down the receiver, his air nowhere near as confident as his telephone voice.

'Another owner full of doubt. Load of rats. Half of them are thinking of leaving without waiting to see if the ship will sink. Half of them, as well, haven't paid their last month's bills.'

'Has Seb?' asked Holly.

Bobby shook his head.

'He's got a cheek, then.'

'That wretched paragraph reached him by post yesterday: just the Intimate Details column. A clipping, he said, not the whole paper. In an ordinary brown envelope, typed. From London, like the others.'

'Did all the owners get a clipping?' I asked.

'It looks like it. Most of them have been on the phone. I haven't exactly rung the rest to ask.'

We sat around for a while, and I borrowed the telephone to pick up my messages from the answering machine in the cottage, and to call in return a couple of trainers who'd offered rides during the week, and to talk to a couple of jockeys who lived in Newmarket, asking for a lift down to Plumpton in Sussex for racing the next day. Two of them were already going together, they said, and would take me.

'Will you come back here?' Holly said, when all was fixed.

I looked at the anxiety in her face and the lack of opposition in Bobby's. I wouldn't have expected him to want me even in the first place, but it seemed I was wrong.

'Stay,' he said briefly, but with invitation, not grudge.

'I haven't been much help.'

'We feel better,' Holly said, 'with you here.'

I didn't much want to stay because of practical considerations. I was due to ride in Devon on the Tuesday, and one reason I preferred to live in Lambourn, not Newmarket, was that from Lambourn one could drive to every racecourse in England and return home on the same day. Lambourn was central.

I said apologetically, 'I'll have to get a lift back to Lambourn from Plumpton, because I need my car to go to Devon on

Tuesday. When I get back to Lambourn on Tuesday evening, we'll see how things are here.'

Holly said, 'All right' dispiritedly, not attempting to persuade.

I looked at her downcast face, more beautiful, as often, in sorrow than in joy. A thought came unexpectedly into my head and I said without reflection, 'Holly, are you pregnant?'

FIVE

Bobby was dumbstruck.

Holly gave me a piercing look from the light brown eyes in which I read both alarm and stimulation.

'Why did you say that?' Bobby demanded.

'I don't know.'

'She's only a short while overdue. We haven't had any tests done yet,' Bobby said; and to Holly, 'You must have told him.'

'No, I haven't.' She shook her head. 'But I was thinking just then how happy I was first thing on Friday, when I woke up feeling sick. I was thinking how ironic it would be. All those months of trying, and the first time it may really have happened, we are in such trouble that the very last thing we need is a baby.'

Bobby frowned. 'You must have told him,' he repeated, and he sounded definitely upset, almost as if he were jealous.

'Well, no, I didn't,' Holly said uncertainly.

'On the way back here yesterday,' he insisted.

'Look,' I said. 'Forget I said it. What does it matter?'

Bobby looked at me with resentment and then more forgivingly at Holly, as if some thought had struck him. 'Is this the sort of thing you meant,' he said doubtfully, 'when you told me once about you and Kit reading each other's minds when you were kids?'

She reluctantly nodded. 'We haven't done it for years, though.'

'It doesn't happen nowadays,' I agreed. 'I mean, this was just a once-off. A throw-back. I don't suppose it will happen again.'

And if it did happen again, I thought, I would be more

57

careful what I said. Stray thoughts would be sieved.

I understood Bobby's jealousy perfectly well because I had felt it myself, extraordinarily strongly, when Holly first told me she had fallen in love. The jealousy had been quickly overlaid by a more normal dismay when she'd confessed just who it was she'd set her heart on, but I still remembered the sharpness of not wanting to share her, not wanting my status as her closest friend to be usurped by a stranger.

I'd been slightly shocked at my jealousy and done a fair amount of soul-searching, never before having questioned my feelings for my sister: and I'd made the reassuring but also rueful discovery that she could sleep with Bobby all she liked and leave me undisturbed: it was the mental intimacy I minded losing.

There had been sexual adventures of my own, of course, both before and after her marriage, but they had been short-lived affairs with no deep involvement, nothing anywhere approaching Holly's commitment to Bobby. Plenty of time, I thought, and maybe, one of these days; and platitudes like that.

Bobby made at least a show of believing that telepathy between me and Holly wouldn't happen again, although both she and I, giving each other the merest flick of a glance, guessed differently. If we chose to tune in, so to speak, the old habit would come back.

The three of us spent the evening trying not to return over and over to the central questions of who and why, and in the end went wearily to bed without any possible answers. I lay down again in jeans, jersey and socks in case Graves should return, but I reckoned that if he'd ever planned it, he had had second thoughts.

I was wrong.

The bell woke me with a clatter at three-thirty-five in the morning, and I was into my shoes, out of the house and running down the drive, in the strategy that Bobby and I had discussed the night before, almost before it stopped ringing.

Out of the open gateway, turn left; and sure enough, on a stretch of roadside grass that sometimes accommodated gypsies, stood the wherewithal for shifting horses. A car, this time, towing a two-horse trailer. A trailer with its rear ramp lowered; ready, but not yet loaded.

I ran straight up to the car and yanked open the driver's door, but there was no one inside to be taken by surprise. Just keys in the ignition; unbelievable.

I lifted up the trailer's ramp and bolted it shut, then climbed into the car, started up, and drove a couple of hundred yards to a side road. I turned into there, parked a short way along, left the keys in the ignition as before, and sprinted back to Bobby's yard.

The scene was almost a repeat of the time before, at least as far as the lights, the shouting and obscenity went. Bobby and Jermyn Graves were standing outside the empty box where the alarm had been rigged and had all but come to blows. A thin boy of perhaps sixteen stood a short distance away, holding a large carrier bag, shifting from foot to foot and looking unhappy.

'Give me my property,' Graves yelled. 'This is stealing.'

'No, it's not,' I said in his ear. 'Stealing is an intention permanently to deprive.'

'What?' He swung round to glare at me. 'You again!'

'If you're talking law,' I said, 'it is within the law to withhold property upon which money is owed, until the debt is discharged.'

'I'll ruin you,' he said vindictively. 'I'll ruin you both.'

'Be sensible, Mr Graves,' I said. 'You're in the wrong.'

'Who the shit cares. I won't have some pipsqueak jockey and some bankrupt little trainer get the better of me, I'll tell you that.'

The attendant boy said nervously, 'Uncle . . .'

'You shut up,' Graves snapped.

The boy dropped the carrier and fell over his feet picking it up.

'Go away, Mr Graves,' I said. 'Calm down. Think it over. Come and fetch your horses when your cheque's been cleared, and that'll be the end of it.'

'No, it won't.'

'Up to you,' I said, shrugging.

Bobby and I watched him try to extricate himself without severe loss of face, which could hardly be done. He delivered a few more threats with a good deal of bluster, and then finally, saying 'Come on, come on' irritably to his nephew, he stalked away down the drive.

'Did you immobilise his horsebox?' Bobby asked.

'It was a car and a trailer, and the key was in it. I just drove it out of sight round the nearest corner. Wonder if they'll find it.'

'I suppose we needn't have bothered,' Bobby said. 'As Graves went to the alarm box first.'

We had thought he might go to his other horse's box first, find it empty, think he had the wrong place, and perhaps remove one of the horses from either side. We thought he might have brought more men. In the event, he hadn't done either. But the precaution, all the same, might have been worth it.

We closed the empty stable and Bobby kicked against something on the ground. He bent to pick it up, and held it out for me to see: a large piece of thick felt with pieces of velcro attached. A silencer for a hoof. Fallen out of the carrier, no doubt.

'Not leather boots,' Bobby said, grimly. 'Home-made.'

He switched off the yard lights and we stood for a while near the kitchen door, waiting. We would hear the car and trailer drive off, we thought, in the quiet night. What we heard instead, however, were hesitant footsteps coming back into the yard.

Bobby turned the lights on again, and the boy stood there, blinking and highly embarrassed.

'Someone's stolen Uncle's car,' he said.

'What's your name?' I asked.

'Jasper.'

'Graves?'

He nodded and swallowed. 'Uncle wants me to ring the police and get a taxi.'

'If I were you,' I said, 'I'd go out of the gate here, turn left, take the first turn to the left along the road a bit, and use the public telephone box you'll find down there.'

'Oh,' he said. 'All right.' He looked at us almost beseechingly. 'It was only supposed to be a lark,' he said. 'It's all gone wrong.'

We gave him no particular comfort, and after a moment he turned and went away again down the drive, his footsteps slowly receding.

'What do you think?' Bobby said.

'I think we should rig the bell so that anyone coming up the drive sets it off.'

'So do I. And I'll disconnect it first thing when I get up.'

We began to run a blackened string tightly across the drive at knee level, and heard Graves's car start up in the distance.

'He's found it,' Bobby said. He smiled. 'There's no telephone box down that road, did you know?'

We finished the elementary alarm system and went yawning indoors to sleep for another couple of hours, and I reflected, as I lay down, about the way a feud could start, as with Graves, and continue through centuries, as with Allardecks and Fieldings, and could expand into political and religious persecutions on a national scale, permanently persisting as a habit of mind, a destructive hatred stuck in one groove. I would make a start in my own small corner, I thought sardonically, drifting off, and force my subconscious to love the Allardecks, of which my own sister, God help her, was one.

Persistence raised its ugliest head first thing in the morning.

I answered the telephone when it rang at eight-thirty because Bobby was out exercising his horses and Holly was again feeling sick: and it was the feed-merchant calling in his Etonian accent to say that he had received a further copy of the *Daily Flag*.

'I've just picked it up,' he said. 'It's today's paper. Monday. There's another piece outlined in red.'

'What does it say?' I asked, my heart sinking.

'I think . . . well . . . you can come and fetch it, if you like. It's longer, this time. And there's a picture of Bobby.'

'I'll be there.'

I drove straight round in Holly's car and found the feed-merchant in his office as before. Silently he handed me the paper, and with growing dismay I looked at the picture which made Bobby seem a grinning fool, and read the damage in Intimate Details.

*Money troubles abound for Robertson (Bobby) Allardeck
(32), still training a few racehorses in his grandfather's
once-bustling stables in Newmarket. Local traders threaten
court action over unpaid bills. Bobby weakly denies the
owners of the remaining horses should be worried, although
the feed-merchant has stopped deliveries. Where will it end?*

Not with manna from heaven from Daddy.

*Maynard 'Moneybags' Allardeck (50), cross with Bobby
for marrying badly, won't come to the rescue.*

*Maynard, known to be fishing for a knighthood, gives
all his spare cash to charity.*

Needy Bobby's opinion? Unprintable.

Watch this space for more.

'If Bobby doesn't sue for libel,' I said, 'his father surely
will.'

'Greater the truth, greater the libel,' the feed-merchant said
dryly, and added, 'Tell Bobby his credit's good with me again.
I've been thinking it over. He's always paid me regularly, even
if always late. And I don't like being manipulated by muck
like that.' He pointed to the paper. 'So tell Bobby I'll supply
him as before. Tell him to tell his owners.'

I thanked him and went back to Bobby's house, and read
Intimate Details again over a cup of coffee in the kitchen.
Then I pensively telephoned the feed-merchant.

'Did you,' I said, 'actually tell anyone that you intended to
stop making deliveries to Bobby?'

'I told Bobby.' He sounded equally thoughtful. 'No one
else.'

'Sure?'

'Positive.'

'Not even your secretary? Or your family?'

'I admit that on Friday I was very annoyed and wanted my
money immediately, but no one overheard my giving Bobby
a talking to about it, I'm quite certain. My secretary doesn't
come in until eleven on Fridays, and as you know, my office
is an annexe. I was alone when I telephoned him, I assure
you.'

'Well, thanks,' I said.

'The informant must be at Bobby's end,' he insisted.

'Yes. I think you're right.'

We disconnected and I began to read the *Daily Flag* from start to finish, which I'd never done before, seeking enlightenment perhaps on what made a newspaper suddenly attack an inoffensive man and aim to destroy him.

The *Flag*'s overall and constant tone, I found, was of self-righteous spite, its message a sneer, its aftertaste guaranteed to send a reader belligerently out looking for an excuse to take umbrage or to spread ill-will.

Any story that would show someone in a poor light was in. Praise was out. The put-down had been developed to a minor art, so that a woman, however prominent or successful, did not 'say'; instead she 'trilled', or she 'shrilled', or she 'wailed'. A man 'chortled', or he 'fumed', or he 'squeaked'.

The word 'anger' appeared on every single page. All sorts of things were 'slammed', but not doors. People were reported as denying things in a way that interpreted 'deny' as 'guilty but won't own up'; and the word 'claims', in the *Flag*'s view, as, for instance, in 'He claims he saw . . .' was synonymous with 'He is lying when he says he saw . . .'

The *Flag* thought that respect was unnecessary, envy was normal, all motives were sleazy and only dogs were loved; and presumably it was what people wanted to read, as the circulation (said the *Flag*) was increasing daily.

On the premise that a newspaper ultimately reflected the personality of its owner, as the *Towncrier* did Lord Vaughnley's, I thought the proprietor of the *Daily Flag* to be destructive, calculating, mean-spirited and dangerous. Not a good prospect. It meant one couldn't with any hope of success appeal to the *Flag*'s better nature to let up on Bobby, because a better nature it didn't have.

Holly came downstairs looking wan but more cheerful, Bobby returned from the Heath with reviving optimism, and I found the necessity of demolishing their fragile recovery just one more reason to detest the *Flag*.

Holly began to cry quietly and Bobby strode about the kitchen wanting to smash things, and still there was the unanswerable question: Why?

'This time,' I said, 'you consult your lawyer, and to hell with the cost. Also this time we are going to pay all your worst bills at once, and we are going to get letters from all your creditors saying they have been paid, and we'll get those letters photocopied by the dozen, and we'll send a set of them out to everyone who got a copy of the *Flag*, and to the *Flag* itself, to Sam Leggatt, the editor, special delivery, and to all the owners, and to anyone else we can think of, and we'll accompany these with a letter of your own saying you don't understand why the *Flag* is attacking you but the attacks have no foundation, the stable is in good shape and you are certainly not going out of business.'

'But,' Holly said, gulping, 'the bank manager won't honour our cheques.'

'Get the worst bills,' I said to Bobby, 'and let's have a look at them. 'Specially the blacksmith, the vets and the transport people. We'll pay those and any others that are vital.'

'What with?' he said irritably.

'With my money.'

They were both suddenly still, as if shocked, and I realised with a thrust of pleasure that that plain solution simply hadn't occurred to them. They were not askers, those two.

Holly couldn't disguise her upsurge of hope, but she said doubtfully, 'Your new house, though. It must be taking you all you've saved. You haven't been paid for the cottage yet.'

'There's enough,' I assured her. 'And let's get started because I'll have to be off to Plumpton pretty soon.'

'But we can't . . .' Bobby said.

'Yes, you must. Don't argue.'

Bobby looked pole-axed but he fetched the bunch of accounts and I made out several cheques.

'Take these round yourself this morning and get watertight receipts, and in a minute we'll write the letter to go with them,' I said. 'And see if you can get them all photocopied and clipped into sets in time to catch this afternoon's post. I know it's a bit of a job, but the sooner very much the better, don't you think?'

'And one set to Graves?' Bobby asked.

'Certainly to Graves.'

'We'll start immediately,' Holly said.

'Don't forget the feed-merchant,' I said. 'He'll write you

something good. He didn't like being made use of by the *Flag*.'

'I don't like to mention it . . .' Holly began slowly.

'The bank?' I asked.

She nodded.

'Leave the bank for now. Tomorrow maybe you can go to the manager with a set of letters and see if he will reinstate you. He darned well ought to. His bank's making enough out of you in interest, especially on the yearling loans. And you do still have the yearlings as security.'

'Unfortunately,' Bobby said.

'One step at a time,' I said.

'I'll telephone my solicitor straight away,' he said, picking up the receiver and looking at his watch. 'He'll be in by now.'

'No, I shouldn't,' I said.

'But you said . . .'

'You've got an informant right inside this house.'

'What do you mean?'

'Your telephone,' I said, 'I should think.'

He looked at it with disgusted understanding and in a half-groan said, 'Oh, God.'

'It's been done before,' I said: and there had in fact been a time in Lambourn when everyone had been paranoid about being overheard and had gone to elaborate lengths to avoid talking on their home telephones. Illegal it might well be to listen uninvited, but it was carried on nevertheless, as everyone knew.

Without more ado we unscrewed all the telephones in the house, but found no limpet-like bugs inside. Horses, however, not electronics, were our speciality, and Bobby said he would go out to a public box and ring up the telephone company and ask them to come themselves to see what they could find.

It happened at one point that Bobby was on his knees by the kitchen wall screwing together the telephone junction there and Holly and I were standing side by side in the centre of the room, watching him, so that when the newcomer suddenly arrived among us unannounced it was my sister and I that he saw first.

A tall man with fair hair fading to grey, immensely well brushed. Neat, good-looking features, smoothly shaven rounded chin; trim figure inside a grey City suit of the most impeccable breeding. A man of fifty, a man of power whose very presence filled the kitchen, a man holding a folded copy of the *Daily Flag* and looking at Holly and me with open loathing.

Maynard Allardeck; Bobby's father.

Known to me, as I to him, as the enemy. Known to each other by frequent sight, by indoctrination, by professional repute. Ever known, never willingly meeting.

'Fieldings,' he said with battering hate; and to me directly, 'What do you think you're doing in this house?'

'I asked him,' Bobby said, straightening up.

His father turned abruptly in his direction, seeing his son for the first time closely face to face for more than four years.

They stared at each other for a long moment as if frozen, as if re-learning familiar features, taking physical stock. Seeing each other perhaps as partial strangers, freshly. Whatever any of us might have expected or wished for in the way of reconciliation, it turned out to be the opposite of what Maynard had in mind. He had come neither to help nor even to commiserate, but to complain.

Without any form of greeting he said, 'How dare you drag me into your sordid little troubles.' He waved his copy of the *Flag*. 'I won't have you whining to the Press about something that's entirely your own fault. If you want to marry into a bunch of crooks, take your consequences and keep me out of it.'

I imagine we all blinked, as Bobby was doing. Maynard's voice was thick with anger and his sudden onslaught out of all proportion, but it was his reasoning above all which had us stunned.

'I didn't,' Bobby said, almost rocking on his feet. 'I mean, I haven't talked to the Press. I wouldn't. They just wrote it.'

'And this part about me refusing you money? How else would they know, if you hadn't told them? Answer me that.'

Bobby swallowed. 'You've always said ... I mean, I thought you meant it, that you wouldn't.'

'Of course I mean it.' His father glared at him. 'I won't. That's not the point. You've no business snivelling about it in public and I won't have it. Do you hear?'

'I haven't,' Bobby protested, but without conviction.

I thought how much father and son resembled each other in looks, and how little in character. Maynard had six times the force of Bobby but none of his sense of fair play. Maynard could make money work for him, Bobby worked to be paid. Maynard could hold a grudge implacably for ever, Bobby could waver and crumble and rethink. The comparative weaknesses in Bobby, I thought, were also his strength.

'You must have been blabbing.' Maynard was uncompromisingly offensive in his tone, and I thought that if Bobby ever wanted to announce to the whole world that his father would let him sink, he would have every provocation and every right.

Bobby said with a rush, 'We think someone may have been tapping our telephone.'

'Oh, you do, do you?' Maynard said ominously, casting an angry look at the silent instrument. 'So it's on the telephone you've been bleating about me, is it?'

'No,' Bobby said, half stuttering. 'I mean, no I haven't. But one or two people said ask your father for money, and I told them I couldn't.'

'And this bit,' Maynard belted the air furiously with the newspaper, 'about me fishing for a knighthood. I won't have it. It's a damned lie.'

It struck me forcibly at that point, perhaps because of an undisguisable edge of fear in his voice, that it was the bit about the knighthood which lay at the real heart of Maynard's rage.

It was no lie, I thought conclusively. It was true. He must indeed be trying actively to get himself a title. Grandfather had said that Maynard at nine had wanted to be a lord. Maynard at fifty was still the same person, but now with money, with influence, with no doubt a line to the right ears. Maynard might be even then in the middle of delicate but entirely unlawful negotiations.

Sir Maynard Allardeck. It certainly rolled well off the tongue. Sir Maynard. Bow down to me, you Fieldings. I am your superior, bow low.

'I didn't say anything about a knighthood,' Bobby protested with more force. 'I mean, I didn't know you wanted one. I never said anything about it. I never thought of it.'

'Why don't you sue the newspaper?' I said.

'You keep quiet,' he said to me vehemently. 'Keep your nose out.' He readdressed himself to Bobby. 'If you didn't mention a knighthood on the telephone, how did they get hold of it? Why did they write that . . . that damned lie? Answer me that.'

'I don't know,' Bobby said, sounding bewildered. 'I don't know why they wrote any of it.'

'Someone has put you up to stirring up trouble against me,' Maynard said, looking hard and mean and deadly in earnest.

We all three stared at him in amazement. How anyone could think that was beyond me.

Bobby said with more stuttering, 'Of course not. I mean, that's stupid. It's not you that's in trouble because of what they wrote, it's me. I wouldn't stir up trouble against myself. It doesn't make sense.'

'Three people telephoned me before seven this morning to tell me there was another paragraph in today's *Flag*,' Maynard said angrily. 'I bought a copy on my way here. I was instantly certain it was your poisonous brother-in-law or his pig of a grandfather who was at the back of it, it's just their filthy sort of thing.'

'No,' Holly said.

Maynard ignored her as if she hadn't spoken.

'I came in here to tell you it served you right,' he said to Bobby, 'and to insist on your forcing the Fieldings to get a full retraction printed in the paper.'

'But,' Bobby said, shaking his head as if concussed, 'it wasn't Kit. He wouldn't do that. Nor his grandfather.'

'You're soft,' Maynard said contemptuously. 'You've never understood that someone can smile into your face while they shove a knife through your ribs.'

'Because of Holly,' Bobby insisted, 'they wouldn't.'

'You're a naive fool,' his father said. 'Why shouldn't they try to break up your marriage? They never wanted it, any more than I did. They're a wily, shifty, vengeful family, the whole lot of them, and if you trust any one of them, you deserve what you get.'

Bobby gave me a quick glance in which I read only discomfort, not doubt. Neither Holly nor I offered any sort of defence because mere words wouldn't dent the opinions that Maynard had held all his life, and nor would hitting him. Moreover we had heard the same sort of invective too often from Grandfather on the subject of the Allardecks. We were more or less immune, by then, to violent reaction. It was Bobby, interestingly, who protested.

'Kit and Holly care what becomes of me,' he said. 'You don't. Kit came to help, and you didn't. So I'll judge as I find, and I don't agree with what you say.'

Maynard looked as if he could hardly believe his ears, and nor, to be honest, could I. It wasn't just that what Bobby was expressing was a heretical defection from his upbringing, but that he also had the courage to stand up to his father and say it to his face.

He looked, as a matter of fact, slightly nervous. Maynard, it was said, inspired wholesale nervousness in the boardroom of any business his eye fell on, and as of that morning I understood why. The unyielding ruthlessness in him, clearly perceptible to all three of us, was central to his success, and for us at least he made no attempt to disguise it or dress it with a façade of charm.

Bobby made a frustrated gesture with both hands, walked over to the sink and began to fill the kettle.

'Do you want any coffee?' he said to his father.

'Of course not.' He spoke as if he'd been insulted. 'I've a committee meeting at the Jockey Club.' He looked at his watch, and then at me. 'You,' he said, 'have attacked me. And you'll suffer for it.'

I said calmly but distinctly, 'If I hear you have said in the Jockey Club that a Fielding is responsible for what has appeared in the *Flag*, I will personally sue you for slander.'

Maynard glared. He said, 'You're filth by birth, you're not worth the fuss that's made of you, and I'd be glad to see you dead.'

I felt Holly beside me begin to spring forward in some passionate explosion of feeling and gripped her wrist tight to stop her. I was actually well satisfied. I had read in Maynard's eyes that he was inclined to take me seriously, but he didn't want me to know it, and I understood also, for the first time, and with unease, that the very fact of my being successful, of being champion, was to him, in his obsession, intolerable.

Along at the Jockey Club, which had its ancient head-quarters in Newmarket's main street, and where he had been one of its members for four or five years, Maynard would with luck now pass off the whole *Flag* thing with a grouchy joke. There, in the organisation which ruled the racing industry, he would show all courtesy and hide the snarl. There, where he served on dogsbody committees while he made his determined way up that particular ladder, aiming perhaps to be a Steward, one of the top triumvirate, before long, he would now perhaps be careful to say nothing that could get back to my ears.

There were no active professional jockeys in the Jockey Club, nor any licensed trainers, though a few retired practitioners of both sorts sprinkled the ranks. There were many racehorse owners, among whom I had real friends. The approximately 140 members, devoted to the welfare of racing, were self-perpetuating, self-elected. If Maynard had ever campaigned quietly to be chosen for membership it might have helped him to be a member of an old-established racing family, and it might have helped him to be rich, but one thing was certain: he would never have unsheathed for the civilised inspection of his peers the raw, brutal anti-Fielding prejudice he had given spleen to in the kitchen. Nothing alienated the courteous members more than ill-mannered excess.

The preserving of Maynard's public good manners was very much my concern.

He went as he'd come, private manners non-existent, walking out of the kitchen without a farewell. We listened to the firm footsteps recede and to the distant slam of a car door, and his engine starting.

'Do you realise,' Bobby said to me slowly, 'that if he's made a Steward and you're still a jockey ... you'd be horribly vulnerable ...?'

'Mm,' I said dryly. 'Very nasty indeed.'

SIX

I rode at Plumpton. A typical day of four rides; one win, one third, one nowhere, one very nearly last, with owner reactions to match.

Far more people than in the previous week seemed to have seen the pieces in Intimate Details, and I spent a good deal of the day assuring all who asked that, no, Bobby wasn't bankrupt, and yes, I was certain, and no, I couldn't say for sure what Bobby's father's intentions were in any respect.

There were the usual small scattering of racing journalists at the meeting, but no one from the *Flag*. The racing column in the *Flag* was most often the work of a sharp young man who wrote disparagingly about what was to come and critically of what was past, and who was avoided whenever possible by all jockeys. On that day, however, I would have been satisfied enough to see him, but had to make do with his equivalent on the *Towncrier*.

'You want to know about the *Flag*? Whatever for? Disgusting rag.' Large and benevolent, Bunty Ireland, the *Towncrier*'s man, spoke with the complacency of a more respectful rag behind him. 'But if you want to know if the parts about your brother-in-law are the work of our sharp-nosed colleague, then no, I'm pretty sure they're not. He was at Doncaster on Friday and he didn't know at first what was in the gossip column. Slightly put out, he was, when he found out. He said the gossip people hadn't consulted him and they should have done. He was his usual endearing sunny self.' Bunty Ireland beamed. 'Anything else?'

'Yes,' I said. 'Who runs Intimate Details?'

'Can't help you there, old son. I'll ask around, if you like. But it won't do Bobby much good, you can't just go and bop us fellows on the nose, however great the provocation.'

Never be too sure, I thought.

I cadged a lift home to Lambourn, ate some lobster and an orange, and thought about telephoning Holly.

Someone, it was certain, would be listening in on the line. Someone had probably been listening in on that line for quite a long period. Long enough to make a list of people Bobby dealt with in Newmarket, long enough to know where he banked, long enough to know how things stood between him and his father. The owner who had telephoned to say he couldn't afford to pay fifty thousand for his yearling must have been listened to, and so must Bobby's unsuccessful attempts to sell it to anyone else.

Someone must indeed have listened also to Bobby's racing plans and to his many conversations with owners and jockeys. There was no trainer alive who wouldn't in the fullness of time have passed unflattering or downright slanderous opinions about jockeys to owners and vice versa, but nothing of that nature had been used in the paper. No 'inside' revelations of betting coups. No innuendoes about regulations broken or crimes committed, such as giving a horse an easy race, a common practice for which one could be fined or even have one's licence suspended if found out. The target hadn't in fact been Bobby's training secrets, but his financial status alone.

Why?

Too many whys.

I pressed the necessary buttons and the bell rang only once at the other end.

'Kit?' Holly said immediately.

'Yes.'

'Did you try earlier?'

'No,' I said.

'That's all right, then. We've left the receiver off for most of the day, the calls were so awful. But it just occurred to me that you might be trying to ring, so I put it back less than a minute ago . . .' Her voice faded away as she realised what she was saying. 'We've done it again,' she said.

'Yes.'

She must have heard the smile in my voice, because it was in hers also when she replied.

'Look,' she said. 'I've been thinking . . . I've got to go out, now. I'll ring you later, OK?'

'Sure,' I said.

'Bye.'

'Bye,' I said, and disconnected. I also waited, wondering where she would go. Where she'd planned. She called back within fifteen minutes and it was unexpectedly from the feed-merchant's office. The feed-merchant, it appeared, had let her in, switched on the heater, and left her in private.

'He's been terribly good,' Holly explained. 'I think he'd been feeling a bit guilty, though he's no need to really. Anyway I told him we thought our telephone might be bugged and he said he thought it highly possible, and I could come in here and use the phone whenever I liked. I said I'd like to ring you this evening . . . and anyway, here I am.'

'Great,' I said. 'How are things going?'

'We spent the whole day doing those letters and we're frankly bushed. Bobby's asleep on his feet. Everyone took your cheque without question and gave us paid-in-full letters, and we photocopied those and also the rebuttal letter we all wrote before you went to Plumpton, and by the time we'd finished putting everything in the envelopes the last post was just going, and in fact the postman actually waited at the post office while I stuck on the last ten stamps, and I saw him take the special delivery one to the editor of the *Flag*, so with luck, with luck, it will be all over.'

'Mm,' I said. 'Let's hope so.'

'Oh, and Bobby went to see the solicitor, who said he would write a strong letter of protest to the editor and demand a retraction in the paper, like Lord Vaughnley told you, but Bobby says he isn't sure that that letter will have gone today, he says the solicitor didn't seem to think it was frantically urgent.'

'Tell Bobby to get a different solicitor.'

Holly almost laughed. 'Yes. OK.'

We made plans and times for me to talk to her again the next evening after I got home from Devon, but it was at eight in the morning when my telephone rang and her voice came sharp and distressed into my ear.

'It's Holly,' she said. 'Get a copy of the *Flag*. I'll be along where I was last night. OK?'

'Yes,' I said.

She disconnected without another word, and I drove to the village for the paper.

The column would have been printed during the past night. The special delivery envelope wouldn't reach the editor until later in the present morning. I thought in hindsight it would have been better for Bobby to have driven the letter to London and specially delivered it himself, which might just possibly have halted the campaign.

The third broadside read:

Don't pity Robertson (Bobby) Allardeck (32), strapped for cash but still trying to train racehorses in Newmarket. It's the small trader who suffers when fat cats run up unpaid bills.

In his luxury home yesterday Bobby refused to comment on reports he came to blows with the owner of one of the horses in the stable, preventing the owner taking his horse away by force. 'I deny everything,' Bobby fumed.

Meanwhile Daddy Maynard ('Moneybags') Allardeck (50) goes on record as prize skinflint of the month. 'My son won't get a penny in aid from me,' he intones piously. 'He doesn't deserve it.'

Instead Moneybags lavishes ostentatious hand-outs on good deserving charities dear to the Government's heart. Can knighthoods be bought nowadays? Of course not!

Bobby wails that while Daddy lashes out the loot on the main chance, he (Bobby) gets threatening letters from Daddy's lawyers demanding repayment of a fourteen-year-old loan. Seems Moneybags advanced a small sum for 18-year-old Bobby to buy a banger on leaving school. With the wheels a long-ago memory on the scrapheap, Daddy wants his money back. Bobby's opinion of Daddy? 'Ruthless swine.'

Can stingy Maynard be extorting interest on top?
Watch this space.

74

Thoughtfully I got the feed-merchant's number from directory enquiries and pressed the buttons: Holly was waiting at the other end.

'What are we going to do?' she said miserably. 'They're such pigs. All those quotes . . . they just made them up.'

'Yes,' I said. 'If you could bear to put together another batch of those letters you sent yesterday, it might do some good to send them to the editors of the other national newspapers, and to the *Sporting Life*. None of them likes the *Flag*. A spot of ridicule from its rivals might make the *Flag* shut up.'

'Might,' Holly said, unconvinced.

'Doing everything one can think of is better than doing nothing,' I said. 'You never know which pellet might kill the bird when you loose off the shot.'

'Poetic,' Holly said sardonically. 'All right. We'll try.'

'And what about the solicitor?' I asked.

'Bobby says he'll find a better one today. Not local. In a London firm. High powered.'

'Some of his owners may know who's best,' I said. 'If not, I could get him a name from one of the people I ride for.'

'Great.'

'But do you know something?' I said.

'What?'

'I'm not so sure that Maynard was very far wrong. All this aggro is aimed as much at him as at Bobby.'

'Yes,' Holly said slowly. 'When we read today's bit of dirt, that's what Bobby thought too.'

'I wouldn't mind betting,' I said, 'that a fair few copies of Intimate Details, episodes one, two and three, will find their way to the attention of the Honours' Secretary in Downing Street. And that this was chiefly what was at the bottom of Maynard's anger yesterday. If Maynard is really being considered for a knighthood, Intimate Details could have put the lid on his chances, at least for just now.'

'Do you think it would? Just a few words in a paper?'

'You never know. The whole Honours thing is so sensitive. Anyway it's about now that they send out those ultra-secret letters asking Mr Bloggs if he would accept a medal if invited. They'll be drawing up the New Year's Honours' List at this moment. And the sixty-four dollar question is, if you were the

Honours' Secretary drawing up a list for the Prime Minister's approval, would you put Maynard on it?'

'But we don't know that anything like that is happening.'

'No, we sure don't.'

'It's probably just the *Flag* being its typically vicious, mean, destructive self.'

'Perhaps,' I said.

'You know how nasty the Press can be, if they want to. And the *Flag* seems to want to, all the time, as a matter of policy.'

'Mm,' I said. 'Maybe you're right.'

'But you don't think so?'

'Well ... It would make more sense if we could see a purpose behind these attacks, and stopping Maynard getting a knighthood would be a purpose. But why they'd want to stop it, and how they got to hear of it ... hell alone knows.'

'They didn't hear about any knighthood from our telephone,' Holly said positively. 'So perhaps they're just making it up.'

'Everything else in those stories is founded on things that have happened or been said,' I pointed out. 'They've taken the truth and distorted it. Shall I write to the Honours' Secretary and ask if Maynard's on his provisional list?'

'Yes, yes, funny joke.'

'Anyway,' I said. 'How did Bobby get on with the telephone people?'

'They said they would look into it. They said telephone tapping is illegal as of 1985. They didn't send anyone here yesterday looking for bugs. They said something about checking our exchange.'

'The exchange? I didn't know people could tap into an exchange.'

'Well, apparently they can.'

'So no actual bugs?'

'We told them we couldn't find any and they said we probably didn't know where to look.'

'Well, at least they're paying attention.'

'They said a lot of people think they're being bugged when they aren't,' Holly said. 'All the same, they did say they would look.'

'Keep them up to it.'

'Yes.'

'I'll ring you this evening when I get back from Devon,' I said. 'If I don't get back . . . I'll ring sometime.'

'Yes,' she said. 'Take care of yourself.'

'Always do,' I said automatically; and both she and I knew it was impossible. If a steeplechase jockey took too much care of himself, he didn't win races, and there were days occasionally when one couldn't drive oneself home. I was superstitious to the extent of not making binding commitments for the evenings of race-days, and like most other jump jockeys accepted invitations with words like 'If I can' and 'With luck'.

I drove the two hours to the Devon and Exeter meeting with my mind more on Holly and Bobby and Maynard than on the work ahead. None of the five horses I was due to ride posed the problems of North Face, and I'd ridden all of them often enough to know their little quirks and their capabilities. All I had to do was help them turn in the best they could do on the day.

The Devon and Exeter racecourse lay on the top of Halden Moor, a majestic sweep of bare countryside with the winds blowing vigorously from the Channel to the Atlantic. The track itself, with its long circuit of almost two miles, stretched away as a green undulating ribbon between oceans of scrub and heather, its far deserted curves as private a place as one could imagine for contest of horse and man.

Unfashionable in Ascot terms, distant geographically, drawing comparatively small crowds, it was still one of my favourite courses; well run, well kept, with welcoming locals, nice people.

The princess liked to go there because friends of hers maintained one of the few private boxes, friends who had a house down by a Devon beach and who invited her to stay regularly for the meetings.

She was there, lunched, fur-coated and discreetly excited, in good time for the first race, accompanied in the parade ring by a small bunch of the friends. Three friends, to be exact. The couple she stayed with, and a young woman.

The princess made introductions. 'Kit . . . you know Mr

77

and Mrs Inscombe . . .' We shook hands. '. . . And my niece. Have you met my niece, Danielle?'

No, I hadn't. I shook the niece's hand.

'Danielle de Brescou,' the niece said. 'Hi. How're you doing?' And in spite of her name she was not French but audibly American.

I took in briefly the white wool short coat, the black trousers, the wide band of what looked like flowered chintz holding back a lot of dark hair. I got in return a cool look of assessment; half interest, half judgment deferred, topped by a bright smile of no depth.

'What shall we expect?' the princess asked. 'Will Bernina win?'

Wykeham, naturally, had not made the journey to Devon. Moreover he had been vague when I'd talked to him on the telephone, seeming almost unclear as to Bernina's identity, let alone her state of readiness, and it had been Dusty, when I'd handed him my saddle to put on to the mare before the race, who had told me she was 'jumping out of her skin and acting up something chronic'.

'She's fit and ready,' I said to the princess.

'And Wykeham's riding instructions?' Mr Inscombe enquired genially. 'What are those?'

Wykeham's instructions to me were zero, as they had been for several years. I said diplomatically, 'Stay handy in fourth place or thereabouts and kick for home at the second last hurdle.'

Inscombe nodded benevolent approval and I caught the ghost of a grin from the princess, who knew quite well that Wykeham's instructions, if any, would have taken the form of 'Win if you can', an uncomplicated declaration of honesty by no means universal among trainers.

Wykeham produced his horses fighting fit from a mixture of instinct, inherited wisdom, and loving them individually as athletes and children. He knew how to bring them to a peak and understood their moods and preferences, and if nowadays he found the actual races less interesting than the preparation, he was still, just, one of the greats.

I had been his retained jockey for the whole of the main part of my career and he frequently called me by the name of

78

my predecessor. He quite often told me I would be riding horses long dead. 'Polonium in the big race at Sandown,' he would say, and, mystified, I would ask who owned the horse as I'd never heard of it. 'Polonium? Don't be stupid. Big chestnut. Likes mints. You won on him last week.' 'Oh . . . Pepperoni?' 'What? Yes, Pepperoni, of course, that's what I said. Big race at Sandown.'

He was almost as old as my grandfather, and gradually, through their eyes, I was coming to see the whole of racing as a sort of stream that rolled onwards through time, the new generations rising and the old floating slowly away. Racing had a longer history than almost any other sport and changed less, and sometimes I had a powerful feeling of repeating in my own person the experience of generations of jockeys before me and of being a transient speck in a passing pageant; vivid today, talked about, fêted, but gone tomorrow, a memory fading into a footnote, until no one alive had seen me race or cared a damn whether I'd won or lost.

Dead humbling, the whole thing.

Bernina, named after the mountain to the south of St Moritz, had by four years old produced none of the grandeur of the Alps, and to my mind was never going to. She could, however, turn in a respectable performance in moderate company, which was all she was faced with on that occasion, and I hoped very much to win on her, as much for the princess's sake as my own. I understood very well that she liked to be able to please the various hosts around the country who offered her multiple invitations, and was always slightly anxious for her horses to do well where she felt they might contribute to her overnight bread and butter. I thought that if people like the Inscombes didn't enjoy her company for its own sake they wouldn't keep on asking her to stay. The princess's inner insecurities were sometimes astonishing.

Bernina, without any of the foregoing complications of intent, took me out of the parade ring and down to the start in her best immoderate fashion which included a display of extravagant head-shaking and some sideways dancing on her toes. These preliminaries were a good sign: on her off days she went docilely to the starting gate, left it without enthusiasm and took her time about finishing. Last time out she'd had me hauled in front of the Stewards and fined for not trying hard enough to win, and I'd said they should have understood that a horse that doesn't want to race won't race; and that mares have dull days like anyone else. They listened, unimpressed. Pay the fine, they said.

The princess had insisted on reimbursing me for that little lot, where other owners might have raged. 'If she wouldn't go, she wouldn't go,' she'd said with finality. 'And she's my horse, so I'm responsible for her debts.' Owners didn't come more illogical or more generous than the princess.

I'd told her never to let her friends back Bernina on the days she went flat-footed to the start, and she'd acknowledged the advice gravely. I hoped, sitting on top of the bravura performance going on in Devon, that she, the Inscombes and the niece would all be at that moment trekking to the bookmakers or the Tote. The mare was feeling good, and, beyond that, competitive.

The event was a two-mile hurdle race, which meant eight jumps over the sort of fencing used for penning sheep: hurdles made of wood and threaded with gorse or brushwood, each section unattached to the hurdle on either side, so that if a horse hit one, it could be knocked over separately. Good jumpers flowed over hurdles easily, rising little in the air but bending up their forelegs sharply; the trick was to get them to take off from where the hurdle could be crossed in mid-stride.

Bernina, graciously accepting my guidance in that matter, went round the whole course without touching a twig. She also attacked the job of beating her opponents with such gusto that one mightn't have blamed the Stewards this time for testing her for dope, such was the contrast.

She would, if she'd had serious talent, have won by twenty lengths, especially as the chief danger had fallen in a flurry of legs about halfway round. As it was, she made enough progress, when I gave her an encouraging kick between the last two hurdles, to reach the last jump upsides of the only horse still in front, and on the run-in she produced a weak burst of speed for just long enough to pass and demoralise her tiring opponent.

Accepting my congratulatory pats on her victorious neck as totally her due, she pulled up and pranced back to the winners' enclosure, and skittered about there restlessly, sweating copiously and rolling her eyes, up on a high like any other triumphant performer.

The princess, relieved and contented, kept out of the way of the powerful body as I unbuckled the girths and slid my saddle off on to my arm. She didn't say much herself as the Inscombes were doing a good deal of talking, but in any case she didn't have to. I knew what she thought and she knew I knew: we'd been through it all a couple of hundred times before.

The niece said, 'Wow,' a little thoughtfully.

I glanced briefly at her face and saw that she was surprised: I didn't know what she was surprised at, and didn't have time to find out as there was the matter of weighing in, changing, and weighing out for the next race. Icicle, the princess's other runner, didn't go until the fourth race, but I had two other horses to ride before that.

Those two, undisgraced, finished fifth and second, and were both for a local trainer who I rode for when I could: besides Wykeham I also often rode for a stable in Lambourn, and when neither of them had a runner, for anyone else who asked. After, that is, having looked up the offered horse in the form book. Constant fallers I refused, saying Wykeham wouldn't give his approval. Wykeham was a handy excuse.

Icicle, like his name, was the palest of greys; also long-backed, angular and sweet-natured. He had been fast and clever over hurdles, the younger horses' sport, but at a mature eight years and running over bigger fences, was proving more cautious than carefree, more dependable than dazzling, willing but no whirlwind.

I went out to the parade ring again in the princess's colours and found her and the friends deep in a discussion that had nothing to do with horses but which involved a good deal of looking at watches.

'The train from Exeter is very fast,' Mrs Inscombe was saying comfortingly; and the niece was giving her a bright look of stifled impatience.

'Most unfortunate,' Mr Inscombe said in a bluff voice. 'But the train, that's the thing.'

The princess said carefully as if for the tenth time, 'But my dears, the train goes too late . . .' She broke off to give me an absent-minded smile and a brief explanation.

'My niece Danielle was going to London by car with friends but the arrangement has fallen through.' She paused. 'I suppose you don't know anyone who is driving straight from here to London after this race?'

'Sorry, I don't,' I said regretfully.

I looked at the niece: at Danielle. She looked worriedly back. 'I have to be in London by six-thirty,' she said. 'In Chiswick. I expect you know where that is? Just as you reach London from the west?'

I nodded.

'Could you possibly ask,' she waved a hand towards the busy door of the weighing room, 'in there?'

'Yes, I'll ask.'

'I have to be at work.'

I must have showed surprise, because she added, 'I work for a news bureau. This week I'm on duty in the evenings.'

Icicle stalked methodically round the parade ring with two and a half miles of strenuous jumping ahead of him. After that, in the fifth race, I would be riding another two miles over hurdles.

After that . . .

I glanced briefly at the princess, checking her expression, which was benign, and I thought of the fine she'd paid for me when she didn't have to.

I said to Danielle, 'I'll take you myself straight after the fifth race . . . if, er, that would be of any use to you.'

Her gaze intensified fast on my face and the anxiety cleared like sunrise.

'Yes,' she said decisively. 'It sure would.'

Never make positive commitments on race-days . . .

'I'll meet you outside the weighing room, after the fifth, then,' I said. 'It's a good road. We should get to Chiswick in time.'

'Great,' she said, and the princess seemed relieved that we could now concentrate on her horse and the immediate future.

'Kind of you, Kit,' she said, nodding.

'Any time.'

'How do you think my old boy will do today?'

'He's got bags of stamina,' I said. 'He should run well.'

She smiled. She knew 'bags of stamina' was a euphemism for 'not much finishing speed'. She knew Icicle's ability as well as I did, but like all owners, she wanted good news from her jockey.

'Do your best.'

'Yes,' I said.

I mounted and took Icicle out on to the track.

To hell with superstition, I thought.

SEVEN

It wasn't Icicle I had trouble with.

Icicle jumped adequately but without inspiration and ran on doggedly at one pace up the straight, more by good luck than anything else hanging on to finish second.

'Dear old slowcoach,' the princess said to him proudly in the unsaddling enclosure, rubbing his nose. 'What a gentleman you are.'

It was the hurdler afterwards that came to grief: an experienced racer but unintelligent. The one horse slightly ahead and to the right of us hit the top of the second hurdle as he rose to the jump and stumbled on to his nose on landing, and my horse, as if copying, promptly did exactly the same.

As falls went, it wasn't bad. I rolled like a tumbler on touching the ground, a circus skill learned by every jump jockey, and stayed curled, waiting for all the other runners to pass. As standing up in the middle of a thundering herd was the surest way to get badly injured, staying on the ground, where horses could more easily avoid one, was almost the first lesson in survival. The bad thing about falls near the start of hurdle races, however, was that the horses were going faster than in steeplechases, and were often bunched up together, with the result that they tended not to see a fallen rider until they were on top of him, by which time there was nowhere else to put their feet.

I was fairly used to hoof-shaped bruises. In the quiet that came after the buffeting I stood slowly and stiffly up with the makings of a new collection, and found the other fallen jockey doing the same.

'You all right?' I said.

'Yeah. You?'

I nodded. My colleague expressed a few obscene opinions of his former mount and a car came along to pick us up and deliver us to the ambulance room to be checked by the doctor on duty. In the old days jockeys had got away easily with riding with broken bones, but nowadays the medical inspections had intensified to safeguard the interests not altogether of the men injured but of the people who bet on them. Appeasing the punter was priority stuff.

Bruises didn't count. Doctors never stopped one from riding for those, and in any case bruises weren't visible when very new. I proved to the local man that all the bits of me that should bend, did, and all the bits that shouldn't bend, didn't, and got passed fit to ride again from then on.

One of the two volunteer nurses went to answer a knock on the door and came back slightly bemused to say I was wanted outside by a woman who said she was a princess.

'Right,' I said, thanking the doctor and turning to go.

'Is she?' the nurse asked dubiously.

'A princess? Yes. How often do you come to race meetings?'

'Today's my first.'

'She's been leading owner three times in the past six jumping seasons, and she's a right darling.'

The young nurse grinned. 'Makes you sick.'

I went outside to find the right darling looking first worried and then relieved at my reappearance. She was certainly not in the habit of enquiring after my health by waiting around outside ambulance room doors, and of course it wasn't my actual well-being which mattered at that point, but my being well enough to drive the niece to work.

The niece was also there and also relieved and also looking at her watch. I said I would change into street clothes and be ready shortly, and the princess kissed the niece and patted my arm, and went away saying she would see me at Newbury on the morrow.

I changed, found the niece waiting outside the weighing room, and took her to my car. She was fairly fidgeting with an impatience which slightly abated when she found the car was a Mercedes, but changed to straight anxiety when she saw me wince as I edged into the driving seat.

'Are you OK? You're not going to pass out, or anything, are you?' she said.

'I shouldn't think so.'

I started the car and extricated ourselves from the close-packed rows. A few other cars were leaving, but not enough to clog the entrance or the road outside. We would have a clear run, barring accidents.

'I guess I thought you'd be dead,' the niece said without emotion. 'How does anyone survive being trampled that way by a stampede?'

'Luck,' I said succinctly.

'My aunt was sure relieved when you stood up.'

I made an assenting noise in my throat. 'So was I.'

'Why do you do it?' she said.

'Race?'

'Uh-huh.'

'I like it.'

'Like getting trampled?'

'No,' I said. 'That doesn't happen all that often.'

We swooped down the hill from the moor and sped unhindered along roads that in the summer were busy with holiday crises. No swaying overloaded caravans being towed that day, no children being sick at the roadside, no radiators boiling and burst, with glum groups on the verges waiting for help. Devon roads in November were bare and fast and led straight to the motorways which should take us to Chiswick with no problems.

'Tell me truthfully,' she said, 'why do you do it?'

I glanced at her face, seeing there a quality of interest suitable for a newsgatherer. She had also large grey eyes, a narrow nose, and a determined mouth. Good-looking in a well-groomed way, I thought.

I had been asked the same question many times by other newsgatherers, and I gave the standard answer.

'I do it because I was born to it. I was brought up in a racing stable and I can't remember not being able to ride. I can't remember not wanting to ride in races.'

She listened with her head on one side and her gaze on my face.

'I guess I never met a jockey until now,' she said reflectively.

'And we don't have much jump racing in America.'

'No,' I agreed. 'In England there are probably more jump races than Flat. Just as many, anyway.'

'So why do you do it?'

'I told you,' I said.

'Yeah.'

She turned her head away to look out at the passing fields.

I raced, I thought fancifully, as one might play a violin, making one's own sort of music from coordinated muscles and intuitive spirit. I raced because the partnership with horses filled my mind with perfections of cadence and rhythmic excitement and intensities of communion: and I couldn't exactly say aloud such pretentious rubbish.

'I feel alive,' I said, 'on a horse.'

She looked back, faintly smiling. 'My aunt says you read their thoughts.'

'Everyone close to horses does that.'

'But some more than others?'

'I don't really know.'

She nodded. 'That makes sense. My aunt says you read the thoughts of people also.'

I glanced at her briefly. 'Your aunt seems to have said a lot.'

'My aunt,' she said neutrally, 'wanted me to understand, I think, that if I went in your car I should arrive unmolested.'

'Good God.'

'She was right, I see.'

'Mm.'

Molesting Danielle de Brescou, I thought, would be my quickest route to unemployment. Not that in other circumstances and with her willing cooperation I would have found it unthinkable. Danielle de Brescou moved with understated long-legged grace and watched the world from clear eyes, and if I found the sheen and scent of her hair and skin fresh and pleasing, it did no more than change the journey from a chore to a pleasure.

Between Exeter and Bristol, while dusk dimmed the day, she told me that she had been in England for three weeks and was staying with her uncle and aunt while she found herself an apartment. She had come because she'd been posted to

London by the national broadcasting company she worked for: she was the bureau coordinator, and as it was only her second week there it was essential not to be late.

'You won't be late,' I assured her.

'No . . . Do you always drive at eighty miles an hour?'

'Not if I'm in a real hurry.'

'Very funny.'

She told me Roland de Brescou, the princess's husband, was her father's eldest brother. Her father had emigrated to California from France as a young man and had married an American girl, Danielle being their only child.

'I guess there was a family ruckus when Dad left home, but he never told me the details. He's been sending greetings cards lately though, nostalgic for his roots, I guess. Anyway, he told Uncle Roland I was coming to London and the princess wrote me to say come visit. I hadn't met either of them before. It's my first trip to Europe.'

'How do you like it?'

She smiled. 'How would you like being cosseted in a sort of mansion in Eaton Square with a cook and maids and a butler? And a chauffeur. All last week the chauffeur drove me to work and picked me up after. Same thing yesterday. Aunt Casilia says it's not safe here after midnight on the subway, the same as it isn't in New York. She fusses worse than my own mother. But I can't live with them for too long. They're both sweet to me. I like her a lot and we get along fine. But I need a place of my own, near the office. And I'll get a car. I guess I'll have to.'

'How long will you be in England?' I asked.

'Don't know. Three years, maybe. Maybe less. The company can shift you around.'

She said I didn't need to tell her much about myself on account of information from her aunt.

She said she knew I lived in Lambourn and came from an old racing family and had a twin sister married to a racehorse trainer in Newmarket. She said she knew I wasn't married. She left the last observation dangling like a question mark, so I answered the unasked query.

'Not married. No present girlfriend. A couple in the past.'

I could feel her smile.

'And you?' I asked.

'Same thing.'

We drove for a good while in silence on that thought, and I rather pensively wondered what the princess would say or think if I asked her niece out to dinner. The close but arms-length relationship I'd had with her for so many years would change subtly if I did, and perhaps not for the better.

Between Bristol and Chiswick, while we sped with headlights on up the M4 motorway, Danielle told me about her job, which was, she said, pretty much a matter of logistics: she sent the camera crews and interviewers to wherever the news was.

'Half the time I'm looking at train schedules and road maps to find the fastest route, and starting from when we did, and taking the road we're on right now, I expected to be late.' She glanced at the speedometer. 'I didn't dream of ninety.'

I eased the car back to eighty-eight. A car passed us effortlessly. Danielle shook her head. 'I guess it'll take a while,' she said. 'How often do you get speeding tickets?'

'I've had three in ten years.'

'Driving like this every day?'

'Pretty much.'

She sighed. 'In dear old US of A we think seventy is sinful. Have you ever been there?'

'America?' I nodded. 'Twice. I rode there once in the Maryland Hunt Cup.'

'That's an amateurs' race,' she said without emphasis, careful, it seemed, not to appear to doubt my word.

'Yes. I started as an amateur. It seemed best to find out if I was any good before I committed my future to what I do.'

'And if it hadn't worked out?'

'I had a place at college.'

'And you didn't take it?' she said incredulously.

'No. I started winning, and that was what I wanted most. I tried for the place at college only in case I couldn't make it as a jockey. Sort of insurance.'

'What subject?'

'Veterinary science.'

It shocked her. 'You mean you passed up being a veterinarian to be a jockey?'

'That's right,' I said. 'Why not?'

'But . . . but . . .'

'Yeah,' I said. 'All athletes . . . sportsmen . . . whatever . . . find themselves on the wrong side of thirty-five with old age staring them point blank in the face. I might have another five years yet.'

'And then?'

'Train them, I suppose. Train horses for others to ride.' I shrugged. 'It's a long way off.'

'It came pretty close this afternoon,' Danielle said.

'Not really.'

'Aunt Casilia says the Cresta Run is possibly more dangerous than the life of a jump jockey. Possibly. She wasn't sure.'

'The Cresta Run is a gold medal or the fright of a lifetime, not a career.'

'Have you been down it?'

'Of course not. It's dangerous.'

She laughed. 'Are all jockeys like you?'

'No. All different. Like princesses.'

She took a deep breath, as if of sea air. I removed my attention from the motorway for a second's inspection of her face, for whatever her aunt might think of my ability to read minds I never seemed to be able to do it with any young woman except Holly . . . I was aware also that I wanted to, that without it, any loving was incomplete. I thought that if I hadn't had Holly I might have married one of the two girls I'd most liked: as it was, I hadn't reached the living-in stage with either of them.

I hadn't wanted to marry Holly, nor to sleep with her, but I'd loved her more deeply. It seemed that sex and telepathy couldn't co-exist in me, and until or unless they did, I probably would stay single.

'What are you thinking?' Danielle asked.

I smiled wryly. 'About not knowing what you were thinking.'

After a pause she said, 'I was thinking that when Aunt Casilia said you were exceptional, I can see what she meant.'

'She said what?'

'Exceptional. I asked her in what way, but she just smiled sweetly and changed the subject.'

'Er . . . when was that?'

'On our way down to Devon this morning. She's been wanting me to go racing with her ever since I came over, so today I did, because she'd arranged that ride back for me, although she herself was staying with the Inscombes tonight for some frantically grand party. She hoped I would love racing like she does, I think. Do you think sometimes she's lonesome, travelling all those miles to racemeets with just her chauffeur?'

'I don't think she felt lonesome until you came.'

'Oh!'

She fell silent for a while, and eventually I said prosaically, 'We'll be in Chiswick in three minutes.'

'Will we?' She sounded almost disappointed. 'I mean, good. But I've enjoyed the journey.'

'So have I.'

My inner vision was suddenly filled very powerfully with the presence of Holly, and I had a vivid impression of her face, screwed up in deep distress.

I said abruptly to Danielle, 'Is there a public telephone anywhere near your office?'

'Yeah, I guess so.' She seemed slightly puzzled by the urgency I could hear in my voice. 'Sure . . . use the one on my desk. Did you remember something important?'

'No . . . er, I . . .' I drew back from the impossibility of rational explanation. 'I have a feeling,' I said lamely, 'that I should telephone my sister.'

'A feeling?' she asked curiously. 'You looked as if you'd forgotten a date with the President, at least.'

I shook my head. 'This is Chiswick. Where do we go from here?'

She gave me directions and we stopped in a parking space labelled 'Staff Only' outside a warehouse-like building in a side street. Six-twenty on the clock; ten minutes to spare.

'Come on in,' Danielle said. 'The least I can do is lend you a phone.'

I stood up stiffly out of the car, and she said with contrition, 'I guess I shouldn't have let you drive all this way.'

'It's not much further than going home.'

'You lie in your teeth. We passed the exit to Lambourn fifty miles back.'

'A bagatelle.'

She watched me lock the car door. 'Seriously, are you OK?'

'It's nothing that a hot bath won't put right.'

She nodded and turned to lead the way into the building, which proved to have glass entrance doors into a hallway furnished with armchairs, potted plants and a uniformed guard behind a reception desk. She and he signed me into a book, gave me a pass to clip to my clothes, and ushered me through a heavy door that opened to an electronic buzz.

'Sorry about the fortress syndrome,' Danielle said. 'The company is currently paranoid about bombs.'

We went down a short corridor into a wide open office inhabited by six or seven desks, mostly with people behind them showing signs of packing up to go home. There was also a sea of green carpet, a dozen or so computers, and on one long wall a row of television screens above head height, all showing different programmes and none of them emitting a sound.

Danielle and the other inhabitants exchanged a few 'Hi's, and 'How're you doing's, and no one questioned my presence. She took me across the room to her own domain, an area of two large desks set at right angles with a comfortable-looking swivelling chair serving both. The desk tops bore several box files, a computer, a typewriter, a stack of newspapers and a telephone. On the wall behind the chair there was a large chart on which things could be written in chinagraph and rubbed off: a chart with columns labelled along the top as SLUG, TEAM, LOCATION, TIME, FORMAT.

'Sit down,' Danielle said, pointing to the chair. She picked up the receiver and pressed a lighted button on the telephone. 'OK. Make your call.' She turned to look at the chart. 'Let's see what's been happening in the world since I left it.' She scanned the segments. Under SLUG someone had written 'Embassy' in large black letters. Danielle called across the room, 'Hank, what's this embassy story?' and a voice answered, 'Someone painted "Yanks Go Home" in red on the US embassy steps and there's a stink about security.'

'Good grief.'

'You'll need to do a follow-up for *Nightline*.'

'Right . . . has anyone interviewed the Ambassador?'

'We couldn't reach him earlier.'

'Guess I'll try again.'

'Sure. It's your baby, baby. All yours.'

Danielle smiled vividly down at me, and I recognised with some surprise that her job was of far higher status than I'd guessed, and that she herself came alive also when she was working.

'Make your call,' she said again.

'Yes.'

I pressed the buttons and at the first ring Holly picked up the receiver.

'Kit,' she said immediately, full of stress.

'Yes,' I said.

Holly's voice had come explosively out of the telephone, loudly enough to reach Danielle's ears.

'How did she know?' she asked. Then her eyes widened. 'She was waiting . . . you knew.'

I half nodded. 'Kit,' Holly was saying. 'Where are you? Are you all right? Your horse fell . . .'

'I'm fine. I'm in London. What's the matter?'

'Everything's worse. Everything's terrible. We're going to lose . . . lose the yard . . . everything . . . Bobby's out walking somewhere . . .'

'Holly, remember the telephone,' I said.

'What? Oh, the bugs? I simply don't care any more. The telephone people are coming to look for bugs in the morning, they've promised. But what does it matter? We're finished . . . It's over.' She sounded exhausted. 'Can you come? Bobby wants you. We need you. You hold us together.'

'What's happened?' I asked.

'It's the bank. The new manager. We went to see him today and he says we can't even have the money for the wages on Friday and they're going to make us sell up . . . he says we haven't enough security to cover all we owe them . . . and we're just slipping further into debt because we aren't making enough profit to pay the interest on the loan for those year-lings, and do you know how much he's charging us for that now? Seven per cent over base rate. Seven. That's about seventeen per cent right now. And he's adding the interest on, so now we're paying interest on the interest . . . it's like a snowball . . . it's monstrous . . . it's bloody unfair.'

A shambles, I thought. Banks were never in the benefaction business.

'He admitted it was because of the newspaper articles,' Holly said wretchedly. 'He said it was unfortunate . . . unfortunate! . . . that Bobby's father wouldn't help us, not even a penny . . . I've caused Bobby all this trouble . . . it's because of me . . .'

'Holly, stop it,' I said. 'That's nonsense. Sit tight and I'll come. I'm at Chiswick. It will take me an hour and a half.'

'The bank manager says we will have to tell the owners to take their horses away. He says we're not the only trainers who've ever had to sell up . . . he says it happens, it's quite common . . . he's so hard-hearted I could kill him.'

'Mm,' I said. 'Well, don't do anything yet. Have a drink. Cook me some spinach or something, I'm starving. I'll be on my way . . . See you soon.'

I put down the receiver with a sigh. I didn't really want to drive on to Newmarket with stiffening bruises and an echoingly empty stomach, and I didn't really want to shoulder all the Allardeck troubles again, but a pact was a pact and that was the end of it. My twin, my bond, and all that.

'Trouble?' Danielle said, watching.

I nodded. I told her briefly about the attacks in the *Flag* and their dire financial consequences and she came swiftly to the same conclusion as myself.

'Bobby's father is crass.'

'Crass,' I said appreciatively, 'puts it in a nutshell.'

I stood up slowly from her chair and thanked her for the telephone.

'You're in no shape for all this,' she said objectively.

'Never believe it.' I leaned forward and kissed her fragrant cheek. 'Will you come racing again, with your aunt?'

She looked at me straightly. 'Probably,' she said.

'Good.'

Bobby and Holly were sitting in silence in the kitchen, staring into space, and turned their heads towards me apathetically when I went in.

I touched Bobby on the shoulder and kissed Holly and said, 'Come on, now, where's the wine? I'm dying of various ills and the first thing I need is a drink.'

My voice sounded loud in their gloom. Holly got heavily to her feet and went over to the cupboard where they kept glasses. She put her hand out towards it and then let it fall again. She turned towards me.

'I had my test results since you phoned,' she said blankly. 'I definitely am pregnant. This should have been the happiest night of our lives.' She put her arms around my neck and began quietly to cry. I wrapped my arms round her and held her, and Bobby stayed sitting down, too defeated, it seemed, to be jealous.

'All right,' I said. 'We'll drink to the baby. Come on, loves, businesses come and go, and this one hasn't gone yet, but babies are for ever, God rot their dear little souls.'

I disentangled her arms and picked out the glasses while she silently wiped her eyes on the sleeve of her jersey.

Bobby said dully, 'You don't understand,' but I did, very well. There was no fight in him, the deflation was too great; and I'd had my own agonising disappointments now and then. It could take a great effort of will not to sit around and mope.

I said to Holly, 'Put on some music, very loud.'

'No,' Bobby said.

'Yes, Bobby. Yes,' I said. 'Stand up and yell. Stick two fingers up at fate. Break something. Swear your guts out.'

'I'll break your neck,' he said with a flicker of savagery.

'All right, then, do it.'

He raised his head and stared at me and then rose abruptly to his feet, power crowding back into his muscles and vigour and exasperation into his face.

'All right then,' he shouted, 'I'll break your fucking Fielding neck.'

'That's better,' I said. 'And give me something to eat.'

Instead he went over to Holly and enfolded her and the two of them stood there half weeping, half laughing, entwined in privacy and back with the living. I resignedly dug in the freezer for something fast and unfattening and transferred it to the microwave oven, and I poured some red wine and drank it at a gulp.

Over the food Bobby admitted that he'd been too depressed to walk round at evening stables, so after coffee he and I both went out into the yard for a last inspection. The night was windy and cold and moonlit behind scurrying clouds. Everything looked normal and quiet, all the horses dozing behind closed doors, scarcely moving when we looked in on them, checking.

The boxes that had contained Jermyn Graves's horses were still empty, and the string which led to the bell had been detached from the door and hung limply from its last guiding staple. Bobby watched while I attached it to the door again.

'Do you think it's still necessary?' he asked dubiously.

'Yes, I do,' I said positively. 'The feed-merchant will have paid in Graves's cheque yesterday, but it won't have been cleared yet. I wouldn't trust Graves out of sight and I'd rig as many strings to the bell as we can manage.'

'He won't come back again,' Bobby said, shaking his head.

'Do you want to risk it?'

He stared at me for a while and then said, 'No.'

We ran three more strings, all as tripwires across pathways, and made sure the bell would fall if any one of them was tugged. It was perhaps not the most sophisticated of systems, but it had twice proved that it worked.

It worked for the third time at one in the morning.

EIGHT

My first feeling, despite what I'd said to Bobby, was of incredulity. My second, that springing out of bed was a bad idea, despite the long hot soaking I'd loosened up with earlier; and I creaked and groaned and felt sore.

As I took basic overnight things with me permanently in a bag in the car – razor, clean shirt, toothbrush – I was sleeping (as usual in other people's houses) in bright blue running shorts. I would have dressed, I think, if I'd felt more supple. Instead I simply thrust my feet into shoes and went out on to the landing, and found Bobby there, bleary-eyed, indecisive, wearing the top half of his pyjamas.

'Was that the bell?' he said.

'Yes. I'll take the drive again. You take the yard.'

He looked down at his half-nakedness and then at mine.

'Wait.' He dived back into his and Holly's bedroom and reappeared with a sweater for me and trousers for himself, and, struggling into these garments en route, we careered down the stairs and went out into the windy night. There was enough moonlight to see by, which was as well, as we hadn't brought torches.

At a shuffle more than a run I hurried down the drive, but the string across that route was still stretched tight. If Graves had come, he hadn't come that way.

I turned back and went to help Bobby in the yard, but he was standing there indecisively in the semi-darkness, looking around him, puzzled. 'I can't find Graves,' he said. 'Do you think the bell just blew off in the wind?'

'It's too heavy. Have you checked all the strings?'

'All except the one across the gate from the garden. But there's no one here. No one's come that way.'

97

'All the same . . .' I set off down the path to the gate to the garden, Bobby following: and we found the rustic wooden barrier wide open. We both knew it couldn't have blown open. It was held shut normally with a loop of chain, and the chain hung there on the gatepost, lifted off the gate by human hands.

We couldn't hear much for the wind. Bobby looked doubtfully back the way we had come and made as if to return to the yard.

I said, 'Suppose he's in the garden.'

'But what for? And how?'

'He could have come through the hedge from the road into the paddock, and over the paddock fence, and then down this path, and he'd have missed all the strings except this one.'

'But it's pointless. He can't get horses out through the garden. There are walls all round it. He wouldn't try.'

I was inclined to agree, but all the same, someone had opened the gate.

The walled garden of Bobby's house was all and only on one side, with the drive, stable yard and outhouses wrapping round the other three; and apart from the gate where we now stood, the only way into the garden was through French windows from the drawing room of the house.

Maybe Bobby was struck by the same unwelcome thought as myself. In any case he followed me instantly through the gate and off the paving-stone path inside on to the grass, which would be quieter underfoot.

We went silently, fast, the short distance towards the French windows, but they appeared shut, the many square glass frames reflecting the pale light from the sky.

We were about to go over to try them to make sure they were still locked when a faint click and a rattle reached my ears above the breeze, followed by a sharp and definite 'Bugger'.

Bobby and I stood stock still. We could see no one, even with eyes fast approaching maximum night vision.

'Get down,' a voice said. 'I don't like it.'

'Shut up.'

Feeling highly visible in my long bare legs and electric blue shorts I moved across the grass in the direction of the shadows

98

which held the voices, and as policemen will tell you, you should not do that; one should go indoors and telephone the force.

We found, Bobby and I, a man standing at the bottom of a ladder, looking upwards. He wore no mask, no hood, simply an ordinary suit – incongruous as a burglar kit.

He was not Jermyn Graves, and he was not the nephew, Jasper.

He was under forty, dark haired, and a stranger.

He didn't see us at all until we were near him, so firmly fixed upwards was his attention, and when I said loudly, 'What the hell do you think you're doing?' he jumped a foot.

Bobby made a flying rugby tackle at his knees and I took hold of the ladder and pushed it sideways. There was a yell from above and a good deal of clattering, and a second stranger tumbled down from the eaves and fell with a thud on to an uninhabited flower bed.

I pounced on that one and pushed his face down into the November mud and with one hand tried to search his pockets for a weapon, with him heaving and threshing about beneath me, and then when I found no weapon, for some sort of identification, for a diary or a letter, for anything. People who came to burgle dressed as for going to the office might not have taken all suitable precautions.

I couldn't get into his pockets – it was too dark and there was too much movement – but somehow I found myself grasping the collar of his jacket, and I pulled it backwards and downwards with both hands, temporarily fastening his arms to his sides. He plunged and kicked and managed to throw my weight off his back, but I held fiercely on to the jacket, which was entangling his arms and driving him frantic.

To get loose he slid right out of the jacket, leaving it in my hands, and before I could do anything he was up from his knees to his feet, and running.

Instead of chasing him I turned towards Bobby, who was rolling on the ground exchanging short jabbing blows and breathless grunts with the man who'd been holding the ladder. Throwing the jacket into the deep shadow against the house wall I went to Bobby's help, and between the two of us we managed to pin the intruder face down on to the grass, Bobby astride his legs and I with a foot on his neck. Bobby delivered several meaningful blows to the kidneys, designed to hurt.

'Something to tie him with,' he said.

I bent down, gripped the collar of that jacket also, and pulled it as before backwards over the burglar's shoulders, pinning his arms, and then yanking it right off, I took my foot off the neck and said to Bobby, 'That's enough.'

'What? Don't be stupid.'

The intruder rolled under him still full of fight. Bobby punched him wickedly on the ear and again in the small of his back.

I shoved a hand into an inside pocket of the jacket and drew out a wallet.

'See,' I said to Bobby, pushing it under his nose. He shook his head, ignoring it, not wanting to be deterred.

I put the wallet back into the jacket and threw that jacket too into the shadows, and for a second watched Bobby and the now shirt-sleeved intruder tearing at each other and punching again, half standing, half falling, the one trying to cling on and hit, the other to escape.

Bobby was tall and strong and angry at having his house attacked, and no doubt erupting also with the suppressed and helpless fury of the past traumatic days: in any case he was hitting his adversary with tangible hatred and very hard, and I thought with spurting sudden alarm that it was too much, he was beating the man viciously and murderously and not merely capturing a burglar.

I caught Bobby's raised wrist and pulled his bunched fist backwards, upsetting his balance, and his victim twisted out of his grasp and half fell on his knees, coughing, retching, clutching his stomach.

Bobby shouted 'You bugger' bitterly and hit me instead, and the intruder got unsteadily to his feet and staggered towards the gate.

Bobby tried to follow and when I grasped at him to stop him he jabbed his fist solidly into my ribs, calling me a bloody Fielding, a bloody sod, a fucking bastard.

'Bobby . . . Let him go.'

I got a frightful cuff on the head and another clout in the ribs along with some more obscene opinions of my character and ancestors, and he didn't calm down, he kicked my shin and shoved me off him, tearing himself away with another direct hit to my head which rattled my teeth.

I caught him again in a couple of strides and he swung at me, swearing and increasingly violent, and I said to him, 'For God's sake, Bobby . . .' and just tried to hang on to his lethal fists and parry them and survive until the fireball had spent itself.

The generations were all there in his intent face: Allardecks and Fieldings fighting with guns and swords and bare knuckles in malice and perpetuity. He had transferred the intruder-born fury on to the older enemy and all rational restraints had vanished. It was me, his blood's foe, that he was at that point trying to smash, I the focus of his anger and fear and despair.

Locked in this futile archaic struggle we traversed the lawn all the way to the gate; and it was there, when I was wedged against the heavy post and finally in serious trouble, that the killing rage went out of his hands from one second to the next, and he let them fall, the passion dying, the manic strength draining away.

He gave me a blank look, his eyes like glass reflecting the moonlight, and he said 'Bastard', but without much force, and he turned and walked away along the path to the yard.

I said 'God Almighty' aloud, and took a few deep breaths of rueful and shaky relief, standing for a while to let my hammering heart settle before shoving off the gatepost to go and fetch the burglars' coats. Bobby's fists hadn't had the same weight as the hurdlers' hooves, but I could well have done without them. Heigh ho, I thought, in about twelve hours I would ride three tricky jumpers at Newbury.

The coats lay where I had thrown them, in the angle of the empty flower bed and the brick wall of the house. I picked them up and stood there looking at the silvery ladder which had reached high up the wall, and then at the wall itself, which stretched in that section right to the roof, smooth and unbroken.

No windows.

Why would burglars try to break into a house at a point where there were no windows?

I frowned, tipping my head back, looking upwards. Beyond

101

the line of the roof, above it, rising like a silhouette against the night sky, there was a sturdy brick chimney, surmounted by a pair of antique pots. It was, I worked out, the chimney from the fireplace in the drawing room. The fireplace was right through the wall from where I stood.

Irresolutely I looked from the ladder to the chimney pots and shivered in the wind. Then, shrugging, I put the jackets back into the shadow, propped the ladder up against the eaves, rooted its feet firmly in the flower bed, and climbed.

The ladder was aluminium, made in telescopic sections. I hoped none of them would collapse.

I didn't much like heights. Halfway up I regretted the whole enterprise. What on earth was I doing climbing an unsteady ladder in the dark? I could fall and hurt myself and not be able to race. It was madness, the whole thing. Crazy.

I reached the roof. The top of the ladder extended beyond that, four or five more rungs going right up to the chimney. On the tiles of the roof lay an opened tool-kit, a sort of cloth roll with spanners, screwdrivers, pliers and so on, all held in stitched pockets. Beside it lay a coil of what looked like dark cord, with one end leading upwards to a bracket on the chimney.

I looked more closely at the chimney and almost laughed. One takes so many things for granted, sees certain objects day by day and never consciously sees them at all. Fixed to the chimney was the bracket and mounted on the bracket were the two terminals of the telephone wires leading to Bobby's house. I had seen them a hundred times and never noticed they were fixed to the chimney.

The wire itself stretched away into darkness, going across the telephone pole out on the road; the old above-ground wiring system of all but modern housing.

Attached to the telephone bracket, at the end of the dark cord leading from the coil, there appeared to be a small square object about the size of a sugar cube, with a thin rod about the length of a finger extending downwards. I stretched out a hand precariously to touch it and found it wobbled as if only half attached.

The moon seemed to be going down just when I needed it most. I fumbled around the small cube and came to what felt like a half-undone screw. I couldn't see it, but it turned easily anti-clockwise and in a few moments slipped out into my hand.

The cube and the rod fell straight off the bracket, and I would have lost them in the night if it hadn't been for the coil of stiff cord attached to them. Some of the cord unwound before I caught it, but not a great deal, and I put the coil, the cube and the rod on to the row of tools and rolled up the canvas kit and fastened it with its buckle.

The flower bed, I thought, wouldn't hurt the tool-kit, so I dropped the rolled bundle straight below, and went down the ladder as slowly as I'd gone up, careful to balance and not to fall. There was no doubt I felt more at home on horses.

Retrieving the jackets and the tool-kit but leaving the ladder, I went out of the garden and walked along the path and round to the kitchen door. Holly in a dressing gown and with wide frightened eyes was standing there, shivering with cold and anxiety.

'Thank goodness,' she said when I appeared. 'Where's Bobby?'

'I don't know. Come on in. Let's make a hot drink.'

We went into the kitchen where it was always warmest and I put the kettle on while Holly looked out of the window for her missing husband.

'He'll come soon,' I said. 'He's all right.'

'I saw two men running . . .'

'Where did they go?'

'Over the fence into the paddock. One first, then the other a bit later. The second one was . . . well . . . groaning.'

'Mm,' I said. 'Bobby hit him.'

'Did he?' She sounded proud. 'Who were they? They weren't Jermyn. Did they come for his horses?'

'Which do you want,' I asked, 'coffee, tea or chocolate?'

'Chocolate.'

I made chocolate for her and tea for myself and brought the steaming cups to the table.

'Come and sit down,' I said. 'He'll be back.'

She came reluctantly and then watched with awakening curiosity while I unbuckled and unrolled the tool-kit.

'See that?' I said. 'That tiny little box with its rod and its

103

coil of cord? I'll bet anything that that's what's been listening to your telephone.'

'But it's minute.'

'Yes. I wish I knew more. Tomorrow we'll find out just how it works.' I looked at my watch. 'Today, I suppose one should say.' I told her where I'd found the bug, and about Bobby and me disturbing the intruders.

She frowned. 'These two men . . . Were they fixing this to our telephone?'

'Taking it away, perhaps. Or changing its battery.'

She reflected. 'I did say to you this evening on the telephone that the telephone people were coming tomorrow to look for bugs.'

'So you did.'

'So perhaps if they heard that, they thought . . . those two men . . . that if they took their bug away first, there wouldn't be anything to find, and we'd never know for sure.'

'Yes,' I said. 'I think you're right.' I picked up the first of the jackets and went through the pockets methodically, laying the contents on the table.

Holly, watching in amazement, said, 'They surely didn't leave their coats?'

'They didn't have much choice.'

'But all those things . . .'

'Dead careless,' I said. 'Amateurs.'

The first jacket produced a notepad, three pens, a diary, a handkerchief, two toothpicks and the wallet I had shown to Bobby in the garden. The wallet contained a moderate amount of money, five credit cards, a photograph of a young woman, and a reminder to go to the dentist. The name on the credit cards was Owen Watts. The diary not only gave the same name but also an address (home) and telephone number (office). The pages were filled with appointments and memos, and spoke of a busy and orderly life.

'Why are you purring like a cat with cream?' Holly said.

'Take a look.'

I pushed Owen Watts's belongings over to her and emptied the pockets of the second jacket. These revealed another notepad, more pens, a comb, cigarettes, throwaway lighter, two letters and a chequebook. There was also, tucked into

104

the outside breast pocket, a small plastic folder containing a gold-coloured card announcing that Mr Jay Erskine was member number 609 of The Press Club, London EC4A 3JB; and Mr Jay Erskine's signature and address were on the back.

Just as well to make absolutely certain, I thought.

I telephoned to Owen Watts's office number, and a man's voice answered immediately.

'*Daily Flag*,' he said.

Satisfied, I put the receiver down without speaking.

'No answer?' Holly said. 'Not surprising, at this hour.'

'The *Daily Flag* neither slumbers nor sleeps. The switchboard, anyway, was awake.'

'So those two really are . . . those pigs.'

'Well,' I said. 'They work for the *Flag*. One can't say if they actually wrote those pieces. Not tonight. We'll find out in the morning.'

'I'd like to smash their faces.'

I shook my head. 'You want to smash the face of whoever sent them.'

'Him too.' She stood up restlessly. 'Where is Bobby? What's he doing?'

'Probably making sure that everything's secure.'

'You don't think those men came back?' she said, alarmed.

'No, I don't. Bobby will come in when he's ready.'

She was worried, however, and went to the outside door and called him, but the wind snatched her voice away so that one could scarcely have heard her from across the yard.

'Go and look for him, will you?' she said anxiously. 'He's been out there so long.'

'All right.' I collected the bugging device, the tools and the pressmen's things together on the table. 'Could you find a box for these, and put them somewhere safe.'

She nodded and began to look vaguely about, and I went out into the yard on the unwelcome errand. Wherever Bobby was, I was probably the last person he wanted to have come after him. I thought that I would simply set about rigging the alarm bell again, and if he wanted to be found, he would appear.

I rigged the bell and got back some night vision, and came across him down by the gate into the garden. He had brought

105

the ladder out so that it lay along the path, and he was simply standing by the gatepost, doing nothing.

'Holly's wondering where you've got to,' I said easily.

He didn't answer.

'Do you think you can hear the bell from here?' I said. 'Would you climb up someone's house if you'd heard an alarm bell?'

Bobby said nothing. He watched in flat calm while I found the string and shut the gate, fastening everything as before so that the bell would fall on the far side of the house if the gate was opened.

Bobby watched but did nothing. Shrugging, I opened the gate.

One could hear the bell if one was listening for it. On a still night it would have been alarming, but in the breeze the intruders had ignored it.

'Let's go in,' I said. 'Holly's anxious.'

I turned away to walk up the path.

'Kit,' he said stiffly.

I turned back.

'Did you tell her?' he asked.

'No.'

'I'm sorry,' he said.

'Come on in. It doesn't matter.'

'Yes, it does matter.' He paused. 'I couldn't help it. That makes it worse.'

'Tell you what,' I said, 'let's go in out of this bloody cold wind. My legs are freezing. If you want to talk, we'll talk tomorrow. But it's OK. Come on in, you old bugger, it's OK.'

I put the journalists' belongings under my bed for safety before I went achingly back to sleep, but their owners seemed to make no attempt to break in to get them back. I derived a great deal of yawning pleasure from picturing their joint states of mind and body, and thought that anything that had happened to them served them very well right.

Owen Watts and Jay Erskine. Jay Erskine, Owen Watts.

They were going to be, I decided hazily, trying to find an unbruised area to lie on, the lever with which to shift the world. Careless, sneaky, callous Owen Watts, battered half unconscious by Bobby, and stupid, snooping, flint-hearted Jay Erskine, fallen off his ladder with his face pressed into the mud. Served them bloody well right.

I dreamed of being run over by a tractor and felt like it a bit when I woke up. The morning after falls like the day before's were always a bore.

It was nearly nine when I made it to the kitchen, but although the lights were on against the grey morning, there was no one else there. I heated myself some coffee and began to read Bobby's daily paper, which was the *Towncrier*, not the *Flag*.

On page seven, which was wholly devoted to the Wednesday comments and opinions of a leading and immensely influential lady columnist, the central headline read:

WHAT PRICE FATHERLY LOVE?

And underneath, in a long spread unmissable by any *Towncrier* reader, came an outline of Maynard Allardeck's upwardly thrusting career.

He had journeyed from commodity broker, she said, to multi-storey magnate, sucking in other people's enterprises and spitting out the husks.

His *modus operandi*, she explained, was to advance smilingly towards an over-extended business with offers of loans of life-saving cash. Easy terms, pay when you can, glad to help. His new partners, the journalist said, welcomed him with open arms and spoke enthusiastically of their benefactor. But oh, the disillusionment! Once the business was running smoothly, Maynard would very pleasantly ask for his money back. Consternation! Disaster! Impossible to pay him without selling up and closing. The workforce redundant. Personal tragedies abounding. Can't have that, Maynard agreed genially. He would take the business instead of the money, how was that? Everyone still had their job. Except, hard luck, the proprietor and the managing director. Maynard presently would sell his now financially stable newly acquired business at a comfortable profit to any big fish looking out for manageable minnows: and so back, one might say, to the start, with Maynard appreciably richer.

How do I know all this? the lady journalist asked; and answered herself; less than three weeks ago on the TV programme *How's Trade*, Maynard himself told us. Classic takeover procedure, he smugly called it. Anyone could do the same. Anyone could make a fortune the same way that he had.

It now seemed, she wrote, that one particular over-extended business in dire need of easy-terms cash was the racehorse training enterprise of Maynard's own and only son, Robertson (32).

Maynard was on record in this one instance as obstinately refusing to offer help.

My advice to someone in Robertson's (known as Bobby) position, said the lady firmly, would be to not touch Daddy's money with a bargepole. To count his rocky blessings. Daddy's fond embrace could find him presently sweeping the streets. Don't forget, she said, this parent is still grasping for car money he lent his son as a kid.

Is Maynard, she asked finally, worth a knighthood for services to industry? And she answered herself again: in her own opinion, definitely not.

There was a photograph of Maynard, polished and handsome, showing a lot of teeth. The word 'shark' sprang to mind. Maynard, I thought, would be apoplectic.

Bobby's first lot of horses clattered back into the yard from their morning exercise on the Heath, and Bobby himself came into the kitchen looking intensely depressed. He fixed himself a cup of coffee and wouldn't look at me, and drank standing by the window, staring out.

'How's Holly?' I asked.

'Sick.'

'Your father's in the paper,' I said.

'I don't want to read it.' He put down his cup. 'I expect you'll be going.'

'Yes. I'm riding at Newbury.'

'I meant . . . because of last night.'

'No, not because of that.'

He came over to the table and sat down, looking not at me but at his hands. There were grazes on the knuckles of both fists, red-raw patches where he'd smashed off his own skin.

'Why didn't you fight?' he said.

'I didn't want to.'

'You could have hurt me to hell and gone. I know that now. Why didn't you? I could have killed you.'

'Over my dead body,' I said dryly.

He shook his head. I looked at his face, at the downcast blue eyes, seeing the trouble, the self-doubt, the confusion.

'What I fight,' I said, 'is being brainwashed. Why should we still jump to that old hate? It was a Fielding you were trying to kill. Any Fielding. Not me, Kit, your brother-in-law who actually likes you, though I can't quite see why after last night. I'll fight my indoctrination, I'll fight my bloody ancestors, but I won't fight you, my sister's husband, with whom I have no quarrel.'

He sat for a while without speaking, still looking at his hands, then in a low voice he said, 'You're stronger than me.'

'No. If it makes you feel better, I don't know what I'd have done if I'd been through all you have in the past week and there had been an Allardeck handy to let it all out on.'

He raised his head, the very faintest of glimmers reappearing. 'Truce, then?' he said.

'Yeah,' I agreed; and wondered if our subconscious minds would observe it.

NINE

The vans swept into the yard as if conducting a race; one red, one yellow. Out of each emerged more slowly a man in dark clothes carrying, from the red van, the day's letters, and from the yellow, a clipboard. The Royal Mail and British Telecom side by side.

Bobby went to the door, accepted the letters, and brought the phone company man back with him into the kitchen.

'Bug-hunting,' the latter said heartily, as the red van roared away again outside. 'Got termites in the telephone, have you? Been hearing clicking noises on the line? No end of people hear them. False alarms, you know.'

He was large, moustached, and too full of unnecessary bonhomie. Bobby, making a great effort, offered tea or coffee, and I went upstairs to fetch the non-imaginary equipment from the chimney.

I could hear the phone man's voice long before I could see him on my way back.

'You get your MI5, of course, but your average left-wing militant, they call us in regular. In Cambridge, now, false alarms all the time.'

'This is not,' Bobby said through gritted teeth, 'a false alarm.'

'We found this,' I said calmingly, putting the tool-kit on the table, unrolling it, and producing for inspection the small metal cube with its rod and its coil of attached stiff cord.

'Ah now,' the telephone man's interest came to life, 'now you know what this is, don't you?'

'A bug,' I said.

'Now that,' he said, 'is your transformer stroke transmitter and your earth. Where's the rest?'

110

'What rest?'

He looked at us with pity. 'You got to have the tap itself. Where did you get this little lot?'

'From the chimney stack, where the phone wires reach the house.'

'Did you now.' He blew down his nose. 'Then that's where we'd better look.'

We took him outside the house rather than through the drawing room, walking down the path from the yard and through the gate. The telescopic aluminium ladder still lay on the path, but the phone man, eyeing the height of the chimney, decided against its fragile support and went back to his van for much sturdier rungs. He returned also with a busy tool-belt buckled round his rotund middle.

Planting and extending his workmanlike ladder he lumbered up it as casually as walking. To each his own expertise.

At the top, with his stomach supported, he reached out to where the telephone wire divided to the two terminals, and with tools from his belt spent some time clamping, clipping and refastening before returning unruffled to earth.

'A neat little job,' he said appreciatively. 'Superior bit of wire-tapping. Looks like its been in place for a couple of weeks. Grimy, but not too bad, see? Been up there just a while in the soot and rain.'

He held out a large palm on which rested a small cylinder with two short wires leading from it.

'See, this picks up the currents from your phone wire and leads them into that transformer you took down last night. See, voice frequencies run at anywhere between fifty Hertz and three kiloHertz, but you can't transmit that by radio, you have to transform it up to about three thousand megaHertz. You need an amplifier which modulates the frequency to something a microwave transmitter can transmit.' He looked at our faces. 'Not exactly electronics experts, are you?'

'No,' we said.

With complacent superiority he led the way back to the yard, carrying his heavy ladder with ease. In the kitchen he put the newly gathered cylinder alongside the previous night's spoils and continued with the lecture.

111

'These two wires from the cylinder plug into the transformer and this short little rod is the aerial.'

'What's all that cord?' I asked.

'Cord?' He smiled largely. 'That's not cord, it's wire. See? Fine wire inside insulation. That's an earth wire, to complete the circuit.'

We looked no doubt blank.

'If you'd have closely inspected your brickwork below your chimney these last weeks you'd have seen this so-called cord lying against it. Running through clips, even. Going down from the transmitter into the earth.'

'Yes,' Bobby said. 'We're never out there much this time of the year.'

'Neat little job,' the telephone man said again.

'Is it difficult to get?' I asked. 'This sort of equipment.'

'Dead easy,' he said pityingly. 'You can send for it from your electronic mail order catalogue any day.'

'And what then?' I asked. 'We've got the tap and the transmitter. Where would we find the receiver?'

The phone man said judiciously, 'This is a low-powered transmitter. Has to be, see, being so small. Runs on a battery, see? So you'd need a big dish-receiver to pick up the signals. Line of sight. Say a quarter-mile away? And no buildings to distort things. Then I'd reckon you'd get good results.'

'A big dish-receiver a quarter of a mile away?' I repeated. 'Everyone would see it.'

'Not inside a van, they wouldn't.' He touched the cube transmitter reflectively. 'Nice high chimney you've got there. Most often we find these babies on the poles out on the road. But the higher you put the transmitter, of course, the further you get good reception.'

'Yes,' I said, understanding that at least.

'This is an unofficial bit of snooping,' he said, happy to instruct. 'Private. You won't get no clicks from this, neither. You'd never know it was there.' He hitched up his tool-belt. 'Right then, you just sign my sheet and I'll be off. And you want to take your binoculars out there now and then and keep a watch on your chimney and your pole in the road, and if you see any more little strangers growing on your wires, you give me a ring and I'll be right back.'

112

Bobby signed his sheet and thanked him and saw him out to his van; and I looked at the silent bug and wondered vaguely whose telephone I could tap with it, if I learned how.

Holly came in as the yellow van departed, Holly looking pale in jeans and sloppy sweater, with hair still damp from the shower.

'Morning sickness is the pits,' she said. 'Did you make any tea?'

'Coffee in the pot.'

'Couldn't face it.' She put the kettle on. 'What happened out there last night between you and Bobby? He said you would never forgive him, but he wouldn't say what for. I don't think he slept at all. He was up walking round the house at five. So what happened?'

'There's no trouble between us,' I said. 'I promise you.'

She swallowed. 'It would just be the end if you and Bobby quarrelled.'

'We didn't.'

She was still doubtful but said no more. She put some bread in the toaster as Bobby came back, and the three of us sat round the table passing the marmalade and thinking our own thoughts, which in my case was a jumble of journalists, Bobby's bank manager, and how was I going to warm and loosen my muscles before the first race.

Bobby with apprehension began opening the day's letters, but his fears were unfounded. There was no blast from the bank and no demands for payment with menaces. Three of the envelopes contained cheques.

'I don't believe it,' he said, sounding stunned. 'The owners are paying.'

'That's fast,' I said. 'They can only have got those letters yesterday. Their consciences must be pricking overtime.'

'Seb's paid,' Bobby said. He mentally added the three totals and then pushed the cheques across to me. 'They're yours.'

I hesitated.

'Go on,' he said. 'You paid our bills on Monday. If those cheques had come on Monday you wouldn't have had to.'

Holly nodded.

'What about the lads' wages this Friday?' I asked.

Bobby shrugged frustratedly. 'God knows.'

'What did your bank manager actually say?' I said.

'Sadistic bully,' Bobby said. 'He sat there with a smirk on his prim little face telling me I should go into voluntary liquidation immediately. Voluntary! He said if I didn't, the bank would have no choice but to start bankruptcy proceedings. No choice! Of course they have a choice. Why did they ever lend the money for the yearlings if they were going to behave like this five minutes later?'

The probable answer to that was because Bobby was Maynard's son. Maynard's millions might have seemed security enough, before the *Flag* fired its broadside.

'Isn't there any trainer in Newmarket who would buy the yearlings from you?' I said.

'Not a chance. Most of them are in the same boat. They can't sell their own.'

I pondered. 'Did the bank manager say anything about bailiffs?'

'No,' Bobby said, and Holly, if possible, went paler.

We might have a week, I thought. I didn't know much about liquidation or bankruptcy: I didn't know the speed of events. Perhaps we had no time at all. No one, however, could expect Bobby to be able to sell all his property overnight.

'I'll take the cheques,' I said, 'and I'll get them cashed. We'll pay your lads this week out of the proceeds and keep the rest for contingencies. And don't tell the bank manager, because he no doubt thinks this money belongs to the bank.'

'They lent it to us quick enough,' Holly said bitterly. 'No one twisted their arm.'

It wasn't only Maynard, I thought, who could lend with a smile and foreclose with a vengeance.

'It's hopeless,' Bobby said. 'I'll have to tell the owners to take their horses. Sack the lads.' He stopped abruptly. Holly, too, had tears in her eyes. 'It's such a mess,' Bobby said.

'Yeah . . . well . . . hold tight for a day or two,' I said.

'What's the point?'

'We might try a little fund-raising.'

'What do you mean?'

I knew only vaguely what I meant and I didn't think I would discuss it with Bobby. I said instead, 'Don't break up the stable before the dragon's breathing fire right in the yard.'

'St George might come along,' Holly said.

'What?' Bobby looked uncomprehending.

'In the story,' Holly said. 'You know. Kit and I had a pop-up book where St George came along and slew the dragon. We used to read it with a torch under the bedclothes and scare ourselves with shadows.'

'Oh.' He looked from one of us to the other, seeing dark-haired twins with a shared and private history. He may have felt another twinge of exclusion because he smothered some reaction with a firming of the mouth, but after a while, with only a hint of sarcasm and as if stifling any hope I might have raised, he came up with an adequate reply. 'OK, St George. Get on your horse.'

I drove to Newbury and solved the stiff muscle problem by borrowing the sauna of a local flat race jockey who spent every summer sweating away his body in there and had thankfully come out for the winter. I didn't like water-shedding in saunas as a daily form of weight-control (still less diuretics), but after twenty minutes of its hot embrace on that cold morning I did feel a good deal fitter.

My first two mounts were for the Lambourn stable I normally rode for, and, given a jockey with smoothly working limbs, they both cleared the obstacles efficiently without covering themselves with either mud or glory. One could say to the hopeful owners afterwards that yes, their horses would win one day; and so they might, when the weights were favourable and the ground was right and a few of the better opponents fell. I'd ridden duds I wouldn't have taken out of the stable and had them come in first.

My final mount of the day belonged to the princess, who was waiting, alone as usual, for me to join her in the parade ring. I was aware of being faintly disappointed that Danielle wasn't with her, even though I hadn't expected it: most illogical. The princess, sable coat swinging, wore a pale yellow silk scarf at her neck with gold and citrine earrings, and although I'd seen her in them often before I thought she was looking exceptionally well and glowing. I made the small bow; shook her hand. She smiled.

'How do you think we'll do today?' she said.

'I think we'll win.'

Her eyes widened. 'You're not usually so positive.'

'Your horses are all in form. And . . .' I stopped.

'And what?'

'And . . . er . . . you were thinking, yourself, that we would win.'

She said without surprise, 'Yes, I was.' She turned to watch her horse walk by. 'What else was I thinking?'

'That . . . well . . . that you were happy.'

'Yes.' She paused. 'Do you think the Irish mare will beat us? Several people have tipped it.'

'She's got a lot of weight.'

'Lord Vaughnley thinks she'll win.'

'Lord Vaughnley?' I repeated, my interest quickening. 'Is he here?'

'Yes,' she said. 'He was lunching in a box near mine. I came down the stairs with him just now.'

I asked her if she remembered which box, but she didn't. I said I would like to talk to him, if I could find him.

'He'll be glad to,' she said, nodding. 'He's still delighted about the Towncrier Trophy. He says literally hundreds of people have congratulated him on this year's race.'

'Good,' I said. 'If I ask him a favour, I might get it.'

'You could ask the world.'

'Not that much.'

The signal came for jockeys to mount, and I got up on her horse to see what we could do about the Irish mare: and what we did was to start out at a fast pace and maintain it steadily throughout, making the mare feel every extra pound she was carrying every stride of the way, and finally to beat off her determined challenge most satisfactorily by a length and a half.

'Splendid,' the princess exclaimed in the winners' enclosure, sparkling. 'Beautiful.' She patted her excited 'chaser. 'Come up to the box, Kit, when you've changed.' She saw my very faint and stifled hesitation and interpreted it. 'I saw Lord Vaughnley up there again. I asked him to my box also.'

'You're amazingly kind.'

'I'm amazingly pleased with winning races like this.'

I changed into street clothes and went up to her familiar box high above the winning post. For once she was there

116

alone, not surrounded by guests, and she mentioned that she was on her way back from Devon, her chauffeur having driven her up that morning.

'My niece telephoned yesterday evening from her bureau to say she had arrived promptly,' the princess said. 'She was most grateful.'

I said I'd been very pleased to help. The princess offered tea, pouring it herself, and we sat on adjacent chairs, as so often, as I described the past race to her almost fence by fence.

'I could see,' she said contentedly. 'You were pushing along just ahead of the mare all the way. When she quickened, you quickened, when she took a breather down the bottom end, so did you. And then I could see you just shake up my horse when her jockey took up his whip . . . I knew we'd win. I was sure of it all the way round. It was lovely.'

Such sublime confidence could come crashing down on its nose at the last fence, but she knew that as well as I did. There had been times when it had. It made the good times better.

She said, 'Wykeham says we're giving Kinley his first try over hurdles at Towcester tomorrow. His first ever race.'

'Yes,' I nodded. 'And Dhaulagiri's taking his first start at a novice 'chase. I rode both of them schooling at Wykeham's last week, did he tell you? They both jumped super. Er . . . will you be there?'

'I wouldn't miss it.' She paused. 'My niece says she will come with me.'

I lifted my head. 'Will she?'

'She said so.'

The princess regarded me calmly and I looked straight back, but although it would have been useful I couldn't read what she was thinking.

'I enjoyed driving her,' I said.

'She said the journey went quickly.'

'Yes.'

The princess patted my arm non-committally, and Lord and Lady Vaughnley appeared in the doorway, looking in with enquiring faces and coming forward with greetings. The princess welcomed them, gave them glasses of port, which it seemed they liked particularly on cold days, and drew Lady Vaughnley away with her to admire something out on the viewing balcony, leaving Lord Vaughnley alone inside with me.

He said how truly delighted he'd been with everyone's response to last Saturday's race, and I asked if he could possibly do me a favour.

'My dear man. Fire away. Anything I can.'

I explained again about Bobby and the attacks in the *Flag*, which by now he himself knew all about.

'Good Lord, yes. Did you see the comment page in our own paper this morning? That woman of ours, Rose Quince, she has a tongue like a rattlesnake, but when she writes, she makes sense. What's the favour?'

'I wondered,' I said, 'if the *Towncrier* would have a file of clippings about Maynard Allardeck. And if you have one, would you let me see it.'

'Good Lord,' he said. 'You'll have a reason, no doubt?'

I said we had concluded that Bobby had been a casualty in a campaign mainly aimed at his father. 'And it would be handy to know who might have enough of a grudge against Maynard to kill off his chance of a knighthood.'

Lord Vaughnley smiled benignly. 'Such as anyone whose business was pulled from beneath them?'

'Such as,' I agreed. 'Yes.'

'You're suggesting that the *Flag* could be pressured in to mounting a hate campaign?' He pursed his mouth, considering.

'I wouldn't have thought it would take much pressure,' I said. 'The whole paper's a hate campaign.'

'Dear, dear,' he said with mock reproof. 'Very well. I can't see how it will directly help your brother-in-law, but yes, I'll see you get access to our files.'

'That's great,' I said fervently. 'Thank you very much.'

'When would suit you?'

'As soon as possible.'

He looked at his watch. 'Six o'clock?'

I shut my mouth on a gasp. He said, 'I have to be at a dinner in the City this evening. I'll be dropping into the *Towncrier* first. Ask for me at the front desk.'

I duly asked at his front desk in Fleet Street and was directed upwards to the editorial section on the third floor, arriving, it seemed, at a point of maximum bustle as the earliest editions of the following day's papers were about to go to press.

Lord Vaughnley, incongruous in tweed jacket, dress trousers, stiff shirt and white tie, stood at the shoulder of a coatless man seated at a central table, both of them intent on the newspaper before them. Around them, in many bays half separated from each other by shoulder-high partitions, were clumps of three or four desks, each bay inhabited by telephones, typewriters, potted plants and people in a faint but continuous state of agitation.

'What do you want?' someone said to me brusquely as I hovered, and when I said Lord Vaughnley, he merely pointed. Accordingly I walked over to the centre of the activity and said neutrally to Lord Vaughnley, 'Excuse me . . .'

He raised his eyes but not his head. 'Ah yes, my dear chap, be with you directly,' he said, and lowered the eyes again, intently scanning what I saw to be tomorrow's front page, freshly printed.

I waited with interest while he finished, looking around at a functional scene which I guessed hadn't changed much since the days of that rumbustious giant, the first Lord Vaughnley. Desks and equipment had no doubt come and gone, but from the brown floor to the yellowing cream walls the overall impression was of a working permanence, slightly old-fashioned.

The present Lord Vaughnley finished reading, stretched himself upwards and patted the shirt-sleeved shoulder of the seated man, who was, I discovered later, that big white chief, the editor.

'Strong stuff, Marty. Well done.'

The seated man nodded and went on reading. Lord Vaughnley said to me, 'Rose Quince is here. You might like to meet her.'

'Yes,' I said, 'I would.'

'Over here.' He set off towards one of the bays, the lair, it proved, of the lady of the rattlesnake tongue who could nevertheless write sense, and who had written that day's judgment on Maynard.

'Rose,' said the paper's proprietor, 'take care of Kit Fielding, won't you?' and the redoubtable Rose Quince assured him that yes, she would.

119

'Files,' Lord Vaughnley said. 'Whatever he wants to see, show him.'

'Right.'

To me he said, 'We have a box at Ascot. The *Towncrier* has, I mean. I understand from the princess that you'll be riding there this Friday and Saturday. No point, I suppose, my dear chap, in asking you to lunch with me on Saturday, which is the day I'll be there, but do come up for a drink when you've finished. You'll always be welcome.'

I said I'd be glad to.

'Good. Good. My wife will be delighted. You'll be in good hands with Rose, now. She was born in Fleet Street the same as I was, her father was Conn Quince who edited the old *Chronicle*; she knows more of what goes on than the Street itself. She'll give you the gen, won't you, Rose?'

Rose, who looked to me to be bristling with reservations, agreed again that yes, she would; and Lord Vaughnley, with the nod of a man who knows he's done well, went away and left me to her serpent mercies.

She did not, it is true, have Medusa snakes growing out of her head, but whoever had named her Rose couldn't have foreseen its incongruity.

A rose she was not. A tiger-lily, more like. She was tall and very thin and fifteen to twenty years older than myself. Her artfully tousled and abundant hair was dark but streaked throughout with blonde, the aim having clearly been two contrasting colours, not overall tortoiseshell. The expertly painted sallow face could never have been pretty but was strongly good-looking, the nose masculine, the eyes noticeably pale blue; and from several feet away one could smell her sweet and heavy scent.

A quantity of bracelets, rings and necklaces decorated the ultimate in fashionable outlines, complemented by a heavy bossed and buckled belt round the hips, and I wondered if the general overstatement was a sort of stockade to frighten off the encroachment of the next generation of writers, a battlement against time.

If it was, I knew how she felt. Every jump jockey over thirty felt threatened by the rising nineteen-year-olds who would supplant them sooner or later. Every jockey, every champion had to prove race by race that he was as good as he'd ever been, and it was tough at the top only because of those hungry to take over one's saddle. I didn't need bangles, but I pulled out grey hairs when they appeared.

Rose Quince looked me up and down critically and said, 'Big for a jockey, aren't you?' which was hardly original, as most people I met said the same.

'Big enough.'

Her voice had an edge to it more than an accent, and was as positive as her appearance.

'And your sister is married to Maynard Allardeck's son.'

'Yes, that's right.'

'The source of Daddy's disapproval.'

'Yes.'

'What's wrong with her? Was she a whore?'

'No, a Capulet.'

Rose took barely three seconds to comprehend, then she shook her head in self-disgust.

'I missed an angle,' she said.

'Just as well.'

She narrowed her eyes and looked at me with her head tilted.

'I watched the Towncrier Trophy on television last Saturday,' she said. 'It would more or less have been treason not to.' She let her gaze wander around my shoulders. 'Left it a bit late, didn't you?'

'Probably.'

She looked back to my face. 'No excuses?'

'We won.'

'Yes, dammit, after you'd given everyone cardiac arrest. Did you realise that half the people in this building had their pay packets on you?'

'No, I didn't.'

'The Sports Desk told us you couldn't lose.'

'Bunty Ireland?'

'Precisely, Bunty Ireland. He thinks the sun shines out of your arse.' She shook an armful of baubles to express dismissal of Bunty's opinions. 'No jockey is that smart.'

'Mm,' I said. 'Could we talk about Maynard?'

Her dark eyebrows rose. 'On first name terms, are you?'

121

'Maynard Allardeck.'

'A prize shit.'

'Olympic gold.'

She smiled, showing well-disciplined teeth. 'You read nothing in the paper, buddy boy. Do you want to see the tape?'

'What tape?'

'The tape of *How's Trade*. It's still here, downstairs. If you want to see it, now's the time.'

'Yes,' I said.

'Right. Come along. I've got the unexpurgated version, the one they cut from to make the programme. Ready for the rough stuff? It's dynamite.'

TEN

She had acquired, it appeared, both the ten-minute edition which had been broadcast as well as the half-hour original.

'Did you see the programme on the box?' Rose said.

I shook my head.

'You'd better see that first, then.'

She had taken me to a small room which contained a semi-circle of comfortable chairs grouped in front of a television set. To each side of the set various makes of video machine sat on tables, with connecting cables snaking about in apparent disorder.

'We get brought or sent unsolicited tapes of things that have happened,' Rose explained casually. 'All sorts of tapes. Loch Ness monsters by the pailful. Mostly rubbish, but you never know. We've had a scoop or sixteen this way. The big white chief swears by it. Then we record things ourselves. Some of our reporters like to interview with video cameras, as I do sometimes. You get the flavour back fresh if you don't write the piece for a week or so.'

While she talked she connected a couple of wandering cable ends to the back of the television set and switched everything on. Her every movement was accompanied by metallic clinks and jingles, and her lily scent filled the room. She picked up a tape cassette which had been lying on the table behind one of the video machines and fed it into the slot.

'Right. Here we go.'

We sat in two of the chairs, she sprawling sideways so she could see my face, and the screen sprang immediately to life with an interesting arrangement of snow. Total silence ensued for ten seconds before the Maynard segment of *How's Trade* arrived in full sharp colour with sound attached. Then we had

123

the benefit of Maynard looking bland and polished through a voice-over introduction, with time to admire the hand-sewn lapels and silk tie.

The interviewer asked several harmless questions, Maynard's slightly condescending answers being lavishly interrupted by views of the interviewer nodding and smiling. The interviewer himself, unknown as far as I was concerned, was perhaps in his mid-thirties, with forgettable features except for calculating eyes of a chilling detachment. A prosecutor, I thought; and disliked him.

In reply to a question about how he got rich Maynard said that 'once or twice' he had come to the rescue of an ailing but basically sound business, had set it back on its feet with injections of liquidity and had subsequently acquired it to save it from closure when it had been unable to repay him. To the benefit, he suavely insisted, of all concerned.

'Except the former owners?' the interviewer asked; but the question was put as merely fact-finding, without bite.

Maynard's voice said that generous compensation was of course paid to the owners.

'And then what?' asked the interviewer, in the same way.

Naturally, Maynard said, if a good offer came along, he would in his turn sell: he could then lend the money to rescue another needy firm. The buying, selling and merging of businesses was advisable when jobs could be saved and a sensible profit made. He had done his modest best for industry and had ensured employment for many. It had been most rewarding in human terms.

Neither Maynard nor the interviewer raised his voice above a civilised monotone, and as an entertainment it was a drag. The segment ended with the interviewer thanking Maynard for a most interesting discussion, and there was a final shot of Maynard looking noble.

The screen, as if bored silly, reverted to black and white snow.

'Allardeck the philanthropist,' Rose said, jangling the bracelets and recrossing her long legs. 'Have you met him?'

'Yes.'

'Well, now for Allardeck the rapacious bully.'

'I've met him too,' I said.

She gave me a quizzical look and watched me watch the snowstorm until we were suddenly alive again with Maynard's charm and with the introduction and the first few harmless questions. It wasn't until the interviewer started asking about takeovers that things warmed up; and in this version the interviewer's voice was sharp and critical, designed to raise a prickly defensive response.

Maynard had kept his temper for a while, reacting self-righteously rather than with irritation, and these answers had been broadcast. In the end however his courtesy disintegrated, his voice rose and a forefinger began to wag.

'I act within the law,' he told the interviewer heavily. 'Your insinuations are disgraceful. When a debtor can't pay, one is entitled to take his property. The state does it. The courts enforce it. It's the law. Let me tell you that in the horse racing business, if a man can't pay his training fees, the trainer is entitled to sell the horse to recover his money. It's the law, and what's more, it's natural justice.'

The interviewer mentioned villainous mortgage holders who foreclosed and evicted their tenants. Hadn't Maynard, he asked, lent money to a hard-pressed family business that owned a block of flats which was costing more to maintain than the rental income, and couldn't afford the repairs required by the authorities? And after the repairs were done, hadn't Maynard demanded his money back? And when the family couldn't pay, hadn't he said he would take the flats instead, which were a loss to the family anyway? And after that, hadn't mysterious cracks developed in the fabric, so that the building was condemned and all the poor tenants had to leave? And after that, hadn't he demolished the flats and sold the freehold land to a development company for ten times his original loan for repairs?

The inquisitorial nature of the interviewer was by now totally laid bare, and the questions came spitting out as accusations, to which Maynard answered variously with growing fury:

'It's none of your business.'

'It was a long time ago.'

'The building subsided because of underground trains.'

'The family was glad to be rid of a mill-stone liability.'

'I will not answer these questions.'

The last statement was practically a shout. The interviewer made calming motions with his hand, leaning back in his chair, appearing to relax, all of which cooling behaviour caused Maynard to simmer rather than seethe. A mean-looking scowl, however, remained in place. Nobility was nowhere to be seen.

The interviewer with subterranean cunning said pleasantly, 'You mentioned racehorses. Am I right in thinking your own father was a racehorse trainer and that you at one time were his assistant?'

Maynard said ungraciously, 'Yes.'

'Give us your opinion of investing in bloodstock.'

Maynard said profits could be made if one took expert advice.

'But in your case,' the interviewer said, 'you must be your own expert.'

Maynard shrugged. 'Perhaps.'

The interviewer said very smoothly, 'Will you tell us how you acquired your racehorse Metavane?'

Maynard said tightly, 'I took him in settlement of a bad debt.'

'In the same way as your other businesses?'

Maynard didn't answer.

'Metavane proved to be a great horse, didn't he? And you syndicated him for at least four million pounds . . . which must be your biggest coup ever – bigger than the Bourne Brothers' patents. Shall we talk about those two enterprises? First, tell me how much you allow either Metavane's former owners or the Bourne Brothers out of the continuing fruits of your machinations.'

'Look here,' Maynard said furiously, 'if you had a fraction of my business sense you'd be out doing something useful instead of sitting here green with envy picking holes.'

He stood up fiercely and abruptly and walked decisively off the set, tearing off the microphone he had been wearing on his tie and flinging it on the ground. The interviewer made no attempt to stop him. Instead he faced the camera and with carefully presented distaste said that some of the other businesses, big and small, known to have benefited from Mr

126

Allardeck's rescue missions were Downs and Co. (a printing works), Benjy's Fast Food Takeout, Healthy Life (sports goods manufacturers), Applewood Garden Centre, Purfleet Electronics and Bourne Brothers (light engineers).

The Bourne Brothers' assets, he said, had proved to include some long overlooked patents for a special valve which had turned out to be just what industry was beginning to need. As soon as it was his, Maynard Allardeck had offered the valve on a royalty basis to the highest bidder, and had been collecting handsomely ever since. The Bourne Brothers? The interviewer shook his head. The Bourne Brothers hadn't realised what they'd owned until they'd irrevocably parted with it. But did Maynard Allardeck know what he was getting? Almost certainly yes. The interviewer smiled maliciously and pushed the knife right in. If Allardeck had told the Bourne Brothers what they owned, collecting dust in a file, they could have saved themselves several times over.

The interviewer's smugly sarcastic face vanished into another section of blizzard, and Rose Quince rose languidly to switch everything off.

'Well?' she said.

'Nasty.'

'Is that all?'

'Why didn't they show the whole tape on *How's Trade*? They obviously meant to needle Maynard. Why did they smother the results?'

'I thought you'd never ask.' Rose hitched a hip on to one of the tables and regarded me with acid amusement. 'I should think Allardeck paid them not to show it.'

'What?'

'Pure as a spring lamb, aren't you? That interviewer and his producer have before this set up a pigeon and then thoroughly shot him down, but without the brawl ever reaching the screen. One politician, I know for certain, was invited by the producer to see his hopelessly damaging tape before it was broadcast. He was totally appalled and asked if there was any way he could persuade the producer to edit it. Sure, the producer said, the oldest way in the world, through your wallet.'

'How do you know?'

'The politician told me himself. He wanted me to write about it, he was so furious, but I couldn't. He wouldn't let me use his name.'

'Maynard,' I said slowly, 'has a real genius for acquiring assets.'

'Oh, sure. And nothing illegal. Not unless he helped the trains to shake the block of flats' foundations.'

'One could never find out.'

'Not a chance.'

'How did the interviewer rake all that up?'

Rose shrugged. 'Out of files. Out of archives. Same as we all do when we're on a story.'

'He'd done a great deal of work.'

'Expecting a great deal of pay-off.'

'Mm,' I said, 'if Maynard was already angling for a knighthood, he'd have paid the earth. They could probably have got more from him than they did.'

'They'll curl up like lemon rind now that they know.' The idea pleased Rose greatly.

'How did you get this tape?' I asked curiously.

'From the producer himself, sort of. He owed me a big favour. I told him I wanted to do a shredding job on Allardeck, and asked to see the interview again, uncut if possible, and he was as nice as pie. I wouldn't tell him I knew about his own little scam, now would I?'

'I suppose,' I said slowly, 'that I couldn't have a copy?'

Rose gave me a long cool look while she considered it. Her eyelids, I noticed, were coloured purple, dark contrast to the pale blue eyes.

'What would you do with it?' she said.

'I don't know yet.'

'It's under copyright,' she said.

'Mm.'

'You shouldn't have it.'

'No.'

She bent over the video machine and pressed the eject button. The large black cassette slid quietly and smoothly into her hand. She slotted it into its case and held it out to me, gold chains tinkling.

'Take this one. This is a copy. I made it myself. The originals

128

never left the building, they're hot as hell about that in that television company, but I'm fairly quick with these things. They left me alone in an editing room to view, with some spare tapes stacked in a corner, which was their big mistake.'

I took the box, which bore a large white label saying 'Do not touch'.

'Now listen to me, buddy boy, if you're found with this, you don't get me into trouble, right?'

'Right,' I said. 'Do you want it back?'

'I don't know why I trust you,' she said plaintively. 'A goddamn jockey. If I want it back I'll ask. You keep it somewhere safe. Don't leave it lying about, for God's sake. Though I suppose I should tell you it won't play on an ordinary video. The tape is professional tape three-quarters of an inch wide, it gives better definition. You'll need a machine that takes that size.'

'What were you going to do with it yourself?' I asked.

'Wipe it off,' she said decisively. 'I got it yesterday morning and played it several times here to make sure I didn't put the uncut version's words into Allardeck's mouth in the paper. I don't need suing. Then I wrote my piece, and I've been busy today . . . but if you'd come one day later, it would all have been wiped.'

'Lucky,' I said.

'Yes. What else? Files? There's more on the tape, but Bill said files, so files you can have.'

'Bill?'

'Bill Vaughnley. We worked together when we were young. Bill started at the bottom, the old Lord made him. So did I. You don't call someone sir when you've shared cigarette butts on a night stint.'

They had been lovers, I thought. It was in her voice.

'He says I have a tongue like a viper,' she said without offence. 'I dare say he told you?'

I nodded. 'Rattlesnake.'

She smiled. 'When he's a pompous fool, I let him know it.'

She stood up, tawny and tinkling like a mobile in a breeze, and we went out of the television room, down a corridor, round a few corners, and found ourselves in an expanse like a library with shelves to the ceiling bearing not books but folders of all sorts, the whole presided over by a severe looking youth in spectacles who signed us in, looked up the indexing and directed us to the section we needed.

The file on Maynard Allardeck was, as Rose had said, less informative than the tape. There were sundry photographs of him, black and white glossy prints, chiefly taken at race meetings, where I supposed he was more accessible. There were three, several years old now, of him leading in his great horse Metavane after its win in the 2000 Guineas, the Goodwood Mile and the Champion Stakes. Details and dates were on flimsy paper strips stuck to the back of the prints.

There were two bunches of newspaper clippings, one from the *Towncrier*, one from other sources such as the *Financial Times* and the *Sporting Life*. Nothing critical had been written, it seemed, before the onslaught in the *Flag*. The paragraphs were mainly dull: Maynard, from one of the oldest racing families ... Maynard, proud owner ... Maynard, member of the Jockey Club ... Maynard, astute businessman ... Maynard, supporter of charity ... Maynard the great and good. Approving adjectives like bold, compassionate, far-sighted and responsible occurred. The public persona at its prettiest.

'Enough to make you puke,' Rose said.

'Mm,' I said. 'Do you think you could ask your producer friend why he hit on Maynard as a target?'

'Maybe. Why?'

'Someone's got it in for Maynard. That TV interview might be an attack that didn't work, God bless bribery and corruption. The attack in the *Flag* has worked well. You've helped it along handsomely yourself. So who got to the *Flag*, and did they also get to the producer?'

'I take it back,' she said. 'Some jockeys are smarter than others.'

'Very few are dumb.'

'They just talk a different language?'

'Dead right.'

She returned the file to its place. 'Anything else? Any dinky little thing?'

'Yes,' I said. 'How would I get to talk to Sam Leggatt, who edits the *Flag*?'

She let out a breath, a cross between a cough and a laugh. 'Sam Leggatt? You don't. '

'Why not?'

'He walks around in a bullet-proof vest.'

'Seriously?'

'Metaphorically.'

'Do you know him?'

'Sure, I know him. Can't say I like him. He was political correspondent on the *Record* before he went to the *Flag*, and he's always thought he was God's gift to Fleet Street. He's a mocker by nature. He and the *Flag* are soulmates.'

'Could you reach him on the telephone?' I asked.

She shook her head over my naivety. 'They'll be printing the first edition by now, but he'll be checking everything again for the second. Adding stuff. Changing it round. There's no way he'd talk to Moses let alone a . . . a jumping bean.'

'You could say,' I suggested, 'that you were your editor's secretary, and it was urgent.'

She looked at me in disbelief. 'And why the hell should I?'

'Because you trade in favours.'

'Jee—sus.' She blinked the pale blue eyes.

'Any time,' I said. 'I'll pay. I took it for granted that this . . .' I held up the tape, 'was on account.'

'The telephone,' she said, 'makes it two favours.'

'All right.'

She said with amusement, 'Is this how you win your races?' She turned without waiting for an answer and led the way back roughly to where we had started from but ending in a small, bare little room furnished only with three or four chairs, a table and a telephone.

'Interview room,' Rose said. 'General purposes. Not used much. I'm not having anyone hear me make this call.'

She sat on one of the chairs looking exotically sensuous and behaving with middle-class propriety, the baroque façade for frighteners, the sensible woman beneath.

'You'll have about ten seconds, if that,' she said, stretching out the bracelets for the telephone. 'Leggatt will know straight away you're not our editor. Our editor comes from Yorkshire and still sounds like it.'

I nodded.

She got an outside line and with long red nails tapped in the *Flag*'s number, which she knew by heart; and within a minute, after out-blarneying the Irish, she handed me the receiver silently.

'Hello, Martin, what goes?' an unenthusiastic voice said.

I said slowly and clearly, 'Owen Watts left his credit cards in Bobby Allardeck's garden.'

'What? I don't see . . .' There was a sudden silence. 'Who is this?'

'Jay Erskine,' I said, 'left his Press Club card in the same place. To whom should I report these losses? To the Press Council, the police or my member of parliament?'

'Who is that?' he asked flatly.

'I'm speaking from a telephone in the *Towncrier*. Will you talk to me in your office, or shall I give the *Towncrier* a scoop?'

There was a long pause. I waited. His voice then said, 'I'll ring you back. Give me your extension.'

'No,' I said. 'Now or never.'

A much shorter pause. 'Very well. Come to the front desk. Say you're from the *Towncrier*.'

'I'll be there.'

He crashed the telephone down as soon as I'd finished speaking, and Rose was staring at me as if alarmed for my wholeness of mind.

'No one speaks to editors like that,' she said.

'Yeah . . . well, I don't work for him. And somewhere along the way I've learned not to be afraid of people. I was never afraid of horses. People were more difficult.'

She said with a touch of seriousness, 'People can harm you.'

'They sure can. But I'd get nowhere with Leggatt by being soft.'

'Where do you want to be?' she asked. 'What's this scoop you're not giving the *Towncrier*?'

'Nothing much. Just some dirty tricks the *Flag* indulged in to get their Allardeck story for Intimate Details.'

She shrugged. 'I doubt if we'd print that.'

'Maybe not. What's the limit journalists will go to to get a story?'

'No limit. Up Everest, into battlefields, along the gutters, anywhere a scandal leads. I've done my crusading time in rotten health farms, corrupt local governments, nutty religions. I've seen more dirt, more famine, more poverty, more tragedy than I need. I've sat through nights with parents of murdered children and I've been in a village of lifeboatmen's widows weeping for their dead. And then some damn fool man expects me to go sit on a prissy gilt chair and swoon over skirt lengths in some goddam Paris salon. I've never been a women's writer and I'm bloody well not starting now.'

She stopped, smiled twistedly, 'My feminism's showing.'

'Say you won't go,' I said. 'If it's a demotion, refuse it. You've got the clout. No one expects you to write about fashion, and I agree with you, you shouldn't.'

She gave me a long look. 'I wouldn't be fired, but he's new, he's a chauvinist, he could certainly make life difficult.'

'You,' I said, 'are one very marketable lady. Get out the famous poison fangs. A little venom might work wonders.'

She stood up, stretching tall, putting her hands on her heavily belted hips. She looked like an Amazon equipped for battle but I could still sense the indecision inside. I stood also, to the same height, and kissed her cheek.

'Very brotherly,' she said dryly. 'Is that all?'

'That's all you want, isn't it?'

'Yes,' she said, mildly surprised. 'You're goddam right.'

The *Daily Flag*, along Fleet Street from the *Towncrier*, had either been built much later or had been done over in Modern Flashy.

There was a fountain throwing out negative ions in the foyer and ceiling-wide chandeliers of thin vertical shimmering glass rods, each emitting light at its downward tip. Also a marble floor, futuristic seating and a security desk populated by four large men in intimidating uniforms.

I told one of them I'd come from the *Towncrier* to see Mr Leggatt and half expected to be thrown out bodily into the street. All that happened, however, was that after a check against a list on the desk I was directed upwards with the same lack of interest as I'd met with on friendlier territory.

Upstairs the decorative contrast continued. Walls in the *Flag* were pale orange with red flecks, the desks shining green plastic, the floor carpeted with busy orange and red zigzags, the whole a study in unrestfulness. Anger on every page, I thought, and no wonder.

Sam Leggatt's office had an opaque glass door marked 'editor' in large lower-case white letters, followed some way below by smaller but similar letters telling callers to ring bell and wait.

I rang the bell and waited, and presently with a buzz the door swung inwards a few inches. Sam Leggatt might not actually wear a bullet-proof vest but his defences against people with grievances were impressive.

I pushed the door open further and went in to another brash display of rotten taste: black plastic desk, red wallpaper flecked in a geometric pattern, and a mottled green carpet, which as a working environment would have sent me screaming to the bottle.

There were two shirt-sleeved men in there, both standing, both apparently impervious to their surroundings. One was short, stubby and sandy-haired, the other taller, stooped, bespectacled and going bald. Both about fifty, I thought. A third man, younger, sat in a corner, in a suit, watchful and quiet.

'Mr Leggatt?' I said.

The short sandy-haired one said, 'I'm Leggatt. I'll give you five minutes.' He inclined his head towards the taller man beside him. 'This is Tug Tunny, who edits Intimate Details. That is Mr Evans from our legal department. So who are you, and what do you want?'

Tug Tunny snapped his fingers. 'I know who he is,' he said. 'Jockey. That jockey.' He searched for the name in his memory and found it. 'Fielding. Champion jockey.'

I nodded, and it seemed to me that they all relaxed. There was a trace of arrogance all the same in the way Leggatt stood, and a suggestion of pugnaciousness, but not more, I supposed, than his eminence and the circumstances warranted, and he spoke and behaved without bluster throughout.

'What do you want?' Leggatt repeated, but lacking quite the same tension as when I'd entered; and it crossed my mind as he spoke that with his passion for security they would be recording the conversation, and that I was speaking into an open microphone somewhere out of sight.

134

I said carefully, 'I came to make arrangements for returning the property of two of your journalists, Owen Watts and Jay Erskine.'

'Return it then,' Leggatt said brusquely.

'I would be so glad,' I said, 'if you would tell me why they needed to climb a ladder set against Bobby Allardeck's house at one in the morning.'

'What's it to you?'

'We found them, you understand, with telephone tapping equipment. Up a ladder, with tools, at the point where the telephone wires enter the Allardecks' house. What were they doing there?'

There was a pause, then Tunny flicked his fingers again.

'He's Allardeck's brother-in-law. Mrs Allardeck's brother.'

'Quite right,' I said. 'I was staying with them last night when your men came to break in.'

'They didn't break in,' Leggatt said. 'On the contrary, they were, I understand, quite savagely attacked. Allardeck should be arrested for assault.'

'We thought they were burglars. What would you think if you found people climbing a ladder set against your house at dead of night? It was only after we'd chased them off that we found they weren't after the silver.'

'Found? How found?'

'They left their jackets behind, full of credit cards and other things with their names on.'

'Which you propose to return.'

'Naturally. But I'd like a proper explanation of why they were there at all. Wire-tapping is illegal, and we disturbed them in the act of removing a tap which had been in place for at least two weeks, according to the telephone engineer who came this morning to complete the dismantling.'

They said nothing, just waited with calculating eyes.

I went on. 'Your paper mounted an unprovoked and damaging attack on Bobby Allardeck, using information gleaned by illegal means. Tell me why.'

They said nothing.

I said, 'You were sent, Mr Leggatt, a special delivery letter containing proof that all of Bobby Allardeck's creditors had been paid and he was not going bankrupt. Why don't you

135

now try to undo a fraction of the misery you've caused him and my sister? Why don't you print conspicuously in Intimate Details an apology for misrepresenting Bobby's position? Why don't you outline the paragraph in red and get your two busy nocturnal journalists to scoot up to Newmarket with the edition hot off the presses like before, and while the town is asleep deliver a copy personally to every recipient who was on their earlier round? And why don't you send a red-inked copy to each of Bobby's owners, as before? That would be most pleasing, don't you think?'

They didn't looked pleased in the slightest.

'It's unfortunate,' I said mildly, 'that it's one's duty as a citizen to report illegal acts to the relevant authorities.'

Without any show of emotion Sam Leggatt turned his head towards the silent Mr Evans. After a pause Mr Evans briefly nodded.

'Do it,' Sam Leggatt said to Tunny.

Tunny was thunderstruck. 'No.'

'Print the apology and get the papers delivered.'

'But . . .'

'Don't you know a barrel when you see one?' He looked back at me. 'And in return?'

'Watts's credit cards and Erskine's Press Club pass.'

'And you'll still have . . .?'

'Their jackets, a chequebook, photos, letters, notebooks, a diary and a neat little bugging system.'

He nodded. 'And for those?'

'Well,' I said slowly, 'how about if you asked your lawyers what you would be forced to pay to Bobby if the wire-tapping came to court? If you cared to compensate him at that level now we would press no charges and save you the bad publicity and the costs and the penalties of a trial.'

'I have no authority for that.'

'But you could get it.'

He merely stared, without assent or denial.

'Also,' I said, 'the answer to why the attack was made. Who suggested it? Did you direct your journalists to break the law? Did they do it at their own instigation? Were they paid to do it, and if so by whom?'

'Those questions can't be answered.'

'Do you yourself know the answers?'

He said flatly, 'Your bargaining position is strong enough only for the apology and the delivery of the apology, and you shall have those, and I will consult on the question of compensation. Beyond that, nothing.'

I knew a stone wall when I saw one. The never-reveal-your-sources syndrome at its most flexible. Leggatt was telling me directly that answering my questions would cause the *Flag* more trouble than my reporting them for wire-tapping, which being so I would indeed get nothing else.

'We'll settle for the compensation,' I said. 'We would have to report the wire-tapping quite soon. Within a few days.' I paused. 'When a sufficient apology appears in the paper on Friday morning, and I've checked on the Newmarket deliveries, I'll see that the credit cards and the Press Club pass reach you here at your front desk.'

'Acceptable,' Leggatt said, smothering a protest from Tunny. 'I agree to that.'

I nodded to them and turned and went out through the door, and when I'd gone three steps felt a hand on my arm and found Leggatt had followed me.

'Off the record,' he said, 'what would you do if you discovered who had suggested the Allardeck attacks?'

I looked into sandy brown eyes, at one with the hair. At the businesslike outward presentation of the man who daily printed sneers, innuendo, distrust and spite, and spoke without showing a trace of them.

'Off the record,' I said, 'bash his face in.'

ELEVEN

I didn't suppose an apology printed in the *Flag* would melt Bobby's bank manager's cash register heart, and I was afraid that the *Flag*'s compensation, if they paid it, wouldn't be enough, or soon enough, to make much difference.

I thought with a sigh of the manager in my own bank, who had seen me uncomplainingly through bad patches in the past and had stuck out his neck later to lend me capital for one or two business excursions, never pressing prematurely for repayment. Now that I looked like being solvent for the foreseeable future he behaved the same as ever, friendly, helpful, a generous source of advice.

Getting the apology printed was more a gesture than an end to Bobby's troubles, but at least it should reassure the owners and put rock back under the quicksands for the tradespeople in Newmarket. If the stable could be saved, it would be saved alive, not comatose.

I'd got from Sam Leggatt a tacit admission that the *Flag* had been at fault, and the certainty that he knew the answers to my questions. I needed those answers immediately and had no hope of unlocking his tongue.

With a sense of failure and frustration I booked into a nearby hotel for the night, feeling more tired than I liked to admit and afraid of falling asleep on the seventy dark miles home. I ordered something to eat from room service and made a great many telephone calls between yawns.

First, to Holly.

'Well done, today,' she said.

'What?'

'Your win, of course.'

'Oh, yes.' It seemed a lifetime ago. 'Thanks.'

'Where are you?' she said. 'I tried the cottage.'

'In London.' I told her the hotel and my room number. 'How are things?'

'Awful.'

I told her about the *Flag* promising to print the apology, which cheered her a little but not much.

'Bobby's out. He's gone walking on the Heath. It's all dreadful. I wish he'd come back.'

The anxiety was raw in her voice and I spent some time trying to reassure her, saying Bobby would certainly return soon, he would know how she worried; and privately wondering if he wasn't sunk so deep in his own despair that he'd have no room for imagining Holly's.

'Listen,' I said after a while. 'Do something for me, will you?'

'Yes. What?'

'Look up in the form books for Maynard's horse Metavane. Do you remember, it won the 2000 Guineas about eight years ago?'

'Vaguely.'

'I want to know who owned it before Maynard.'

'Is it important?' She sounded uninterested and dispirited.

'Yes. See if you can find out, and ring me back.'

'All right.'

'And don't worry.'

'I can't help it.'

No one could help it, I thought, disconnecting. Her unhappiness settled heavily on me as if generated in my own mind.

I telephoned Rose Quince at the home number she had given me on my way out, and she answered breathlessly at the eighth ring saying she had just that minute come through the door.

'So they didn't throw you to the presses?' she said.

'No. But I fear I got bounced off the flak jacket.'

'Not surprising.'

'All the same, read Intimate Details on Friday. And by the way, do you know a man called Tunny? He edits Intimate Details.'

'Tunny,' she said. 'Tug Tunny. A memory like a floppy disc, instant recall at the flick of a switch. He's been in the gossip business all his life. He probably pulled the wings off butterflies as a child and he's fulfilled if he can goad any poor slob to a messy divorce.'

'He didn't look like that,' I said dubiously.

'Don't be put off by the parsonage exterior. Read his column. That's *him*.'

'Yes. Thanks. And what about Owen Watts and Jay Erskine?'

'The people who left their belongings in your sister's garden?'

'That's right.'

'Owen Watts I've never heard of before today,' Rose said. 'Jay Erskine . . . if it's the same Jay Erskine, he used to work on the *Towncrier* as a crime reporter.'

There were reservations in her voice, and I said persuasively, 'Tell me about him.'

'Hm.' She paused, then seemed to make up her mind. 'He went to jail some time ago,' she said. 'He was among criminals so much because of his job, he grew to like them, like policemen sometimes do. He got tried for conspiracy to obstruct the course of justice. Anyway, if it's the same Jay Erskine, he was as hard as nails but a terrific writer. If he wrote those pieces about your brother-in-law, he's sold out for the money.'

'To eat,' I said.

'Don't get compassionate,' Rose said critically. 'Jay Erskine wouldn't.'

'No,' I said. 'Thanks. Have you been inside the *Flag* building?'

'Not since they did it up. I hear it's gruesome. When Pollgate took over he let loose some decorator who'd been weaned on orange kitchen plastic. What's it like?'

'Gruesome,' I said, 'is an understatement. What's Pollgate like himself?'

'Nestor Pollgate, owner of the *Flag* as of a year ago,' she said, 'is reported to be a fairly young upwardly mobile shit of the first water. I've never met him myself. They say a charging rhinoceros is safer.'

'Does he have editorial control?' I asked. 'Does Sam Leggatt print to Pollgate's orders?'

'In the good old days proprietors never interfered,' she said nostalgically. 'Now, some do, some still don't. Bill Vaughnley gives general advice. The old Lord edited the *Towncrier* himself in the early years, which was different. Pollgate bought the *Flag* over several smarting dead bodies and you'll see old-guard *Flag* journalists weeping into their beer in Fleet Street bars over the whipped-up rancour they have to dip their pens in. The editor before Sam Leggatt threw in the sponge and retired. Pollgate has certainly dragged the *Flag* to new heights of depravity, but whether he stands over Leggatt with a whip, I don't know.'

'He wasn't around tonight, I don't think,' I said.

'He spends his time putting his weight about in the City, so I'm told. Incidentally, compared with Pollgate, your man Maynard is a babe in arms with his small takeovers and his saintly front. They say Pollgate doesn't give a damn what people think of him, and his financial bullying starts where Maynard's leaves off.'

'A right darling.'

'Sam Leggatt I understand,' she said. 'Pollgate I don't. If I were you I wouldn't twist the *Flag*'s tail any further.'

'Perhaps not.'

'Look what they did to your brother-in-law,' she said, 'and be warned.'

'Yes,' I said soberly. 'Thank you.'

'Any time.'

She said goodbye cheerfully and I sat drinking a glass of wine and thinking of Sam Leggatt and the fearsome manipulator behind him: wondering if the campaign against Maynard had originated from the very top, or from Leggatt or from Tunny, or from Watts and Erskine, or from outside the *Flag* altogether, or from one of Maynard's comet-trail of victims.

The telephone rang and I picked up the receiver, hearing Holly's voice saying without preamble, 'Maynard got Metavane when he was an unraced two-year-old, and I couldn't find the former owners in the form book. But Bobby has come back now, and he says he thinks they were called Perryside. He's sure his grandfather used to train for them, but they seem to have dropped right out of racing.'

'Um,' I said. 'Have you got any of those old *Racing Who's Whos*? They had pages of owners in them, with addresses.

141

I've got them, but they're in the cottage, which isn't much good tonight.'

'I don't think we've got any from ten years ago,' she said doubtfully, and I heard her asking Bobby. 'No, he says not.'

'Then I'll ring up Grandfather and ask him. I know he's kept them all, back to the beginning.'

'Bobby wants to know what's so important about Metavane after all these years.'

'Ask him if Maynard still owns any part of Metavane.'

The murmuring went on and the answer came back. 'He thinks Maynard still owns one share. He syndicated the rest for millions.'

I said, 'I don't know if Metavane's important. I'll know tomorrow. Keep the chin up, won't you?'

'Bobby says to tell you the dragon has started up the drive.'

I put the receiver down smiling. If Bobby could make jokes he had come back whole from the Heath.

Grandfather grumbled that he was ready for bed but consented to go downstairs in his pyjamas. 'Perryside,' he said, reading, 'Major Clement Perryside, The Firs, St Albans, Hertfordshire, telephone number attached.' Disgust filled the old voice. 'Did you know the fella had his horses with Allardeck?'

'Sorry, yes.'

'To hell with him, then. Anything else? No? Then goodnight.'

I telephoned to the Perryside number he'd given me and a voice at the other end said, Yes, it was The Firs, but the Perrysides hadn't lived there for about seven years. The voice had bought the house from Major and Mrs Perryside, and if I would wait they might find their new address and telephone number.

I waited. They found them. I thanked them; said goodnight.

At the new number another voice said, No, Major and Mrs Perryside don't live here any more. The voice had bought the bungalow from them several months back. They thought the Perrysides had gone into sheltered housing in Hitchin. Which sheltered housing? They couldn't say, but it was definitely in Hitchin. Or just outside. They thought.

Thank you, I said, sighing, and disconnected.

Major and Mrs Perryside, growing older and perhaps

poorer, knowing Maynard had made millions from their horse: could they still hold a grievance obsessional enough to set them tilting at him at this late stage? But even if they hadn't, I thought it would be profitable to talk to them.

If I could find them; in Hitchin, or outside.

I telephoned to my answering machine in the cottage and collected my messages: four from various trainers, the one from Holly, and a final unidentified man asking me to ring him back, number supplied.

I got through to Wykeham Harlowe first because he, like my grandfather, went early to bed, and he, too, said he was in his pyjamas.

We talked for a while about that day's runners and those for the next day and the rest of the week, normal more or less nightly discussions. And as usual nowadays he said he wouldn't be coming to Towcester tomorrow, it was too far. Ascot, he said, on Friday and Saturday. He would go to Ascot, perhaps only on one day, but he'd be there.

'Great,' I said.

'You know how it is, Paul,' he said. 'Old bones, old bones.'

'Yes,' I said. 'I know. This is Kit.'

'Kit? Of course you're Kit. Who else would you be?'

'No one,' I said. 'I'll ring you tomorrow night.'

'Good, good. Take care of those novices. Goodnight, then, Paul.'

'Goodnight,' I said.

I talked after that with the three other trainers, all on the subject of the horses I'd be riding for them that week and next, and finally, after ten o'clock and yawning convulsively, I got through to the last, unidentified, number.

'This is Kit Fielding,' I said.

'Ah.' There was a pause, then a faint but discernible click. 'I'm offering you,' said a civilised voice, 'a golden opportunity.'

He paused. I said nothing. He went on, very smoothly, 'Three thousand before, ten thousand after.'

'No,' I said.

'You haven't heard the details.'

I'd heard quite enough. I disconnected without saying another word and sat for a while staring at walls I didn't see.

I'd been propositioned before, but not quite like that. Never for such a large sum. The before-and-after merchants were always wanting jockeys to lose races to order, but I hadn't been approached by any of them seriously for years. Not since they'd tired of being told no.

Tonight's was an unknown voice, or one I hadn't heard often enough to recognise. High in register. Education to match. Prickles wriggled up my spine. The voice, the approach, the amount, the timing, all of them raised horrid little suggestions of entrapment.

I sat looking at the telephone number I'd been given.

A London number. The exchange 722. I got through to the operator and asked whereabouts in London one would find exchange 722, general information printed in London telephone directories. Hold on, she said, and told me almost immediately; 722 was Chalk Farm stroke Hampstead.

I thanked her. Chalk Farm stroke Hampstead meant absolutely nothing, except that it was not an area known for devotion to horse racing. Very much the reverse, I would have thought. Life in Hampstead tended to be intellectually inward-looking, not raucously open-air.

Why Hampstead . . .

I fell asleep in the chair.

After a night spent at least half in bed I drank some coffee in the morning and went out shopping, standing in draughty doorways in Tottenham Court Road, waiting for the electronic wizards to unbolt their steel-mesh shutters.

I found a place that would re-record Rose's professional three-quarter-inch tape of Maynard on to a domestic size to fit my own player, no copyright questions asked. The knowingly obliging youth who performed the service seemed disgusted and astounded that the contents weren't pornographic, but I cheered him up a little by buying a lightweight video-recording camera, a battery pack to run it off and a number of new tapes. He showed me in detail how to work everything and encouraged me to practise in the shop. He could point me to a helpful little bachelor club, he said, if I needed therapy.

I declined the offer, piled everything in the car, and set off

144

north to Hitchin, which was not exactly on the direct route to Towcester but at least not in a diametrically opposite direction.

Finding the Perrysides when I got there was easy: they were in the telephone book. Major C. Perryside, 14 Conway Retreat, Ingle Barton. Helpful locals pointed me to the village of Ingle Barton, three miles outside the town, and others there explained how to find number 14 in the retirement homes.

The houses themselves were several long terraces of small one-storey units, each with its own brightly painted front door and strip of minute flower bed. Paths alone led to the houses: one had to park one's car on a tarmac area and walk along neatly paved ways between tiny segments of grass. Furniture removal men, I thought, would curse the lay-out roundly, but it certainly led to an air of unusual peace, even on a cold damp morning in November.

I walked along to number 14, carrying the video camera in its bag. Pressed the bell push. Waited.

Everywhere was quiet, and no one answered the door. After two or three more unsuccessful attempts at knocking and ringing I went to the door of the right-hand neighbour and tried there.

An old lady answered, round, bright-eyed, interested.

'They walked round to the shop,' she said.

'Do you know how long they'll be?'

'They take their time.'

'How would I know them?' I asked.

'The Major has white hair and walks with a stick. Lucy will be wearing a fishing hat, I should think. And if you're thinking of carrying their groceries home for them, young man, you'll be welcomed. But don't try to sell them encyclo-paedias or life insurance. You'll be wasting your time.'

'I'm not selling,' I assured her.

'Then the shop is past the car park and down the lane to the left.' She gave me a sharp little nod and retreated behind her lavender door, and I went where she'd directed.

I found the easily recognisable Perrysides on the point of emerging from the tiny village stores, each of them carrying a basket and moving extremely slowly. I walked up to them without haste and asked if I could perhaps help.

'Decent of you,' said the Major gruffly, holding out his basket.

'What are you selling?' Lucy Perryside said suspiciously, relinquishing hers. 'Whatever it is, we're not buying.'

The baskets weren't heavy: the contents looked meagre.

'I'm not selling,' I said, turning to walk with them at the snail's pace apparently dictated by the Major's shaky legs. 'Would the name Fielding mean anything to you?'

They shook their heads.

Lucy under the battered tweed fishing hat had a thin imperious-looking face, heavily wrinkled with age but firm as to mouth. She spoke with clear upper-class diction and held her back ramrod straight as if in defiance of the onslaughts of time. Lucy Perryside, in various guises and various centuries, had pitched pride against bloody adversity and come through unbent.

'My name is Kit Fielding,' I said. 'My grandfather trains horses in Newmarket.'

The Major stopped altogether. 'Fielding. Yes. I remember. We don't like to talk about racing. Better keep off the subject, there's a good chap.'

I nodded slightly and we moved on as before, along the cold little lane with the bare trees fuzzy with the foreboding of drizzle; after a while Lucy said, 'That's why he came, Clement, to talk about racing.'

'Did you?' asked the Major apprehensively.

'I'm afraid so, yes.'

This time, however, he went on walking, with, it seemed to me, resignation; and I had an intense sense of the disappointments and downward adjustments he had made, swallowing his pain and behaving with dignity, civil in the face of disasters.

'Are you a journalist?' Lucy asked.

'No . . . a jockey.'

She gave me a sweeping glance from head to foot. 'You're too big for a jockey.'

'Steeplechasing,' I said.

'Oh.' She nodded. 'We didn't have jumpers.'

'I'm making a film,' I said. 'It's about hard luck stories in

146

racing. And I wondered if you would help with one segment. For a fee, of course.'

They glanced at each other, searching each other's reactions, and in their private language apparently decided not to turn down the offer without listening.

'What would we have to do?' Lucy asked prosaically.

'Just talk. Talk to my camera.' I indicated the bag I was carrying along with the baskets. 'It wouldn't be difficult.'

'Subject?' the Major asked, and before I could tell him he sighed and said, 'Metavane?'

'Yes,' I said.

They faced up to it as to a firing squad, and Lucy said eventually, 'For a fee. Very well.'

I mentioned an amount. They made no audible comment, but it was clear from their nods of acceptance that it was enough, that it was a relief, that they badly needed the money.

We made our slow progress across the car park and down the path and through their bright blue front door, and at their gestured invitation I brought out the camera and fed in a tape.

They grouped themselves naturally side by side on the sofa whose chintz cover had been patched here and there with different fabrics. They sat in a room unexpectedly spacious, facing large sliding windows which let out on to a tiny secluded paved area where in summer they could sit in the sun. There was a bedroom, Lucy said, and a kitchen and a bathroom, and they were comfortable, as I could see.

I could see that their furniture, although sparse, was antique, and that apart from that it looked as if everything saleable had been sold.

I adjusted the camera in the way I'd been taught and balanced it on a pile of books on a table, kneeling behind it to see through the viewfinder.

'OK,' I said, 'I'll ask you questions. Would you just look into the camera lens while you talk?'

They nodded. She took his hand: to give courage, I thought, rather than to receive.

I started the camera silently recording and said, 'Major, would you tell me how you came to buy Metavane?'

The Major swallowed and blinked, looking distinguished but unhappy.

147

'Major,' I repeated persuasively, 'please do tell me how you bought Metavane?'

He cleared his throat. 'I er . . . we . . . always had a horse, now and then. One at a time. Couldn't afford more, do you see? But loved them.' He paused. 'We asked our trainer . . . he was called Allardeck . . . to buy us a yearling at the sales. Not too expensive, don't you know. Not more than ten thousand. That was always the limit. But at that price we'd had a lot of fun, a lot of good times. A few thousand for a horse every four or five years, and the training fees. Comfortably off, do you see.'

'Go on, Major,' I said warmly as he stopped. 'You're doing absolutely fine.'

He swallowed. 'Allardeck bought us a colt that we liked very much. Not brilliant to look at, rather small, but good blood lines. Our sort of horse. We were delighted. He was broken in during the winter and during the spring he began to grow fast. Allardeck said we shouldn't race him then until the autumn, and of course we took his advice.' He paused. 'During the summer he developed splendidly and Allardeck told us he was very speedy and that we might have a really good one on our hands if all went well.'

The ancient memory of those heady days lit a faint glow in the eyes, and I saw the Major as he must have been then, full of boyish enthusiasm, inoffensively proud.

'And then, Major, what happened next?'

The light faded and disappeared. He shrugged. He said, 'Had a bit of bad luck, don't you know.'

He seemed at a loss to know how much to say, but Lucy, having contracted for gain, proved to have fewer inhibitions.

'Clement was a member of Lloyd's,' she said. 'He was in one of those syndicates which crashed . . . many racing people were, do you remember? He was called upon, of course, to make good his share of the losses.'

'I see,' I said, and indeed I did. Underwriting insurance was fine as long as one never actually had to pay out.

'A hundred and ninety-three thousand pounds,' the Major said heavily, as if the shock was still starkly fresh, 'over and above my Lloyd's deposit, which was another twenty-five. Lloyd's took that, of course, straight away. And it was a bad time to sell shares. The market was down. We cast about, do you see, to know what to do.' He paused gloomily, then went on, 'Our house was already mortgaged. Financial advisors, you understand, had always told us it was best to mortgage one's house and use the money for investments. But the investments had gone badly down ... some of them never recovered.'

The flesh on his old face drooped at the memory of failure. Lucy looked at him anxiously, protectively stroking his hand with one finger.

'It does no good to dwell on it,' she said uneasily. 'I'll tell you what happened. Allardeck got to hear of our problems and said his son Maynard could help us, he understood finance. We'd met Maynard once or twice and he'd been charming. So he came to our house and said if we liked, as we were such old owners of his father, he would lend us whatever we needed. The bank had agreed to advance us fifty thousand on the security of our shares, but that still left a hundred and forty. Am I boring you?'

'No, you are not,' I said with emphasis. 'Please go on.'

She sighed. 'Metavane was going to run in about six weeks and I suppose we were clutching at straws, we hoped he would win. We needed it so badly. We didn't want to have to sell him unraced for whatever we could get. If he won he would be worth very much more. So we were overwhelmed by Maynard's offer. It solved all our problems. We accepted. We were overjoyed. We banked his cheque and Clement paid off his losses at Lloyd's.'

Sardonic bitterness tugged at the corners of her mouth, but her neck was still stretched high.

'Was Maynard charging you interest?' I asked.

'Very low,' the Major said. 'Five per cent. Damned good of him, we thought.' The downward curve of his mouth matched his wife's. 'We knew it would be a struggle, but we were sure we would get back on our feet somehow. Economise, do you see. Sell things. Pay him back gradually. Sell Metavane, when he'd won.'

'Yes,' I said. 'What happened next?'

'Nothing much for about five weeks,' Lucy said. 'Then Maynard came to our house again in a terrible state and told us he had two very bad pieces of news for us. He said he would have to call in some of the money he had just lent us as he was in difficulties himself, and almost worse, his father had asked him to tell us that Metavane had lamed himself out at exercise so badly that the vet said he wouldn't be fit to run before the end of the season. It was late September by then. We'd counted on him running in October. We were absolutely, completely shattered, because of course we couldn't afford any longer to pay training fees for six months until racing started again in March, and worse than that, a lame unraced two-year-old at the end of the season isn't worth much. We wouldn't be able to sell him for even what we'd paid for him.'

She paused, staring wretchedly back to the heartbreak.

'Go on,' I said.

She sighed. 'Maynard offered to take Metavane off our hands.'

'Is that how he put it?'

'Yes. Exactly. Take him off our hands is what he said. He said moreover he would knock ten thousand off our debt, just as if the colt was still worth that much. But, he said, he desperately needed some cash, and couldn't we possibly raise a hundred thousand for him at once.' She looked at me bleakly. 'We simply couldn't. We went through it all with him, explaining. He could see that we couldn't pay him without borrowing from a moneylender at a huge interest and he said in no way would he let us do that. He was understanding and charming and looked so worried that in the end we found ourselves comforting him in his troubles, and assuring him we'd do everything humanly possible to repay him as soon as we could.'

'And then?'

'Then he said we'd better make it all legal, so we signed papers transferring ownership of Metavane to him. He changed the amount we owed him from a hundred and forty to a hundred and thirty thousand, and we signed a banker's order to pay him regularly month by month. We were all unhappy, but it seemed the best that could be done.'

'You let him have Metavane without contingencies?' I

150

asked. 'You didn't ask for extra relief on your debt if the horse turned out well?'

Lucy shook her head wearily. 'We didn't think about contingencies. Who thinks about contingencies for a lame horse?'

'Maynard said he would have to put our interest payments up to ten per cent,' the Major said. 'He kept apologising, said he felt embarrassed.'

'Perhaps he was,' I said.

Lucy nodded. 'Embarrassed at his own wickedness. He went away leaving us utterly miserable, but it was nothing to what we felt two weeks later. Metavane ran in a two-year-old race at Newmarket and won by three lengths. We couldn't believe it. We saw the result in the paper. We telephoned Allardeck at once. And I suppose you'll have guessed what he said?'

I half nodded.

'He said he couldn't think why we thought Metavane was lame. He wasn't. He never had been. He had been working brilliantly of late on the Heath.'

TWELVE

'You hadn't thought, I suppose,' I said gently, 'to ask to see the vet's report? Or even to check with Allardeck?'

Lucy shook her head. 'We took Maynard's word.'

The Major nodded heavily. 'Trusted him. Allardeck's son, do you see.'

Lucy said, 'We protested vigorously, of course, that Maynard had told us a deliberate lie, and Maynard said he hadn't. He just denied he'd ever told us Metavane wouldn't run before spring. Took our breath away. Clement complained to the Jockey Club, and got nowhere. Maynard charmed them too. Told them we had misunderstood. The Stewards were very cool to Clement. And do you know what I think? I think Maynard told them we were trying to screw yet more money out of him, when he'd been so generous as to help us out of a dreadful hole.'

They were both beginning to look distressed and I had a few twinges of conscience of my own. But I said, 'Please tell me the state of your debt now, and how much Maynard shared with you out of his winnings and the syndication of Metavane as a stallion.'

They both stared.

The Major said as if surprised, 'Nothing.'

'How do you mean, nothing?'

'He didn't give us a farthing.'

'He syndicated the horse for several millions,' I said.

The Major nodded. 'We read about it.'

'I wrote to him,' Lucy said, her cheeks slightly pink. 'I asked him to at least release us from what we owed him.'

'And?'

'He didn't answer.'

152

'Lucy wrote twice,' the Major said uncomfortably. 'The second time, she sent it special delivery, to be handed to him personally, so we know he must have received it.'

'He didn't reply,' Lucy said.

'We borrowed the money and that's that,' the Major said with resignation. 'Repayments and interest take most of our income, and I don't think we will ever finish.'

Lucy stroked his hand openly. 'We are both eighty-two, you see,' she said.

'And no children?' I asked.

'No children,' Lucy said regretfully. 'It wasn't to be.'

I packed away the camera, thanking them and giving them the cash I'd collected for paying Bobby's lads, proceeds of cashing one of Bobby's cheques with my valet at Newbury. My valet, a walking bank, had found the service routine and had agreed to bring cash for the other cheques to Towcester.

The Major and Lucy accepted the money with some embarrassment but more relief, and I wondered if they had feared I might not actually pay them once I'd got what I wanted. They'd learned in a hard school.

I looked at my watch and asked if I could make a quick credit card call on their telephone. They nodded in unison, and I got through to the manager where I banked.

'John,' I said.

'Kit.'

'Look, I'm in a hurry, on my way to ride at Towcester, but I've been thinking ... It's true, isn't it, that money can be paid into my account without my knowing?'

'Yes, by direct transfer from another bank, like your riding fees. But you'd see it on your next statement.'

'Well,' I said, 'except for my riding fees, could you see to it that nothing gets paid in? If anything else arrives, can you refuse to put it into my account?'

'Yes, I can,' he said doubtfully, 'but why?'

'Someone offered me a bribe last night,' I said. 'It felt too much like a set-up. I don't want to find I've been sneakily paid by a back door for something I don't intend to do. I don't want to find myself trying to tell the Stewards I didn't take the money.'

He said after a short pause, 'Is this one of your intuitions?'

'I just thought I'd take precautions.'

'Yes,' he said. 'All right. If anything comes, I'll check with you before crediting your account.'

'Thanks,' I said. 'Until further notice.'

'And perhaps you would drop me a line putting your instructions in writing? Then you would be wholly safe, if it came to the Stewards.'

'I do not know,' I said, 'what I would do without you.'

I said goodbye to the Perrysides and drove away, reflecting that it was their own total lack of sensible precautions which had crystallised in me the thought that I should prudently take my own.

They should have insured in the first place against a catastrophic loss at Lloyd's and they should have brought in an independent vet to examine Metavane. It was easy to see these things after the event. The trick for survival was to imagine them before.

Towcester was a deep-country course, all rolling green hills sixty miles to the north-west of London. I drove there with my mind on anything except the horses ahead.

Mostly I thought about precautions.

With me in the car, besides my overnight bag, I had the tapes of Maynard, the tape of the Perrysides, the video camera and a small hold-all of Holly's containing the jackets and other belongings of Jay Erskine and Owen Watts. Without all those things I would not be able to get any sort of compensation or future for Bobby and Holly, and it occurred to me that I should make sure that no one stole them.

Sam Leggatt or anyone else at the *Flag* would see that repossessing the journalists' belongings would be a lot cheaper and less painful than coughing up cash and printing and distributing humble apologies.

Owen Watts and Jay Erskine were bound to be revengeful after the damage they had suffered, and they could be literally anywhere, plotting heaven knew what.

I was driving to a time and place printed in more than half the daily newspapers: my name plain to see on the racing pages, declared overnight for the one-thirty, two o'clock, three o'clock and three-thirty races.

If I were Jay Erskine, I thought, I would be jemmying open Kit Fielding's Mercedes at one-thirty, two o'clock, three o'clock or three-thirty.

If I were Owen Watts, perhaps at those times, I would be breaking into Kit Fielding's cottage in Lambourn.

They might.

They might not.

I didn't think a little active breaking and entering would disturb their consciences in the least, especially as the current penalties for a conviction for wire-tapping ran to a two thousand pound fine or up to two years in prison, or both.

I didn't know that I would recognise them from the mêlée in the dark. They could however make it their business to know me. To watch for my arrival in the jockeys' car park. To note my car.

It took forty-five minutes to drive from the Perrysides' village to Towcester racecourse and for half the journey I thought I was being unnecessarily fanciful.

Then abruptly I drove into the centre of the town of Bletchley and booked myself into an old and prosperous looking hotel, the Golden Lion. They took an impression of my credit card and I was shown to a pleasant room, where I hung Watts's and Erskine's jackets in the closet, draped my night things around the bathroom and stowed everything else in a drawer. The receptionist nodded pleasantly and impersonally when I left the key at the desk on my way out, and no one else took any notice; and with a wince at my watch but feeling decidedly safer I broke the speed limit to Towcester.

The princess's novices were the first and last of my booked rides, with another for Wykeham and one for the Lambourn trainer in between.

The princess was waiting with her usual lambent patina in the parade ring when I went out there, and so was Danielle, dressed on that damp day in a blazing red shiny coat over the black trousers. I suppose my pleasure showed. Certainly both of them smiled down their noses in the way women do when they know they're admired, and Danielle, instead of shaking my hand, gave me a brief peck of a kiss on the cheek, a half

155

touch of skin to skin, unpremeditated, the sensation lingering surprisingly in my nerve endings.

She laughed. 'How're you doing?' she said.

'Fine. And you?'

'Great.'

The princess said mildly, 'What do we expect from Kinley, Kit?'

I had a blank second of non-comprehension before remembering that Kinley was her horse. The one I was about to ride: three years old, still entire, a dappled grey going to the starting gate as second favourite for the first race of his life. High time, I thought, that I concentrated on my job.

'Dusty says he's travelled well; he's excited but not sweating,' I said.

'And that's good?' Danielle asked.

'That's good,' said the princess, nodding.

'He's mature for three, he jumps super at home and I think he's fast,' I said.

'And it all depends, I suppose, on whether he enjoys it today.'

'Yes,' I said. 'I'll do my best.'

'Enjoys it?' Danielle asked, surprised.

'Most horses enjoy it,' I said. 'If they don't, they won't race.'

'Do you remember Snowline?' the princess said. I nodded, and she said to Danielle, 'Snowline was a mare I had a long time ago. She was beautiful to look at and had won two or three times on the Flat, and I bought her to be a hurdler, partly, I must confess, because of her name, but she didn't like jumping. I kept her in training for two years because I had a soft spot for her, but it was a waste of money and hope.' She smiled. 'Wykeham tried other jockeys, do you remember, Kit? For the second of those she wouldn't even start. I learned a great lesson. If a horse doesn't like racing, cut your losses.'

'What became of Snowline?' Danielle said.

'I sold her as a brood mare. Two of her foals have been winners on the Flat.'

Danielle looked from her aunt to me and back again. 'You both totally love it, don't you?'

156

'Totally,' said the princess.

'Totally,' I agreed.

I got up on Kinley and walked him slowly up past the stands to let him take in the sounds and smells, and then down towards the start, giving him a long close look at a flight of hurdles, letting him stand chest-high, almost touching, looking out over the top. He pricked his ears and extended his nostrils, and I felt the instinct stir in him most satisfactorily, the in-bred compulsion that ran in the blood like a song, the surging will to race and win.

You, Kinley, I thought, know all I've been able to teach you about jumping, and if you mess it up today you'll be wasting all those mornings I've spent with you on the schooling grounds this autumn.

Kinley tossed his head. I smoothed a hand down his neck and took him on to the start, mingling there with two or three other complete novices and about ten who had run at least once before but never won. The youngest a horse was allowed to go jump racing in Britain was in the August of its three-year-old year, and Kinley's was a two-mile event for three-year-olds who hadn't yet won.

Some jockeys avoided doing schooling sessions, but I'd never minded, on the basis that if I'd taught the horse myself I'd know what it could and wouldn't do. Some trainers sent green horses to crash around racecourses with only the haziest idea of how to meet a jump right, but Wykeham and I were in accord: it was no good expecting virtuoso jumping in public without arpeggios at home.

Wykeham was in the habit of referring to Kinley as Kettering, a horse he'd trained in the distant past. It was amazing, I sometimes thought, that the right horses turned up at the meetings: Dusty's doing, no doubt.

Kinley circled and lined up with only an appropriate amount of nervousness and when the tapes went up, set off with a fierce plunge of speed. Everything was new to him, everything unknown; nothing on the home gallops ever prepared a horse for the first rocketing reality. I settled him gradually with hands and mind, careful not to do it too much, not to teach him that what he was really feeling was wrong but just to control it, to keep it simmering, to wait.

He met the first hurdle perfectly and jumped it cleanly and I clearly felt his reaction of recognition, his increase in confidence. He let me shorten his stride a little approaching the second hurdle so as to meet it right and avoid slowing to jump, and at the third flight he landed so far out on the other side that my spirits rose like a bird. Kinley was going to be good. One could tell sometimes right from the beginning, like watching a great actor in his first decent role.

I let him see every obstacle clearly, mostly by keeping him to the outside. Technically the inside was the shortest way, but also the more difficult. Time for squeezing through openings when he could reliably run straight.

Just keep it going, Kinley old son, I told him; you're doing all right. Just take a pull here, that's right, to get set for the next jump, and now go for it, go for it . . . dear bloody hell, Kinley, you'll leave me behind, jumping like that, just wait while I get up here over your shoulders, I don't see why we can't kick for home, first time out, why not, it's been done, get on there, Kinley, you keep jumping like that and we'll damned near win.

I gave him a breather on the last uphill section and he was most aggrieved at my lack of urging, but once round the last bend, with one jump left before the run-in, I shook him up and told him aloud to get on with it, squeezing him with the calves of my legs, sending him rhythmic messages through my hands, telling him OK, my son, now fly, now run, now stretch out your bloody neck, this is what it's all about, this is your future, take it, embrace it, it's all yours.

He was bursting with pride when I pulled him up, learning at once that he'd done right, that the many pats I gave him were approval, that the applause greeting his arrival in the winners' enclosure was the curtain call for a smash hit. Heady stuff for a novice; and I reckoned that because of that day he would run his guts out to win all his life.

'He enjoyed it,' the princess said, glowing with pleasure.

'He sure did.'

'Those jumps . . .'

I unbuckled my saddle and drew it off on to my arm.

'He's very good,' I said. 'You have seriously got a good horse.'

She looked at me with speculation, and I nodded. 'You never know. Too soon to be sure.'

'What on earth are you talking about?' Danielle demanded.

'The Triumph Hurdle,' said her aunt.

I went to weigh in, change and weigh out and go through the whole rigmarole again with Wykeham's second runner, which didn't belong to the princess but to a couple in their seventies who cared just as much.

They owned only the one horse, an ageing 'chaser who'd been retired once and had pined until he'd been sent back into training, and I was truly pleased for them when, because of his experience, he stood up throughout the three miles as others fell, and against all the odds thundered along insouciantly into first place.

Wykeham might not go to the meetings, I thought, gratefully pulling up, he might have his mental grooves stuck in the past, but he sure as hell could still train winners.

I watched the next race after that from the jockeys' stand, and won the one after for the Lambourn trainer. One of those days, I thought contentedly. A treble. It happened once or twice a season, not much more.

It occurred to me as I was unbuckling my saddle in the winners' enclosure that Eric Olderjohn, the owner of the horse, who was present and quietly incandescent with delight, was something to do with the Civil Service on a high level, a fact I knew only because he occasionally lamented that government business would keep him away from seeing his pride and joy run.

I asked him on an impulse if I could talk to him for a few minutes after I'd weighed in and changed for the next race, and rather in the Vaughnley mould he said 'Anything' expansively, and was waiting there as promised when I went out.

We talked for a bit about his win, which was uppermost in his mind, and then he asked what I wanted. I wanted, I said, the answers to a couple of questions, and I wondered if he could – or would – get them for me.

'Fire away,' he said. 'I'm listening.'

I explained about the newspaper attacks on Bobby and Maynard, and to my surprise he nodded.

'I've heard about this, yes. What are your questions?'

159

'Well, first, whether Maynard was in fact being considered for a knighthood, and second, if he was, who would have known?'

He half laughed. 'You don't want much, do you?' He shook his head. 'Patronage is not my department.' He looked up at the sky and down at the colours I wore, which were by then the princess's. 'What good would it do you to find out?'

'I don't know,' I said frankly. 'But someone ought to make reparation to Bobby and my sister.'

'Hm. Why don't they ask these questions themselves?'

I said blankly, 'But they wouldn't.'

'They wouldn't, but you would.' His eyes were half assessing, half amused.

'Those newspaper articles were maliciously unfair,' I said positively. 'Bobby and my sister Holly are gentle well-intentioned people trying to make a success of training and doing no harm to anyone.'

'And the newspaper attack on them makes you angry?'

'Yes, it does. Wouldn't it you?'

He considered it. 'An attack on my daughter would, yes.' He nodded briefly. 'I don't promise, but I'll ask.'

'Thank you very much,' I said.

He smiled, turned to go and said, 'Win for me again next time out.'

I said I hoped to, and wondered why I'd described Bobby as gentle when the marks of his fists lay scattered on my body among the dark red attentions of the hurdlers. Bobby was brother to the wind, the seed of the tornado dormant in the calm.

I went back into the changing room for my helmet and stick and then out to the parade ring again for the sixth and last race of the day, the two-mile novice 'chase.

'Totally awesome,' Danielle said, standing there.

'What is?' I asked.

'We went down in the medic's car to one of the fences. We stood right by there watching you jump. That speed . . . so fast . . . you don't realise, from the stands.'

'In the three-mile 'chase,' the princess said, nodding.

'The medic said you were all going over there at better than thirty miles an hour. He says you're all crazy. He's right.'

160

The princess asked me if I thought I'd be making it four for the day, but I thought it unlikely: this one, Dhaulagiri, hadn't as much talent as Kinley.

'There's a woman riding in this race,' Danielle observed, watching the other jockeys standing in groups with the owners. She looked at me without archness. 'What do you think if you're beaten in a race by a woman?'

'That she had a faster horse,' I said.

'Ouch.'

The princess smiled but made no comment. She knew I didn't like racing against the very few women who rode professionally over jumps, not for fear of a male ego-battering, but because I couldn't rid myself of protectiveness. A male opponent could take his bumps, but I'd never learned to ride ruthlessly against a female; and moreover I didn't like the idea of what falls and horses' hooves could do to their faces and bodies. The women jockeys despised my concern for them, and took advantage of it if they could.

Dhaulagiri was looking well, I thought, watching him walk round. Better than when I'd schooled him the previous week. Tauter. A new lean line of muscle on the haunch. Something in the carriage of the head.

'What is it, Kit?' the princess asked.

I looked from the horse to her enquiring face. 'He's improved since last week,' I said.

'Wykeham said he seemed to like jumping fences better than hurdles.'

'Yes, he did.'

Her eyes smiled. 'Do you think, then . . .?'

'It would be nice, wouldn't it?'

'Exquisite,' she said.

I nodded and went away on Dhaulagiri to the start, and in some odd way it seemed a jaunt to the horse as much as to me. Three winners raised my spirits euphorically. Dhaulagiri could jump. So why not, why bloody not make it four. Dhaulagiri took the mood from his jockey, as all horses do. I reckon Dhaulagiri on that afternoon would have light-heartedly jumped off a cliff if I'd asked him.

It wasn't the most advisable tactic for a horse running for the first time over the bigger fences and I dared say Wykeham would have deplored it, but Dhaulagiri and I went round the whole two miles in friendly fully stretched recklessness, and at the winning post I thought for nearly the thousandth time in my life that there was nothing in existence comparable to the shared intense joy of victory. Better perhaps, but comparable, no. I was laughing aloud when we pulled up.

The exhilaration lasted all the way back to the changing room and in and out of the shower, and only marginally began to abate when my valet handed me a zipped webbing belt stuffed full of Bobby's money. Jockeys' valets washed one's breeches and took one's saddles and other belongings from racecourse to racecourse, turning up with everything clean every day. Besides that they were the grapevine, the machine oil, the comforters and the bank. My valet said he was lending me the money-belt he used himself on holidays, as he didn't like the idea of me walking around with all those thousands in my pockets.

Bobby, I thought, sighing. I would drive to Bletchley and collect my stuff from the Golden Lion, and then go on to Newmarket to give the money to Bobby so he could pay his lads at the normal time the next day and stack the rest away in his safe. I would sleep there and go direct to Ascot in the morning.

I strapped the belt against my skin and buttoned my shirt over it, the valet nodding approval. It didn't show, he said.

I thanked him for his thoughtfulness, finished dressing, and went out for a briefer than usual talk with the princess, whose eyes were still sparkling behind the sheltering lashes.

Vague thoughts I'd had of asking Danielle to help celebrate my four winners over dinner disintegrated when she said she was again due at her bureau at six-thirty, and they would be leaving for London at any moment.

'Do you work at week-ends?' I asked.

'No.'

'Could . . . er, could I ask you out on Saturday evening?'

She glanced at her aunt, and so did I, but as usual one could tell nothing from the princess's face that she didn't want one to see. I felt no withdrawal, though, coming from her mind, and nor, it seemed, did her niece.

'Yes,' Danielle said, 'you could. I'll be coming to Ascot. After the races, we might make plans.'

Extraordinary, I thought. She understood. She had of course come close to seeing her ride from Devon to London evaporate at the third hurdle two days ago. Two days. That too was extraordinary. I seemed to have known her for longer.

'Tomorrow at Ascot,' the princess said to me, shaking my hand in goodbye. 'How long can we go on winning?'

'Until Christmas.'

She smiled. 'Christmas Fielding.'

'Yes.'

Danielle said, 'What do you mean, Christmas Fielding?'

'It's my name,' I said.

'What? I mean, I know it says C. Fielding on the number boards, but I took it for granted that Kit was for Christopher.'

I shook my head. 'We were born on Christmas morning. Christmas and Holly. No accounting for parents.'

There was warmth in her eyes as well as in the princess's. I left them saying their thanks to their hosts for the day before starting home, and with swelling contentment walked out to my own car.

At the sight of it most of the contentment vanished into anger. All four tyres were flat, the window on the driver's side was broken, and the lid of the boot hovered halfway open.

I said aloud and precisely about four obscene words and then shrugged and turned to go back into the racecourse to telephone. The AA could deal with it. I could hire another car. The things I'd feared losing were safe in the Golden Lion and if that was what the vandals had been looking for, they were out of luck.

Most people had already left, but there were still a few cars in the park, still a person or two moving about. I was thinking chiefly of inconvenience and paying little attention to anything else, and very suddenly there was a voice at my left ear saying, 'Stand still, Fielding', and another man crowding against my right elbow with the same message.

I did stand still, too taken by surprise to think of doing anything else.

From each side the message reached me clearly.

Reached throught my jacket, through my shirt and into my skin, somewhere above the money-belt.

'That's right,' said the one who'd spoken before. 'We've come to repossess some property. You don't want to get cut, do you?'

THIRTEEN

I certainly didn't.

'See that grey Ford over there right by the road,' said the man on my left. 'We're going to get into it, nice and easy. Then you'll tell us where to go for some jackets and the things in the pockets. We'll be sitting one each side of you on the back seat, and we're going to tie your hands, and if you make any sudden moves we'll slice your tendons so you won't stand again, never mind ride horses. You got that?'

Dry mouthed, I nodded.

'You've got to learn there's people you can't push around. We're here to teach you. So now walk.'

They were not Owen Watts and Jay Erskine. Different build, different voices, older and much heavier. They underlined their intentions with jabs against my lower ribs, and I did walk. Walked stiff-legged towards the grey Ford.

I would give them what they wanted: that was simple. Owen Watts's credit cards and Jay Erskine's Press Club pass weren't worth being crippled for. It was what would happen after the Golden Lion that seized up the imagination and quivered in the gut. They weren't going to release me with a handshake and a smile. They had as good as said so.

There was a third man, a driver, sitting in the Ford. At our approach he got out of the car and opened both rear doors. The car itself was pointing in the direction of the way out to the main road.

There seemed to be no one within shouting distance. No one near enough to help. I decided sharply and suddenly that all the same I wouldn't get into the car. I would run. Take my chances in the open air. Better under the sky than in some little dark corner; than on the back seat of a car with my hands tied. I would have given them the jackets but their priority was damage, and their intention of it was reaching me like shock waves.

It came to the point of now or never, and I was already tensing my muscles for it to be now, when a large quiet black car rolled along the road towards the racecourse exit and stopped barely six feet away from where I stood closely flanked. The nearside rear window slid down and a familiar voice said, 'Are you in trouble, Kit?'

I never was more pleased to see the princess in all my life.

'Say no,' the man on the left directed into my ear, screwing his knife round a notch. 'Get rid of them.'

'Kit?'

'Yes,' I said.

The princess's face didn't change. The rear door of her Rolls swung widely open and she said economically, 'Get in.'

I leapt. I jumped. I dived into her car head first, landing on my hands as lightly as possible across her ankles and Danielle's, flicking from there to the floor.

The car was moving forward quite fast even before the princess said, 'Drive on, Thomas' to her chauffeur, and I saw the angry faces of my three would-be captors staring in through the windows, heard their fists beating on the glossy bodywork, their hands trying to open the already centrally locked doors.

'They've got knives,' Danielle said in horror. 'I mean . . . knives.'

Thomas accelerated further, setting the heavy men running alongside and then leaving them behind, and I fumbled my way up on to one of the rear-facing folding seats and said I was sorry.

'Sorry!' Danielle exclaimed.

'For involving you in such a mess,' I said to the princess. I rubbed my hand across my face. 'I'm very sorry.'

Thomas said without noticeable alarm, 'Madam, those three men are intending to follow us in a grey Ford car.'

I looked out through the tinted rear window and saw that he was right. The last of them was scrambling in, fingers urgently pointing.

'Then we'd better find a policeman,' the princess said

calmly; but as on every other racing day the police had left the racecourse as soon as the crowds had gone. There was no one at the racecourse gate directing traffic, since there was no longer any need. Thomas slowed and turned in the direction of London and put his foot smoothly on the accelerator.

'If I might suggest, madam?' he said.

'Yes. Go on.'

'You would all be safer if we kept going. I don't know where the police station is in Stony Stratford, which is the first town we come to. I would have to stop to ask directions.'

'If we go to a police station,' Danielle said anxiously, 'they'll keep us there for ages, taking statements, and I'll be terribly late.'

'Kit?' the princess asked.

'Keep going,' I said. 'If that's all right.'

'Keep going then, Thomas,' said the princess, and Thomas, nodding, complied. 'And now, Kit,' she said, 'tell us why you needed to be rescued in such a melodramatic fashion.'

'They had knives on him,' Danielle said.

'So I observed. But why?'

'They wanted something I've got.' I took a deep breath, trying to damp down the incredible relief of not being a prisoner in the car behind, trying to stop myself trembling. 'It started with some newspaper articles about my brother-in-law, Bobby Allardeck.'

She nodded. 'I heard about those from Lord Vaughnley yesterday, after you'd gone.'

'I've got blood on my leg,' Danielle said abruptly. 'How did I get . . .' She was looking down at her ankles, and then lifted her head suddenly and said to me, 'When you flew in like an acrobat, were you bleeding? Are you still bleeding?'

'I suppose so.'

'What do you mean, you suppose so? Can't you feel it?'

'No.' I looked inside my jacket, right and left.

'Well?' Danielle demanded.

'A bit,' I said.

Maybe the heavies hadn't expected me to jump with their knives already in. Certainly they'd reacted too slowly to stop me, ripping purposefully, but too late. The sting had been momentary, the aftermath ignorable. A little blood, however, went a long way.

The princess said resignedly, 'Don't we carry a first-aid box, Thomas?'

Thomas said 'Yes, madam' and produced a black box from a built-in compartment. He held it over his shoulder, and I took it, opened it, and found it contained useful-sized padded absorbent sterile dressings and all manner of ointments and sticky tapes. I took out one of the thick dressings and found two pairs of eyes watching.

'Excuse me,' I said awkwardly.

'You're embarrassed!' Danielle said.

'Mm.'

I was embarrassed by the whole situation. The princess turned her head away and studied the passing fields while I groped around under my shirt for somewhere to stick the dressing. The cuts, wherever they were, proved to be too far round for me to see them.

'For heaven's sake,' Danielle said, still watching, 'let me do it.'

She removed herself from the rear seat facing me to the folding seat by my side, took the dressing out of my hand and told me to hold my shirt and jacket up so that she could see the action. When I did she lifted her head slowly and looked at me directly.

'I simply don't believe you can't feel that.'

I smiled into her eyes. Whatever I felt was a pinprick to what I'd been facing. 'Stick the dressing on,' I said.

'All right.'

She stuck it on, and we changed places so she could do the other one, on my left. 'What a mess,' she said, wiping her hands and returning to the rear seat while I tucked my shirt untidily into my trousers. 'That first cut is long and horribly deep and needs stitches.'

The princess stopped staring out of the window and looked at me assessingly.

'I'll be all right for racing tomorrow,' I said.

Her mouth twitched. 'I would expect you to say that, if you had two broken legs.'

'I probably would.'

168

'Madam,' Thomas said, 'we're approaching the motorway and the grey Ford is still on our tail.'

The princess made an indecisive gesture with her hands. 'I suppose we'd better go on,' she said. 'What do you think?'

'On,' Danielle said positively, and Thomas and I nodded.

'Very well. On to London. And now, Kit, tell us what was happening.'

I told them about Bobby and me finding the journalists dismantling their wire-tap, and about removing their jackets before letting them go.

The princess blinked.

I said I had offered to return the jackets if the *Flag* would print an apology to Bobby and also pay some compensation. I explained about finding my car broken into, and about the suddenness with which my assailants had appeared.

'They wanted those jackets,' I said. 'And although I'd thought about robbery, I hadn't expected violence.' I couldn't think why not, after the violence of Bobby's assault on Owen Watts. I paused. 'I can't thank you enough.'

'Thank Thomas,' the princess said. 'Thomas said you were in trouble. I wouldn't have known.'

'Thank you, Thomas.'

'You could see it a mile off,' he said.

'You were pretty quick getting away.'

'I went to a lecture once about how not to get your employer kidnapped.'

'Thomas!' said the princess. 'Did you really?'

He said seriously, 'I wouldn't want to lose you, madam.'

The princess was moved and for once without an easy surface answer. Thomas, who had driven her devotedly for years, was a large quiet middle-aged Londoner with whom I talked briefly most days in racecourse car parks, where he sat and read books in the Rolls. I'd asked him once long ago if he didn't get bored going to the races every day when he wasn't much interested in horses and didn't gamble, and he'd said no, he liked the long journeys, he liked his solitude and most of all he liked the princess. He and I both, in many ways opposites, would I dare say have died for the lady.

I thought, all the same, that she wouldn't much care for the alarms of the continuing present. I looked back to the grey car still steadfastly following and began to consider what to do to vanish. I was thinking about perhaps diving down into thick undergrowth once we'd left the motorway, when the car behind suddenly swerved dangerously from the centre lane, cut across the slow lane to a wild blowing of horns and disappeared down a side road.

Thomas made a sort of growl in his throat and said, 'They've gone into the service station' with relief.

'You mean we've lost them?' Danielle said, twisting to look back.

'They peeled off.' To telephone, I supposed, a no-success story.

The princess said 'Good' as if that ended the matter entirely, and, greatly released, began to talk of her horses, of the day's triumphs, of more pleasing excitements, tracking with intent and expertise away from the alien violent terror of maiming steel back to the safe familiar danger of breaking one's neck.

By the time we reached central London she had returned the atmosphere to a semblance of full normality, behaving as if my presence in her car were commonplace, the tempestuous entrance overlooked. She would have gone with good manners to the scaffold, I thought, and was grateful for the calm she had laid upon us.

Within the last mile home, with dusk turning to full night, the princess asked Thomas if he would drive her niece to Chiswick as usual and return for her when she'd finished work.

'Certainly, madam.'

'Perhaps,' I said, 'I could fetch Danielle instead? Save Thomas the trip.'

'At two in the morning?' Danielle said.

'Why not?'

'OK.'

The princess made no comment, showed no feeling. 'It seems you have the night off, Thomas' was all she said; and to me, 'If you are wanting to go to the police, Thomas will drive you.'

I shook my head. 'I'm not going to the police.'

'But,' she said doubtfully, 'those horrid men . . .'

'If I go to the police, you will be in the newspapers.'

170

She said 'Oh' blankly. Cavorting about saving her jockey from a bunch of knife-wielding heavies was not the sort of publicity she yearned for. 'Do what you think best,' she said faintly.

'Yes.'

Thomas braked to a halt outside her house in Eaton Square and opened the car door for us to disembark. On the pavement I thanked the princess for the journey. Politeness conquered all. With the faintest gleam of amusement she said she would no doubt see me at Ascot, and as on ordinary days held out her hand for a formal shake, accepting the sketch of a bow.

'I don't believe it,' Danielle said.

'If you get the form of things right,' the princess said to her sweetly, 'every peril can be tamed.'

I bought a shirt and an anorak and booked into a hotel for the night, stopping in the lobby to rent a car from an agency booth there.

'I want a good one,' I said. 'A Mercedes, if you have one.'

They would try, they assured me.

Upstairs I changed from the slashed bloodstained shirt and jacket into the new clothes, and began another orgy of telephoning.

The Golden Lion via directory enquiries said there was no problem, they would hold my room for another day, they had my credit card number, too bad I'd been unexpectedly detained, my belongings would be perfectly safe.

The AA said not to worry, they would rescue my car from Towcester racecourse within the hour. If I phoned in the morning, they would tell me where they'd taken it for repairs.

My answering system in the cottage had been hard-worked with please-ring-back messages from the police, my neighbour, my bank manager, Rose Quince, three trainers and Sam Leggatt.

My neighbour, an elderly widow, sounded uncommonly agitated, so I called her back first.

'Kit, dear, I hope I did right,' she said. 'I saw a strange man moving about in your cottage and I told the police.'

'You did right,' I agreed.

'It was lunchtime and I knew you'd be at Towcester, I always follow your doings. Four winners! It was on the radio just now. Well done.'

'Thanks . . . What happened at the cottage?'

'Nothing, really. I went over when the police came to let them in with my key. They couldn't have been more than five minutes getting there, but there wasn't anyone in the cottage. I felt so foolish, but then one of the policemen said a window was broken, and when they looked around a bit more they said someone had been in there searching. I couldn't see anything missing. Your racing trophies weren't touched. Just the window broken in the cloakroom.'

I sighed. 'Thank you,' I said. 'You are a dear.'

'I got Pedro from down the road to mend the window. I didn't like to leave it. I mean, anyone could get in.'

'I'll take you for a drink in the pub when I get back.'

She chuckled. 'Thank you, dear. That'll be nice.'

The police themselves had nothing to add. I should return, they said, to check my losses.

I got through to my bank manager at his home and listened to him chewing while he spoke. 'Sorry. Piece of toast,' he said. 'A man came into the bank at lunchtime to pay three thousand pounds into your account.'

'What man?'

'I didn't see him, unfortunately. I was out. It was a banker's draft, not a personal cheque.'

'Damn,' I said feelingly.

'Don't worry, it won't appear on your account. I've put a stop on anything being paid into it, as we agreed. The banker's draft is locked in the safe in my office. What do you want me to do with it?'

'Tear it up in front of witnesses,' I said.

'I can't do that,' he protested. 'Someone paid three thousand pounds for it.'

'Where was it issued?'

'At a bank in the City.'

'Can you ask them if they remember who bought it?'

'Yes, I'll try tomorrow. And be a good chap, let me have the no-paying-in instruction in writing pronto.'

'Yes,' I said.

'And well done with the winners. It was on the radio.'

I thanked him and disconnected, and after some thought left the hotel, walked down the street to an Underground station and from a public phone rang Sam Leggatt at the *Flag*.

There was no delay this time. His voice came immediately on the line, brisk and uncompromising.

'Our lawyers say that what you said here yesterday was tantamount to blackmail.'

'What your reporters did at my brother-in-law's house was tantamount to a jail sentence.'

'Our lawyers say if your brother-in-law thinks he has a case for settlement out of court, his lawyers should contact our lawyers.'

'Yeah,' I said. 'And how long would that take?'

'Our lawyers are of the opinion that no compensation should be paid. The information used in the column was essentially true.'

'Are you printing the apology?'

'Not yet. We haven't gone to press yet.'

'Will you print it?'

He paused too long.

'Did you know,' I said, 'that today someone searched my cottage, someone smashed their way into my car, two men attacked me with knives, and someone tried to bribe me with three thousand pounds, paid directly into my bank account?'

More silence.

'I'll be telling everyone I can think of about the wire-tapping,' I said. 'Starting now.'

'Where are you?' he said.

'At the other end of the telephone line.'

'Wait,' he said. 'Ring me back will you?'

'How long?'

'Fifteen minutes.'

'All right.'

I put the receiver down and stood looking at it, drumming my fingers and wondering if the *Flag* really did have equipment which could trace where I'd called from, or whether I was being fanciful.

I couldn't afford, I thought, any more punch-ups. I left the

Underground station, walked along the street for ten minutes, went into a pub, rang the *Flag*. My call was again expected: the switchboard put me straight through.

When Sam Leggatt said 'Yes' there were voices raised loudly in the background.

'Fielding,' I said.

'You're early.' The background voices abruptly stopped.

'Your decision,' I said.

'We want to talk to you.'

'You're talking.'

'No. Here, in my office.'

I didn't answer immediately, and he said sharply, 'Are you still there?'

'Yes,' I said. 'What time do you go to press?'

'First edition, six-thirty, to catch the West Country trains. We can hold until seven. That's the limit.'

I looked at my watch. Fourteen minutes after six. Too late, to my mind, for talking.

'Look,' I said. 'Why don't you just print and distribute the apology? It's surely no big deal. It'll cost you nothing but the petrol to Newmarket. I'll come to your office when you assure me that you're doing that.'

'You'd trust my word?'

'Do you trust mine?'

He said grudgingly, 'Yes, I suppose I do expect you to return what you said.'

'I'll do it. I'll act in good faith. But so must you. You seriously did damage Bobby Allardeck, and you must at least try to put it right.'

'Our lawyers say an apology would be an acknowledgment of liability. They say we can't do it.'

'That's it, then,' I said. 'Goodbye.'

'No, Fielding, wait.'

'Your lawyers are fools,' I said, and put down the receiver.

I went out into the street and rubbed a hand over my head, over my hair, feeling depressed and a loser.

Four winners, I thought. It happened so seldom. I should be knee-deep in champagne, not banging myself against a brick wall that kicked back so viciously.

The cuts on my ribs hurt. I could no longer ignore them.

I walked dispiritedly along to yet another telephone and rang up a long-time surgical ally.

'Oh, hello,' he said cheerfully. 'What is it this time? A little clandestine bone-setting?'

'Sewing,' I said.

'Ah. And when are you racing?'

'Tomorrow.'

'Toddle round, then.'

'Thanks.'

I went in a taxi and got stitched.

'That's not a horseshoe slash,' he observed, dabbing anaesthetic into my right side. 'That's a knife.'

'Yeah.'

'Did you know the bone is showing?'

'I can't see it.'

'Don't tear it open again tomorrow.'

'Then fix it up tight.'

He worked for a while before patting my shoulder. 'It's got absorbable stitches, also clips and gripping tape, but whether it would stand another four winners is anyone's guess.'

I turned my head. I'd said nothing about the winners.

'I heard it on the news,' he said.

He worked less lengthily on the other cut and said lightly, 'I didn't think getting knifed was your sort of thing.'

'Nor did I.'

'Want to tell me why it happened?'

He was asking, I saw, for reassurance. He would come to my aid on the quiet, but it was important to him that I should be honest.

'Do you mean,' I said, 'have I got myself into trouble with gamblers and race-fixers and such?'

'I suppose so.'

'Then no, I promise you.' I told him briefly of Bobby's problems and felt his reservations fade.

'And the bruises?' he said.

'I fell under some hurdlers the day before yesterday.'

He nodded prosaically. I paid his fee in cash and he showed me to his door.

'Good luck,' he said. 'Come back when you need.'

I thanked him, caught a taxi and rode back to the hotel

thinking of the *Flag* thundering off the presses at that moment without carrying the apology. Thinking of Leggatt and the people behind him; lawyers, Nestor Pollgate, Tug Tunny, Owen Watts and Jay Erskine. Thinking of the forces and the furies I had somehow unleashed. You've got to learn there's people you can't push around, one of the knifemen had said.

Well, I was learning.

The rented car booth in the lobby told me I was in luck, they'd got me a Mercedes; here were the keys, it was in the underground car park; the porter would show me when I wanted to go out. I thanked them. We try harder, they said.

Up in my room I ordered some food from room service and telephoned Wykeham to tell him how his winners had won, catching at least an echo of the elation of the afternoon.

'Did they get home all right?' I asked.

'Yes, they all ate up. Dhaulagiri looks as if he had a hard race but Dusty said he won easy.'

'Dhaulagiri ran great,' I said. 'They all did. Kinley's as good as any you've got.'

We talked of Kinley's future and of the runners at Ascot the next day and Saturday. For Wykeham the months of October, November and December were the peak: his horses came annually into their best form then, the present flourish of successes expected and planned for.

Between 30 September and New Year's Day he ran every horse in his charge as often as he could. 'Seize the moment,' he would say. After Christmas, with meetings disrupted by frost and snow, he let his stable more or less hibernate, resting, regrouping, aiming for a second intense flowering in March. My life followed his rhythms to a great extent, as natural to me as to his horses.

'Get some rest, now,' he said jovially. 'You've got six rides tomorrow, another five on Saturday. Get some good sleep.'

'Yes,' I said. 'Goodnight, Wykeham.'

'Goodnight, Paul.'

My food came and I ate bits of it and drank some wine while I got through to the other trainers who'd left messages, and after that I rang Rose Quince.

'Four winners,' she said. 'Laying it on a bit thick, aren't you?'

'These things happen.'

'Of sure. Just hold on to your moment of glory, buddy boy, because I've some negative news for you.'

'How negative?'

'A firm and positive thumbs down from the producer of *How's Trade*. There's no way on earth he's going to say who sicked him on to Maynard Allardeck.'

'But someone did?'

'Oh, sure. He just won't say who. I'd guess he got paid to do it as well as paid not to, if you see what I mean.'

'Whoever paid him to do it must be feeling betrayed.'

'Too bad,' she said. 'See you.'

'Listen,' I said hastily, 'what did Jay Erskine go to jail for?'

'I told you. Conspiracy to obstruct the course of justice.'

'But what did he actually do?'

'As far as I remember, he put some frighteners on to a chief prosecution witness who then skipped the country and never gave evidence, so the villain got off. Why?'

'I just wondered. How long did he get?'

'Five years, but he was out in a lot less.'

'Thanks.'

'You're welcome. And by the way, one of the favours you owed me is cancelled. I took your advice. The venom worked a treat and I'm freed, I'm no longer under the jurisdiction of the chauvinist. So thanks, and goodnight.'

'Goodnight.'

If the *Flag* wanted frighteners, Jay Erskine could get them.

I sighed and rubbed my eyes and thought about Holly, who had been hovering in my mind for ages, telling me to ring her up. She would want the money I still wore round my waist and I was going to have to persuade her and Bobby to come to London or Ascot in the morning to fetch it.

I was going to have to tell her that I hadn't after all managed to get the apology printed. That hers and Bobby's lawyers could grind on for ever and get nothing. That reporting the wire-tapping to all and sundry might inconvenience the *Flag*, but would do nothing to change their bank manager's mind. I put the call through to Holly reluctantly.

'Of course we'll come to fetch the money,' she said. 'Will you please stop talking about it and listen.'

177

'OK.'

'Sam Leggatt telephoned. The editor of the *Flag*.'

'Did he? When?'

'About an hour ago. An hour and a half. About seven o'clock. He said you were in London, somewhere in the Knightsbridge area, and did I know where you would be staying?'

'What did you say?' I asked, alarmed.

'I told him where you stayed last night. I told him to try there. He said that wasn't in Knightsbridge and I said of course not, but hadn't he heard of taxis. Anyway he wanted to get a message to you urgently, he said. He wanted me to write it down. He said to tell you the apology was being printed at that moment and will be delivered.'

'What! Why on earth didn't you say so?'

'But you told me last night it was going to happen. I mean, I thought you knew.'

'Christ Almighty,' I said.

'Also,' Holly said, 'he wants you to go to the *Flag* tonight. He said if you could get there before ten there would be someone there you wanted to meet.'

FOURTEEN

When I pressed the buzzer and walked unannounced through his unlatching door he was sitting alone in his office, shirt-sleeved behind his shiny black desk, reading the *Flag*.

He stood up slowly, his fingers spread on the paper as if to give himself leverage, a short solid man with authority carried easily, as of right.

I was not who he'd expected. A voice behind me was saying, 'Here it is, Sam', and a man came walking close, waving a folder.

'Yes, Dan, just leave it with me, will you?' Leggatt said, stretching out a hand and taking it. 'I'll get back to you.'

'Oh? OK.' The man Dan went away, looking at me curiously, closing the door with a click.

'I got your message,' I said.

He looked down at his copy of the *Flag*, turned a page, reversed the paper and pushed it towards me across the desk.

I read the Intimate Details that would be titillating a few million Friday breakfasts and saw that at least he'd played fair. The paragraph was in bold black type in a black-outlined box.

It said:

The Daily Flag *acknowledges that the Newmarket racing stable of Robertson (Bobby) Allardeck (32) is a sound business and is not in debt to local traders. The* Daily Flag *apologises to Mr Allardeck for any inconvenience he may have suffered in consequence of reports to the contrary printed in this column earlier.*

'Well,' he said, when I'd read.

'Thank you.'

'Bobby Allardeck should thank God for his brother-in-law.'

I looked at him in surprise, and I thought of Bobby's schizophrenic untrustable regard for me, and of my sister, for whom I truly acted. That paragraph should at least settle the nerves of the town and the owners and put the stable back into functionable order: given, of course, that its uneasy underlying finances could be equally sorted out.

'What changed your mind?' I asked.

He shrugged. 'You did. The lawyers said you would back down. I said you wouldn't. They think they can intimidate anybody with their threats of long expensive lawsuits.' He smiled twistedly. 'I said you'd be real poisonous trouble if we didn't print, and you would have been, wouldn't you?'

'Yes.'

He nodded. 'I persuaded them we didn't want Jay Erskine and Owen Watts in court, where you would put them.'

'Particularly as Jay Erskine has a criminal record already.'

He was momentarily still. 'Yes,' he said.

It had been that one fact, I thought, that had swayed them.

'Did Jay Erskine write the attacks on Bobby?' I asked.

After a slight hesitation he nodded. 'He wrote everything except the apology. I wrote that myself.'

He pressed a button on an intercom on his desk and said, 'Fielding's here' neutrally to the general air.

'Where are the credit cards, now we've printed?' he asked.

'You'll get them tomorrow, after the newspapers have been delivered, like I said.'

'You never let up, do you? Owen Watts has set off to Newmarket already and the others are in the post.' He looked at me broodingly. 'How did you find out about the bank?'

'I thought you might try to discredit me. I put a stop on all ingoing payments.'

He compressed his mouth. 'They can't see what they're dealing with,' he said.

The buzzer on his door sounded and he pushed the release instantly. I turned and saw a man I didn't know walking in with interest and no caution. Fairly tall, with a receding hairline over a pale forehead, he wore an ordinary dark suit with a brightly striped tie and had a habit of rubbing his fingers together, like a schoolmaster brushing off chalk.

'David Morse, head of our legal department,' said Sam Leggatt briefly.

No one offered to shake hands. David Morse looked me over as an exhibit, up and down, gaze wandering over the unzipped anorak and the blue shirt and tie beneath.

'The jockey,' he said coolly. 'The one making the fuss.'

I gave no reply, as none seemed useful, and through the open door behind him came another man who brought power with him like an aura and walked softly on the outsides of his feet. This one, as tall as the lawyer, had oiled dark hair, olive skin, a rounded chin, a small mouth and eyes like bright dark beads: also heavy shoulders and a flat stomach in smooth navy suiting. He was younger than either Sam Leggatt or Morse and was indefinably their boss.

'I'm Nestor Pollgate,' he announced, giving me a repeat of the Morse inspection and the same absence of greeting. 'I am tired of your antics. You will return my journalists' possessions immediately.'

His voice, like his body, was virile, reverberatingly bass in unaccented basic English.

'Did you ask me here just for that?' I said.

Don't twist their tail, Rose Quince had said. Ah well.

Pollgate's mouth contracted and he moved round to Leggatt's side of the desk, and the lawyer also, so that they were ranged there in a row like a triumvirate of judges with myself before them, as it were on the carpet.

I had stood before the racing Disciplinary Stewards once or twice in that configuration, and I'd learned to let neither fright nor defiance show. Every bad experience, it seemed, could bring unexpected dividends. I stood without fidgeting and waited.

'Your contention that we mounted a deliberate campaign to ruin your brother-in-law is rubbish,' Pollgate said flatly. 'If you utter that opinion in public we will sue you.'

'You mounted a campaign to ruin Maynard Allardeck's chance of a knighthood,' I said. 'You aimed to destroy his credibility and you didn't give a damn who else you hurt in the process. Your paper was ruthlessly callous. It often is. I will utter that opinion as often as I care to.'

Pollgate perceptibly stiffened. The lawyer's mouth opened a little and Leggatt looked on the verge of inner amusement.

'Tell me why you wanted to wreck Maynard Allardeck,' I said.

'None of your business.' Pollgate answered with the finality of a bank-vault door, and I acknowledged that if I ever found out it wouldn't be by straightforward questions put to anyone in that room.

'You judged,' I said instead, 'that a sideways swipe at Maynard would be most effective, and you decided to get at him through his son. You gave not a thought to the ruin you were bringing on the son. You used him. You should compensate him for that use.'

'No,' Pollgate said.

'We admit nothing,' the lawyer said. A classically lawyer-like phrase. We may be guilty but we'll never say so. He went on, 'If you persist in trying to extort money by menaces, the *Daily Flag* will have you arrested and charged.'

I listened not so much to the words as to the voice, knowing I'd heard it somewhere recently, sorting out the distinctive high pitch and the precision of consonants and the lack of belief in any intelligence I might have.

'Do you live in Hampstead?' I said thoughtfully.

'What's that got to do with anything?' Pollgate said, coldly impatient.

'Three thousand before, ten after.'

'You're talking gibberish,' Pollgate said.

I shook my head. David Morse was looking as if he'd bitten a wasp.

'You were clumsy,' I said to him. 'You don't know the first thing about bribing a jockey.'

'What is the first thing?' Sam Leggatt asked.

I almost smiled. 'The name of the horse.'

'You admit you take bribes, then,' Morse said defensively.

'No I don't, but I've been propositioned now and then, and you didn't sound right. Also you were recording your offer on tape. I heard you start the machine. True would-be corrupters wouldn't do that.'

'I did advise caution,' Sam Leggatt said mildly.

'You've no proof of any of this,' Pollgate said with finality.

'My bank manager's holding a three thousand pound draft issued in the City. He intends on my behalf to ask questions about its origins.'

'He'll get nowhere,' Pollgate said positively.

'Then perhaps he'll do what I asked him first, which is to tear it up.'

There was a short stark silence. If they asked for the draft back they would admit they'd delivered it, and if they didn't, their failed ploy would have cost them the money.

'Or it could be transferred to Bobby Allardeck, as a first small instalment of compensation.'

'I've heard enough,' Pollgate said brusquely. 'Return the property of our journalists immediately. There will be no compensation, do you understand? None. You will come to wish, I promise you, that you had never tried to extort it.'

Under the civilised suiting he hunched his shoulders like a boxer, rotating them as a physical warning of an imminent onslaught, a flexing of literal muscles before an explosion of mental aggression. I saw in his face all the brutality of his newspaper and also the arrogance of absolute power. No one, I thought, could have defied him for too long, and he didn't intend that I should be an exception.

'If you make trouble for us in the courts,' he said grittily, 'I'll smash you. I mean it. I'll see to it that you yourself are accused of some crime that you'll hate, and I'll get you convicted and sent to prison, and you'll go down, I promise you, dishonoured and reviled, with maximum publicity and disgrace.'

The final words were savagely biting, the intention vibratingly real.

Both Leggatt and Morse looked impassive and I wondered what any of them could read on my own face. Show no fright . . . ye gods.

He surely wouldn't do it, I thought wildly. The threat must be only to deter. Surely a man in his position wouldn't risk his own status to frame and jail an adversary who wanted so little, who represented no life-or-death danger to his paper or to himself, who wielded no corporate power.

All the same, it looked horrible. Jockeys were eternally vulnerable to accusations of dishonesty and it took little to disillusion a cynical public. The assumption of guilt would be strong. He could try harder and more subtly to frame me for taking bribes, and certainly for things worse. What his paper had already set their hand to, they could do again and more thoroughly. A crime I would hate.

I could find no immediate words to reply to him, and while I stood there in the lengthening silence the door alarm buzzed fiercely, making Morse jump.

Sam Leggatt flicked a switch. 'Who is it?' he said.

'Erskine.'

Leggatt looked at Pollgate, who nodded. Leggatt pressed the button that unlatched the door, and the man I'd shaken off the ladder came quietly in.

He was of about my height, reddish haired going bald, with a drooping moustache and chillingly unsmiling eyes. He nodded to the triumvirate as if he'd been talking to them earlier and turned to face me directly, chin tucked in, stomach thrust out, a man with a ruined life behind him and a present mind full of malice.

'You'll give me my stuff,' he said. Not a question, not a statement: more a threat.

'Eventually,' I said.

There was a certain quality of stillness, of stiffening, on the far side of Leggatt's desk. I looked at Pollgate's thunderous expression and realised that I had almost without intending it told him with that one word that his threat, his promise, hadn't immediately worked.

'He's yours, Jay,' he said thickly.

I didn't have time to wonder what he meant. Jay Erskine caught hold of my right wrist and twisted my arm behind my back with a strength and speed that spoke of practice. I had done much the same to him in Bobby's garden, pressing his face into the mud, and into my ear with the satisfaction of an account paid he said, 'You tell me where my gear is or I'll break your shoulder so bad you'll ride no more races this side of Doomsday.'

His vigour hurt. I checked the three watching faces. No surprise, not even from the lawyer. Was this, I wondered fleetingly, a normal course of events in the editor's office of the *Daily Flag*?

'Tell me,' Erskine said, shoving.

I took a sharp half-pace backwards, cannoning into him. I went down in a crouch, head nearly to the floor, then straightened my legs with the fiercest possible jerk, pitching Jay Erskine bodily forwards over my shoulders, where he let go of my wrist and sailed sprawlingly into the air. He landed with a crash on a potted palm against the far wall while I completed the rolling somersault and ended upright on my feet. The manoeuvre took a scant second in the execution: the stunned silence afterwards lasted at least twice as long.

Jay Erskine furiously tore a leaf from his mouth and struggled pugnaciously to right himself, almost pawing the carpet like a bull for a second charge.

'That's enough,' I said. 'That's bloody enough.'

I looked directly at Nestor Pollgate. 'Compensation,' I said. 'Another of your banker's drafts. One hundred thousand pounds. Tomorrow. Bobby Allardeck will be coming to Ascot races. You can give it to him there. It could cost you about that much to manufacture a crime I didn't commit and have me convicted. Why not save yourself the trouble.'

Jay Erskine was upright and looking utterly malignant.

I said to him, 'Pray the compensation's paid . . . Do you want another dose of the slammer?'

I walked to the door and looked briefly back. Pollgate, Leggatt and Morse had wiped-slate faces: Jay Erskine's was glitteringly cold.

I wondered fearfully for a second if the door's unlatching mechanism also locked and would keep me in; but it seemed not. The handle turned easily, came smoothly towards me, opening the path of escape.

Out of the office, along the passage to the lifts my feet felt alarmingly detached from my legs. If I believed Pollgate's threats I was walking into the bleakest of futures: if I believed Erskine's malevolence it would be violent and soon. Why in God's name, I thought despairingly, hadn't I given in, given them the jackets, let Bobby go bust.

There were running footsteps behind me across the mock-marble hallway outside the lifts, and I turned fast, expecting Erskine and danger, but finding, as once before, Sam Leggatt.

His eyes widened at the speed with which I'd faced him.

'You expected another attack,' he said.

'Mm.'

'I'll come down with you.' He pressed the button for descent and stared at me for a while without speaking while we waited.

'One hundred thousand,' he said finally, 'is too much. I thought you meant less.'

'Yesterday, I did.'

'And today?'

'Today I met Pollgate. He would sneer at a small demand. He doesn't think in peanuts.'

Sam Leggatt went back to staring, blinking his sandy lashes, not showing his unspoken thoughts.

'That threat,' I said slowly, 'about sending me to prison. Has he used that before?'

'What do you mean?'

'On someone else.'

'What makes you think so?'

'You and your lawyer,' I said, 'showed no surprise.'

The lift purred to a halt inside the shaft and the doors opened. Leggatt and I stepped inside.

'Also,' I said, as the doors closed, 'the words he used sounded almost rehearsed. "You'll go down, I promise you, dishonoured and reviled, with maximum publicity and disgrace." Like a play, don't you think?'

He said curiously, 'You remember the exact words?'

'One wouldn't easily forget them.' I paused. 'Did he mean it?'

'Probably.'

'What happened before?'

'He wasn't put to the test.'

'Do you mean, the threat worked?' I asked.

'Twice.'

'Jesus,' I said.

I absent-mindedly rubbed my right shoulder, digging in under the anorak with the left thumb and fingers to massage. 'Does he always get his way by threats?'

186

Leggatt said evenly, 'The threats vary to suit the circumstances. Does that hurt?'

'What?'

'Your shoulder.'

'Oh. Yes, I suppose so. Not much. No worse than a fall.'

'How did you do that? Fling him off you, like that?'

I half grinned. 'I haven't done it since I was about fifteen, same as the other guy. I wasn't sure it would work with a grown man, but it did, a treat.'

We reached the ground floor and stepped out of the lift.

'Where are you staying?' he asked casually.

'With a friend,' I said.

He came with me halfway across the ornate entrance hall, stopping beside the small fountain.

'Why did Nestor Pollgate want to crunch Maynard Allardeck?' I said.

'I don't know.'

'Then it wasn't your idea or Erskine's? It came from the top?'

'From the top.'

'And beyond,' I said.

'What do you mean?'

I frowned. 'I don't know. Do you?'

'As far as I know, Nestor Pollgate started it.'

I said ruefully, 'Then I didn't exactly smash his face in.'

'Not far off.'

There was no shade of disloyalty in his voice, but I had the impression that he was in some way apologising: the chief's sworn lieutenant offering comfort to the outcast. The chief's man, I thought. Remember it.

'What do you plan to do next?' he said.

'Ride at Ascot.'

He looked steadily into my eyes and I looked right back. I might have liked him, I thought, if he'd steered any other ship.

'Goodbye,' I said.

He seemed to hesitate a fraction but in the end said merely, 'Goodbye' and turned back to the lifts: and I went out into Fleet Street and breathed great gulps of free air under the stars.

187

I walked the two miles back to the hotel and sat in my room for a while there contemplating the walls, and then I went down to find the rented Mercedes in the underground park and drove it out to Chiswick.

'You're incredibly early,' Danielle said, faintly alarmed at my arrival. 'I did say two a.m., not half after eleven.'

'I thought I might just sit here and watch you, as no one seemed to mind me being here last time.'

'You'll be bored crazy.'

'No.'

'OK.'

She pointed to a desk and chair close to hers. 'No one's using that tonight. You'll be all right there. Did you get that cut fixed?'

'Yes, it's fine.'

I sat in the chair and listened to the mysteries of newsgathering, American style, for the folks back home. The big six-thirty evening slot, eastern US time, was being aired at that moment, it appeared. The day's major hassle had just ended. From now until two, Danielle said, she would be working on anything new and urgent which might make the eleven o'clock news back home, but would otherwise be on the screens at breakfast.

'Does much news happen here at this time of night?' I asked.

'Right now we've got an out-of-control fire in an oil terminal in Scotland and at midnight Devil-Boy goes on stage at a royal charity gala to unveil a new smash.'

'Who?' I said.

'Never mind. A billion teenagers can't be wrong.'

'And then what?' I said.

'After we get the pictures? Transmit them back here from a mobile van, edit them, and transmit the finished article to the studios in New York. Sometimes at midday here we do live interviews, mostly for the seven-to-nine morning show back home, but nothing live at nights.'

'You do edit the tapes here?'

'Sure. Usually. Want to see?'

'Yes, very much.'

'After I've made these calls.' She gestured to the telephone and I nodded, and subsequently listened to her talking to someone at the fire.

'The talent is on his way back by helicopter from the race riot and should be with you in ten minutes. Get him to call me when he can. How close to the blaze are you? OK, when Cervano gets to you try to go closer, from that distance a volcano would look like a sparkler. OK, tell him to call me when he's reached you. Yeah, OK, get him to call me.'

She put down the receiver, grimacing. 'They're a good mile off. They might as well be in Brooklyn.'

'Who's the talent?' I said.

'Ed Cervano. Oh ... the talent is any person behind a microphone talking to the camera. News reporter, anchor, anyone.'

She looked along the headings on the board on the wall behind her chair. 'Slug. That's the story we're working on. Oil fire. Devil-Boy. Embassy. So on.'

'Yes,' I said.

'Locations, obvious. Time, obvious. Crew. That's the camera crew which is allocated to that story, and also the talent. Format, that's how fully we're covering a story. Package means the works, camera crew, talent, interviews, the lot. Voice-over is just a cameraman, with the commentary tagged on later. So on.'

'And it's you who decides who goes where for what?'

She half nodded. 'The bureau chief, and the other coordinators, who work in the daytime, and me, yes.'

'Some job,' I said.

She smiled with her eyes. 'If we do well, the company's ratings go up. If we do badly, we get fired.'

'The news is the news, surely,' I said.

'Oh yes? Which would you prefer, an oil fire from a mile off or to think you feel the flames?'

'Mm.'

Her telephone rang. 'News,' she said, and listened. 'Look,' she said, sounding exasperated, 'if he's late, it's news. If he's sick, it's news. If he doesn't make it on to the stage at a royal gala, it's news. You just stay there, whatever happens is news, OK? Get some shots of royalty leaving, if all else fails.' She put down the receiver. 'Devil-Boy hasn't arrived at the theatre and it takes him a good hour to dress.'

'The joys of the non-event.'

'I don't want to be scooped by one of the other broadcasting companies, now do I?'

'Where do you get the news from in the first place?'

'Oh . . . the press agencies, newspapers, police broadcasts, publicity releases, things like that.'

'I guess I never wondered before how the news arrived on the box.'

'Ten seconds' worth can take all day to gather.'

Her telephone rang again, with the helicoptering Ed Cervano now down to earth at the other end. Danielle asked him in gentle tones to go get himself a first degree burn, and from her smile it seemed he was willing to go up in flames entirely for her sake.

'A sweet-talking guy,' she said, putting down the receiver. 'And he writes like a poet.' Her eyes were shining over the talent's talents, her mouth curving from his honey.

'Writes?' I said.

'Writes what he says on the news. All our news reporters write their own stuff.'

Another message came through from the royal gala: Devil-Boy, horns and all, was reported on his way to the theatre in a bell-ringing ambulance.

'Is he sick?' Danielle asked. 'If it's a stunt, make sure you catch it.' She disconnected, shrugging resignedly. 'The hip-wriggling imp of Satan will get double the oil fire exposure. Real hell stands no chance against the fake. Do you want to see the editing rooms?'

'Yes,' I said, and followed her across the large office and down a passage, admiring the neatness of her walk and wanting to put my hands deep into her cloud of dark hair, wanting to kiss her, wanting quite fiercely to take her to bed.

She said, 'I'll show you the studio first, it's more interesting', and veered down a secondary passage towards a door warningly marked 'If red light shows, do not enter'. No red light shone. We went in. The room was moderate in size, furnished barely with a couple of armchairs, a coffee table, a television camera, a television set, a teleprompter and a silent coffee machine with paper cups. The only surprise was the window, through which one could see a stretch of the Thames and Hammersmith Bridge, all decked with lights and busily living.

'We do live interviews in here in front of the window,' Danielle said. 'Mostly politicians but also actors, authors, sportsmen, anyone in the news. Red buses go across the bridge in the background. It's impressive.'

'I'm sure,' I said.

She gave me a swift look. 'Am I boring you?'

'Absolutely not.'

She wore pink lipstick and had eyebrows like wings. Dark smiling eyes, creamy skin, long neck to hidden breasts like apples on a slender stem . . . For Christ's sake, Kit, I thought, drag your mind off it and ask some sensible questions.

'How does your stuff get from here to America?' I said.

'From in here.' She walked over to a closed door in one of the walls, and opened it. Beyond it was another room, much smaller, dimly lit, which was warm and hummed faintly with walls of machines.

'This is the transmitter room,' she said. 'Everything goes from in here by satellite, but don't ask me how, we have a man with a haunted expression twiddling the knobs and we leave it to him.'

She closed the transmitter room door and we went through the studio, into the passage and back to the editing rooms, of which there were three.

'OK,' she said, switching a light on and revealing a small area walled on one side by three television screens, several video recorders and racks of tape cassettes, 'this is what we still use, though I'm told there's a load of new technology round the corner. Our guys here like these machines, so I guess we'll have them around for a while yet.'

'How do they work?' I asked.

'You run the unedited tape through on the left-hand screen and pick out the best bits, then you record just those on to the second tape, showing on the second screen. You can switch it all around until it looks good and you get a good feeling. We transmit it like that, but New York often cuts it shorter. Depends how much else they've got to fit in.'

'Can you work these machines yourself?' I asked.

'I'm slow. If you really want to know now, you can watch Joe later when we get the oil fire and Devil-Boy tapes – he's one of the best.'

'Great,' I said.

'I'm surprised you're so interested.'

'Well, I've some tapes I want to edit myself. It would be nice to learn how.'

'Is that why you came here so early?' She sounded as if I might say yes without at all offending her.

I said, 'Partly. Mostly to see you . . . and what you do.'

She was close enough to hug and I had no insight at all into what she was thinking. A brick wall between minds. Disconcerting.

She looked with friendliness but nothing else into my face, and the only thing I was sure of was that she didn't feel as I did about a little uninhibited love-making on the spot.

She asked if I would like to see the library and I said yes please: and the library turned out to be not books but rows and rows of recorded tapes, past years of news stories forgotten but waiting like bombs in the dark, records of things said, undeniable.

'Mostly used for obituaries,' Danielle said. 'Reactivated scandals. Things like that.'

We returned to her news desk, where over the next hour I sat and listened to the progress of events. (Devil-Boy had arrived at the stage door, fit, well and fully made-up in a blaze of technicolor lights to the gratified hysterics of a streetful of fans) and met Danielle's working companions, the bureau chief, Joe the editor, the gaunt transmitter expert, two spare cameramen and a bored and unallocated female talent. About sixty people altogether worked for the bureau, Danielle said, but of course never all at one time. The day shift, from ten to six-thirty, was much bigger: in the daytime there were two to do her job.

At one o'clock Ed Cervano telephoned to say they'd gotten a whole load of spectacular shots of the oil fire but the blaze was now under control and the story was as dead as tomorrow's ashes.

'Bring back the tapes anyway,' Danielle said. 'We don't have any oil fire stock shots in the library.'

She put down the receiver resignedly. 'So it goes.'

The crew from the royal gala returned noisily bearing Devil-Boy's capers themselves, and at the same time a delivery man brought a stock of morning newspapers to put on Danielle's desk for her to look through for possible stories. The *Daily Flag*, as it happened, lay on top, and I opened it at Intimate Details to re-read Leggatt's words.

'What are you looking at?' Danielle asked.

I pointed. She read the apology and blinked.

'I didn't think you stood a chance,' she said frankly. 'Did they agree to the compensation also?'

'Not so far.'

'They'll have to,' she said. 'They've practically admitted liability.'

I shook my head. 'British courts don't award huge damages for libel. It's doubtful whether Bobby would actually win if he sued, and even if he won, unless the *Flag* was ordered to pay his costs, which also isn't certain, he simply couldn't afford the lawyers' fees.'

She gazed at me. 'Back home you don't pay the lawyers unless you win. Then the lawyers take their slice of the damages. Forty per cent, sometimes.'

'It's not like that here.'

Here, I thought numbly, one bargained with threats. On the one side: I'll get your wrist slapped by the Press Council, I'll get questions asked in Parliament, I'll see your ex-convict journalist back in the dock. And on the other, I'll slice your tendons, I'll lose you your jockey's licence for taking bribes, I'll put you in prison. Reviled, dishonoured, and with publicity, disgraced.

Catch me first, I thought.

FIFTEEN

I watched Joe the editor, dark-skinned and with rapid fingers, sort his way through a mass of noisy peacock footage, clicking his tongue as a sort of commentary to himself, punctuating the lifted sections he was stringing together to make the most flamboyant impact. Kaleidoscope arrival of Devil-Boy, earlier entrance of royals, wriggling release of new incomprehensible song.

'Thirty seconds,' he said, running through the finished sequence. 'Maybe they'll use it all, maybe they won't.'

'It looks good to me.'

'Thirty seconds is a long news item.' He took the spooled tape from the machine, put it into an already labelled box and handed it to the gaunt transmitter man, who was waiting to take it away. 'Danielle says you want to learn to edit, so what do you want to know?'

'Er . . . what these machines will do, for a start.'

'Quite a lot.' He fluttered his dark fingers over the banks of controls, barely touching them. 'They'll take any size tape, any make, and record on any other. You can bring the sound up, cut it out, transpose it, superimpose any sounds you like. You can put the sound from one tape on to the pictures of another, you can cut two tapes together so that it looks as if the people are talking to each other when they were recorded hours and miles apart, you can tell lies and goddam lies and put a false face on truth.'

'Anything else?'

'That about covers it.'

He showed me how to achieve some of his effects, but his speed confounded me.

'Have you got an actual tape you want to edit?' he asked finally.

'Yes, but I want to add to it first, if I can.'

He looked at me assessingly, a poised black man of perhaps my own age with a touch of humour in the eyes but a rarely smiling mouth. I felt untidy in my anorak beside his neat suit and cream shirt; also battered and sweaty and dim. It had been, I thought ruefully, too long a day.

'Danielle says you're OK,' he said surprisingly. 'I don't see why you can't ask the chief to rent you the use of this room some night we're not busy. You tell me what you want, and I'll edit your tapes for you, if you like.'

'Joe's a nice guy,' Danielle said, stretching lazily beside me in the rented Mercedes on her way home. 'Sure, if he said he'd edit your tape, he means it. He gets bored. He waited three hours tonight for the Devil-Boy slot. He loves editing. Has a passion for it. He wants to work in movies. He'll enjoy doing your tape.'

The bureau chief, solicited, had proved equally generous. 'If Joe's using the machines, go ahead.' He'd looked over to where Danielle was eyes down marking paragraphs in the morning papers. 'I had New York on the line this evening congratulating me on the upswing of our output recently. That's her doing. She says you're OK, you're OK.'

For her too it had been a long day.

'Towcester,' she said, yawning, 'seems light years back.'

'Mm,' I said. 'What did Princess Casilia say after you went in, when you got back to Eaton Square?'

Danielle looked at me with amusement. 'In the hall she told me that good manners were a sign of strength, and in the drawing room she asked if I thought you would really be fit for Ascot.'

'What did you say?' I asked, faintly alarmed.

'I said yes, you would.'

I relaxed. 'That's all right, then.'

'I did not say,' Danielle said mildly, 'that you were insane, but only that you didn't appear to notice when you'd been injured. Aunt Casilia said she thought this to be fairly typical of steeplechase jockeys.'

'I do notice,' I said.

'But?'

'Well . . . if I don't race, I don't earn. Almost worse, if I miss a race on a horse and it wins, the happy owner may put up that winning jockey the next time, so I can lose not just the one fee but maybe the rides on that horse for ever.'

She looked almost disappointed. 'So it's purely economic, this refusal to look filleted ribs in the face?'

'At least half.'

'And the rest?'

'What you feel for your job. What Joe feels for his. Much the same.'

She nodded, and after a pause said, 'Aunt Casilia wouldn't do that, though. Keep another jockey on, after you were fit again.'

'No, she never has. But your aunt is special.'

'She said,' Danielle said reflectively, 'that I wasn't to think of you as a jockey.'

'But I am.'

'That's what she said this morning on the way to Towcester.'

'Did she explain what she meant?'

'No. I asked her. She said something vague about essences.' She yawned. 'Anyway, this evening she told Uncle Roland all about those horrid men with knives, as she put it, and although he was scandalised and said she shouldn't get involved in such sordid brawls, she seemed quite serene and unaffected. She may look like porcelain, but she's quite tough. The more I get to know her, the more, to be honest, I adore her.'

The road from Chiswick to Eaton Square, clogged by day with stop–go traffic, was at two-fifteen in the morning regrettably empty. Red lights turned green at our approach and even sticking rigidly to the speed limit didn't much seem to lengthen the journey. We slid to a halt outside the princess's house far too soon.

Neither of us made a move to spring at once out of the car: we sat rather for a moment letting the day die in peace.

I said, 'I'll see you then, on Saturday.'

'Yes,' she sighed for no clear reason. 'I guess so.'

'You don't have to,' I said.

'Oh no,' she half laughed. 'I suppose I meant . . . Saturday's some way off.'

I took her hand. She let it lie in mine, passive, waiting.

'We might have,' I said, 'a lot of Saturdays.'

'Yes, we might.'

I leaned over and kissed her mouth, tasting her pink lipstick, feeling her breath on my cheek, sensing the tremble somewhere in her body. She neither drew back nor clutched forward, but kissed as I'd kissed, as an announcement, as a promise perhaps; as an invitation.

I sat away from her and smiled into her eyes, and then got out of the car and went round to open her door.

We stood briefly together on the pavement.

'Where are you sleeping?' she said. 'It's so late.'

'In a hotel.'

'Near here?'

'Less than a mile.'

'Good . . . you won't have far to drive.'

'No distance.'

'Goodnight, then,' she said.

'Goodnight.'

We kissed again, as before. Then, laughing, she turned away, walked across the pavement and let herself through the princess's porticoed front door with a latchkey: and I drove away thinking that if the princess had disapproved of her jockey making approaches to her niece, she would by now have let both of us know.

I slept like the dead for five hours, then rolled stiffly out of bed, blinked blearily at the heavy cold rain making a mess of the day, and pointed the Mercedes towards Bletchley.

The Golden Lion was warm and alive with the smells of breakfast, and I ate there while the desk processed my bill. Then I telephoned the AA for news of my car (ready Monday) and to Holly to check that the marked *Flag* copies had been delivered as promised (which they had: the feed-merchant had telephoned) and after that I packed all my gear into the car and headed straight back towards the hotel I'd slept in.

No problem, they said helpfully at reception, I could retain my present room for as long as I wanted, and yes, certainly, I could leave items in the strongroom for safe-keeping.

Upstairs I put Jay Erskine's Press Club pass and Owen

Watts's credit cards into an envelope and wrote 'URGENT DELIVER TO MR LEGGATT IMMEDIATELY' in large letters on the outside. Then I put the video recordings and all of the journalists' other possessions, except their jackets, into one of the hotel's laundry bags, rolling it into a neat bundle which downstairs was fastened with sticky-tape and labelled before vanishing into the vault.

After that I drove to Fleet Street, parked where I shouldn't, ran through the rain to leave the envelope for Sam Leggatt at the *Flag* front desk, fielded the car from under the nose of a traffic warden, and went lightheartedly to Ascot.

It was a rotten afternoon there in many ways. Sleet fell almost ceaselessly, needle-sharp, ice-cold and slanting, soaking every jockey to the skin before the start and proving a blinding hazard thereafter. Goggles were useless, caked with flying mud; gloves slipped wetly on the reins; racing boots clung clammily to waterlogged feet. A day for gritting one's teeth and getting round safely, for meeting fences exactly right and not slithering along on one's nose on landing. Raw November at its worst.

The crowd was sparse, deterred before it started out by the visible downpour and the drenching forecast, and the few people standing in the open were huddled inside dripping coats looking like mushrooms with their umbrellas.

Holly and Bobby both came but wouldn't stay, arriving after I'd won the first race more by luck than inspiration, and leaving before the second. They took the money out of the money-belt, which I returned to the valet with thanks.

Holly hugged me. 'Three people telephoned, after I'd talked to you, to say they were pleased about the apology,' she said. 'They're offering credit again. It's made all the difference.'

'Take care how you go with running up bills,' I said.

'Of course we will. The bank manager haunts us.'

I said to Bobby, 'I borrowed some of that money. I'll repay it next week.'

'It's all yours, really.' He spoke calmly in friendship, but the life-force was again at a low ebb. No vigour. Too much apathy. Not what was needed.

Holly looked frozen and was shivering. 'Keep the baby warm,' I said. 'Go into the trainers' bar.'

'We're going home.' She kissed me with cold lips. 'We would stay to watch you, but I feel sick. I feel sick most of the time. It's the pits.'

Bobby put his arm round her protectively and took her away under a large umbrella, both of them leaning head down against the icy wind, and I felt depressed for them, and thought also of the risks that lay ahead, before they could be safe.

The princess had invited to her box the friends of hers that I cared for least, a quartet of aristocrats from her old country, and as always when they were there I saw little of her. With two of them she came in red oilskins down to the parade ring before the first of her two runners, smiling cheerfully through the freezing rain and asking what I thought of her chances, and with the other two she repeated the enquiry an hour and a half later.

In each case I said, 'Reasonable.' The first runner finished reasonably fourth, the second runner, second. Neither time did she come down to the unsaddling enclosure, for which one couldn't blame her, and nor did I go up to her box, partly because it was a perfunctory routine when those friends were there, but mostly on account of crashing to the ground on the far side of the course in the last race. By the time I got in and changed, she would be gone.

Oh well, I thought dimly, scraping myself up; six rides, one winner, one second, one fourth, two also-rans, one fall. You can't win four every day, old son. And nothing broken. Even the stitches had survived without leaking. I waited in the blowing sleet for the car to pick me up, and took off my helmet to let the water run through my hair, embracing in a way the wild day, feeling at home. Winter and horses, the old song in the blood.

There was no fruit cake left in the changing room.

'Rotten buggers,' I said.

'But you never eat cake,' my valet said, heaving off my sodden boots.

'Every so often,' I said, 'like on freezing wet Fridays after a fall in the last race.'

'There's some tea still. It's hot.'

I drank the tea, feeling the warmth slide down, heating

from inside. There was always tea and fruit cake in the changing rooms; instant energy, instant comfort. Everyone ate cake now and then.

An official put his head through the door: someone to see you, he said.

I pulled on a shirt and shoes and went out to the door from the weighing room to the outside world. No one all day had appeared with a banker's draft from Pollgate, and I suppose I went out with an incredulous flicker of hope. Hope soon extinguished. It was only Dusty, huddled in the weighing room doorway, blue of face, eyes watering with cold.

'Is the horse all right?' I asked. 'I heard you caught him.'

'Yes. Useless bugger. What about you?'

'No damage. I got passed by the doctor. I'll be riding tomorrow.'

'Right, I'll tell the guv'nor. We'll be off, then. So long.'

'So long.'

He scurried away into the leaden early dusk, a small dedicated man who liked to check for himself after I'd fallen that I was in good enough shape to do his charges justice next time out. He had been known to advise Wykeham to stand me down. Wykeham had been known to take the advice. Passing Dusty was sometimes harder than passing the medics.

I showered and dressed and left the racecourse via the cheaper enclosures, walking from there into the darkening town, where I'd left the rented Mercedes in a public parking place in the morning. Maybe it was unlikely that a repeat ambush would be set in the nearly deserted jockeys' car park long after the last race, but I was taking no chances. I climbed unmolested into the Mercedes and drove in safety to London.

There in my comfortable bolthole I again made additions to my astronomical phone bill, arranging first for my obliging neighbour to go into my cottage in the morning and pack one of my suits and some shirts and other things into a suitcase.

'Of course I will, Kit dear, but I thought you'd be back here for sure tonight, after riding at Ascot.'

'Staying with friends,' I said. 'I'll get someone to pick up the suitcase from your place tomorrow morning to take it to Ascot. Would that be all right?'

'Of course, dear.'

I persuaded another jockey who lived in Lambourn to collect the case and bring it with him, and he said sure he would, if he remembered.

I telephoned Wykeham when I judged he'd be indoors after his evening tour of the horses and told him his winner had been steadfast, the princess's two as good as could be hoped for, and one of the also-rans disappointing.

'And Dusty says you made a clear balls-up of the hurdle down by Swinley Bottom in the last.'

'Yeah,' I said. 'If Dusty can see clearly half a mile through driving sleet in poor light he's got better eyesight than I thought.'

'Er . . .' Wykeham said. 'What happened?'

'The one in front fell. Mine went down over him. He wouldn't have won, if that's any consolation. He was beginning to tire already, and he was hating the weather.'

Wykeham grunted assent. 'He's a sun-lover, true-bred. Kit, tomorrow there's Inchcape for the princess in the big race and he's in grand form, jumping out of his skin, improved a mile since you saw him last week.'

'Inchcape,' I said resignedly, 'is dead.'

'What? Did I say Inchcape? No, not Inchcape. What's the princess's horse?'

'Icefall.'

'Icicle's full brother,' he said, not quite making it a question.

'Yes.'

'Of course.' He cleared his throat. 'Icefall. Naturally. He should win, Kit, seriously.'

'Will you be there?' I asked. 'I half expected you today.'

'In that weather?' He sounded surprised. 'No, no, Dusty and you and the princess, you'll do fine.'

'But you've had a whole bunch of winners this week and you haven't seen one of them.'

'I see them here in the yard. I see them on video tapes. You tell Inchcape he's the greatest, and he'll jump Ben Nevis.'

'All right,' I said. Icefall, Inchcape, what did it matter?

'Good. Great. Goodnight, Kit.'

'Goodnight, Wykeham,' I said.

I got through to my answering machine and collected the messages, one of which was from Eric Olderjohn, the civil servant owner of the horse I'd won on for the Lambourn trainer at Towcester.

I called him back without delay at the London number he'd given, and caught him, it seemed, on the point of going out.

'Oh, Kit, yes. Look, I suppose you're in Lambourn?'

'No, actually. In London.'

'Really? That's fine. I've something you might be interested to see, but I can't let it out of my hands.' He paused for thought. 'Would you be free this evening after nine?'

'Yes,' I said.

'Right. Come round to my house, I'll be back by then.' He gave me directions to a street south of Sloane Square, not more than a mile from where I was staying. 'Coffee and brandy, right? Got to run. Bye.'

He disconnected abruptly and I put down my own receiver more slowly saying 'Wow' to myself silently. I hadn't expected much action from Eric Olderjohn, civil servant, and certainly none with such speed.

I sat for a while thinking of the tape of Maynard, and of the list of companies at the end, of those who had suffered from Maynard's philanthropy. Short of finding somewhere to replay the tape, I would have to rely on memory, and the only name I could remember for certain was Purfleet Electronics; chiefly because I'd spent a summer sailing holiday with a schoolfriend there long ago.

Purfleet Electronics, directory enquiries told me, was not listed.

I sucked my teeth a bit and reflected that the only way to find things was to look in the right place. I would go to Purfleet, as to Hitchin, in the morning.

I filled in the evening with eating and more phone calls, and by nine had walked down Sloane Street and found Eric Olderjohn's house. It was narrow, two storeys, one of a long terrace built for low-income early Victorians, now inhabited by the affluent as pieds-à-terre: or so Eric Olderjohn affably told me, opening his dark green front door and waving me in.

From the street one stepped straight into the sitting room, which stretched from side to side of the house; all of four metres. The remarkably small space glowed with pinks and light greens, textured trellised wallpaper, swagged satin curtains, round tables with skirts, china birds, silver photograph frames, fat buttoned armchairs, chinese creamy rugs on the floor. There were softly glowing lamps, and the trellised wallpaper covered the ceiling also, enclosing the crowded contents in an impression of a summer grotto.

My host watched my smile of appreciation as if the reaction were only what he would have expected.

'It's great,' I said.

'My daughter did it.'

'The one you would defend from the *Flag*?'

'My only daughter. Yes. Sit down. Has it stopped raining? You'd like a brandy, I dare say?' He moved the one necessary step to a silver tray of bottles on one of the round tables and poured cognac into two modest balloon glasses. 'I've set some coffee ready. I'll just fetch it. Sit down, do.' He vanished through a rear door camouflaged by trellis and I looked at the photographs in the frames, seeing a well-groomed young woman who might be his daughter, seeing the horse that he owned, with myself on its back.

He returned with another small tray, setting it alongside the first.

'My daughter,' he said, nodding, as he saw I'd been looking. 'She lives here part of the time, part with her mother.' He shrugged. 'One of those things.'

'I'm sorry.'

'Yes. Well, it happens. Coffee?' He poured into two small cups and handed me one. 'Sugar? No, I suppose not. Sit down. Here's the brandy.'

He was neat in movement as in dress, and I found myself thinking 'dapper'; but there was purposefulness there under the surface, the developed faculty of getting things done. I sat in one of the armchairs with coffee and brandy beside me, and he sat also, and sipped, and looked at me over his cup.

'You were in luck,' he said finally. 'I put out a few feelers this morning and was told a certain person might be lunching at his club.' He paused. 'I was sufficiently interested in your problem to arrange for a friend of mine to meet and sound out that person, whom he knows well, and their conversation was, one might say, fruitful. As a result I myself went to a certain person's office this afternoon, and the upshot of that meeting was some information which I'll presently show you.'

His care over the choice of words was typical, I supposed, of the stratosphere of the civil service: the wheeler-dealers in subtlety, obliqueness and not saying quite what one meant. I never discovered the exact identity of the certain person, on the basis no doubt that it wasn't something I needed to know, and in view of what he'd allowed me a sight of, I could scarcely complain.

'I have some letters,' Eric Olderjohn said. 'More precisely, photocopies of letters. You can read them, but I am directly commanded not to let you take them away. I have to return them on Monday. Is all that . . . er . . . quite clear?'

'Yes.' I said.

'Good.'

Without haste he finished his coffee and put down the cup. Then, raising the skirt of the table which bore the trays, he bent and brought out a brown leather attaché case, which he rested on his knees. He snapped open the locks, raised the lid and paused again.

'They're interesting,' he said, frowning.

I waited.

As if coming to a decision which until that moment he had left open, he drew a single sheet of paper out of the case and passed it across.

The letter had been addressed to the Prime Minister and had been sent in September from a company which made fine china for export. The chairman, who had written the letter, explained that he and the other directors were unanimous in suggesting some signal honour for Mr Maynard Allardeck, in recognition of his great and patriotic services to industry.

Mr Allardeck had come generously to the aid of the historic company, and thanks entirely to his efforts the jobs of two hundred and fifty people had been saved. The skills of many of these people were priceless and included the ability to paint and gild porcelain to the world's highest standards. The company was now exporting more than before and was looking forward to the brightest of futures.

The board would like to propose a knighthood for Mr Allardeck.

I finished reading and looked over at Eric Olderjohn.

'Is this sort of letter normal?' I asked.

'Entirely.' He nodded. 'Most awards are the result of recommendations to the Prime Minister's office. Anyone can suggest anyone for anything. If the cause seems just, an award is given. The patronage people draw up a list of awards they deem suitable, and the list is passed to the Prime Minister for approval.'

I said, 'So all these people in the honours lists who get medals . . . firefighters, music teachers, postmen, people like that, it's because their mates have written in to suggest it?'

'Er, yes. More often their employers, but sometimes their mates.'

He produced a second letter from his briefcase and handed it over. This one also was from an exporting company and stressed Maynard's invaluable contributions to worthwhile industry, chief among them the saving of very many jobs in an area of great local unemployment.

It was impossible to overestimate Mr Allardeck's services to his country in industry, and the firm unreservedly recommended that he should be offered a knighthood.

'Naturally,' I said, 'the patronage people checked that all this was true?'

'Naturally,' Eric Olderjohn said.

'And of course it was?'

'I am assured so. The certain person with whom I talked this afternoon told me that occasionally, if they receive six or seven similar letters all proposing someone unknown to the general public, they may begin to suspect that the person is busily proposing himself by persuading his friends to write in. The writers of the two letters I've shown you were specifically asked, as their recommendations were so similar, if Maynard himself had suggested they write. Each of them emphatically denied any such thing.'

'Mm,' I said. 'Well they would, wouldn't they, if they stood to gain from Maynard for his knighthood.'

'That's a thoroughly scurrilous remark.'

'So it is,' I said cheerfully. 'And your certain person, did he put Maynard down for his Sir?'

He nodded. 'Provisionally. To be considered. Then they

received a third letter, emphasising substantial philanthropy that they already knew about, and the question mark was erased. Maynard Allardeck was definitely in line for his K. The letter inviting him to accept the honour was drafted, and would have been sent out in about ten days from now, at the normal time for the New Year's list.'

'Would have been?' I said.

'Would have been.' He smiled twistedly. 'It is not now considered appropriate, as a result of the stories in the *Daily Flag* and the opinion page in the *Towncrier*.'

'Rose Quince,' I said.

He looked uncomprehending.

'She wrote the piece in the *Towncrier*,' I said.

'Oh . . . yes.'

'Would your, er, certain person,' I asked, 'really take notice of those bits in the newspapers?'

'Oh, definitely. Particularly as in each case the paragraphs were delivered by hand to his office, outlined in red.'

'They weren't!'

Eric Olderjohn raised an eyebrow. 'That means something to you?' he asked.

I explained about the tradespeople and the owners all receiving similarly marked copies.

'There you are, then. A thorough job of demolition. Nothing left to chance.'

'You mentioned a third letter,' I said. 'The clincher.'

He peered carefully into his case and produced it. 'This one may surprise you,' he said.

The third letter was not from a commercial firm but from a charitable organisation with a list of patrons that stretched half the way down the left side of the page. The recipients of the charity appeared to be the needy dependants of dead or disabled public servants. Widows, children, the old and the sick.

'How do you define a public servant?' I asked.

'The Civil Service, from the top down.'

Maynard Allardeck, the letter reported, had worked tirelessly over several years to improve the individual lives of those left in dire straits through no fault of their own. He unstintingly poured out his own fortune in aid, besides giving his time and extending a high level of compassionate ongoing care to families in need. The charitable organisation said it would itself feel honoured if the reward of a knighthood should be given to one of its most stalwart pillars: to the man they had unanimously chosen to be their next chairman, the appointment to be effective from 1 December of that year.

The letter had been signed by no fewer than four of the charity's officers: the retiring chairman, the head of the board of management, and two of the senior patrons. It was the fourth of these signatures which had me lifting my head in astonishment.

'Well?' Eric Olderjohn asked, watching.

'That's odd,' I said blankly.

'Yes, curious, I agree.'

He held out his hand for the letters, took them from me, snapped them safely back into his case. I sat with thoughts tumbling over themselves and unquestioned assumptions melting like wax.

Was it true, I had wanted to know, if Maynard Allardeck was being considered for a knighthood, and if so, who knew?

The people who had proposed him; they knew.

The letter from the charity, dated 1 October, had been signed by Lord Vaughnley.

SIXTEEN

'Why,' I said, 'did your certain person allow you to show these letters to me?'

'Ah.' Eric Olderjohn joined his fingers together in a steeple and studied them for a while. 'Why do you think?'

'I would suppose,' I said, 'he might think it possible I would stir up a few ponds, get a few muddy answers, without him having to do it himself.'

Eric Olderjohn switched his attention from his hands to my face. 'Something like that,' he said. 'He would like to know for sure Maynard Allardeck isn't just the victim of a hate campaign, for instance. He wants to do him justice. To put him back on the list, perhaps, for a knighthood next time around, in the summer.'

'He wants proof?' I asked.

'Can you supply it?'

'Yes, I think so.'

'What are you planning to do,' he asked with dry humour, 'when you have to give up race-riding?'

'Jump off a cliff, I dare say.'

I stood up, and he also. I thanked him sincerely for the trouble he'd taken. He said he would expect me to win again on his horse next time out. Do my best, I said, and took a last appreciative glance round his bower of a sitting room before making my way back to the hotel.

Lord Vaughnley, I thought.

On 1 October he had recommended Maynard for a knighthood. By the end of that month or the beginning of November there had been a tap on Bobby's telephone.

The tap had been installed by Jay Erskine, who had listened for two weeks and then written the articles in the *Flag*.

Jay Erskine had once worked for Lord Vaughnley, as crime reporter on the *Towncrier*.

But if Lord Vaughnley had got Jay Erskine to attack Maynard Allardeck, why was Nestor Pollgate so aggressive?

Because he didn't want to have to pay compensation, or to admit his paper had done wrong.

Well . . . perhaps.

I went round in circles and came back always to the central and unexpected question: Was it really Lord Vaughnley who had prompted the attacks, and if so, why?

From my hotel room I telephoned Rose Quince's home, catching her again soon after she had come in.

'Bill?' she said. 'Civil Service charity? Oh, sure, he's a patron of dozens of things. All sorts. Keeps him in touch, he says.'

'Mm,' I said. 'When you wrote that piece about Maynard Allardeck, did he suggest it?'

'Who? Bill? Yes, sure he did. He put the clippings from the *Flag* on my desk and said it looked my sort of thing. I may know him from way back, but he's still the ultimate boss. When he wants something written, it gets written. Martin, our big white chief, always agrees to that.'

'And, er, how did you get on to the *How's Trade* interview? I mean, did you see the programme when it was broadcast?'

'Do me a favour. Of course not.' She paused. 'Bill suggested I try the television company, to ask for a private re-run.'

'Which you did.'

'Yes, of course. Look,' she demanded, 'what's all this about? Bill often suggests subjects to me. There's nothing strange in it.'

'No,' I said. 'Sleep well, Rose.'

'And goodnight to you, too.'

I slept soundly and long, and early in the morning took the video camera and drove to Purfleet along the flat lands just north of the Thames estuary. The rains of the day before had drawn away, leaving the sky washed and pale, and there were seagulls wheeling high over the low-tide mud.

I asked in about twenty places, post office and shops, before I found anyone who had heard of Purfleet Electronics, but was finally pointed towards someone who had worked there. 'You want George Tarker . . . he owned it,' he said.

Following a few further instructions from helpful locals, I eventually pulled up beside a shabby old wooden boatshed optimistically emblazoned with a sign-board saying 'George Tarker Repairs All'.

Out of the car and walking across the pot-holed entrance yard to the door one could see that the sign had once had a bottom half, which had split off and was lying propped against the wall, and which read 'Boats and Marine Equipment'.

With a sinking feeling of having come entirely to the wrong place I pushed open the rickety door and stepped straight into the untidiest office in the world, a place where every surface and every shelf was covered with unidentifiable lumps of ships' hardware in advanced age, and where every patch of wall was occupied by ancient calendars, posters, bills and instructions, all attached not by drawing pins but by nails.

In a sagging old chair, oblivious to the mess, sat an elderly grey-bearded man with his feet up on a desk, reading a newspaper and drinking from a cup.

'Mr Tarker?' I said.

'That's me.' He lowered the paper, looking at me critically from over the soles of his shoes. 'What do you want repaired?' He looked towards the bag I was carrying, which contained the camera. 'A bit off a boat?'

'I'm afraid I've come to the wrong place,' I said. 'I was looking for Mr George Tarker who used to own Purfleet Electronics.'

He put his cup down carefully on the desk, and his feet on the floor. He was old, I saw, from an inner weariness as much as from age: it lay in the sag of his shoulders and the droop of his eyes and shouted from the disarray of everything around him.

'That George Tarker was my son,' he said.

Was.

'I'm sorry,' I said.

'Do you want anything repaired, or don't you?'

'No,' I said. 'I want to talk about Maynard Allardeck.'

The cheeks fell inwards into shadowed hollows and the eyes seemed to recede darkly into the sockets. He had scattered grey hair, uncombed, and below the short beard, in the thin neck inside the unbuttoned and tieless shirt, the tendons tightened and began to quiver.

'I don't want to distress you,' I said: but I had. 'I'm making a film about the damage Maynard Allardeck has done to many people's lives. I hoped you . . . I hoped your son . . . might help me.' I gestured vaguely with one hand. 'I know it wouldn't sway you one way or another, but I'm offering a fee.'

He was silent, staring at my face but seeing, I thought, another scene altogether, looking back into memory and finding it almost past bearing. The strain in his face deepened to the point when I did actively regret having come.

'Will it destroy him, your film?' he said huskily.

'In some ways, yes.'

'He deserves hellfire and damnation.'

I took the video camera out of its bag and showed it to him, explaining about talking straight at the lens.

'Will you tell me what happened to your son?' I asked.

'Yes, I will.'

I balanced the camera on a heap of junk and started it running; and with few direct questions from me he repeated in essence the familiar story. Maynard had come smiling to the rescue in a temporary cash crisis caused by a rapid expansion of the business. He had lent at low rates, but at the last and worst moment demanded to be repaid; had taken over the firm and ousted George Tarker, and after a while had stripped the assets, sold the freehold and put the workforce on the dole.

'Charming,' George Tarker said. 'That's what he was. Like a con man, right to the end. Reasonable. Friendly. Then he was gone, and everything with him. My son's business, gone. He started it when he was only eighteen and worked and worked . . . and after twenty-three years it was growing too fast.'

The gaunt face stared starkly into the lens, and water stood in the corner of each eye.

'My son George . . . my only child . . . he blamed himself for everything . . . for all his workers losing their jobs. He began to drink. He knew such a lot about electricity.' The tears spilled over the lower eyelids and rolled down the lined cheeks to be lost in the beard. 'My son wired himself up . . . and hit the switch . . .'

211

The voice stopped as if with the jolt that had stopped his son's heart. I found it unbearable. I wished with an intensity of pity that I hadn't come. I turned off the camera and stood there in silence, not knowing how to apologise for such an intrusion.

He brushed the tears away with the back of his hand. 'Two years ago, just over,' he said. 'He was a good man, you know, my son George. That Allardeck . . . just destroyed him.'

I offered him the same amount that I'd given the Perrysides, setting it down in front of him on the desk. He stared at the flat bunch of banknotes for a while, and then pushed it towards me.

'I didn't tell you for money,' he said. 'You take it back. I told you for George.'

I hesitated.

'Go on,' he said. 'I don't want it. Doesn't feel right. Any time you have a boat, you pay me then for repairs.'

'All right,' I said.

He nodded and watched while I picked up the notes.

'You make your film good,' he said. 'Make it for George.'

'Yes,' I said; and he was still sitting there, staring with pain into the past, when I left.

I went to Ascot with the same precautions as before, leaving the Mercedes down in the town and walking into the race-course from the opposite direction to the jockeys' official car park. No one that I could see took any notice of my arrival, beyond the gatemen with their usual good mornings.

I had rides in the first five of the six races; two for the princess, two others for Wykeham, one for the Lambourn trainer. Dusty reported Wykeham to have a crippling migraine headache which would keep him at home watching on television. Icefall, Dusty said, should zoom in, and all the lads had staked their wages. Dusty's manner to me was as usual a mixture of deference and truculence, a double attitude I had long ago sorted into components: I might do the actual winning for the stable, but the fitness of the horses was the gift of the lads in the yard, and I wasn't to forget it. Dusty and I had worked together for ten years in a truce founded on mutual need, active friendship being neither sought nor necessary. He said the guv'nor wanted me to give the princess and the other owners his regrets about his headache. I'd tell them, I said.

I rode one of Wykeham's horses in the first race with negligible results, and came third in the second race, for the Lambourn trainer. The third race was Icefall for the princess, and she and Danielle were both waiting in the parade ring, rosily lunched and sparkling-eyed, when I went out there to greet them.

'Wykeham sends his regrets,' I said.

'The poor man.' The princess believed in the migraines as little as I did, but was willing to pretend. 'Will we give him a win to console him?'

'I'm afraid he expects it.'

We watched Icefall walk round, grey and well muscled under his coroneted rug, more compact than his full brother Icicle.

'I schooled him last week,' I said. 'Wykeham says he's come on a ton since then. So there's hope.'

'Hope!' Danielle said. 'He's hot favourite.'

'Odds on,' nodded the princess. 'It never makes one feel better.'

She and I exchanged glances of acknowledgement of the extra pressure that came with too much expectation, and when I went off to mount she said only, 'Get round safely, that's all.'

Icefall at six was at the top of his hurdling form with a string of successes behind him, and his race on that day was a much publicised, much sponsored two-mile event which had cut up, as big-prize races tended occasionally to do, into no more than six runners: Icefall at the top of the handicap, the other five at the bottom, the centre block having decided to duck out for less taxing contests.

Icefall was an easy horse to ride, as willing as his brother and naturally courageous, and the only foreseeable problem was the amount of weight he carried in relation to the others: twenty pounds and more. Wykeham never liked his horses to be front runners and had tried to dissuade me sometimes from running Icefall in that way; but the horse positively preferred it and let me know it at every start, and even with the weights so much against us, when the tapes went up we were there where he wanted to be, setting the pace.

I'd learned in my teens from an American flat-race jockey how to start a clock in my head, to judge the speed of each section of the race against the clock, and to judge how fast I could go in each section in order to finish at or near the horse's own best time for the distance.

Icefall's best time for two miles at Ascot at almost the same weights on the same sort of wet ground was three minutes forty-eight seconds, and I set out to take him to the finish line in precisely that period, and at a more or less even speed the whole way.

It seemed to the crowd on the stands, I was told afterwards, that I'd set off too fast, that some of the lightweights would definitely catch me; but I'd looked up their times also in the form book, and none of them had ever completed two miles as fast as I aimed to.

All Icefall had to do was jump with perfection, and that he did, informing me of his joy in mid-air at every hurdle. The lightweights never came near us, and we finished ahead, without slackening, by eight lengths, a margin that would do Icefall's handicap no good at all next time out.

Maybe, I thought, pulling up and patting the grey neck hugely, it would have been better for the future not to have won by so far, but the present was what mattered, and with those weights one couldn't take risks.

The princess was flushed and laughing and delighted, and as usual intensified my own pleasure in winning. Victories for glum and grumbling owners were never so sweet.

'My friends say it's sacrilege,' she said, 'for a top-weight to set off so fast and try to make all the running after rain like yesterday's. They were pitying me up in the box, telling me you were mad.'

I smiled at her, unbuckling my saddle. 'When he jumps like today, he can run this course even on wet gound in three minutes forty-eight seconds. That's what we did, more or less.'

Her eyes widened. 'You planned it! You didn't tell me. I didn't expect you to go off so fast, even though he likes it in front.'

214

'If he'd made a hash of any of the hurdles, I'd have looked a right idiot.' I patted the grey neck over and over. 'He understands racing,' I said. 'He's a great horse to ride. Very generous. He enjoys it.'

'You talk as if horses were people,' Danielle said, standing behind her aunt, listening.

'Yes, they are,' I said. 'Not human, but individuals, all different.'

I took the saddle in and sat on the scales, and changed into other colours and weighed out again for the next race. Then put the princess's colours back on, on top of the others, and went out bareheaded for the sponsors' presentations.

Lord Vaughnley was among the crowd round the sponsors' table of prizes, and he came straight over to me when I went out.

'My dear chap, what a race! I thought you'd gone off your rocker, I'm sorry to say. Now, you are coming to our box, aren't you? Like we agreed?'

He was a puzzle. His grey eyes smiled blandly in the big face, full of friendliness, empty of guile.

'Yes,' I said. 'Thank you. After the fifth race, when I'll have finished for the day, if that's all right?'

Lady Vaughnley appeared at his elbow, reinforcing the invitation. 'Delighted to have you. Do come.'

The princess, overhearing, said, 'Come along to me after,' taking my compliance for granted, not expecting an answer. 'Did you know,' she said with humour, 'the time Icefall took?'

'No, not yet.'

'Three minutes forty-nine seconds.'

'We were one second late.'

'Yes, indeed. Next time, go faster.'

Lady Vaughnley looked at her in astonishment. 'How can you say that?' she protested, and then understood it was merely a joke. 'Oh. For a moment . . .'

The princess patted her arm consolingly, and I watched Danielle, on the far side of the green-baized pot-laden table, talking to the sponsors as to the winning habit born. She turned her head and looked straight at me, and I felt the tingle of that visual connection run right down my spine. She's beautiful, I thought. I want her in bed.

It seemed that she had broken off in the middle of whatever she was saying. The sponsor spoke to her enquiringly. She looked at him blankly, and then with another glance at me seemed to sort out her thoughts and answer whatever he'd asked.

I looked down at the trophies, afraid that my feelings were naked. I had two races and a lot of box-talk to get through before we could be in any real way together, and the memory of her kisses was no help.

The presentations were made, the princess and the others melted away, and I pealed off the princess's colours and went out and rode another winner for Wykeham, scrambling home that time by a neck, all elbows, no elegance, practically throwing the horse ahead of himself, hard on him, squeezing him, making him stretch beyond where he thought he could go.

'Bloody hell,' said his owner, in the winners' unsaddling area. 'Bloody hell, I'd not like you on my back.' He seemed pleased enough all the same, a Sussex farmer, big and forthright, surrounded by chattering friends. 'You're a bloody demon, lad, that's what you are. Hard as bloody nails. He'll know he's had a race, I'll tell you.'

'Yes, well, Mr Davis, he can take it, he's tough, he'd not thank you to be soft. Like his owner, wouldn't you say, Mr Davis?'

He gave a great guffaw and clapped me largely on the shoulder, and I went and weighed in, and changed into the princess's colours again for the fifth race.

The princess's runner, Allegheny, was the second of her only two mares (Bernina being the other), as the princess, perhaps because of her own femininity, had a definite preference for male horses. Not as temperamental as Bernina, Allegheny was a friendly old pudding, running moderately well always but without fire. I'd tried to get Wykeham to persuade the princess to sell her but he wouldn't: Princess Casilia, he said, knew her own mind.

Allegheny's seconds, thirds, fourths, fifths, sixths, also-rans never seemed to disappoint her. It wasn't essential to her, he said, for all her children to be stars.

Allegheny and I set off amicably but as usual my attempts

216

to jolly her into *joie de vivre* got little response. We turned into the straight for the first time lying fourth, going easily, approaching a plain fence, meeting it right, launching into the air, landing, accelerating away . . .

In one of her hind legs a suspensory ligament tore apart at the fetlock, and Allegheny went lame in three strides, all rhythm gone; like driving a car on a suddenly flat tyre. I pulled her up and jumped off her back, and walked her a few paces to make sure she hadn't broken a bone.

Just the tendon, I thought in relief. Bad enough, but not a death sentence. Losing a horse to the bolt of a humane killer upset everyone for days. Wykeham had wept sometimes for dead horses, and I also, and the princess. One couldn't help it, sometimes.

The vet sped round in his car, looked her over and pronounced her fit to walk, so I led her back up the course, her head nodding every time she put the injured foot to the ground. The princess and Danielle came down anxiously to the unsaddling area and Dusty assured them the guv'nor would get a vet to Allegheny as soon as soon.

'What do you think?' the princess asked me in depression, as Dusty and the mare's lad led her, nodding, away.

'I don't know.'

'Yes, you do. Tell me.'

The princess's eyes were deep blue. I said, 'She'll be a year off the racecourse, at least.'

She sighed. 'Yes, I suppose so.'

'You could patch her up,' I said, 'and sell her as a brood mare. She's got good blood lines. She could breed in the spring.'

'Oh!' She seemed pleased. 'I'm fond of her, you know.'

'Yes, I know.'

'I do begin to see,' Danielle said, 'what racing is all about.'

My neighbour and the Lambourn fellow jockey having come up trumps in the matter of a suitcase of clothes, I went up to Lord Vaughnley's box in a change for the better. I appeared to have chosen, though, the doldrums of time between events when everyone had gone down to look at the horses or to bet, and not yet returned to watch the race.

There was only one person in there, standing nervously beside the table now laid for tea, shifting from foot to foot: and I was surprised to see it was Hugh Vaughnley, Lord Vaughnley's son.

'Hello,' I said. 'No one's here . . . I'll come back.'

'Don't go.'

His voice was urgent. I looked at him curiously, thinking of the family row which had so clearly been in operation on the previous Saturday, seeing only trouble still in the usually cheerful face. Much thinner than his father, more like his mother in build, he had neat features well placed, two disarming dimples, and youth still in the indecision of his mouth. Around nineteen, I thought. Maybe twenty. Not more.

'I . . . er . . .' he said. 'Do stay. I want someone here, to be honest, when they come back.'

'Do you?'

'Er . . .' he said. 'They don't know I'm here. I mean . . . Dad might be furious, and he can't be, can he, in front of strangers? That's why I came here, to the races. I mean, I know you're not a stranger, but you know what I mean.'

'Your mother will surely be glad to see you.'

He swallowed. 'I hate quarrelling with them. I can't bear it. To be honest, Dad threw me out almost a month ago. He's making me live with Saul Bradley, and I can't bear it much longer, I want to go home.'

'He threw you out?' I must have sounded as surprised as I felt. 'You always seemed such a solid family. Does he think you should stand on your own two feet? Something like that?'

'Nothing like that. I just wish it was. I did something . . . I didn't know he'd be so desperately angry . . . not really . . .'

I didn't want to hear what it was, with so much else on my mind.

'Drugs?' I said, without sympathy.

'What?'

'Did you take drugs?'

I saw from his face that it hadn't been that. He was simply bewildered by the suggestion.

'I mean,' he said plaintively, 'he thought so much of him. He said so. I mean, I thought he approved of him.'

'Who?' I said.

He looked over my shoulder however and didn't answer, a fresh wave of anxiety blotting out all else.

I turned. Lord and Lady Vaughnley had come through the door from the passage and were advancing towards us. I saw their expressions with clarity when they caught sight of their son. Lady Vaughnley's face lifted into a spontaneous uncomplicated smile.

Lord Vaughnley looked from his son to myself, and his reaction wasn't forgiveness, apathy, irritation or even anger.

It was alarm. It was horror.

SEVENTEEN

He recovered fast to some extent. Lady Vaughnley put her arms around Hugh and hugged him, and her husband looked on, stony-faced and displeased. Others of their guests came in good spirits back to the box, and Hugh was proved right to the extent that his father was not ready to fight with him in public.

Lord Vaughnley, in fact, addressed himself solely to me, fussing about cups of tea and making sure I talked no more to his son, seemingly unaware that his instant reaction and his current manner were telling me a good deal more than he probably meant.

'There we are,' he said heartily, getting a waitress to pass me a cup. 'Milk? Sugar? No? Princess Casilia's mare is all right, isn't she? So sad when a horse breaks down in a race. Sandwich?'

I said the mare wouldn't race again, and no thanks to the sandwich.

'Hugh been bothering you with his troubles, has he?' he said.

'Not really.'

'What did he say?'

I glanced at the grey eyes from where the blandness had flown and watchfulness taken over.

'He said he had quarrelled with you and wanted to make it up.'

'Hmph.' An unforgiving noise from a compressed mouth. 'As long as he didn't bother you?'

'No.'

'Good. Good. Then you'll be wanting to talk to Princess Casilia, eh? Let me take your cup. Good of you to come up. Yes. Off you go, then. Can't keep her waiting.'

Short of rudeness I couldn't have stayed, and rudeness at that point, I thought, would accomplish no good that I could think of. I went obediently along to the princess's well-populated box and drank more tea and averted my stomach from another sandwich, and tried not to look too much at Danielle.

'You're abstracted,' the princess said. 'You are not here.'

'I was thinking of Lord Vaughnley . . . I just came from his box.'

'Such a nice man.'

'Mm.'

'And for Danielle, this evening, what are your plans?'

I shut out the thoughts of what I would like. If I could read the princess's mind, she could also on occasion read mine.

'I expect we'll talk, and eat, and I'll bring her home.'

She patted my arm. She set me to talk to her guests, most of whom I knew, and I worked my way round to Danielle scattering politeness like confetti.

'Hi,' she said. 'Am I going back with Aunt Casilia, or what?'

'Coming with me from here, if you will.'

'OK.'

We went out on to the balcony with everyone else to watch the sixth race, and afterwards said goodbye correctly to the princess and left.

'Where are we going?' Danielle asked.

'For a walk, for a drink, for dinner. First of all we're walking to Ascot town, where I left the car, so as not to be carved up again in the car park.'

'You're too much,' she said.

I collected my suitcase from the changing room and we walked down through the cheaper enclosures to the furthest gate, and from there again safely to the rented Mercedes.

'I guess I never gave a thought to it happening again,' she said.

'And next time there would be no princess to the rescue.'

'Do you seriously think they'd be lying in wait?'

'I still have what they wanted.' And I'd twisted their tail

fiercely, besides. 'I just go where they don't know I'm going, and hope.'

'Yes, but,' she said faintly, 'for how long?'

'Um,' I said, 'I suppose Joe doesn't work on Sundays?'

'No. Not till Monday night, like me. Not week-ends. What's that got to do with how long?'

'Tuesday or Wednesday,' I said.

'You're not making much sense.'

'It's because I don't know for sure.' We got into the car and I started the engine. 'I feel like a juggler. Half a dozen clubs in the air and all likely to fall in a heap.'

'With you underneath?'

'Not,' I said, 'if I can help it.'

I drove not very fast to Henley, and stopped near a telephone box to try to reach Rose Quince, who was out. She had an answering machine which invited me to give a number for her to call back. I would try later, I said.

Henley-on-Thames was bright with lights and late Saturday afternoon shopping. Danielle and I left the car in a parking place and walked slowly along in the bustle.

'Where are we going?' she asked.

'To buy you a present.'

'What present?'

'Anything you'd like.'

She stopped walking. 'Are you crazy?'

'No.' We were outside a shop selling sports goods. 'Tennis racket?'

'I don't play tennis.'

I waved at the next shop along. 'Piano?'

'I can't play a piano.'

'Over there,' I pointed at a flower shop. 'Orchids?'

'In their place, but not to pin on me.'

'And over there, an antique chair?'

She laughed, her eyes crinkling. 'Tell me, too, what you like, and what you don't.'

'All right.'

We walked along the shopfronts, looking and telling. She liked blues and pinks but not yellow, she liked things with flowers and birds on, not geometric patterns, she liked baskets and nylon-tipped pens and aquamarines and seedless grapes

222

and books about Leonardo da Vinci. She would choose for me, she said, something simple. If I were giving her a present, I would have to have one as well.

'OK,' I said. 'Twenty minutes. Meet me back at the car. Here's the key, in case you get there first.'

'And not expensive,' she said, 'or I'm not playing.'

'All right.'

When I returned with my parcel she was sitting in the car already, and smiling.

'You've been half an hour,' she said. 'You're disqualified.'

'Too bad.'

I climbed into the car beside her and we sat looking at each other's packages, mine to her in brown paper, hers to me flatter, in a carrier bag.

'Guess,' she said.

I tried to, and nothing came. I said with regret, 'I don't know.'

She eyed the brown-wrapped parcel in my hands. 'Three books? Three pounds of chocolates? A jack-in-a-box?'

'All wrong.'

We exchanged the presents and began to unwrap them. 'More fun than Christmas,' she said. 'Oh. How odd. I'd forgotten it was your name.' She paused very briefly for thought and said it the other way round. 'Christmas is more fun.'

It sounded all right in American. I opened the paper carrier she'd given me and found that our walk along the street had taught her a good deal about me, too. I drew out a soft brown leather zipped-around case which looked as if it would hold a pad of writing paper and a few envelopes: and it had KIT stamped in gold on the top.

'Go on, open it,' she said. 'I couldn't resist it. And you like neat small things, the way I do.'

I unzipped the case, opened it flat, and smiled with pure pleasure. It contained on one side a tool-kit and on the other pens, a pocket calculator and a notepad; all in slots, all of top quality, solidly made.

'You do like it,' she said with satisfaction. 'I thought you would. It had your name on it, literally.'

She finished taking off the brown paper and showed me

that I had pleased her also, and as much. I'd given her a baby antique chest of drawers which smelled faintly of polish, had little brass handles, and ran smoothly as silk. Neat, small, well-crafted, useful, good-looking, efficient: like the kit.

She looked long at the implications of the presents, and then at my face.

'That,' she said slowly, 'really is amazing, that we should both get it right.'

'Yes, it is.'

'And you broke the rules. That chest's not cheap.'

'So did you. Nor's the kit.'

'God bless credit cards.'

I kissed her, the same way as before, the gifts still on our laps. 'Thank you for mine.'

'Thank you for mine.'

'Well,' I said, reaching over to put my tool-kit on the back seat. 'By the time we get there, the pub might be open.'

'What pub?'

'Where we're going.'

'Anyone who wants to know what you're not about to tell them,' she said, 'has a darned sticky time.'

I drove in contentment to the French Horn at Sonning, where the food was legendary and floodlights shone on willow trees drooping over the Thames. We went inside and sat on a sofa, and watched ducks roast on a spit over an open fire, and drank champagne. I stretched and breathed deeply, and felt the tensions of the long week relax: and I'd got to phone Rose Quince.

I went and phoned her. Answering machine again. I said, 'Rose, Rose, I love you. Rose, I need you. If you come home before eleven, please, I beg you, ring me at the French Horn Hotel, the number is 0734 692204, tell them I'm in the restaurant having dinner.'

I telephoned Wykeham. 'Is the headache better?' I said.

'What?'

'Never mind. How's the mare?'

The mare was sore but eating, Mr Davis's horse was exhausted, Inchcape hardly looked as if he'd had a race.

'Icefall,' I said.

'What? I wish you wouldn't ride him from so far in front.'

'He liked it. And it worked.'

'I was watching on TV. Can you come and school on Tuesday? We have no runners that day, I'm not sending any to Southwell.'

'Yes, all right.'

'Well done, today,' he said with sincerity. 'Very well done.'

'Thanks.'

'Yes. Er. Goodnight then, Paul.'

'Goodnight, Wykeham,' I said.

I went back to Danielle and we spent the whole evening talking and later eating in the restaurant with silver and candlelight gleaming on the tables and a living vine growing over the ceiling; and at the last minute Rose Quince called me back.

'It's after eleven,' she said, 'but I just took a chance.'

'You're a dear.'

'I sure am. So what is so urgent, buddy boy?'

'Um,' I said. 'Does the name Saul Bradfield or Saul Bradley ... something like that ... mean anything to you?'

'Saul Bradley? Of course it does. What's so urgent about him?'

'Who is he?'

'He used to be the sports editor of the *Towncrier*. He retired last year ... everyone's universal father-figure, an old friend of Bill's.'

'Do you know where he lives?'

'Good heavens. Wait while I think. Why do you want him?'

'In the general area of demolishing our business friend of the tapes.'

'Oh. Well, let's see. He moved. He said he was taking his wife to live by the sea. I'd've thought it would drive him mad but no accounting for taste. Worthing, or somewhere. No. Selsey.' Her voice strengthened. 'I remember, Selsey, in Sussex.'

'Terrific,' I said. 'And Lord Vaughnley. Where does he live?'

'Mostly in Regent's Park, in one of the Nash terraces. They've a place in Kent too, near Sevenoaks.'

'Could you tell me exactly?' I said. 'I mean ... I'd like to

225

write to thank him for my Towncrier trophy, and for all his other help.'

'Sure,' she said easily, and told me both his addresses right down to the postal codes, tacking on the telephone numbers for good measure. 'You might need those. They're not in the directory.'

'I'm back in your debt,' I said, writing it all down.

'Deep, deep, buddy boy.'

I replaced the receiver feeling perfidious but unrepentant, and went to fetch Danielle to drive her home. It was midnight, more or less, when I pulled up in Eaton Square: and it wasn't where I would have preferred to have taken her, but where it was best.

'Thank you,' she said, 'for a great day.'

'What about tomorrow?'

'OK.'

'I don't know what time,' I said. 'I've something to do first.'

'Call me.'

'Yes.'

We sat in the car looking at each other, as if we hadn't been doing that already for hours. I've known her since Tuesday, I thought. In five days she'd grown roots in my life. I kissed her with much more hunger than before, which didn't seem to worry her, and I thought not long, not long . . . but not yet. When it was right, not before.

We said goodnight again on the pavement, and I watched her go into the house, carrying her present and waving as she closed the door. Princess Casilia, I thought, you are severely inhibiting, but I said I'd bring your niece home, and I have; and I don't even know what Danielle wanted, I can't read her mind and she didn't tell me in words, and tomorrow . . . tomorrow maybe I'd ask.

Early in the morning I drove to Selsey on the South Coast and looked up Saul Bradley in the local telephone book, and there he was, address and all, 15 Sea View Lane.

His house was on two floors and looked more suburban than seaside with mock-Tudor beams in its cream plastered gables. The mock-Tudor door, when I rang the bell, was opened by a grey-haired bespectacled motherly looking person in a flowered overall, and I could smell bacon frying.

'Hugh?' she said in reply to my question. 'Yes, he's still here, but he's still in bed. You know what boys are.'

'I'll wait,' I said.

She looked doubtful.

'I do very much want to see him,' I said.

'You'd better come in,' she said. 'I'll ask my husband. I think he's shaving, but he'll be down soon.'

She led me across the entrance hall into a smallish kitchen, all yellow and white tiles, with sunlight flooding in.

'A friend of Hugh's?' she said.

'Yes . . . I was talking to him yesterday.'

She shook her head worriedly. 'It's all most upsetting. He shouldn't have gone to the races. He was more miserable than ever when he came back.'

'I'll do my best,' I said, 'to make things better.'

She attended to the breakfast she was frying, pushing the bacon round with a spatula. 'Did you say Fielding, your name was?' She turned from the cooker, the spatula in the air, motion arrested. 'Kit Fielding? The jockey?'

'Yes.'

She didn't know what to make of it, which wasn't surprising. She said uncertainly, 'I'm brewing some tea', and I said I'd wait until after I'd seen her husband and Hugh.

Her husband came enquiringly into the kitchen, hearing my voice, and he knew me immediately by sight. A sports editor would, I supposed. Bunty Ireland's ex-boss was comfortably large with a bald head and shrewd eyes and a voice grown fruity, as from beer.

My presence nonplussed him, as it had his wife.

'You want to help Hugh? I suppose it's all right. Bill Vaughnley was speaking highly of you a few days ago. I'll go and get Hugh up. He's not good in the mornings. Want some breakfast?'

I hesitated.

'Like that, is it?' He chuckled. 'Starving and daren't put on an ounce.'

He went away into the house and presently returned, followed shortly by Hugh, tousle-haired, in jeans and a T-shirt, his eyes puffed from sleep

227

'Hello,' he said, bewildered. 'How did you find me?'

'You told me where you were staying.'

'Did I? I suppose I did. Er . . . sorry and all that, but what do you want?'

I wanted, I said, to take him out for a drive, to talk things over and see what could be done to help him: and with no more persuasion, he came.

He didn't seem to realise that his father had made sure he didn't speak to me further on the previous day. It had been done too skilfully for him to notice, especially in the anxiety he'd been suffering.

'Your father made you come back here,' I said, as we drove along Sea View Lane. 'Wouldn't let you go home?'

'It's so unfair.' There was self-pity in his voice, and also acceptance. The exile had been earned, I thought, and Hugh knew it.

'Tell me, then,' I said.

'Well, you know him. He's your father-in-law. I mean, no, he's your sister's father-in-law.'

I breathed deeply. 'Maynard Allardeck.'

'Yes. He caused it all. I'd kill him, if I could.'

I glanced at the good-looking immature face, at the dimples. Even the word kill came oddly from that mouth.

'I mean,' he said in an aggrieved voice, 'he's a member of the Jockey Club. Respected. I thought it was all right. I mean, he and Dad are patrons of the same charity. How was I to know? How was I?'

'You weren't,' I said. 'What happened?'

'He introduced me to his bookmaker.'

Whatever I'd imagined he might say, it wasn't that. I rolled the car to a halt in a parking place which at that time on a Sunday November morning was deserted. There was a distant glimpse of shingle banks and scrubby grass and sea glittering in the early sun, and nearby there was little but an acre of tarmac edged by a low brick wall, and a summer ice-cream stall firmly shut.

'I've got a video camera,' I said. 'If you'd care to speak into that, I'll show the tape to your father, get him to hear your side of things, see if I can persuade him to let you go home.'

'Would you?' he said, hopefully.

'Yes, I would.'

I stretched behind my seat for the bag with the camera. 'Let's sit on the wall,' I said. 'It might be a bit chilly, but we'd get a better picture than inside the car.'

He made no objection, but came and sat on the wall, where I steadied the camera on one knee bent up, framed his face in the viewfinder and asked him to speak straight at the lens.

'Say that again,' I prompted, 'about the bookmaker.'

'I was at the races with my parents one day and having a bet, and a bookmaker was saying I wasn't old enough and making a fuss, and Maynard Allardeck was there and he said not to worry, he would introduce me to his own bookmaker instead.'

'How do you mean, he was there?'

Hugh's brow furrowed. 'He was just standing there. I mean, I didn't know who he was, but he explained he was a friend of my father.'

'And how old were you, and when did this happen?'

'That's what's so silly. I was twenty. I mean, you can bet on your eighteenth birthday. Do I look seventeen?'

'No,' I said truthfully. 'You look twenty.'

'I was twenty-one, actually, in August. It was right back in April when I met Maynard Allardeck.'

'So you started betting with Maynard Allardeck's book-maker . . . regularly?'

'Well, yes,' Hugh said unhappily. 'He made it so easy, always so friendly, and he never seemed to worry when I didn't pay his accounts.'

'There isn't a bookmaker born who doesn't insist on his money.'

'This one didn't,' Hugh said defensively. 'I used to apologise. He'd say never mind, one day, I know you'll pay when you can, and he used to joke . . . and let me bet again . . .'

'He let you bet until you were very deeply in debt?'

'Yes. Encouraged me. I mean, I suppose I should have known . . . but he was so friendly, you see. All the summer . . . Flat racing, every day . . . on the telephone.'

'Until all this happened,' I said, 'did you bet much?'

'I've always liked betting. Studying the form. Picking the good things, following hunches. Never any good, I suppose, but probably any money I ever had went on horses. I'd get someone to put it on for me, on the Tote, when I was ten, and so on. Always. I mean, I won often too, of course. Terrific wins, quite often.'

'Mm.'

'Everyone who goes racing bets,' he said. 'What else do they go for? I mean, there's nothing wrong with a gamble, everyone does it. It's fun.'

'Mm,' I said again. 'But you were betting every day, several bets a day, even though you didn't go.'

'I suppose so, yes.'

'And then one day,' I said, 'it stopped being fun?'

'The Hove Stakes at Brighton,' he said. 'In September.'

'What about it?'

'Three runners. Slateroof couldn't be beaten. Maynard Allardeck told me. Help yourself, he said. Recoup your losses.'

'When did he tell you?'

'Few days before. At the races. Ascot. I went with my parents, and he happened to be there too.'

'And did you go to Brighton?'

'No.' He shook his head. 'Rang up the bookmaker. He said he couldn't give me a good price, Slateroof was a certainty, everyone knew it. Five to one on, he said. If I bet twenty, I could win four.'

'So you bet twenty pounds?'

'No.' Hugh looked surprised. 'Twenty thousand.'

'Twenty ... thousand.' I kept my voice steady, unemotional. 'Was that, er, a big bet, for you, by that time?'

'Biggish. I mean, you can't win much in fivers, can you?'

You couldn't lose much either, I thought. I said, 'What was normal?'

'Anything between one thousand and twenty. I mean, I got there gradually, I suppose. I got used to it. Maynard Allardeck said one had to think big. I never thought of how much they really were. They were just numbers.' He paused, looking unhappy. 'I know it sounds stupid to say it now, but none of it seemed real. I mean, I never had to pay anything out. It was all done on paper. When I won, I felt great. When I lost I didn't really worry. I don't suppose you'll understand. Dad didn't. He couldn't understand how I could have been so stupid. But it just seemed like a game ... and everyone smiled ...'

'So Slateroof got beaten?'

'He didn't even start. He got left flat-footed in the stalls.'

'Oh yes,' I said. 'I remember reading about it. There was an enquiry and the jockey got fined.'

'Yes, but the bets stood, of course.'

'So what happened next?' I said.

'I got this frightful account from the bookmaker. He'd totted up everything, he said, and it seemed to be getting out of hand, and he'd like to be paid. I mean, there were pages of it.'

'Records of all the bets you'd made with him?'

'Yes, that's right. Winners and losers. Many more losers. I mean, there were some losers I couldn't remember backing; though he swore I had, he said he would produce his office records to prove it, if I liked, but he said I was ungenerous to make such a suggestion when he'd been so accommodating and patient.' Hugh swallowed. 'I don't know if he cheated me, I just don't. I mean, I did bet on two horses in the same race quite often, I know that, but I didn't realise I'd done it so much.'

'And you'd kept no record, yourself, of how much you'd bet, and what on?'

'I didn't think of it. I mean, I could remember. I mean, I thought I could.'

'Mm. Well, what next?'

'Maynard Allardeck telephoned me at home and said he'd heard from our mutual bookmaker that I was in difficulties, and could he help, as he felt sort of responsible, having introduced me, so to speak. He said we could meet somewhere and perhaps he could suggest some solutions. So I met him for lunch in a restaurant in London, and talked it all over. He said I should confess to my father and get him to pay my debts but I said I couldn't, he would be so angry, he'd no idea I'd gambled so much, he was always lecturing me about taking care of money. And I didn't want to disappoint him, if you can understand that? I didn't want him to be upset. I mean, I expect it sounds silly, but it wasn't really out of fear, it was, well, sort of love, really, only it's difficult to explain.'

231

'Yes,' I said, 'go on.'

'Maynard Allardeck said not to worry, he could see why I couldn't tell my father, it reflected well on me, he said, and he would lend me the money himself, and I could pay him back slowly, and he would just charge me a little over, if I thought that was fair. And I did think it was fair, of course. I was so extremely relieved. I thanked him a lot, over and over.'

'So Maynard Allardeck paid your bookmaker?'

'Yes.' Hugh nodded. 'I got a final account from him marked "Paid with thanks", and a note saying it would be best if I laid off betting for a while, but if I needed him in the future, he would accommodate me again. I mean, I thought it very fair and kind, wouldn't you?'

'Mm,' I said dryly. 'And then after a while Maynard Allardeck told you he was short of money himself and would have to call in the debt?'

'Yes,' Hugh said in surprise. 'How did you know? He was so apologetic and embarrassed I almost felt sorry for him, though he was putting me in a terrible hole. Terrible. And then he suggested a way round it, which was so easy . . . so simple . . . like the sun coming out. I couldn't think why I hadn't thought of it myself.'

'Hugh,' I asked slowly, 'what did you have, that he wanted?'

'My shares in the *Towncrier*,' he said.

EIGHTEEN

He took my breath away. Oh my Christ, I thought. Bloody bingo.

Talk about the sun coming out. So simple, so easy. Why hadn't I thought of it myself.

'Your shares in the *Towncrier* . . .'

'Yes,' Hugh said. 'They were left to me by my grandfather. I mean, I didn't know I had them, until I was twenty-one.'

'In August.'

'Yes. That's right. Anyway, it seemed to solve everything. I mean it did solve everything, didn't it? Maynard Allardeck looked up the proper market value and everything, and gave me two or three forms to sign, which I did, and then he said that was fine, we were all square, I had no more debts. I mean, it was so easy. And it wasn't all of my shares. Not even half.'

'How much were the shares worth, that you gave Allardeck?'

He said as if such figures were commonplace, 'Two hundred and fifty-four thousand pounds.'

After a pause I said, 'Didn't it upset you . . . so much money?'

'Of course not. It was only on paper. And Maynard Allardeck laughed and said if I ever felt like gambling again, well, I had the collateral, and we could always come to the same arrangement again, if it was necessary. I begged him not to tell my father, and he said no, he wouldn't.'

'But your father found out?'

'Yes, it was something to do with voting shares, or preference shares or debentures. I'm really not sure, I didn't know what they were talking about, but they were busy fending off a takeover. They're always fending off takeovers, but this one

233

had them all dead worried, and somewhere in the *Towncrier* they discovered that half of my shares had gone, and Dad made me tell him what I'd done . . . and he was so angry . . . I'd never seen him angry . . . never like that . . .'

His voice faded away, his eyes stark with remembrance.

'He sent me here to Saul Bradley and he said if I ever bet on anything ever again I could never go home . . . I want him . . . I do . . . to forgive me. I want to go home.'

He stopped. The intensity of his feelings stared into the lens. I let the camera run for a few silent seconds, and then turned it off.

'I'll show him the film,' I said.

'Do you think . . .?'

'In time he'll forgive you? Yes, I'd say so.'

'I could go back to just the odd bet in cash on the Tote.' His eyes were speculative, his air much too hopeful. The infection too deep in his system.

'Hugh,' I said, 'would you mind if I gave you some advice?'

'No. Fire away.'

'Take some practical lessons about money. Go away without any, find out it's not just numbers on a page, learn it's the difference between eating and hunger. Bet your dinner, and if you lose, see if it's worth it.'

He said earnestly, 'Yes, I do see what you mean. But I might win.' And I wondered doubtfully whether one could ever reform an irresponsible gambler, be he rich, poor, or the heir to the *Towncrier*.

I drove back to London, added the Hugh Vaughnley tape to the others in the hotel's care, and went upstairs for another session of staring blindly at the walls. Then I telephoned Holly, and got Bobby instead.

'How's things,' I said.

'Not much different. Holly's lying down, do you want to talk to her?'

'You'll do fine.'

'I've had some more cheques from the owners. Almost everyone's paid.'

'That's great.'

234

'They're a drop in the ocean.' His voice sounded tired. 'Will your valet cash them again?'

'Sure to.'

'Even then,' he said, 'we're right at the end.'

'I suppose,' I said, 'you haven't heard any more from the *Flag*? No letter? No money?'

'Not a thing.'

I sighed internally and said, 'Bobby, I want to talk to your father.'

'It won't do any good. You know what he was like the other day. He's stubborn and mean, and he hates us.'

'He hates me,' I said, 'and Holly. Not you.'

'One wouldn't guess it,' he said bitterly.

'I've no rides on Tuesday,' I said. 'Persuade him to come to your house on Tuesday afternoon. I'm schooling at Wykeham's place in the morning.'

'It's impossible. He wouldn't come here.'

'He might,' I said, 'if you tell him he was right all along, every Fielding is your enemy, and you want his help in getting rid of me, out of your life.'

'Kit!' he was outraged. 'I can't do that. It's the last thing I want.'

'And if you can bring yourself to it, tell him you're getting tired of Holly, as well.'

'No. How can I? I love her so much . . . I couldn't make it sound true.'

'Bobby, nothing less will bring him. Can you think of anything else? I've been thinking for hours. If you can get him there some other way, we'll do it your way.'

After a pause he said, 'He would come out of hate. Isn't that awful? He's my father . . .'

'Yes. I'm sorry.'

'What do you want to talk to him about?'

'A proposition. Help for you in return for something he'd want. But don't tell him that. Don't tell him I'm coming. Just get him there, if you can.'

He said doubtfully, 'He'll never help us. Never.'

'Well, we'll see. At least give it a try.'

'Yes, all right, but for heaven's sake, Kit . . .'

'What?'

235

'It's dreadful to say it, but where you're concerned . . . I think he's dangerous.'

'I'll be careful.'

'It goes back so far . . . When I was little he taught me to hit things . . . with my fists, with a stick, anything, and he told me to think I was hitting Kit Fielding.'

I took a breath. 'Like in the garden?'

'God, Kit . . . I've been so sorry.'

'I told you. I mean it. It's all right.'

'I've been thinking about you, and remembering so much. Things I'd forgotten, like him telling me the Fieldings would eat me if I was naughty . . . I must have been three or four. I was scared stiff.'

'When you were four, I was two.'

'It was your father and your grandfather who would eat me. Then when you were growing up he told me to hit Kit Fielding, he taught me how, he said one day it would be you and I, we would have to fight. I'd forgotten all that . . . but I remember it now.'

'My grandfather,' I sighed, 'gave me a punchbag and taught me how to hit it. That's Bobby Allardeck, he said. Bash him.'

'Do you mean it?'

'Ask Holly. She knows.'

'Bloody, weren't they.'

'It's finished now,' I said.

We disconnected and I got through to Danielle and said how about lunch and tea and dinner.

'Are you planning to eat all those?' she said.

'All or any.'

'All, then.'

'I'll come straight round.'

She opened the Eaton Square front door as I braked to a halt and came across the pavement with a spring in her step, an evocation of summer in a flower-patterned jacket over cream trousers, the chintz band holding back the fluffy hair.

She climbed into the car beside me and kissed me as if from old habit.

'Aunt Casilia sends her regards and hopes we'll have a nice day.'

'And back by midnight?'

236

'I would think so, wouldn't you?'

'Does she notice?'

'She sure does. I go past their rooms to get to mine – she and Uncle Roland sleep separately – and the floors creak. She called me in last night to ask if I'd enjoyed myself. She was sitting in bed, reading, looking a knock-out as usual. I told her what we'd done and showed her the chest of drawers . . . we had quite a long talk.'

I studied her face. She looked seriously back.

'What did she say?' I asked.

'It matters to you, doesn't it, what she thinks?'

'Yes.'

'I guess she'd be glad.'

'Tell me, then.'

'Not yet.' She smiled swiftly, almost secretly. 'What about this lunch?'

We went to a restaurant up a tower and ate looking out over half of London. 'Consommé and strawberries . . . you'll be good for my figure,' she said.

'Have some sugar and cream.'

'Not if you don't.'

'You're thin enough,' I said.

'Don't you get tired of it?'

'Of not eating much? I sure do.'

'But you never let up?'

'A pound overweight in the saddle,' I said wryly, 'can mean a length's difference at the winning post.'

'End of discussion.'

Over coffee I asked if there was anywhere she'd like to go, though I apologised that most of London seemed to shut on Sundays, especially in November.

'I'd like to see where you live,' she said. 'I'd like to see Lambourn.'

'Right,' I said, and drove her there, seventy miles westwards down the M4 motorway, heading back towards Devon, keeping this time law-abidingly within the speed limit, curling off into the large village, small town, where the church stood at the main crossroads and a thousand thoroughbreds lived in boxes.

'It's quiet,' she said.

'It's Sunday.'

'Where's your cottage?'

'We'll drive past there,' I said. 'But we're not going in.'

She was puzzled, and, it seemed, disappointed, looking across at me lengthily. 'Why not?'

I explained about the break in, and the police saying the place had been searched. 'The intruders found nothing they wanted, and they stole nothing. But I'd bet they left something behind.'

'What do you mean?'

'Creepy-crawlies.'

'Bugs?'

'Mm,' I said. 'That's it over there.'

We went past slowly. There was no sign of life. No sign of heavy men lying in the bushes with sharp knives, which they wouldn't be by then, not after three days. Too boring, too cold. Listening somewhere, though, those two, or others.

The cottage was brick-built, rather plain, and would perhaps have looked better in June, with the roses.

'It's all right inside,' I said.

'Yuh.' She sounded downcast. 'OK. That's that.'

I drove around and up a hill and took her to the new house instead.

'Whose is this?' she said. 'This is great.'

'This is mine.' I got out of the car, fishing for keys. 'It's empty. Come and look.'

The bright day was fading but there was enough direct sunlight to shine horizontally through the windows and light the big empty rooms, and although the air inside was cold, the central heating, when I switched it on, went into smooth operation with barely a hiccup. There were a few light sockets with bulbs in, but no shades. No curtains. No carpets. Wood-block floor everywhere, swept but not polished. Signs of builders all over the place.

'They're just starting to paint,' I said, opening the double doors from the hall to the sitting room. 'I'll move in alongside, if they don't hurry up.'

There were trestles in the sitting room set up for reaching the ceiling, and an army of tubs of paint, and dustsheets all over the flooring to avoid spatters.

'It's huge,' she said. 'Incredible.'

'It's got a great kitchen. An office. Lots of things.' I explained about the bankrupt builder. 'He designed it for himself.'

We went around and through everywhere and ended in the big room which led directly off the sitting room, the room where I would sleep. It seemed that the decorators had started with that: it was clean, bare and finished, the bathroom painted and tiled, the wood-blocks faintly gleaming with the first layer of polish, the western sun splashing in patches on the white walls.

Danielle stood by the window looking out at the muddy expanse which by summer would be a terrace, with geraniums in pots. The right person . . . in the right place . . . at the right time.

'Will you lie in my bedroom?' I said.

She turned, silhouetted against the sun, her hair like a halo, her face in shadow, hard to read. It seemed that she was listening still to what I'd said, as if to be sure that she had heard right and not misunderstood.

'On the bare floor?' Her voice was steady, uncommitted, friendly and light.

'We could, er, fetch some dustsheets, perhaps.'

She considered it.

'OK,' she said.

We brought a few dustsheets from the sitting room and arranged them in a rough rectangle, with pillows.

'I've seen better marriage beds,' she said.

We took all our clothes off, not hurrying, dropping them in heaps. No real surprises. She was as I had thought, flat and rounded, her skin glowing now in the sun. She stretched out her fingers, touching lightly the stitches, the fading bruises, the known places.

She said, 'When you looked at me at the races yesterday, over those cups, were you thinking of this?'

'Something like this. Was it so obvious?'

'Blinding.'

'I was afraid so.'

We didn't talk a great deal after that. We stood together for a while, and lay down, and on the hard cotton surface

239

learned the ultimate things about each other, pleasing and pleased, with advances and retreats, with murmurs and intensities and breathless primeval energy.

The sunlight faded slowly, the sky lit still with afterglow, gleams reflecting in her eyes and on her teeth, darknesses deepening in hollows and in her hair.

At the end of a long calm afterwards she said prosaically, 'I suppose the water's not hot?'

'Bound to be,' I said lazily. 'It's combined with the heating. Everything's working, lights, plumbing, the lot.'

We got up and went into the bathroom, switching on taps but not lights. It was darker in there and we moved like shadows, more substance than shape.

I turned on the shower, running it warm. Danielle stepped into it with me, and we made love again there in the spray, with tenderness, with passion and in friendship, her arms round my neck, her stomach flat on mine, united as I'd never been before in my life.

I turned off the tap, in the end.

'There aren't any towels,' I said.

'Always the dustsheets.'

We took our bed apart and dried ourselves, and got dressed, and kissed again with temperance, feeling clean. In almost full darkness we dumped the dust sheets in the sitting room, switched off the heating, and went out of the house, locking it behind us.

Danielle looked back before getting into the car. 'I wonder what the house thinks,' she said.

'It thinks holy wow.'

'As a matter of fact, so do I.'

We drove back to London along the old roads, not the motorway, winding through the empty Sunday evening streets of a string of towns, stopping at traffic lights, stretching the journey. I parked the car eventually in central London and we walked for a while, stopping to read menus, and eating eventually in a busy French bistro with red checked tablecloths and an androgynous guitarist; sitting in a corner, holding hands, reading the bill of fare chalked on a blackboard.

'Aunt Casilia,' Danielle said, sometime later over coffee, her eyes shining with amusement, 'said last night, among other things, that while decorum was essential, abstinence was not.'

I laughed in surprise, and kissed her, and in a while and in decorum drove her back to Eaton Square.

I raced at Windsor the next day, parking the car at the railway station and taking a taxi from there right to the jockeys' entrance gate near the weighing room on the racecourse.

The princess had no runners and wasn't expected: I rode two horses each for Wykeham and the Lambourn trainer and got all of them round into the first or second place, which pleased the owners and put grins on the stable-lads. Bunty Ireland, beaming, told me I was on the winning streak of all time, and I calculated the odds that I'd come crashing down again by Thursday, and hoped that I wouldn't, and that he was right.

My valet said, sure, he would return me to the station in his van – a not too abnormal service. He was reading aloud from the *Flag* with disfavour. 'Reality is sweaty armpits, sordid sex, junkies dead in public lavatories, it says here.' He threw the paper on to the bench. 'Reality is the gas bill, remembering the wife's birthday, a beer with your mates, that's more like it. Get in the van, Kit, it's right outside the weighing room. I've just about finished here.'

Reality, I thought, going out, was speed over fences, a game of manners, love in a shower: to each his own.

I travelled without incident back to the hotel and telephoned on time to Wykeham.

'Where are you?' he said. 'People keep asking for you.'

'Who?' I said.

'They don't say. Four fellows, at least. All day. Where are you?'

'Staying with friends.'

'Oh.' He didn't ask further. He himself didn't care. We talked about his winner and his second, and discussed the horses I would be schooling in the morning.

'One of those fellows who rang wanted you for some lunch party or other in London,' he said, as if suddenly remembering. 'They invited me, too. The sponsors of Inch-cape's race, last Saturday. The princess is going, and they wanted us as well. They said it was a great opportunity as they could see from tomorrow's race programmes that we hadn't any runners.'

'Are you going?'

'No, no. I said I couldn't. But it might be better if you came here early, and do the schooling in good time.'

I agreed, and said goodnight.

'Goodnight, Kit,' he said.

I got through to my answering machine, and there among the messages were the sponsors of Icefall's race, inviting me to lunch the next day. They would be delighted if I could join them and the princess in celebrating our victory in their race, please could I ring back at the given number.

I rang the number and got an answering machine referring me on, reaching finally the head of the sponsors himself.

'Great, great, you can come?' he said. 'Twelve-thirty at the Guineas restaurant in Curzon Street. See you there. That's splendid.'

Sponsors got advertising from racing and in return pumped in generous cash. There was an unspoken understanding among racing people that sponsors were to be appreciated, and that jockeys should turn up if possible where invited. Part of the job. And I wanted to go, besides, to talk to the princess.

I answered my other messages, none of which were important, and then got through to Holly.

'Bobby spoke to his father,' she said. 'The beast said he would come only if you were there. Bobby didn't like it.'

'Did Bobby say I would be there anyway?'

'No, he waited to know what you wanted him to say. He has to ring back to his father.'

I didn't like it any more than Bobby. 'Why does Maynard want me?' I said. 'I didn't think he would come at all if he knew I'd be there.'

'He said he would help Bobby get rid of you once and for all, but that you had to be there.'

Bang, I thought, goes any advantage of surprise. 'All right,' I said. 'Tell Bobby to tell him I'll be coming. At about four o'clock, I should think. I'm going to a sponsors' lunch in London.'

'Kit . . . whatever you're planning, don't do it.'

'Must.'

'I've a feeling . . .'

'Stifle it. How's the baby?'

'Never have one,' she said. 'It's the pits.'

I collected all four recorded video tapes from the hotel's vaults and took them with six others, unused, to Chiswick: and kissed Danielle with circumspection at her desk.

'Hi,' she said, smiling deeply in her eyes.

'Hi, yourself.'

'How did it go, today?'

'Two wins, two seconds.'

'And no crunches.'

'No crunches.'

She seemed to relax. 'I'm glad you're OK.'

Joe appeared from the passage to the editing rooms saying he was biting his fingernails with inactivity and had I by any chance brought my tapes. I picked the four recorded tapes off Danielle's desk and he pounced on them, bearing them away.

I followed him with the spare tapes into an editing room and sat beside him while he played the interviews through, one by one, his dark face showing shock.

'Can you stick them together?' I asked, when he'd finished.

'I sure can,' he said sombrely. 'What you need is some voice-over linkage. You got anything else? Shots of scenery, anything like that?'

I shook my head. 'I didn't think of it.'

'It's no good putting a voice-over on a black screen,' he explained. 'You've got to have pictures, to hold interest. We're bound to have something here in the library that we can use.'

Danielle appeared at the doorway, looking enquiring.

'How's it going?' she said.

'I guess you know what's on these tapes,' Joe said.

'No. Kit hasn't told me.'

'Good,' Joe said. 'When I've finished, we'll try it out on you. Get a reaction.'

'OK,' she said. 'It's a quiet night for news, thank goodness.'

She went away and Joe got me to speak into a microphone, explaining who the Perrysides were, giving George Tarker a location, introducing Hugh Vaughnley. I wanted them in that order, I said.

'Right,' he said. 'Now you go away and talk to Danielle and leave it to me, and if you don't like the result, no problem, we can always change it.'

'I brought these unused tapes,' I said, giving them to him. 'Once we've settled on the final version, could we make copies?'

He took one of the new tapes, peeled off the cellophane wrapping and put it into a machine. 'A breeze,' he said.

He spent two or three hours on it, coming out whistling a couple of times to see if the station chief was still happy (which he appeared to be), telling me Spielberg couldn't do better, drinking coffee from a machine, going cheerfully back.

Danielle worked sporadically on a story about a police hunt for a rapist who lurked in bus shelters and had just been arrested, which she said would probably not make it on to network news back home, but kept everyone working, at least. No Devil-Boys, no oil fires that night.

Aunt Casilia, Danielle said, was looking forward to tomorrow's lunch party and hoped I would be there.

'Will you be going?' I asked.

'Nope. Aunt Casilia would have gotten me invited, but I've a college friend passing through London. We're having lunch. Long time date, I can't break it.'

'Pity.'

'You're going? Shall I tell her?'

I nodded. 'I'm schooling some of her horses in the morning, and I'll be coming along after.'

Joe came out finally, stretching his backbone and flexing his fingers.

'Come on, then,' he said. 'Come and see.'

We all went, the station chief as well, sitting in chairs collected from adjoining rooms. Joe started his machine, and there, immediately, was the uncut version of the television interview of Maynard and his tormentor, followed by the list of firms Maynard had acquired. At the end of that the tape returned to repeat the interviewer's outline of Metavane's story, and then came my voice, superimposed on views of horses exercising on Newmarket Heath, explaining who

244

Major and Mrs Perryside were, and where they now lived.

The Perrysides apeared in entirety, poignant and brave; and at the end the tape returned to the television interviewer again repeating the takeover list. This time it stopped after the mention of Purfleet Electronics, and then, over a view of mudflats in the Thames estuary, my voice introduced George Tarker. The whole of that interview was there also, and when he said in tears about his son wiring himself up, Danielle's own eyes filled..

Joe left the shot of George Tarker's ravaged face running as long as I'd taped it, and then there was my voice again, this time over a printing press in full production, explaining that the next person to appear would be the son of Lord Vaughnley, who owned the *Daily* and *Sunday Towncrier* newspapers.

All of Hugh's tape was there, ending with his impassioned plea to come home. On the screen after that came a long shot taken from the cut televised version of *How's Trade*, of Maynard smiling and looking noble. The sound track of that had been erased, so that one saw him in silence. Then the screen went silently into solid black for about ten seconds before reverting to snow and background crackle.

Even though I'd recorded three of the main segments myself, the total effect was overpowering. Run together they were a punch to the brain, emotional, damning the wicked.

The station chief said, 'Christ', and Danielle blew her nose.

'It runs for one hour, thirteen minutes,' Joe said to me, 'if you're interested.'

'I can't thank you enough.'

'I hope the bastard burns,' he said.

In the morning I went to Wykeham's place south of London and on the Downs there spent two profitable hours teaching his absolute novices how to jump and refreshing the memories of others. We gave the one who had fallen at Ascot a pop to help him get his confidence back after being brought down, and talked about the runners for the rest of that week.

'Thank you for coming,' he said. 'Good of you.'

'A pleasure.'

'Goodbye P . . . er . . . Kit.'

'Goodbye Wykeham,' I said.

I went back to London, showered, dressed in grey suit, white shirt, quiet tie, presenting a civilised face to the sponsors.

I put one of the six copies Joe had made of the Allardeck production into a large envelope, sticking it shut, and then zipped a second of them into the big inside pocket of my blue anorak. The other four I took downstairs and lodged in the hotel vault, and carrying both the envelope and the anorak went by taxi to Eric Olderjohn's terrace house behind Sloane Square.

The taxi waited while I rang the bell beside the green door, and not much to my surprise there was no one at home. I wrote on the envelope: 'Mr Olderjohn, Please give this to a Certain Person, for his eyes only. Regards, Kit Fielding' and pushed it through the letter-box.

'Right,' I said to the taxi driver. 'The Guineas restaurant, Curzon Street.'

The Guineas, where I'd been several times before, was principally a collection of private dining rooms of various sizes, chiefly used for private parties such as the one I was bound for. Opulent and discreet, it went in for dark green flocked wallpaper, gilded cherubs and waiters in gloves. Every time I had been there, there had been noisettes of lamb.

I left my anorak in the cloakroom downstairs and put the ticket in my pocket, walked up the broad stairs to the next floor, turned right, went down a passage and ended, as directed, at the sponsors' party in the One Thousand Room.

The sponsors greeted me effusively. 'Come in, come in. Have some champagne.' They gave me a glass.

The princess was there, dressed in a cream silk suit with gold and citrines, dark hair piled high, smiling.

'I'm so pleased you've come,' she said, shaking my hand.

'I wouldn't have missed it.'

'How are my horses? How is Icefall? How is my poor Allegheny? Did you know that Lord Vaughnley is here?'

'Is he?'

I looked around. There were about thirty people present, more perhaps than I'd expected. From across the room Lady Vaughnley saw me, and waved.

'The *Towncrier* joined forces with the Icefall people,' the princess said. 'It's a double party, now.'

The Icefall sponsors came to bear her away. 'Do come . . . may I present . . .'

Lord Vaughnley approached, looking blander than bland.

'Now, everybody,' said one of the sponsors loudly, 'we're all going into another room to see films of our two races, both won by our most honoured guest, Princess Casilia.'

There was a little light applause, and everyone began to move to the door. Lord Vaughnley stood at my elbow. The princess looked back. 'You're coming, Kit?'

'In a minute,' Lord Vaughnley said. 'Just want to ask him something.'

The princess smiled and nodded and went on. Lord Vaughnley shepherded everyone out, and when the room was empty, closed the door and stood with his back to it.

'I wanted to reach you,' I said; but I don't think he heard. He was looking towards a second door, set in a side wall.

The door opened, and two people came through it.

Nestor Pollgate.

Jay Erskine.

Pollgate looked satisfied and Jay Erskine was smirking.

NINETEEN

'Neatly done,' Pollgate said to Lord Vaughnley.

'It worked out well,' he replied, his big head nodding.

He still stood four-square in front of the door. Erskine stood similarly, with folded arms, in front of the other.

There were chairs and tables round the green walls, tables with white cloths bearing bowls of nuts and cigarette-filled ashtrays. Champagne goblets all over the place, some still with bubble contents. There would be waiters, I thought, coming to clear the rubble.

'We won't be disturbed,' Pollgate told Lord Vaughnley. 'The "do not enter" signs are on both doors, and Mario says we have the room for an hour.'

'The lunch will be before that,' Lord Vaughnley said. 'The films take half an hour, no more.'

'He's not going to the lunch,' Pollgate said, meaning me.

'Er, no, perhaps not. But I should be there.'

I thought numbly: catch me first.

It had taken five days . . . and the princess.

'You are going to give us,' Pollgate said to me directly, 'The wire-tap and my journalists' belongings. And that will be the end of it.'

The power of the man was such that the words themselves were a threat. What would happen if I didn't comply wasn't mentioned. My compliance was assumed; no discussion.

He walked over to Jay Erskine, producing a flat box from a pocket and taking Jay Erskine's place guarding the door.

Jay Erskine's smirk grew to a twisted smile of anticipation. I disliked intensely the cold eyes, the drooping moustache, his callous pen and his violent nature; and most of all I disliked the message in his sneer.

Pollgate opened the box and held it out to Jay Erskine, who took from it something that looked like the hand-held remote control of a television set. He settled it into his hand and walked in my direction. He came without the wariness one might have expected after I'd thrown him across a room, and he put the remote control thing smoothly between the open fronts of my jacket, on to my shirt.

I felt something like a thud, and the next thing I knew I was lying flat on my back on the floor, wholly disorientated, not sure where I was or what had happened.

Jay Erskine and Lord Vaughnley bent down, took my arms, helped me up, and dropped me on to a chair.

The chair had arms. I held on to them. I felt dazed, and couldn't work out why.

Jay Erskine smiled nastily and put the black object again against my shirt.

The thud had a burn to it that time. And so fast. No time to draw breath.

I would have shot out of the chair if they hadn't held me in it. My wits scattered instantly to the four winds. My muscles didn't work. I wasn't sure who I was or where I was, and nor did I care. Time passed. Time was relative. It was minutes, anyway. Not very quick.

The haze in my brain slowly resolved itself to the point where I knew I was sitting in a chair, and knew the people round me were Nestor Pollgate, Lord Vaughnley and Jay Erskine.

'Right,' Pollgate said. 'Can you hear me?'

I said, after a pause, 'Yes.' It didn't sound like my voice. More a croak.

'You're going to give us the wire-tap,' he said. 'And the other things.'

Some sort of electricity, I thought dimly. Those thuds were electric shocks. Like touching a cold metal doorknob after walking on nylon carpet, but magnified monstrously.

'You understand?' he said.

I didn't answer. I understood, but I didn't know whether I was going to give him the things or not.

'Where are they?' he said.

To hell with it, I thought.

'Where are they?'

Silence.

I didn't even see Jay Erskine put his hand against me the third time. I felt a great burning jolt and went shooting into space, floating for several millennia in a disorientated limbo, ordinary consciousness suspended, living as in dream-state, docile and drifting. I could see them in a way, but I didn't know who they were. I didn't know anything. I existed. I had no form.

Whatever would be done, wherever they might take me, whatever God-awful crime they might plant me in, I couldn't resist.

Thought came back again slowly. There were burns somewhere, stinging. I heard Lord Vaughnley's voice saying something, and Pollgate answering, 'Five thousand volts.'

'He's awake,' Erskine said.

Lord Vaughnley leaned over me, his face close and worried. 'Are you sure he's all right?'

'Yes,' Pollgate said. 'There'll be no permanent harm.'

Thank you, I thought wryly, for that. I felt dizzy and sick. Just as well that with lunch in view I had missed breakfast.

Pollgate was looking at his watch and shaking his head. 'He was dazed for twelve minutes that time. A three-second shock is too much. The two-second is better, but it's taking too long. Twenty minutes already.' He glared down at me. 'I can't waste any more time. You'll give me those things, now, at once.'

It was he who held the electric device now, not Erskine.

I thought I could speak. Tried it. Something came out: the same sort of croak. I said 'It will take . . . days.'

It wasn't heroics. I thought vaguely that if they believed it would take days they would give up trying, right there and then. Logic, at that point, was at a low ebb.

Pollgate stepped within touching distance of me and showed me five thousand volts at close range.

'Stun gun,' he said.

It had two short flat metal prongs protruding five centimetres apart from one end of a flat plastic case. He squeezed some switch or other, and between the prongs leapt an electric spark the length of a thumb, bright blue, thick and crackling.

250

The spark fizzed for a long three seconds of painful promise and disappeared as fast as it had come.

I looked from the stun gun up to Pollgate's face, staring straight at the shiny-bead eyes.

'Weeks,' I said.

It certainly nonplussed him. 'Give us the wire-tap,' he said; and he seemed to be looking, as I was, at a long, tiring battle of wills, much of which I would half sleep through, I supposed.

Lord Vaughnley said to Pollgate uncomfortably, 'You can't go on with this.'

A certain amount of coherence returned to my brain. The battle of wills, I thought gratefully, shouldn't be necessary.

'He's going to give us those things,' Pollgate said obstinately. 'I'm not letting some clod like this get the better of me.' Pride, loss of face, all the deadly intangibles.

Lord Vaughnley looked down at me anxiously.

'I'll give you,' I said to him, 'something better.'

'What?'

My voice was steadier. Less hoarse, less slow. I moved in the chair, arms and legs coming back into coordination. It seemed to alarm Jay Erskine but I was still a long way from playing judo.

'What will you give us?' Lord Vaughnley said.

I concentrated on making my throat and tongue work properly. 'It's in Newmarket,' I said. 'We'll have to go there for it. Now, this afternoon.'

Pollgate said with impatience, 'That's ridiculous.'

'I'll give you,' I said to Lord Vaughnley, 'Maynard Allardeck.'

A short burst of stun couldn't have had more effect.

'How do you mean?' he said; not with puzzlement, but with hope.

'On a plate,' I said. 'In your power. Where you want him, don't you?'

They both wanted him. I could see it in Pollgate's face just as clearly as in Lord Vaughnley's. I suppose that I had guessed in a way that it would be both.

Jay Erskine said aggressively, 'Are our things in Newmarket, then?'

I said with an effort, 'That's where you left them.'

251

'All right, then.'

He seemed to think that the purpose of their expedition had been achieved, and I didn't tell him differently.

Nestor Pollgate said, 'Jay, fetch the car to the side entrance, will you?' and the obnoxious Erskine went away.

Pollgate and Lord Vaughnley agreed that Mario, whoever he was, should tell Icefall's sponsors not to expect their guests back for lunch, saying I'd had a bilious attack and Lord Vaughnley was helping me. 'But Mario can't tell them until after we've gone,' Lord Vaughnley said, 'or you'll have my wife and I daresay the princess out here in a flash to mother him.'

I sat and listened lethargically, capable of movement but not wanting to move, no longer sick, all right in my head, peaceful, extraordinarily, and totally without energy.

After a while Jay Erskine came back, the exasperating smirk still in place.

'Can you walk?' Pollgate asked me.

I said, 'Yes' and stood up, and we went out of the side door, along a short passage and down some gilded deeply carpeted backstairs, where no doubt many a Guineas visitor made a discreet entrance and exit, avoiding public eyes in the front hall.

I went down the stairs shakily, holding on to the rail.

'Are you all right?' Lord Vaughnley said solicitously, putting his hand supportively under my elbow.

I glanced at him. How he could think I would be all right was beyond me. Perhaps he was remembering that I was used to damage, to falls, to concussion: but bruises and fractures were different from that day's little junket.

'I'm all right,' I said though, because it was true where it counted, and we went safely down to the bottom.

I stopped there. The exit door stood open ahead, a passage stretching away indoors to the right.

'Come along,' Pollgate said, gesturing to the door. 'If we're going, let's go.'

'My anorak,' I said, 'is in the cloakroom.' I produced the ticket from my pocket. 'Anorak,' I said.

'I'll get it,' Lord Vaughnley said, taking the ticket. 'And I'll see Mario. Wait for me in the car.'

It was a large car. Jay Erskine was driving. Nestor Pollgate sat watchfully beside me on the back seat, and Lord Vaughnley, when he returned, sat in the front.

'Your anorak,' he said, holding it out, and I thanked him and put it by my feet, on the floor.

'The films of the races have just ended, Mario says,' he reported to Pollgate. 'He's going straight in to make our apologies. It's all settled. Off we go.'

It took ages to get out of London, partly because of thick traffic, mostly because Jay Erskine was a rotten driver, all impatience and heavy on the brakes. An hour and a half to Newmarket, at that rate: and I would have to be better by then.

No one spoke much. Jay Erskine locked all the doors centrally and Nestor Pollgate put the stun gun in its case in his right-hand jacket pocket, hidden but available; and I sat beside him in ambiguity, half prisoner, half ringmaster, going willingly but under threat, waiting for energy to return, physical, mental and psychic.

Stun guns, I thought. I'd heard of them, never seen one before. Used originally by American police to subdue dangerous violent criminals without shooting them. Instantaneous. Effective. You don't say.

I remembered from long-ago physics lessons that if you squeezed piezo-electric crystals you got sparks, as in the flickering lighters used for gas cookers. Maybe stun guns were like that, multiplied. Maybe not. Maybe I would ask someone. Maybe not. Five thousand volts . . .

I looked with speculation at the back of Lord Vaughnley's head, wondering what he was thinking. He was eager, that was for sure. They had agreed to the journey like thirsty men in a drought. They were going without knowing for sure why, without demanding to be told. Anything that could do Maynard Allardeck harm must be worth doing, in their eyes: that had to be why, at the beginning, Lord Vaughnley had been happy enough to introduce me to Rose Quince, to let me loose on the files. The destruction of Maynard's credibility could only be helped along, he might have thought, by pinpricks from myself.

I dozed, woke with a start, found Pollgate's face turned my

way, his eyes watching. He was looking, if anything, puzzled.

In my rag-doll state I could think of nothing useful to say, so I didn't, and presently he turned his head away and looked out of the window, and I still felt very conscious of his force, his ruthlessness, and of the ruin he could make of my life if I got the next few hours wrong.

I thought of how they had set their trap in the Guineas.

Icefall's sponsors, on my answering machine, inviting me to lunch. The sponsors hadn't said where, but they'd said tomorrow, Tuesday: today. The message would have been overheard and despatched to Pollgate, and sent from him to Lord Vaughnley, who would have said, Nothing simpler, my dear fellow, I'll join forces with those sponsors, which they can hardly refuse, and Kit Fielding will definitely come, he'd do anything to please the princess . . .

Pollgate had known the Guineas. Known Mario. Known he could get an isolated room for an hour. The sort of place he would know, for sure.

Maybe Lord Vaughnley had suggested the Guineas to Icefall's sponsors. Maybe he hadn't had to. There were often racing celebration parties at the Guineas. The sponsors would very likely have chosen it themselves, knowing they could show the films there.

Unprofitable thoughts. However it had been planned, it had worked.

I thought also about the alliance between Lord Vaughnley and Nestor Pollgate, owners of snapping rival newspapers, always at each other's throats in print, and acting in private accord.

Allies, not friends. They didn't move comfortably around each other, as friends did.

On 1 October Lord Vaughnley had signed the charity letter recommending Maynard for a knighthood: signed it casually perhaps, not knowing him well.

Then later in October his son Hugh had confessed to his dealings with Maynard, and Lord Vaughnley, outraged, had sought to unzip Maynard's accolade by getting Pollgate and his *Flag* to do the demolition; because it was the *Flag*'s sort of thing . . . and Jay Erskine, who had worked for Lord Vaughnley once, was in place there in the *Flag*, and was known not to be averse to an illegal sortie, now and then.

I didn't know why Lord Vaughnley should have gone to Pollgate, should have expected him to help. Somewhere between them there was a reason. I didn't suppose I would get an answer, if I asked.

Lord Vaughnley, I thought, could have been expected to tell the charity he wanted to recant his approval of Maynard Allardeck's knighthood: but they might have said too bad, your son was a fool, but Allardeck definitely helped him. Lord Vaughnley might as a newspaperman have seen a few destructive paragraphs as more certain, and more revengefully satisfying, besides.

Before that, though, I guessed it had been he who had gone to the producers of *How's Trade*, who said dig up what you can about Allardeck, discredit him, I'll pay you: and had been defeated by the producer himself, who according to Rose Quince was known for taking more money in return for helping his victims off the hook.

The *How's Trade* programme on Maynard had gone out loaded in Maynard's favour, which hadn't been the plan at all. And it was after that, I thought, that Lord Vaughnley had gone to Pollgate.

I shut my eyes and drifted. The car hummed. They had the heater on. I thought about horses; more honest than men. Tomorrow I was due to ride at Haydock. Thank God the racecourse doctor hadn't been at the Guineas.

Takeovers, I thought inconsequentially. Always fending off takeovers.

Pollgate would bury me if I didn't get it right.

Towards the end of the journey both mental and physical power came seeping slowly back, like a tide rising, and it was an extraordinary feeling: I hadn't known how much power I did have until I'd both lost it and felt its return. Like not realising how ill one had been, until one was well.

I stretched thankfully with the renewed strength in my muscles and breathed deeply from the surge in my mind, and Pollgate, for whom the consciousness of power must have been normal, sensed in some way the vital recharging in me and sat up more tensely himself.

Erskine drove into Bobby's stableyard at five minutes past

three, and in the middle of what should have been a quiet snooze in the life of the horses, it seemed that there were people and movement all over the place. Erskine stopped the car with his accustomed jerk, and Pollgate having told him to unlock the doors, we climbed out.

Holly was looking distractedly in our direction, and there were besides three or four cars, a horse trailer with the ramp down and grooms wandering about with head-collars.

There was also, to my disbelief, Jermyn Graves.

Holly came running across to me and said, 'Do something, he's a madman, and Bobby's indoors with Maynard, he came early and they've been shouting at each other and I don't want to go in, and thank God you're here, it's a farce.'

Jermyn Graves, seeing me, followed Holly. His gaze swept over Pollgate, Jay Erskine and Lord Vaughnley and he said belligerently, 'Who the hell are these people? Now see here, Fielding, I've had enough of your smart-arse behaviour, I've come for my horses.'

I put my arm around Holly. 'Did his cheque go through?' I asked her.

'Yes, it bloody well did,' Graves said furiously.

Holly nodded. 'The feed-merchant told us. The cheque was cleared yesterday. He has his money.'

'Just what is all this?' Pollgate said heavily.

'You keep out of it,' Graves said rudely. 'It's you, Fielding, I want. You give me my bloody horses or I'll fetch the police to you.'

'Calm down, Mr Graves,' I said. 'You shall have your horses.'

'They're not in their boxes.' He glared with all his old fury; and it occurred to me that his total disregard of Pollgate was sublime. Perhaps one had to know one should be afraid of someone before one was.

'Mr Graves,' I said conversationally to the two proprietors and one journalist, 'is removing his horses because of what he read in Intimate Details. You see here in action the power of the Press.'

'Shut your trap and give me my horses,' Graves said.

'Yes, all right. Your grooms are going in the wrong direction.'

'Jasper,' Graves yelled. 'Come here.'

The luckless nephew approached, eyeing me warily.

'Come on,' I jerked my head. 'Round the back.'

Jay Erskine would have prevented my going, but Pollgate intervened. I took Jasper round to the other yard and pointed out the boxes that contained Graves's horses. 'Awfully sorry,' Jasper said.

'You're welcome,' I said, and I thought that but for him and his uncle we wouldn't have rigged the bell, and but for the bell we wouldn't have caught Jay Erskine up the ladder, and I felt quite grateful to the Graveses, on the whole.

I went back with Jasper walking behind me leading the first of the horses, and found them all standing there in much the same places, Jermyn Graves blustering on about not having faith when the trainer couldn't meet his bills.

'Bobby's better off without you, Mr Graves,' I said. 'Load your horses up and hop it.'

Apoplexy hovered. He opened and shut his mouth a couple of times and finally walked over to his trailer to let out his spleen on the luckless Jasper.

'Thank God for that,' Holly said. 'I can't stand him. I'm so glad you're here. Did you have a good time at your lunch?'

'Stunning,' I said.

They all heard and looked at me sharply.

Lord Vaughnley said, mystified, 'How can you laugh . . .?'

'What the hell,' I said. 'I'm here. I'm alive.'

Holly looked from one to the other of us, sensing something strongly, not knowing what. 'Something happened?' she said, searching my face.

I nodded a fraction. 'I'm OK.'

She said to Lord Vaughnley, 'He risks his life most days of the week. You can't frighten him much.'

They looked at her speechlessly, to my amusement.

I said to her, 'Do you know who you're talking to?' and she shook her head slightly, half remembering but not sure.

'This is Lord Vaughnley who owns the *Towncrier*. This is Nestor Pollgate who owns the *Flag*. This is Jay Erskine who wrote the paragraphs in Intimate Details and put the tap on your telephone.' I paused, and to them I said, 'My sister, Bobby's wife.'

257

She moved closer beside me, her eyes shocked.

'Why are they here? Did you bring them?'

'We sort of brought each other,' I said. 'Where are Maynard and Bobby?'

'In the drawing room, I think.'

Jasper was crunching across the yard with the second horse, Jermyn shouting at him unabated. The other groom who had come with them was scurrying in and out of the trailer, attempting invisibility.

Nestor Pollgate said brusquely, 'We're not standing here watching all this.'

'I'm not leaving Holly alone to put up with that man,' I said. 'He's a menace. It's because of you that he's here, so we'll wait.'

Pollgate stirred restlessly, but there was nowhere particular for him to go. We waited in varying intensities of impatience while Jasper and the groom raised the ramp and clipped it shut, and while Jermyn Graves walked back several steps in our direction and shook his fist at me with the index finger sticking out, jabbing, and said no one messed with him and got away with it, and he'd see I'd be sorry. I'd pay for what I'd done.

'Kit,' Holly said, distressed.

I put my arm round her shoulders and didn't answer Graves, and after a while he turned abruptly on his heel, went over to his car, climbed in, slammed the door, and overburdened his engine, starting with a jerk that must have rocked his horses off their feet in the trailer.

'He's a pig,' Holly said. 'What will he do?'

'He's more threat than action.'

'I,' Pollgate said, 'am not.'

I looked at him, meeting his eyes.

'I do know that,' I said.

The time, I thought, had inescapably come.

Power when I needed it. Give me power, I thought.

I let go of Holly and lent into the car we had come in, picking up my anorak off the floor.

I said to Holly, 'Will you take these three visitors into the sitting room? I'll get Bobby . . . and his father.'

She said with wide apprehensive eyes, 'Kit, do be careful.'

258

'I promise.'

She gave me a look of lingering doubt, but set off with me towards the house. We went in by long habit through the kitchen: I don't think it occurred to either of us to use the formal front door.

Pollgate, Lord Vaughnley and Jay Erskine followed, and in the hall Holly peeled them off into the sitting room, where in the evenings she and Bobby watched television sometimes. The larger drawing room lay ahead, and there were voices in there, or one voice, Maynard's, continuously talking.

I screwed up every inner resource to walk through that door, and it was a great and appalling mistake. Bobby told me afterwards that he saw me in the same way as in the stable and in the garden, the hooded, the enemy, the old foe of antiquity, of immense and dark threat.

Maynard was saying monotonously as if he had already said it over and over, '. . . And if you want to get rid of him you'll do it, and you'll do it today . . .'

Maynard was holding a gun, a hand gun, small and black.

He stopped talking the moment I went in there. His eyes widened. He saw, I supposed, what Bobby saw: Fielding, satanic.

He gave Bobby the pistol, pressing it into his hand.

'Do it,' he said fiercely. 'Do it now.'

His son's eyes were glazed, as in the garden.

He wouldn't do it. He couldn't . . .

'Bobby,' I said explosively, beseechingly: and he raised the gun and pointed it straight at my chest.

TWENTY

I turned my back on him.

I didn't want to see him do it; tear our lives apart, mine and his, and Holly's and the baby's. If he was going to do it, I wasn't going to watch.

Time passed, stretched out, uncountable. Danielle, I thought.

I heard his voice, close behind my shoulder.

'Kit . . .'

I stood rigidly still. You can't frighten him much, Holly had said. Bobby with a gun frightened me into immobility and despair.

He came round in front of me, as white as I felt. He looked into my face. He was holding the gun flat, not aiming, and put it into my hand.

'Forgive me,' he said.

I couldn't speak. He turned away blindly and made for the door. Holly appeared there, questioning, and he enfolded her and hugged her as if he had survived an earthquake, which he had.

I heard a faint noise behind me and turned, and found Maynard advancing, his face sweating, his teeth showing, the charming image long gone. I turned holding the gun, and he saw it in my hand and went back a pace, and then another and another, looking fearful, looking sick.

'You incited,' I said bitterly, 'your own son to murder. Brainwashed him.'

'It would have been an accident,' he said.

'An Allardeck killing a Fielding would not have been believed as an accident.'

'I would have sworn it,' he said.

I loathed him. I said, 'Go into the sitting room' and I stood back to let him pass, keeping the gun pointing his way all the while.

He hadn't had the courage to shoot me himself. Making Bobby do it . . . that crime was worse.

It hadn't been a good idea to draw him there with the express purpose of getting rid of me once and for all. He'd too nearly succeeded. My own stupid fault.

We went down the hall and into the sitting room. Pollgate and Erskine and Lord Vaughnley were all there, standing in the centre, with Bobby and Holly, still entwined, to one side. I went in there feeling I was walking into a cageful of tigers, and Holly said later that with the gun in my hand I looked so dangerous she hardly recognised me as her brother.

'Sit down,' I said. 'You,' I pointed to Maynard, 'over there in that chair at the end.' It was a deep chair, enveloping, no good for springing out of suddenly. 'You next, beside him,' I said to Erskine. 'Then Lord Vaughnley, on the sofa.'

Pollgate looked at the spare place beside Lord Vaughnley and took it in silence.

'Take out the stunner,' I said to him. 'Put it on the floor. Kick it this way.'

I could feel the refusal in him, see it in his eyes. Then he shrugged, and took out the flat black box, and did as I'd said.

'Right,' I said, 'you're all going to watch a video.' I glanced down at the pistol. 'I'm not a good shot. I don't know what I'd hit. So stay sitting down.' I held out the anorak in Bobby's direction. 'The tape's zipped into one of the pockets.'

'Put it on now?' he said, finding it and bringing it out. His hands were shaking, his voice unsteady. Damn Maynard, I thought.

'Yes, now,' I said. 'Holly, close the curtains and put on a lamp, it'll be dark before we're finished.'

No one spoke while she shut out the chilly day, while Bobby switched on the video machine and the television, and fed the tape into the slot. Pollgate looked moodily at the anorak which Bobby had laid on a chair and Lord Vaughnley glanced at the gun, and at my face, and away again.

'Ready,' Bobby said.

'Start it off,' I said, 'and you and Holly sit down and watch.'

261

I shut the door and leaned against it as Lord Vaughnley had done in the Guineas, and Maynard's face came up bright and clear and smiling on the television screen.

He started to struggle up from his deep chair.

'Sit down,' I said flatly.

He must have guessed that what was coming was the tape he thought he'd suppressed. He looked at the gun in my hand and judged the distance he would have to cover to reach me, and he subsided into the cushions as if suddenly weak.

The interview progressed and went from smooth politeness into direct attack, and Lord Vaughnley's mouth slowly opened.

'You've not seen this before?' I said to him.

He said, 'No, no' with his gaze uninterruptedly on the screen, and I supposed that Rose wouldn't have seen any need to go running to the proprietor with her purloined tape, the two days she had had it in the *Towncrier* building.

I looked at all their faces as they watched. Maynard sick, Erskine blank, Lord Vaughnley riveted, Pollgate awakening to acute interest, Bobby and Holly horrified. Bobby, I thought ruefully, was in for some frightful shocks: it couldn't be much fun to find one's father had done so much cruel damage.

The interview finished, to be replaced by the Perrysides telling how they'd lost Metavane, with George Tarker and his son's suicide after, and Hugh Vaughnley, begging to go home; and finally Maynard again, smugly smiling.

The impact of it all on me was still great, and in the others produced something like suspended animation. Their expressions at the end of the hour and thirteen minutes were identical, of total absorption and stretched eyes, and I thought Joe would have been satisfied with the effect of his cutting, and of his hammer blow of final silence.

The trial was over: the accused, condemned. The sentence alone remained to be delivered.

The screen ran from black into snow, and no one moved.

I peeled myself off the door and walked across and switched off the set.

'Right,' I said, 'now listen.'

The eyes of all of them were looking my way with

262

unadulterated concentration, Maynard's dark with humiliation, his body slack and deep in the chair.

'You,' I said to Lord Vaughnley, 'and you,' I said to Nestor Pollgate. 'You or your newspapers will each pay to Bobby the sum of fifty thousand pounds in compensation. You'll write promissory notes, here and now, in this room, in front of witnesses, to pay the money within three days, and those notes will be legal and binding.'

Lord Vaughnley and Nestor Pollgate simply stared.

'And in return,' I said, 'you shall have the wire-tap and the other evidence of Jay Erskine's criminal activity. You shall have complete silence from me about your various assaults on me and my property. You shall have back the draft for three thousand pounds now lodged in my bank manager's safe. And you shall have the tape you've just watched.'

Maynard said, 'No' in anguished protest, and no one took any notice.

'You,' I said to Maynard, 'will write a promissory note promising to pay to Bobby within three days the sum of two hundred and fifty thousand pounds, which will wipe out the overdrafts and the loans and mortgages on this house and stables, which you and your father made Bobby pay for, and which should rightfully be his by inheritance.'

Maynard's mouth opened, but no sound came out.

'You will also,' I said, 'give to Major and Mrs Perryside the one share you still own in Metavane.'

He began to shake his head weakly.

'And in return,' I said, 'you will have my assurance that many copies of this tape will not turn up simultaneously in droves of sensitive places, such as with the Senior Steward of the Jockey Club, or among the patrons of the civil service charity of which you are the new chairman, or in a dozen places in the City.' I paused. 'When Bobby has the money safe in the bank, you will be safe from me also. But that safety will always be conditional on your doing no harm either to Bobby and Holly or to me in future. The tapes will always exist.'

Maynard found his voice, hoarse and shaken.

'That's extortion,' he said aridly. 'It's blackmail.'

'It's justice,' I said.

There was silence. Maynard shrank as if deflated into the chair, and neither Pollgate nor Lord Vaughnley said anything at all.

'Bobby,' I said, 'take the tape out of the machine and out of this room and put it somewhere safe, and bring back some writing paper for the notes.'

Bobby stood up slowly, looking numb.

'You said we could have the tape,' Pollgate said, demurring.

'So you can, when Bobby's been paid. If the money's all safely in the bank by Friday, you shall have it then, along with Erskine's escape from going to jail.'

Bobby took the tape away, and I contemplated Pollgate's and Lord Vaughnley's expressionless faces and thought they were being a good deal too quiet. Maynard, staring at me blackly from his chair, was simple by comparison, his reactions expected. Erskine looked his usual chilling self, but without the smirk, which was an improvement.

Bobby came back with some large sheets of the headed writing paper he used for the bills for the owners, and gave a sheet each to Nestor Pollgate and Lord Vaughnley, and with stiff legs and an arm outstretched as far as it would go, gave the third to his father with his head turned away, not wanting to look at his face.

I surveyed the three of them sitting there stonily holding the blank sheets, and into my head floated various disjointed words and phrases.

'Wait,' I said. 'Don't write yet.'

The words were 'invalid', and 'obtained by menaces', and 'invalid by reason of having been extorted at gun point'.

I wondered if the thought had come on its own or been generated somewhere else in that room, and I looked at their faces carefully, one by one, searching their eyes.

Not Maynard. Not Erskine. Not Lord Vaughnley

Nestor Pollgate's eyelids flickered.

'Bobby,' I said, 'pick that black box up off the floor and drop it out of the window, into the garden.'

He looked bewildered, but did as I asked, the November air blowing in a great gust through the curtains into the room.

'Now the gun,' I said, and gave it to him.

He took it gingerly and threw it out, and shut the window again.

'Right,' I said, putting my hands with deliberation into my pockets, 'you've all heard the propositions. If you accept them, please write the notes.'

For a long moment no one moved. Then Lord Vaughnley stretched out an arm to the coffee table in front of him and picked up a magazine. He put the sheet of writing paper on the magazine for support. With a slightly pursed mouth but in continued quiet he lifted a pen from a pocket inside his jacket, pressed the top of it with a click, and wrote a short sentence, signing his name and adding the date.

He held it out towards Bobby, who stepped forward hesitantly and took it.

'Read it aloud,' I said.

Bobby's voice said shakily, 'I promise to pay Robertson Allardeck fifty thousand pounds within three days of this date.' He looked up at me. 'It is signed William Vaughnley, and the date is today's.'

I looked at Lord Vaughnley.

'Thank you,' I said neutrally.

He gave the supporting magazine to Nestor Pollgate, and offered his own pen. Nestor Pollgate took both with a completely unmoved face and wrote in his turn.

Bobby took the paper from him, glanced at me, and read aloud, 'I promise to pay Robertson Allardeck fifty thousand pounds within three days of this date. It's signed Nestor Pollgate. It's dated today.'

'Thank you,' I said to Pollgate.

Bobby looked slightly dazedly at the two documents he held. They would clear the debt for the unsold yearlings, I thought. When he sold them, anything he got would be profit.

Lord Vaughnley and Jay Erskine, as if in some ritual, passed the magazine and the pen along to Maynard.

With fury he wrote, the pen jabbing hard on the paper. I took the completed page from him myself and read it aloud, 'I promise to pay my son Robertson two hundred and fifty thousand pounds within three days. Maynard Allardeck. Today's date.'

I looked up at him. 'Thank you,' I said.

'Don't thank me. Your thanks are an insult.'

I was careful, in fact, to show no triumph, though in his case I did feel it: and I had to admit to myself ruefully that in that triumph there was a definite element of the old feud. A Fielding had got the better of an Allardeck, and I dared say my ancestors were gloating.

I gave Maynard's note to Bobby. It would clear all his debts and put him on a sure footing to earn a fair living as a trainer, and he held the paper unbelievingly, as if it would evaporate before his eyes.

'Well, gentlemen,' I said cheerfully, 'bankers' drafts by Friday, and you shall have the notes back, properly receipted.'

Maynard stood up, his greying fair hair still smooth, his face grimly composed, his expensive suit falling into uncreased shape; the outer shell intact, the man inside in shreds.

He looked at nobody, avoiding eyes. He walked to the door, opened it, went out, didn't look back. A silence lengthened behind his exit like the silence at the end of the tape; the enormity of Maynard struck one dumb.

Nestor Pollgate rose to his feet, tall, frowning, still with his power intact. He looked at me judiciously, gave me a brief single nod of the head, and said to Holly, 'Which way do I go out?'

'I'll show you,' she said, sounding subdued, and led the way into the hall.

Erskine followed, his face pinched, the drooping reddish moustache in some way announcing his continuing inflexible hatred of those he had damaged.

Bobby went after him, carrying his three notes carefully as if they were brittle, and Lord Vaughnley, last of all, stood up to go. He shook his head, shrugged his shoulders, spread his hands in a sort of embarrassment.

'What can I say?' he said. 'What am I to say when I see you on racecourses?'

'Good morning, Kit,' I said.

The grey eyes almost smiled before awkwardness returned. 'Yes, but,' he said, 'after what we did to you in the Guineas . . .'

I shrugged. 'Fortunes of war,' I said. 'I don't resent it, if that's what you mean. I took the war to the *Flag*. Seek the battle, don't complain of the wounds.'

He said curiously, 'Is that how you view race-riding? How you view life?'

'I hadn't thought of it, but yes, perhaps.'

'I'm sorry all the same,' he said. 'I had no idea what it would be like. Jay Erskine got the stun gun . . . he said two short shocks and you'd be putty. I don't think Nestor realised himself how bad it would be . . .'

'Yeah,' I said dryly, 'but he agreed to it.'

'That was because,' Lord Vaughnley explained with a touch of earnestness, wanting me to understand, perhaps to absolve, 'because you ignored all his threats.'

'About prison?' I said.

He nodded. 'Sam Leggatt warned him you were intelligent . . . he said an attempt to frame you could blow up in their faces, that you would get the *Flag* and Nestor himself into deep serious gritty trouble . . . David Morse, their lawyer, was of the same opinion, so he agreed not to try. Sam Leggatt told me. But you have to understand Nestor. He doesn't like to be crossed. He said he wasn't going to be beaten by some . . . er . . . jockey.'

Expletives deleted, I thought, amused.

'You were elusive,' he said. 'Nestor was getting impatient . . .'

'And he had a tap on my telephone?'

'Er, yes.'

'Mm,' I said. 'Is it Maynard Allardeck who is trying to take over the *Towncrier*?'

He blinked, and said 'Er —' and recovered. 'You guessed?'

'It seemed likely. Maynard got half of Hugh's shares by a trick. I thought it just might be him who was after the whole thing.'

Lord Vaughnley nodded. 'A company . . . Allardeck is behind it. When Hugh confessed, I got people digging up Allardeck's contacts. Just digging for dirt. I'd no idea until then that he owned the company . . . his name hadn't surfaced. All I knew was that it was the same company that nearly acquired the *Flag* a year ago. Very aggressive. It cost Nestor a fortune to cap their bid, far more than he would have had to pay otherwise.'

Holy wow, I thought.

'So when you found out that Maynard was the ultimate enemy,' I said, 'and knew also that he'd recently been proposed for a knighthood, you thought at least you could put paid to that, and casually asked Pollgate to do it in the *Flag*?'

'Not all that casually. Nestor said he'd be pleased to, if it was Allardeck who had cost him so much.'

'Didn't you even consider what hell you were manufacturing for Bobby?'

'Erskine found he couldn't get at Allardeck's phone system . . . they decided on his son.'

'Callous,' I said.

'Er . . . yes.'

'And appallingly spiteful to deliver all those copies to Bobby's suppliers.'

He said without much apology, 'Nestor thought the story would make more of a splash that way. Which it did.'

We began to walk from the sitting room into the hall. He'd told me what I hadn't asked: where the alliance began. In common enmity to Maynard, who had cost them both dear.

'Will you use the tape,' I asked, 'to stop Maynard now in his tracks?'

He glanced at me. 'That would be blackmail,' he said mildly.

'Absolutely.'

'Fifty thousand pounds,' he said. 'That tape's cheap at the price.'

We went into the kitchen and paused again.

'The *Towncrier* is the third newspaper,' he said, 'that has had trouble with Allardeck's company. One paper after another . . . he won't give up till he's got one.'

'He's obsessive,' I said. 'And besides, he's wanted all his life to have power over others . . . to be kowtowed to. To be a lord.'

Lord Vaughnley's mouth opened. I told him about my grandfather, and Maynard at nine. 'He hasn't changed,' I said. 'He still wants those things. Sir first, Lord after. And

268

don't worry, he won't get them. I sent a copy of the tape to where you sent your charity letter.'

He was dumbstruck. He said weakly, 'How did you know about that letter?'

'I saw it,' I said. 'I was shown it. I wanted to know who knew Maynard might be up for a knighthood, and there it was, with your name.'

He shook his head: at life in general, it seemed.

We went on through the kitchen and out into the cold air. All the lights were on round the yard and some of the box doors were open, the lads working there in the routine of evening stables.

'Why did you try to stop me talking to Hugh?' I asked.

'I was wrong, I see that now. But at the time . . . by then you were pressing Nestor for large compensation. He wanted us simply to get back the wire-tap and shut you up.' He spread his hands. 'No one imagined, you see, that you would do all that you've done. I mean, when it was just a matter of disgracing Allardeck in the public eye, no one could have foreseen . . . no one even thought of your existence, let alone considered you a factor. No one knew you would defend your brother-in-law, or be . . . as you are.'

We walked across the yard to the car where Pollgate and Erskine were waiting, shadowy figures behind glass.

'If I were you,' I said, 'I'd find out if Maynard owns the bookmakers that Hugh bet with. If he does, you can threaten him with fraud, and get Hugh's shares back, I should think.'

We stopped a few feet from the car.

'You're generous,' he said.

We stood there, face to face, not knowing whether or not to shake hands.

'Hugh had no chance against Maynard,' I said.

'No.' He paused. 'I'll let him come home.'

He looked at me lengthily, the mind behind the grey eyes perhaps totting up, as I was, where we stood.

Even if he hadn't intended it, he had set in motion the attacks on Bobby; yet because of them Bobby would be much better off. From the dirt, gold.

If he offered his hand, I thought, I would take it.

Tentatively, unsure, that's what he did. I shook it briefly; an acknowledgement, a truce.

'See you at the races,' I said.

When they had gone I went and found the pistol and the stun gun outside the sitting-room window, and with them in my pockets returned to the kitchen, where Holly and Bobby were looking more dazed than happy.

'Tea?' I said hopefully.

They didn't seem to hear. I put the kettle on and got out some cups.

'Kit . . .' Holly said. 'Bobby told me . . .'

'Yeah . . . well . . . have you a lemon?' I said.

She dumbly fetched me one from the refrigerator, and sliced it.

Bobby said, 'I nearly killed you.'

His distress, I saw, was still blotting out any full realisation – or celebration – of the change in his fortunes. He still looked pale, still gaunt round the eyes.

'But you didn't,' I said.

'No . . . when you turned your back on me, I thought, I can't shoot him in the back . . . not in the back . . . and I woke up. Like waking from a nightmare. I couldn't . . . how could I . . . I stood there with that gun, sweating at how near I'd come . . .'

'You frightened me silly,' I said. 'Let's forget it.'

'How can we?'

'Easily.' I punched his arm lightly. 'Concentrate, my old chum, on being a daddy.'

The kettle boiled and Holly made the tea; and we heard a car driving into the yard.

'They've come back,' Holly said in dismay.

We went out to see, all of us fearful.

The car was large and bewilderingly familiar. Two of its doors opened and from one came Thomas, the princess's chauffeur, in his best uniform, and from the other, scrambling and running, Danielle.

'Kit . . .' She ran headlong into my arms, her face screwed up with worry. 'Are you . . . are you really OK?'

'Yes, I am. You can see.'

270

She put her head on my shoulder and I held her close, and felt her trembling, and kissed her hair.

Thomas opened a third door of the car and helped out the princess, holding the sable coat for her to put on over the silk suit against the cold.

'I am glad, Kit,' she said calmly, snuggling into the fur, 'to see you are alive and well.' She looked from me to Bobby and Holly. 'You are Bobby, you are Holly, is that right?' She held out her hand to them, which they blankly shook.

'We are here,' she said, 'because my niece Danielle insisted that we come.' She was explaining, half apologising for her presence. 'When I went home after the Icefall luncheon,' she said to me, 'Danielle was waiting on the pavement. She said you were in very great danger, and that you were at your sister's house in Newmarket. She didn't know how she knew, but she was certain. She said that we must come at once.'

Bobby and Holly looked astounded.

'As I know that with you, Kit, telepathy definitely exists,' the princess said, 'and as you had disappeared from the lunch and were reported to be ill, and as Danielle was distraught . . . we came. And I see she was right in part at least. You are here, at your sister's house.'

'She was right about the rest,' Holly said soberly. 'He was in that danger . . . a split second from dying.' She looked at my face. 'Did you think of her then?'

I swallowed. 'Yes, I did.'

'Holy wow,' Holly said.

'Kit says that too,' Danielle said, lifting her head from my neck and beginning to recover. 'It's awesome.'

'We always did,' Holly said. She looked at Danielle with growing interest and understanding, and slowly smiled with pleasure.

'She's like us, isn't she?' she said.

'I don't know,' I said. 'I've never known what she was thinking.'

'You might, after this'; and to Danielle, with friendship, she said, 'Think of something. See if he can tell what it is.'

'OK.'

There was a silence. The only thought in my head was that

271

telepathy was unpredictable and only sometimes worked to order.

I looked at the princess, and at Bobby and Holly, and saw in their faces the same hope, the same expectation, the same realisation that this moment might matter in all our futures.

I smiled into Danielle's eyes. I knew, for a certainty.

'Dustsheets.' I said.